ELIZABETH

OBSTINATE, HEADSTRONG GIRL

ELIZABETH ADAMS   CHRISTINA BOYD

KAREN M COX   J. MARIE CROFT   AMY D'ORAZIO

LEIGH DREYER   JENETTA JAMES

CHRISTINA MORLAND   BEAU NORTH

JOANA STARNES

Foreword by

TESSA DARE

Edited by

CHRISTINA BOYD

Elizabeth: Obstinate Headstrong Girl

Library of Congress Control Number: 2019916200

ISBN: 978-0-9986540-5-8

Cover design by Shari Ryan of MadHat Books

Front Cover images: Period Images; also, Irina Bg via Shutterstock

Additional images: Marcus via Adobe Stock; digitalskillet1 via Adobe Stock; Kathy via Adobe Stock; Daria Shevstova via Pexels; RetroAtelier via iStock; Giovanni Boldini, *Portrait of Princess Marthe-Lucile Bibesco* (1842-1931); Frédéric Soulacroix, *Meditation* (1858-1930); Edmund Blair Leighton, *The Request* (1853-1922); Ernst Meissel, *Ein fescher Galan* (1838-1895); Frédéric Soulacroix, *The Afternoon Visitor* (1858-1933).

Layout by Karen M Cox, Adalia Street Press

CONTENTS

N.B. For authenticity, each author has written in the style and spelling pertaining to their story and era or proclivity to their prose. In the spirit of the collective and for consistency throughout, this anthology adheres to US style and punctuation. Additionally, as this is a work inspired by Jane Austen, her own words and phrases may be found herein.

PRAISE FOR THE AUTHORS

ELIZABETH ADAMS

Green Card, "You know the characters are interesting and well-crafted when four hundred pages doesn't feel like enough."
—Austenesque Reviews

On Equal Ground, "This book marks her literary signature; she is not afraid to risk controversial stories and executes them beautifully!"—From Pemberley to Milton

The 26th of November, "I had a smile on my face the whole time I was reading this book. I sighed wistfully after finishing it and went back to my favorite scenes to enjoy it again." —Of Pens and Pages

CHRISTINA BOYD

Dangerous to Know: Jane Austen's Rakes & Gentlemen Rogues, "Each tells a story that was left out of Austen's original works. They manage to tell each in such a way it feels authentic to her vision and style." —Silver Petticoat Review

Rational Creatures, "…impressive anthology introduces the works of sixteen gifted Jane Austen-inspired authors, whose stories reimagine adventures of Austen's characters and glow with the beloved novelist's timeless blend of romantic intrigue, witticisms, and biting social commentary on life's absurdities. Each author's style matches the elegance of the Regency period; Austen fans will be pleased." —Publishers Weekly

The Darcy Monologues, "Think of *The Darcy Monologues* as your JAFF gateway drug. Don't worry, experts agree; it lowers anxiety, increases imagination, and is very good for health." —Period Drama Madness

Yuletide: A Jane Austen-inspired Collection of Stories, "…a special collection of Austen-y romance set in the snow, ripe with carriage rides and mistletoe, but staying close enough to the original work to be enjoyable and fun." —Drunk Austen

KAREN M COX

1932, "A sexy and exciting story, *1932* is a truly fresh take on this timeless tale." —Bustle

I Could Write a Book, "...with eloquent style, grace, and insight Karen Cox has proven, once again, she can indeed 'write a book!'" —Austenesque Reviews

Son of a Preacher Man, originally published as *At the Edge of the Sea*, "...intoxicating and heartfelt romance." —Publishers Weekly

Undeceived: Pride and Prejudice in the Spy Game, "Love it when an author can surprise me." —Delighted Reader

J. MARIE CROFT

A Little Whimsical in His Civilities, "If there's an Austen hero that deserves a good chuckle at himself, I can think of none other more deserving than the proud and staid Mr. Darcy. Ms. Croft helps him loosen up his cravat in a manner that is playful, poetic, and utterly romantic." —Just Jane 1813

Love at First Slight, "There was not a single thing I did not like about this novel. The author's sharp wit could rival that of Jane Austen...a pure delight to read." —Addicted to Austen

AMY D'ORAZIO

A Lady's Reputation, "Be still my beating heart!" –Babblings of a Bookworm

A Short Period of Exquisite Felicity, "...a rollercoaster ride of emotions—angst, heartbreak, anger, then awe, shock, and love." —Of Pens and Pages

The Best Part of Love, "...reels with intense drama and is so emotionally charged." —Readers' Favorite

LEIGH DREYER

The Best Laid Flight Plans: A Modern Pride and Prejudice Variation, "I loved this interpretation of Lizzy so much—she was intently focused...she still had her lively spirit, wry sense of humor, loyalty to loved ones, and yet, was a tenacious pilot in training. Lieutenant Bennet is my hero!" —Austenesque Reviews

The Path Less Traveled: A Modern Pride and Prejudice Variation, "This is a very well researched glimpse into a world just as foreign to me as any sci-fi story but written in such a way that I never felt out of place. Highly recommended." —Amazon Reviewer

JENETTA JAMES

Lovers Knot, "...intriguing. There are plenty of red herrings, devious characters, and of course, there is romance." —Olga, Rosie's Book Review Team

Suddenly Mrs. Darcy, "...a touching, sometimes dark, often playfully sexy interpretation of what might have been..." —Jane Austen's Regency World Magazine

The Elizabeth Papers, "...a novel that will appeal to fans of Jane Austen and romantic mysteries." —Publishers Weekly

CHRISTINA MORLAND

A Remedy Against Sin: A Pride and Prejudice Variation, "One of my favourite novels!" —Of Pens and Pages

Seasons of Waiting: A Pride and Prejudice Variation, "This variation has depth that reaches into the soul and one that will stay with me." —Amazon Reviewer

This Disconcerting Happiness: A Pride and Prejudice Variation, "Their love affair is a thing of beauty, I sometimes felt I was intruding—but I would have loved to intrude for another 500 pages!" —Top 1000 Amazon Reviewer

BEAU NORTH

Longbourn's Songbird, "North gives a voice to a whole new demographic of characters and expertly navigates the social confines of conservative Southern expectations of the times." —San Francisco Book Review

Modern Love, "...a love story that cuts through to the heart of what we're looking for as we futilely swipe right—someone who knows us, all the parts of us, and loves us all the more for it." —Maureen Lee Lenker of Entertainment Weekly

The Colonel: A Longbourn's Songbird Novel, "Every so often, a book comes along that will stay with a reader long after the book is finished. *The Colonel* is one of those books. —InD'Tale Magazine

The Many Lives of Fitzwilliam Darcy, "...possibly one of my all-time favorites..." —Diary of an Eccentric

JOANA STARNES

Mr. Bennet's Dutiful Daughter, "'She did it again,' I told myself as I savored the feelings whirling around inside of me." —Just Jane 1813

The Falmouth Connection, "Joana Starnes writes with great verve and affection about the familiar characters—and an intriguing cast of unfamiliar ones." —Jane Austen's Regency World Magazine

The Journey Home to Pemberley, "Prose like that keep me coming back to Austen-inspired fiction!" —The Quill Ink

The Unthinkable Triangle, "...full of feeling...a book full of soul." —From Pemberley to Milton

FOREWORD BY TESSA DARE

As readers, we all have books we wish we could read again for the first time. Jane Austen's *Pride and Prejudice* will forever sit at the top of my list.

When I picked up the book from a library shelf, I was a teenager in the early 1990s—which most diehard Janeites will recognize to be a few years BC. As in, Before Colin (Firth). In 1995, the six-hour BBC adaptation of *Pride and Prejudice* acquainted the world with the very great pleasure a fine gentleman in a pond-drenched shirt can bestow. I, too, was bewitched body and soul.

But long before Firth's earthy, sex-symbol Mr. Darcy made his sweaty dive into the pond, my heart belonged to Elizabeth Bennet.

On my first reading of the book, I began with no knowledge whatsoever of the plot or characters. I went into the story as Lizzy did, knowing nothing but what she learned, and guessing at nothing but what she inferred. Wickham seemed a nice, handsome fellow. Mr. Darcy was an arrogant arse. I was as secure in my judgments of their characters as Elizabeth was in hers.

Then—out of nowhere—Mr. Darcy proposed to her at Hunsford. The shock! The horror! My indignation was extreme. How *dare* he. He did not deserve her, *could* not deserve her... And truthfully, up until the end of the book, I was still not sure that he *did* deserve her.

But I had to admit, the man could grovel.

> *I have been a selfish being all my life, in practice, though not in principle. ... Such I was, from eight to eight and twenty; and such I might still have been but for you, dearest, loveliest Elizabeth! What do I not owe you! You taught me a lesson, hard indeed at first, but most advantageous. By you, I was properly humbled. I came to you without a doubt of my reception. You showed me how insufficient were all my pretensions to please a woman worthy of being pleased.*

"A woman worthy of being pleased." With those words, I was won over. Mr. Darcy could stay.

To paraphrase Jennifer Lynn Barnes, an academic psychologist who studies fandom, readers are drawn to characters who feel "just like us, but *awesome*." That was Lizzy for me. I identified with her opinionated nature, her impatience with the world around her, and—of course—her love of books. I also envied her fearlessness in speaking her mind, her unshakeable belief that she deserved respect, love, and happiness, and her unwillingness to settle for anything less.

She was just like me, but *awesome*.

In fact, when the senior yearbook survey came around, I looked at the question "Who is the person you most admire?" and answered with two words: "Elizabeth Bennet."

Difficult as it may be to believe, not every great writer admired Elizabeth Bennet—or, by extension, Jane Austen. Poet W.H. Auden bemoaned the unflinching honesty with which Austen mingled financial realities and heartfelt emotions.

> *You could not shock her more than she shocks me;*
> *Beside her Joyce seems innocent as grass.*
> *It makes me most uncomfortable to see.*
> *An English spinster of the middle class*
> *Describe the amorous effects of "brass,"*

Reveal so frankly and with sobriety
The economic basis of society.

It's undeniable that from first page to last, *Pride and Prejudice* acknowledges the realities of "brass" in a 19th century woman's life. Austen does not permit her characters (or the reader) the fantasy that true love somehow renders poverty joyful—or even bearable. Money matters, her novels freely admit. But so does love. So does earning the respect of others, and maintaining respect for oneself. Acknowledging the pressing realities of her family's financial situation only serves to make Elizabeth's characterization stronger. She is more admirable, not less.

If Elizabeth were motivated by financial concerns, *Pride and Prejudice* could have come to any of a dozen swift and unsatisfying endings. She could have married the insufferable Mr. Collins. She could have nudged Jane to reveal her feelings and encourage Mr. Bingley. She could have courted Lady Catherine's favor at Rosings and openly pursued Colonel Fitzwilliam during their walks about the park. She could have accepted Mr. Darcy's shocking, arrogant proposal through gritted teeth.

And yet, Lizzy's spirit would not allow any of these. Only love would persuade her to marriage, she resolved. Once she found that love, she was equally resolved to never relinquish or deny it—ultimately prompting Lady Catherine de Bourgh's iconic exclamation: "Obstinate, headstrong girl!"

Lady Catherine might have found a sympathetic friend in Mark Twain, who famously wrote, "Every time I read *Pride and Prejudice*, I want to dig [Austen] up and beat her over the skull with her own shinbone." Colorful as that image is, it's hard to believe Twain gave Austen a fair reading, since by his own admission he never read her novels through to the end.

> *She makes me detest all her people, without reserve. Is that her intention? It is not believable. Then is it her purpose to make the reader detest her people up to the middle of the book and love them in the rest of the chapters? That could*

be. That would be high art. It would be worthwhile, too. Some day I will examine the other end of her books and see.

If Twain had ever overcome his own pride and prejudice and read through to the end of the novel, would he, like me, have been won over by Elizabeth's bravery and Darcy's groveling? Would he have come to love the characters as I do? I'm not sure. However, I hope he would have come to *know* Elizabeth and Darcy in all their complexity —each one an alloy of admitted flaws and admirable strengths.

This is the gift Jane Austen gave us in Elizabeth Bennet. She created a heroine in which "obstinate, headstrong girl" inhabits the same space as "dearest, loveliest Elizabeth." Four strong qualities, all indivisible parts of a whole. She is opinionated and adored, stubborn and respected, imperfect and loved. Is it any wonder she has delighted and inspired readers for over two centuries? I'd go so far as to say Lizzy deserves credit for Mr. Darcy's devoted following, too. We love Darcy because he's smart enough to love Elizabeth—a woman worthy of being pleased.

In this anthology, the authors have given Elizabeth new paths to walk in Regency England and beyond—reimagining her as a modern-day electrical engineering student, an actress in Golden-Age Hollywood, or an Edwardian-era suffragette. Yet in every story Lizzy is possessed of a keen intellect and an irrepressible spirit, and she is loved by Darcy for those very same qualities Lady Catherine scorned.

"I take no leave of you," Lady Catherine went on to add in that acrimonious conversation. "I send no compliments to your mother."

Lady Catherine was right to withhold any compliments to Lizzy's mother. Not merely because Mrs. Bennet is the embodiment of absurdity, but because Elizabeth is, and always has been, her own person. As countless t-shirts, coffee mugs, and this anthology can attest, generations of readers have embraced the epithet "obstinate, headstrong girl" as the compliment Jane Austen surely intended it to be.

TESSA DARE is the *New York Times* and *USA Today* bestselling author of more than twenty historical romances.

Mixing wit, sensuality, and emotion, Tessa writes Regency-set romance novels that feel relatable to modern readers. With her bestselling "Spindle Cove", "Castles Ever After", and "Girl Meets Duke" series, she has had great fun creating heroines who defy the conventions of their time—engaging in "unladylike" pursuits that range from paleontology to beer-making—and dreaming up the strong-willed, sexy heroes who find their hearts ensnared by them.

A librarian by training and a booklover at heart, Tessa makes her home in Southern California, where she lives with her husband, their two children, and a trio of cosmic kitties.

For the Elizabeth Bennet in all of us...

Elizabeth: Obstinate Headstrong Girl

Resolution

Amy D'Orazio

"I am only resolved to act in that manner, which will, in my own opinion, constitute my happiness, without reference to you, or to any person so wholly unconnected with me." –Chapter LVI

RESOLUTION
Amy D'Orazio

ONE FORTNIGHT BEFORE THE WEDDING

*I*t was two weeks until the wedding when by chance I saw him. Being exceedingly careful to keep myself in the shadows of the curtains, I peered out onto the street below. There was a carriage, not Bingley's, and there was Bingley on the side, laughing and talking.

And there was he.

My blood ran cold, then hot, and I had to pause a moment, leaning against the dressing table in Jane's guest apartment until the fever had abated. Was it really him?

I could not see very much of him from where I stood, but there was no mistaking; it was him. The little curl of hair beneath his hat, his form, long and lean under his greatcoat—there was and is no one else like him. My heart pounded in my throat, and without thinking, I raised my hand to press against my chest, trying to calm the unruly beast.

Bingley laughed, and Mr. Darcy did too, a low chuckle, barely audible.

I pressed my fist to my mouth and scarcely breathed while I watched the two old friends conclude their conversation. Then the two men tipped their hats to one another; Mr. Darcy climbed into his carriage and Bingley entered the house. I heard the front door close behind my brother-in-law just as I stared at the back of Mr. Darcy's chaise being pulled away by four horses which seemed damnably, regrettably quick.

I was still staring at the spot where he was last visible when Jane burst into my bedchamber, already in a fine lather. "You are not even dressed!" she cried out in dismay. "Where is Vickery? I declare I shall wring that woman's neck if she does not stop disappearing at the most inconvenient times!"

I had to laugh; she sounded so much like my mother. "Jane, calm down. Is it not hours until the first guests arrive?"

"*One* hour! And pray do not tell me to calm down. My husband seems to think he can simply go about Town all afternoon inviting anyone he sees to come to the house for dinner! And people accept it! I declare, I never knew anything like it. It is as if all of society has collectively decided good manners mean nothing and they should all just wander about, stopping hither and yon wherever they feel so moved to dine!"

While she ranted, Jane had managed to push me into the seat by the vanity. Evidently my sister, not seeing her maid instantly before her, had decided she would dress me herself. Her nimble fingers began to plait wildly even as she continued her diatribe.

"I said to him, 'Charles, my love, surely Mr. Darcy has already plans for this evening—'"

"Jane, you are hurting my head—"

"And just as happy as you please, my husband tells me—"

"What the devil! My head!" I said with extra emphasis, in case she had not heard me before.

"'Oh but I persuaded him to send his regrets to them and come to our party.' I declare sometimes I think marriage turns a man into a half-wit! And then—"

"Mr. Darcy? Mr. Darcy is coming here tonight?"

Jane gave me a cross look in the mirror. "Are you listening to anything I am telling you? Yes! Charles just came home from his club, told me he saw Mr. Darcy, and has invited Mr. Darcy to the party!"

"Oh no!" It felt as though my heart had plummeted into my shoes.

Perversely, Jane seemed even more vexed by my protest. In a trice, she neatly switched to the other side of the argument. "Surely you do not still despise him? You need to grow up and stop holding such silly grudges against people."

"I do not hold grudges!"

"Then what difference does it make if he comes to your engagement dinner or not? He is Charles's dear friend, and Charles has not seen him in an age; I am sure I should be delighted to have him here as should you."

Vickery entered then in a flurry of apologies and excuses, and Jane was able to take herself off to do whatever wifely duties were required of her. Vickery immediately set to work on my hair, clucking mournfully over the frantic plaits my sister had installed, and I was left to my thoughts.

Mr. Darcy. After all this time.

We had a strange history, Mr. Darcy and I. He had insulted me at an assembly, and I responded by teasing him and tormenting him—it seemed a sure spur to my genius to dislike him so heartily when all the others were fawning around him. But then he proposed to me— forever ago, really, an April night at Hunsford parsonage that surely everyone has forgot but me—and then gave me a letter revealing his whole self. As it was, I had been wrong about everything I thought I knew about him. Was it any surprise that I found myself falling in love with him when we met in Derbyshire that summer? As Shakespeare himself said: "My only love sprung from my only hate! Too early seen unknown, and known too late!"

But then came Lydia's big mistake which nearly ruined her and my entire family—I say nearly because he saved her and us. After that, he corrected his error with Bingley, leading to Jane's ultimate happiness when she was reunited with and married to her true love.

What he did not do, however, was return to me. For whatever feelings he once had, they seemed to have died somewhere between late summer in Derbyshire and autumn in Hertfordshire. It plagued me for a long time, wondering why he forgot me, but after too many months repining, I decided I must put it aside or risk ending a spinster, living on the charity of my relations.

That was when Mr. Julius Timpson came along.

My Timpson is a banker, not a gentleman but wealthy enough that the gentlemen do not much care about the distinction. He has a banker's looks, tidy hair and a slender bearing. He lives in London, in an elegant house at Berkeley Square, and in the heat of summer, when no one is in Town, he takes a house in Cheltenham or Brighton and enjoys himself there until business requires him to do otherwise. He is older than I am by ten years and is fond of music—and the sound of his own opinions—in equal measure. He had been something of a dedicated bachelor, and there were many broken hearts when our engagement was announced.

I am not in love with him, but I like him, and I think we shall live out our lives in contentment and harmony.

He awaited me at the bottom of Jane's stairs, looking very elegant in a new suit that was modish without being foppish. "Looking as beautiful as ever, Miss Bennet."

"Thank you, sir." I descended the final stair and placed my hand on his arm. "Is everyone here?"

"Mrs. Bingley's drawing room is nearly bursting with them all," he said, sounding amused. "She told me we must wait here until we are announced. Wants to give them all the proper chance to felicitate us, I suppose."

I laughed at that, though I was nearly eaten up with dismay over the prospect. I had wished to see Mr. Darcy before he saw me; instead, I would be on display, like some sort of horse at auction, whilst he lingered in a corner, no doubt.

I espied him almost immediately as the doors were flung wide and we stood, Timpson and I, awaiting our acclaim. Cheers and cries of congratulation rang out around us as my eyes went immediately to him. He stood next to Bingley, tall and handsome and unsmiling as ever. His eyes flicked over me, then landed for a moment on Timpson. Then he turned, slightly, but enough so that his back was to us. Why did that still pain me?

"You are very dull this evening." Miss Bingley sipped her wine and regarded me coolly. Naturally Miss Bingley noticed my listlessness.

Time had taught us to forget our enmity but to say we were friends would have stretched the truth. We were two ladies whose lives had intertwined too closely to avoid some degree of intimacy. "I should think you would be crowing your victory. I hear he told you that you should decorate the entire house to suit you."

I shrugged. "The present furnishings suit me well enough."

"And this?" She reached out and gently touched the sapphires at my throat. "Does this suit you too?"

"Stop." I gave her a little frown. "You know that is not why I am marrying him."

"Heaven knows I would have taken him for much less," she said with shocking honesty. "I simply cannot decide if I should go have Mr. Darcy rebuff me—it is rather our custom—or go permit Mr. Clay to slaver over me. Oh! But it seems Darcy is coming to us."

I resisted every impulse to turn and look, instead waiting until I saw Caroline's face bend into her usual flirtatious moue. Then I turned, finding myself very close to him. He bowed, and Caroline and I curtsied. "How do you do, ladies? Miss Bennet, may I offer my sincerest wishes for your happiness?"

"And you as well," I replied, then cursed myself inwardly for such a stupid remark. "That is to say, I hope you are well?"

"Yes, Mr. Darcy, you terrible man. Where have you been hiding from us?" Caroline managed to simper, pout, and pry all at once.

"I have been travelling with my sister," he said. "Here and there. Such places as I thought she should see."

"Oh, dear Georgiana!" Miss Bingley exclaimed, closing her eyes to convey her rapture. "I simply must see her! When does she receive callers?"

I permitted Miss Bingley to have her way, to flirt and cajole and press Mr. Darcy into extending an invitation for her to wait upon his sister. I said nothing, gave no indication of interest in the schemes, and for the most part, kept my gaze fixed on Caroline. But any time I chanced a quick peek at the third in our tête-à-tête, I saw his eyes trained upon me.

What I wanted to do was grab him by the cravat and demand

some answers. Why had he not returned? Was there someone else he loved? Was it Lydia's affair which drove him from me? The questions got louder and more insistent in my head until I needed to excuse myself, nearly running across the room for the safety of Timpson's side.

When I arrived there and had tucked myself neatly on his arm, right by his side, I looked back at Mr. Darcy. He remained entrapped in Miss Bingley's conversation, but his eyes had followed me. *Why do you still stare, Mr. Darcy? I cannot make you out.*

As it was an engagement party, I was permitted to sit beside Timpson at dinner. Mr. Darcy was too far away for me to speak with, but I reminded myself often that it did not signify where Mr. Darcy was sat, for I was an engaged woman. The only man whose position I need concern myself with was Timpson.

But no one could ever doubt where Timpson was in any case. He enjoyed parties, large and small; he was the sort of man who was filled with diverting stories. At times, his voice was rather too loud, his laugh too hearty, and I do admit that he had a decided tendency to dominate the conversation—but people liked him. He was just *that* sort of man, the kind people drew to, like moths to a flame, me included.

It seemed, however, that Mr. Darcy was immune to his charms. I did not look his way often, but the few times I did, he was either looking at Timpson or at me; neither of us seemed to please him.

THE SEPARATION OF THE SEXES SEEMED INTERMINABLE THAT EVENING. We could hear, often, bursts of laughter coming from the dining room. They were enjoying themselves too well to hurry to us, it seemed, but oddly it was the fact that Mr. Darcy lingered, rather than Timpson, that annoyed me.

When the men came in, two were absent: Bingley and Darcy. Timpson came to me at once, where I stood in a group with three other young ladies.

I was mad to know where Darcy was. No doubt with Bingley, but where, and why? Fortune smiled on me when one of my friends asked about a book of poetry Timpson had given me.

"I know exactly where it is," I said, already moving towards the door.

"Send a maid, Eliza," said Miss Bingley.

"No, no, it will take me longer to explain it to Vickery than it will to just run up there myself." I smiled over my shoulder, almost running out into the hall. I slowed then, forcing my feet to be utterly silent as I sought some hint of where he was.

No sound escaped from the dining room, save the noises of the servants going about the business of clearing the table. Puzzled, I went to the stair nearest the front of the house, stopping myself when I heard them in the vestibule. I felt a little guilty for eavesdropping until I realised I was the subject of their conversation.

"...approve of the marriage?"

"Who am I to approve or disapprove?" Bingley chuckled. "Mr. Bennet signed the papers, and Lizzy is nearly twenty-three years old. She knew her mind at twenty and has only grown more definite with each passing year."

"And this is her choice?"

"Of course!"

I had stepped into the light before I knew what I was about. "Mr. Darcy, something tells me you disapprove of my choice of husband."

He straightened immediately and, even in the dim light, I could see that he flushed scarlet.

"Lizzy, do not misunderstand us," Bingley said, always quick to intercede if he suspected a row should ensue. "Mr. Darcy merely noted that your spirits were rather low tonight for an engagement party."

"I assure you that nothing is further from the truth," I said icily. "Indeed, were I any happier, it could scarce be borne."

"I am glad to hear it," said Darcy with his customary hauteur. "All is as it should be then."

"I am not surprised my intended husband does not meet your approval," I told him. "After all, he cannot trace his ancestors back to the Conquest, nor does he own half of Derbyshire, or any county for that matter."

"On the contrary," said Darcy, meeting my biting wit head on. "By all accounts, most of the gentry and the nobility are bound to him. It seems he owns most of everyone."

By now, Bingley's man, Hodges, had come to tug his master away. He left us with a worried glance back, but he likely recalled too many of our spats at Netherfield to be genuinely fearful.

"I am not mercenary," I retorted. "Nor have I ever been, as you well know."

"Yes, I do." The conversation paused then, and Mr. Darcy allowed himself to stare at me, to really consider me.

"In any case, what is it to you?"

"Do you love him?"

"I am marrying him," I said, which is no answer at all, and we both knew it. I wondered at his meaning, speaking to Bingley of me, asking such impertinent questions. My anger rose, and I found myself quite unable to resist tossing a bit of it in his direction. "In any case, none of this is any of your concern."

"I am very concerned," he said in a sympathetic tone. "He is going to make you miserable."

"What?" I laughed more heartily than I intended. "I beg your pardon. He makes me very happy indeed."

"Once the thrill of baubles and fripperies wears off, you will wish you had never met him," said Darcy.

"You have no idea of him, nor do you have any idea of me. He is a good man and would never be vicious or cruel to me."

Something changed in Darcy's eyes then. My words seemed to have smitten him although it was not at all my intention. "He has that advantage," he said, seeming far off, almost as if he only spoke to himself. "But he could not possibly love you in the way that I do."

With a little shake of his head, he seemed to recall himself to where he was, what he did. His eyes widened, briefly, with alarm.

"Love me? How can you speak so?"

But Mr. Darcy was turning away, wanting nothing more it seemed than to get away from me. "Congratulations, Miss Bennet, and do enjoy your new life."

"Mr. Darcy, wait—"

But it was too late. He was gone.

THIRTEEN DAYS UNTIL THE WEDDING

THE PARTY WENT ON UNTIL DAWN, AS BINGLEY'S PARTIES TENDED TO DO. Jane and Bingley afforded Timpson and I some bit of privacy, retiring as we said our farewells to one another. As soon as the door closed behind them, Timpson pulled me into his embrace.

I had had too much wine, and I stumbled a little. He caught me, and pressed me close, kissing me in a way that showed me he too was feeling the effects of the evening. As we kissed, I began to do something positively horrid. I began to imagine it was not he, but Darcy, who kissed me.

My ardency rose within me as I envisioned sliding my hands into the curls at Darcy's nape, pressing myself against his long, lean form. I imagined his arms, taut and muscular, clasping me to his chest, and I found myself pressing against him—no, not him, Timpson—but I ignored that bit of my mind which tried to interject.

"Whoa," said Timpson, pulling away at last. "Any more of that and I may need to run off with you."

His voice was a rude intrusion into my fantasies. "Of course." I stepped back, again stumbling as my heel caught on my skirts.

He chuckled indulgently. "Remind me to give you some wine at the breakfast. It seems to be calming your bridal jitters nicely."

Perversely, this vexed me, even more so when he pulled me in for one last kiss, whispering, "A fortnight more, my beloved, and then you are all mine."

HORRID, SCANDALOUS, WANTON, IMMORAL… THE LIST OF CENSURING adjectives I applied to myself was unending. Who would do such a thing? Who would permit liberties to one man while imagining another? A harlot, that was who.

The worst of it all was that I was not very ashamed of myself. Certainly nowhere near what I should have been, and I knew that if I told myself I would never do it again, I would be lying.

Minutes later, I fell into my bed. The room was spinning around me, and I was exhausted, yet I had no expectation of restful sleep. Until this afternoon, I had been happy to marry Timpson. I had been happy, period. And now? Now I was filled with anger, anxiety, doubt, and regret—courtesy of one dinner party.

He never came back. Thinking about it, trying to understand it, had plagued me these many years. Having done so much for my sisters, he had been content to walk away.

At the time, I had persuaded myself that he still loved me. I attributed his kindness to my aunt and uncle and I at Pemberley to ardent love. Perhaps I had been wrong. Maybe he had been only as he was and, as before, I was mistaken in understanding him.

It hardly mattered, did it? I was marrying Timpson, if even now the idea of that felt unnatural and even a little abhorrent. I would be happy with Timpson. *I would!*

But I could not rest. Darcy had invaded my head, and I could not banish him, not while addled with wine and confusion, vexation and grief and far, far too many memories. Somewhere along the way, I found myself out of bed, sitting at the desk in my bedchamber and writing to him.

I did not write much, only his name and these eight words:

Why did you never come back to me?

I HAD A HEADACHE WHEN I WOKE AND HAD COME NO CLOSER TO comprehending any way out of my furious confusion. I kept reminding myself of all the reasons I intended to marry Timpson—

and reminding myself that Darcy had made his wishes clear to me—but nothing seemed to help.

As I sat alone, toying with a plate of eggs and tea, Vickery entered the breakfast room, looking about her as if she expected that the walls had eyes.

"Good day, Vickery," I said.

She came to me immediately, still looking all around her. She leant close over me and murmured against my ear, "I have your reply, miss."

"My reply? What reply?" I turned and gave her a smile, though I had no idea what she meant. Vickery was sweet, but she would have been let go long ago by anyone less forbearing than my sister.

"Not to worry. I have not told your sister a thing."

"A thing about what?" I reached my hand out, expecting some note. "Is it from Timpson?"

"Go to your bedchamber, p'raps? I shall bring it to you."

Mystified, I agreed. Minutes later, as I stood by the fireplace in my bedchamber, Vickery entered, an air of delighted complicity wreathing her. She proudly thrust a folded page towards me, and I took it, unfolding it while still wondering what on earth she was about.

I did as I believe you wished. FD

"FD?"

Vickery looked around her as if someone might have sneaked into the bedchamber. In a lowered voice, she said, "Mr. Darcy, ma'am."

I looked at the page again. *I did as I believe you wished.* "What is the meaning of this?" I asked her in bewilderment. "What on earth would possess him to write me a letter, even a short, utterly incomprehensible one like this?"

Vickery seemed less confident now. "Why, I suppose he felt it gentleman-like to reply to yours."

"To mine!" I stared at her. "I have never written Mr. Darcy a letter."

"Erm, forgive me but the one you left out last night? It said 'Mr. Darcy' and so I—"

Horror shot through me as I realised what she spoke of. "Not the page on my desk?"

"Aye, ma'am." Vickery nodded. "Mrs. Bingley, she tells me I must anticipate a lady's needs, and I saw you had it writ and said, 'Vickery, here is your chance to show Mrs. Bingley you hear her advisements,' and so I took it for you. Sent it over just this morn, and he was quick to reply."

I fell back into a chair that was fortunately nearby, panic immediately thrumming through me. "Oh no. Oh no, no, no. But what did it say?" I searched my mind frantically trying to recall exactly what my note said.

"I cannot say, Miss Bennet. Erm...I hope I did not make some mistake?"

Yes, she certainly had made an enormous mistake, but it was nowhere near the error I had made in writing to Mr. Darcy while under the influence of wine and a late night!

I dismissed Vickery after some indifferent reassurances about her error, though I did mention that in the future she might wish to send only those letters that had been given to her. Then I admonished myself that in the future I should refrain from writing such things as would be utterly disastrous if sent.

TWELVE DAYS BEFORE THE WEDDING

HE DID AS HE BELIEVED I WISHED...? THAT MADE NO SENSE AT ALL. WHAT else could I have done, save for something utterly scandalous like writing to him or tossing myself into his carriage?

But one thing was certain: it did not signify. Whatever whims and inclinations possessed that man, I was going to marry Timpson, and that would be that. I was firmly resolved, even if my heart had not yet caught on to the scheme.

I was reading a letter from Charlotte when Hodges entered the saloon. "Miss Bennet, Mr. Bingley has a caller; and as Mr. Bingley is absent, he has asked to pay his regards to you."

I took the card that Hodges offered, surprised and yet unsurprised to see it belonged to Mr. Darcy. It vexed me how the very sight of his name electrified me. "Send him in," I told Hodges.

He entered the room with an agitated air that immediately brought his proposal at Hunsford to my mind. I invited him to sit, and he did, seeming determined to appear composed.

"You find me alone, sir," I informed him. "Mrs. Bingley has gone out with Miss Bingley, and Mr. Bingley is at his club."

"I know," said he. "For I only just left him there."

"Then why did you come to call on him here?" The question escaped me before I could censure my curiosity.

In reply, he would only quirk an eyebrow.

"Mr. Darcy, you were given a communication which was written while I was indisposed. It was never intended to be sent."

"I am not concerned with the fact that it was sent," he said. "I am only curious about the sentiments it contained."

"How so?"

He rose, his agitation more apparent, and paced towards the window where he leant against the sash and beheld me. Finally, he said, "You wondered that I did not return."

I nodded.

"Did you want me to?"

"Mr. Darcy, I am very nearly a married woman. It hardly signifies."

"*Very nearly* is not at all, in my opinion, and in any case, I ask for nothing more than an answer."

"Perhaps you had no wish to return," I said. "You were silent, grave, and indifferent when you visited Longbourn with Bingley."

"A man who felt less might have spoken more."

"I believed you felt nothing at all."

He stared at me, his incredulity writ plain upon his countenance. "You made little attempt to draw my notice."

I had to lower my eyes. "I was embarrassed," I admitted. "Knowing what my family owed you—"

"Your family owed me nothing." This was said with vehemence.

"And my mother was scarcely civil to you. The entire party seemed to form some design to separate us."

"But all of this," he said, "might have been overcome had I not my aunt's report to know your heart."

His aunt's report? How well I remembered that dark day when Lady Catherine had condescended to visit Longbourn. I had often wondered what she told her nephew, and it seemed now I would know.

Mr. Darcy joined me on my sofa.

"I cannot doubt that your aunt's report of my impertinence, and her strong disapproval of all I said to her, must have made firm your resolve to stay away."

"On the contrary," he said. "Nothing could have made me stay away save for one thing—your vow to never accept me."

"What?" So amazed was I that I leapt to my feet.

He stood with me. "Lady Catherine came to me in London immediately after meeting with you. She told me of her visit, relating in minute detail the subject of your conversation with her. She told me she demanded a promise from you to never accept an offer of marriage from me."

"Indeed she did," I said, angry warmth flooding me. "And I told her I could promise nothing of the sort."

"You refused her?"

"In the strongest possible terms," I said.

The air between us went still as we both began to comprehend what had gone on. Lady Catherine, never one to be gainsaid, had done what she could to separate us...and had succeeded.

"Are you saying my aunt lied to me?"

"I informed Lady Catherine in no uncertain terms that I would not promise her that I would never accept a proposal from you." I shrugged. "How could I when it was my dearest wish, at that time, you would return to Hertfordshire and renew your addresses?"

He said nothing to that, leaving me to resume his post by the window. Minutes went by as I stared at his back, my mind whirling, trying to make sense of what we had only just learnt. I suppose he did likewise. At length, he turned to face me again.

"Forgive me, but I must ask you again. You refused to give her the assurances she sought?"

"Unquestionably," I said. "I remember it as clear as yesterday. She asked for my promise that I would never enter into an engagement with you, and I said I would make no promise of that kind. She did not misunderstand me: my refusal angered her, made her insult me and my family even further than she already had."

Mr. Darcy was clenching his hands into fists so tightly I thought he was going to break his own bones. "I will never speak to her again," he spat. "Her interference, her treatment of you cannot be forgiven."

"It cannot signify," I said gently, with more sedateness than I truly felt. "I am getting married to Timpson. She has had her way with us."

He looked at me for a long moment then quit the room with not a syllable more. When he had gone, I went to my bedchamber, intending to watch him leave. I would say goodbye as I wished to say it, with tears in my eyes and regret, deep regret, on my face.

I was there in time to see him exit the house, to view his confident step which seemed to have lost nothing of its surety. He came to the street and then paused, turning back for a moment and seeming to stand in contemplation of the Bingley's front door. The pain it gave me was considerable, and yet, I could not cry. The ache in my chest would not give way to the sweet relief of physical agony.

In a sudden burst of movement, Darcy yanked the hat from his head, throwing it violently against the ground and kicking it. I gasped, then pressed my hand to my mouth, watching as he remained, shoulders slumped and chest heaving for several long moments.

At length, he retrieved his hat, brushing at it as no doubt he wished it should not show evidence of its recent abuse. Then he placed it back on his head and began again to walk, his gait slow and not at all confident.

"I love you," I whispered to his retreating form.

TEN DAYS BEFORE THE WEDDING

A FAMILY DINNER WAS PLANNED FOR TEN DAYS BEFORE THE WEDDING, just Jane and Bingley, and Miss Bingley, as well as Timpson and me. It was, in some sense, given in my honour. The occasion: my birthday. I am three-and-twenty today. Timpson gave me an extraordinarily large necklace, replete with diamonds and rubies along with a matching bracelet. I thanked him—though privately I thought them rather gaudy—but I took off the small amber cross I customarily wore and put on his jewels. They were heavy on me, and I could not forget that they were there for an instant.

My dismay grew throughout dinner. I set out trying to list, in my mind, all the reasons that I should marry Timpson. *Because I am three and twenty* and *do not want to be a spinster* seemed to be the best I could come up with.

There were things which vexed me about Timpson, had always vexed me, but which seemed painfully glaring given my recent inter-actions with Mr. Darcy. I cared nothing for the fact that he was not a gentleman, but I cared very much that he did not act like one.

He had a decided tendency to talk too much and often he spoke of things he ought not—he was too direct, too bold in his pronounce-ments. He would forget himself sometimes and walk in front of me or neglect to stand when I did. Such behaviour embarrasses me which in turn alarms me. I have spent a great deal of my life embarrassed by my mother, and I just do not know if I have fortitude sufficient to be humiliated by the ill-manners of my husband for the rest of my life.

And I do not love him. I love Darcy. I know not the exact moment when my heart became his, but it has been thus for some years now, and it does not seem it will ever change.

Timpson and I were again granted some moments of privacy at the end of the evening, and I found my spirits revolting against it. Nevertheless, I submitted to his kisses and caresses, and if he found my enthusiasm wanting, he said nothing of it.

When I retired, I sat in my bed, my knees pulled tight against my chest and my nightgown stretched over them. Jane and I used to do this as children, pretending we had enormous breasts. I did it now for comfort, drawing myself tight and hearing a litany in my head, wondering what on earth I had done.

SIX DAYS BEFORE THE WEDDING

I HAD NOT BEEN SLEEPING OR EATING SINCE I SAW HIM, AND MY GOWN, the one I was meant to wear to my wedding, showed it. It folded and gaped where once it was smooth and tight, and neither the modiste nor Jane was happy about it.

We had already been there an hour when the seamstress stuck me with a pin. I was off in a world of my own making by that point and hardly registered the slight pain, and thus, by the time anyone knew what had happened, blood had already seeped onto the fine silk. Both Madame Marseille and Jane exclaimed in horror. There was an immediate flurry of fussing and clucking, but I could scarcely rouse the least morsel of concern.

"You cannot even see it," I said.

Jane was far more interested in the gown than I was. It was pale blue picked out in silver thread, and in truth, it was a *Jane-gown*. It would have made her look like an angel, but it made me look like the angel's sickly cousin.

Jane came to inspect the spot and make dire pronouncements and judgements until it was determined that a bit of extra embroidery and beading might be sufficient to hide the dreadful blemish. I still did not care. Let them do as they wished to me; nothing seemed to matter anymore.

The ordeal was completed after three hours, and Jane, relieved and happy, invited me to take tea nearby. I kissed her cheek; no matter how disinterested I might be about my wedding, I could not forget her kindness. "Above all, I think I need a walk," I told her. "The fresh air will help, I think."

Jane's hand flew to my head. "Oh Lizzy, do anything but get a fever!"

"I shall do all I can to avoid it." I smiled gently. "I have been too much indoors of late."

"You have been hiding," Jane scolded. "But yes, my mother shall come into Town tomorrow so I daresay you should get your time to yourself while you still can."

So, Jane climbed into the carriage alone—she knew me too well to make any futile protest against a solitary ramble—and I set off on my way to the park. Hyde Park is the best thing about London in my estimation, uniting several of my favourites in one place—fresh air, nature, and an ample supply of characters to study.

Despite these charms, however, Hyde Park failed to lift my spirits. I wandered for some time, laggard and dull, until I decided it was all quite useless and turned to go back to Bingley's house. In so doing, I nearly collided with Mr. Darcy.

"Sir!" My hand flew to my bonnet, though our collision was nowhere near so severe as to send it flying. "Forgive me, I did not see you."

His face was lined and grave. Belatedly, he made a short bow to me. "No, the fault was entirely mine. I beg you would excuse my blunder." He paused for a moment, then said, "I have been behind you for some time. I see your enthusiasm for rambles has not diminished."

With a half-smile and a little shrug, I said, "The park has had difficulty in rendering its usual state of enchantment upon me today. I had just decided to return home."

"May I escort you?" On my nod of consent, he offered his arm, and my hand slid into it, quickly and happily. We strolled for a time in silence, and I said not a word when he guided me down a path which led away from the direction I needed to return to Bingley's house.

"I must offer my apologies…"

"For what?"

After another short pause, he said, "For believing in my aunt. After much contemplation over these last days, I have realised I can only blame myself for our present circumstance. I was a coward. No matter what she said, I should have come back to you and seen how things were for myself."

"Do not blame yourself for trusting someone who you believed had your best interests at heart."

"It was not my best interests which directed her," he said sharply. Then, he stopped himself. "But no. I cannot allow my resentment of her to consume me. I wish only to apologise for my shortcomings and to assure you that I wish you every happiness with Tim— Timpson."

I pretended not to notice how he stumbled over Timpson's name. "Thank you."

"Indeed, I began to be philosophical about the whole thing," said he. "I have endeavoured to persuade myself that it is how Fate would have it."

"Then Fate is a bacon-brained imbecile." The words escaped me before I knew what I was saying, but he only looked at me and chuckled.

"I agree."

We continued walking, and I could not help but reflect on the comfort I felt at his side. It seemed right and good to be with him in this way, even as my mind fought against feeling so.

"You will be an excellent husband to some fortunate lady." My words startled us both out of our reflections.

"Me? No, I will never marry."

"You must!" I said, forcing a little laugh. "Do you not require an heir?"

"I suppose that is the way to get one. It is beyond belief how I will find anyone to like well enough to marry, not with you occupying every thought in my heart."

"So, you do still love me?"

He was shocked by the question. "Did you doubt it?"

"Yes, of course, I did." It was not easy to be so open and artless, but he had confessed his feelings, and I knew I had to confess mine. "It has troubled me deeply these months to try and understand why you never came back to me. I could only presume that the difficulties with my family had dimmed your ardour."

"Never," he said quietly. "I curse my cowardice and my faith in my aunt's word. You would have accepted me then?"

"Before you could get the words out of your mouth," I said with a smile.

Reason intruded then, and I recognised that no good would come of this conversation such as it was. The past was past, and what was done was done. I could not walk in this park, speaking of love and romance with one man while on the verge of marriage to another.

"But never mind that. All of this will be forgot, a tale of youthful folly that in time will scarcely be thought of. In any case, you have been abroad for a long time. I daresay I was scarcely considered these months of your absence."

He stopped immediately, turning to face me, his mien intent and serious. "There was not one day, not so much as an hour, when I did not think of you. If nothing else, I have learnt that time is a poor healer for such fevers as mine."

His confession, and the feeling with which he rendered it, softened me and tossed aside all my good resolve. I reached up and touched his cheek with my fingertips. Quick as a wink, he turned his head, kissing my hand and, with equal rapidity, I pulled it back. Though my hand was gloved, his kiss seared me. I began to walk long strides that he matched easily.

"Forgive me. I should not have done that."

"I can forgive you more easily than I forgive myself."

He looked at me, questioning my meaning, and I said in a soft voice, "I have thought of you…you and I. Together. Heaven forbid I should have some substance to add to my imaginings."

Now he understood me. His eyes grew dark and intent, and his gaze shifted to my lips, once, then twice, before he turned his head away from me. I heard a deep sigh.

It was a good place to leave him, and I knew if I did not, I would do something regrettable. The path which would take me to the street was upon us, and the conversation had taken us to places better untrodden.

"I must get home."

"Does Timpson await you even now?"

"Perhaps," I admitted. "Promise me one thing?"

"What?"

"Promise you will find someone to love?"

"I already did," he said flatly before turning and walking away from me.

FIVE DAYS BEFORE THE WEDDING

MY MOTHER'S ARRIVAL IN LONDON COULD ONLY DEPRESS ME FURTHER. She swept in with the airs of a duchess—my sister's marriage had impressed upon her deeply the sense of her own grandeur—and began at once to criticise me. Having long lamented my rather ungenerous curves, she was appalled to find me "positively emaciated" and wondered aloud, often, how Timpson could find me appealing.

It was too much. When she said, "It will be a wonder if he does not throw you over," I immediately retorted, "Perhaps I shall throw him over first, and then we will not have to fret about it."

I turned and fled, seeking the sanctuary of my bedchamber. As I went, I envisioned myself wrapped in a blanket, hiding from the world but once I arrived, I could not sit. I stood in the middle of the room, wanting and needing something that I could not name.

I am only resolved to act in that manner, which will, in my own opinion, constitute my happiness, without reference to you, or to any person so wholly unconnected with me.

I said those words to Lady Catherine boldly and assuredly that autumn in the little wilderness next to Longbourn. But had I held true to myself? Was this happiness? What if I could never be happy again, knowing that I had been denied my real life by one meddlesome old crone?

Could I see him about Town and be his acquaintance? Would I tolerate being at the theatre, perhaps, me with my husband and he with his wife? The very notion of it made me want to scream.

"I love Mr. Darcy." There, it had been spake aloud.

I had not, naturally, been in earnest when I spoke to my mother of jilting Timpson—but when the words had been uttered, I felt relief flood me. Cool, sweet relief, unlike anything I had felt these past days.

Timpson did not deserve to be jilted but neither did he deserve a wife who held another man in her heart. I knew what I had to do and though it would not be easy, it was right.

FOUR DAYS BEFORE THE WEDDING

TIMPSON TOOK IT WELL, FAR BETTER THAN I DESERVED. I HAD TO BE honest with him; I told him my heart was, and still is, Darcy's, and I apologised for the pain I caused. Timpson was too good, consoling me as I wept, even trying to refuse the return of the jewels he had given me. I could not allow it and insisted he accept them.

My mother did not take it well. She alternated between haranguing me, wailing and lamenting to Jane, and stony silence. She spoke of her intention to find me a position as a governess or companion, and she informed me that I would have no part of her four thousand pounds when she died. She said she would rather see me starve than give me a farthing and then mentioned again my deplorably slim figure.

Darcy had hied off to Pemberley it seemed, the very day after we had said our goodbyes in the park. I wondered if he even knew I had thrown over Timpson.

Jane, who was the only person who really understood all the particulars of my disaster, only once asked, "Have you considered what will happen if Darcy does not...?"

"If again he does not come back?" I finished for her. "Yes, I have. But I was determined to be true to myself. To have one man in my heart and another in my bed would make me a liar and a harlot. I could not abide it."

ONE MONTH AFTER THE WEDDING THAT DID NOT HAPPEN

Bingley came home from his club looking peculiarly sober. He asked me to join him in his book room, and my heart pulsed with fear. Was it Darcy? What news?

I joined him, sitting when asked, though my heart wanted to leap from my chest. My hands, of their own mind, began to twist and churn in my lap, but I stopped them. Bingley saw and his face folded into compassion.

"Lizzy," he began. "I must tell you something, but it is not easy news to impart."

"Just tell me," I begged. "The anticipation is worst of all."

"Very well." He drew in a deep breath. "He is engaged."

"What?" I gasped, flooded with dismay. "No! But...." Images flooded my mind: Darcy and his cousin? Darcy and some beautiful London society miss? Would I see them often? When would they marry? It made me sick to my stomach. "But...but how? Who?"

"Miss Jenny Bosworth," he said gently, reaching out with one hand to lay it atop mine. "Are you well? Shall I call Jane?"

"Miss Bosworth!" I shrieked. "She is sixteen!"

"Seventeen." Bingley looked awkward. "Or so I have been told."

"She is younger than his sister! I could not have thought it of him."

Bingley drew back, giving me a confused look. "Timpson has a sister?"

"No." His confusion cut through my distress, and we both took a moment to collect our wits. I used my finger to remove some moisture which had collected in my eyes and forced my breathing to become regular. "No, Timpson does not have a sister."

"Whose sister do you mean?" Bingley asked.

"Forgive me. Tell me again—who is engaged? Miss Bosworth and—"

"Timpson." Bingley sounded as if he thought me mad. "Who did you think I meant?"

"Ah...I do not know. In any case, Timpson will marry Miss Bosworth. Is that what you heard?"

"Yes," said Bingley with his brow contracted and his eyes still muddled. "The wedding is next week."

"Good for him," I said. "I would not wish him to languish."

"It is only a month," Bingley protested. "Rather indecent if you ask me."

"Oh, who cares about that. He was supposed to be married by now anyway."

"To you! Not just to any likely lady who appeared eligible."

I waved away that concern. "I am glad for him."

"But it seemed you were upset before?"

"Upset?" I shook my head, feeling light of heart and much relieved. "Not at all. I wish him joy."

I rose then to leave but before I went, I asked, "Have you heard from Mr. Darcy?"

Bingley nodded. "I have but I must admit, I have lagged dreadfully in replying to him. Oh! He asked me to offer his felicitations to the new Mr. and Mrs. Timpson."

"I believe you still can but pray be sure he knows that the new Mrs. Timpson is not the former Miss Elizabeth Bennet." I smiled. "Perhaps you will do it even now?"

"I shall!" replied Bingley cheerfully.

FIVE DAYS LATER

My days were spent at the window, looking for callers, and on the fifth day, my vigil was gratified. He was shown in by Hodges, his spirits in clear agitation. For some long moments, we merely stood staring at one another.

"You came back," I said with a smile.

"As fast as I could without killing my horse." He came to me then, pulling me tight into his chest with no further ceremony. I inhaled deeply, feeling the comfort of him surround me and wondered that I ever thought, for even a moment, that I might be married to anyone else.

"Are you well? I am sure the gossip has been difficult."

"It has," I said into his shoulder. "But not more difficult than living a lie. I would rather be an honest spinster than a deceitful wife."

"You shall be no kind of spinster," he said, pulling away to look at me. "You will be Mrs. Darcy."

"Is that a proposal?" I teased. "It has the flavour of an order."

"Miss Bennet, I am incomplete without you. I yearn for you every second of the day so pray make me the happiest of men and grant me your hand."

It was a pretty speech if delivered with a dash of impatience, but I was just as impatient to accept him. "You do not mind a scandalous bride?"

"I intend to take you back to Pemberley. We will content ourselves there until the next scandal comes along. I have it on good authority that Sir Alistair White may elope with his children's governess, so there is that to anticipate."

"Perhaps we should wait," I said to him. "Some time for any questions to abate."

"I am willing to wait as long as a se'nnight," he said. "Anything more would be insupportable. We have waited long enough."

And so it was. We were married in St. George's by common licence as soon as was permissible. I had given the Jane-gown to Jane (Vickery proved adept at removing the little stain) and I wore a gown of palest cream to marry him. We went to Pemberley the day after our wedding and stayed there for many months.

Tongues did wag, and they continued to wag when we returned to Town the following spring. People thought I had married too quickly, and had utterly destroyed poor Timpson, though in my mind, Timpson seemed rather jovial going about with his young pregnant wife. I had to wonder that the poor dear did not simply topple over from the size of her stomach and the weight of the jewels Timpson insisted on draping around her neck. In any case, they seemed very happy and I was happy for him.

At times, I felt it rather debauched to be so ridiculously happy. Each day was another day to know my husband better, to spend more time with him, and with dear Georgiana, and to begin building our family. I woke with a smile on my face and slept with laughter in my heart. As I had assured Lady Catherine so long ago, this Mrs. Darcy had absolutely nothing to repine.

AMY D'ORAZIO IS A FORMER SCIENTIST AND CURRENT STAY-AT-home mom who is addicted to Austen and Starbucks in equal measure. While she adores Mr. Darcy, she is married to Mr. Bingley, and their Pemberley is in Pittsburgh, Pennsylvania. She has two daughters devoted to sports with long practices and began writing stories as a way to pass the time spent at their various gyms and studios. She firmly believes that all stories should have long looks, stolen kisses, and happily-ever-afters. Like her favorite heroine, she dearly loves a laugh and considers herself an excellent walker. She is the author of *The Best Part of Love* and *A Short Period of Exquisite Felicity*.

The House Party

Jenetta James

"Do not consider me now as an elegant female intending to plague you, but as a rational creature speaking the truth from her heart."
—Chapter XIX

THE HOUSE PARTY
Jenetta James

PART I: THE EVENING

*L*izzy and Jane had arrived after luncheon, just as the thin winter sun broke through the clouds over Netherfield Park. Jane had been quietly hoping that Father might get the motor out, but in the end, Bridges took them in the cart. Save for her sister's embarrassment, Lizzy didn't mind. She relished the feeling of the wind in her hair and cared not a jot what people might think. The rickety, old contraption clattered up to the house and deposited them like packages at the bottom of the great stone steps. There had been nobody to meet them, but no matter. Within a moment or two, a maid appeared and then the butler, and more besides. Servants seemed to pop up like flowers which made a change from Longbourn. A tall, rather dashing footman picked up their bags and vanished like a phantom. Neither Bennet sister was artful enough to pretend anything other than bewilderment at such luxury. They were shown, wide-eyed, to the chamber they were to share. The room was enormous, vast. It had the most marvellous vantage point at the front of the house, and altogether they were quite thrilled. They were not the sort of girls to expect a set each.

"Oh, Lizzy," gasped Jane as she placed her hat on the bed. "What a large party must be expected."

She turned out to be on the nose about that.

They watched from their window as the gathering took shape. The enormous door below opening and closing, chaps going here and there. A positive army of servants, all clad in black and white, appearing and disappearing. A succession of motor cars roaring up the approach, glinting red, blue, racing green. Lizzy had never seen the like. She had read of it, of course, but that was different. How close to home they were, Lizzy reflected, and how far.

Dusk had begun to gather the light of the day, and Lizzy was standing at the window with her hair down. A shiny black motor drew up below, and a tall, rather handsome gentleman alighted. Dark hair, long limbs, swift confident movements. The first word that came into her mind was "fine," and she wondered who he was, where he was from. Many men, she had observed, were well-looking enough. But few were sufficiently handsome to be noticeable at a distance, to engage one without even a word. He exchanged greetings with a footman and nodded to a man who must surely have been his valet. They moved aside, and he advanced upon the house as all the other guests had done.

But just before he ascended the steps, he looked up.

That face was well-drawn and lightly tanned. But his expression was not altogether a kindly one. It was proud, lofty, rather stern. *How odd*, thought Lizzy. His lips did not smile and nor did they seem to want to. His eyes were most arresting, piercing even. Lizzy felt a jolt, a shocking zing of force chase through her. *Whoosh.* Her sense trailing her emotions, she stepped back from the glass.

"What's the matter, Lizzy?"

Jane looked up from her seat at the dressing table.

"Nothing. Not a bit of it."

Her sister approached her and rested her chin upon Lizzy's shoulder as they looked down upon Netherfield's grand driveway. Yet more motors had appeared, their engines belching out roars. Ladies in furs, dapper chaps with canes. Maids, drivers, valets staggering about with chests. The place was a positive throng.

"Why do you suppose Miss Bingley invited us, Lizzy?" Jane gazed dreamily, absently almost.

"To show herself to best effect? After all, it is in the manner of weekend parties that there must be some poor relations in among the terribly smart ones. Who better than neighbours in penury?"

She spoke acidly, but they both knew that neither of them had ever been to a weekend house party before. Indeed, it had taken some persuasion for Father to agree to it. Days of unceasing work, in fact. Assurances, promises, barefaced, handwringing pleas. Mother had been an ally. Their sister Mary had not.

"Don't be mean. I cannot think that of Miss Bingley. In any case, she looks perfectly wonderful as she is. And so does her sister. To my eye at any rate."

Lizzy laughed. "And to Mother's! What a lecture she gave on the matter of Louisa Hurst's stole. Let me be more forgiving. I think that Caroline has many rich and fashionable friends, but she and her brother have settled here, and she wishes to establish firm acquaintances closer to home. Of all the neighbourhood, she rather liked you, and who can blame her for that? She cannot, for propriety's sake, invite you to a weekend party on your own, so she invited me as well. And here we are."

Jane said not a word but pushed a broad brush through her blonde hair.

"There is also Mr. Bingley."

Jane remained silent, clipping her hair with a bronze slide in the shape of a feather. She could be maddeningly reserved sometimes.

"Mr. Bingley, who I am sure was gazing at you in church last Sunday."

"I say that is excessive, Lizzy. Mr. Bingley is an attentive neighbour to everyone."

"Maybe."

Lizzy stood and regarded her outline in the glass.

Languidly, for there was no need to hurry, the sisters dressed. Jane had a fine gown, blush pink, the lace of the trim so delicate it might almost have been taken for her skin. It had started life as one of Aunt Madeleine's but Mother and Sarah, their maid, had made it up new, and one would never have guessed it was old. Lizzy had a blue dress, stitched with little beads, and Sarah had dressed up her slippers to match.

Their outfits arranged, it was time to go down for drinks.

On their way down the stairs, they met a young woman with a lisp and a sweet expression. Her name, she told them, was Mary King, and she was visiting from Northamptonshire. Her uncle knew Mr. Bingley, or some such. She looked awfully nervous, but perfectly nice, so Lizzy offered out her arm, and the three of them entered the grand gathering together.

The room in which drinks were held was chocker-block and warm with it. Fashionable ladies with strident laughs and gentlemen in coloured waistcoats appeared on all sides. Gingerly, footmen edged about the room, carrying silver trays with wine twinkling in crystal glasses. There was a hum in the air, of tales told and gales of laughter and people saying, "Excuse me, my lord" and "I had no idea, really?" and "Well, that is typical of the palace." Lizzy felt quite as though she were in another land, for all that she lived only three miles across the fields.

Within moments of their arrival in the room, Mr. Bingley and his sister found them. They all shook hands decorously and commented on the weather, and Mr. Bingley, who wished to be called "Charles," asked after their parents and Mary King's uncle. Happy chatter ensued and Lizzy began to be glad she was there. At some point, Mr. Bingley sauntered off towards the punch bowl, with Jane on one arm and Mary King on the other. Lizzy did not mind this a bit, but she did rather mind being unable to detach herself from his stately sister as a consequence. Caroline Bingley was an enormously tall lady, dressed from head to toe in peacock blue. Her features were bold, as though they had been chiselled out of her face by a master craftsman atop a ladder. They had already asked after one another's health, so conversation was getting a bit thin.

It was then that the gentleman with the stern face appeared and was greeted with a shriek of "Fitzwilliam! My dear man!" from Caroline as she flung herself in his path. Lizzy said not a word but regarded him carefully. He was jolly handsome, but he lacked joy in a way she altogether suspected. She recognised him immediately as the man she had observed arriving earlier. His greeting to his hostess was perfectly polite but wanted for any real enthusiasm.

"Caroline. How are you?"

His voice was velvety, deep, commanding somehow.

Caroline Bingley began to babble, and it was then that his eyes flicked over her shoulder to Lizzy standing there like a lemon with no introduction. Suddenly, she felt the heat of his gaze upon her, a sense of static energy crackling inside. She was furious with herself for reacting thus, even if it was known only to her.

His expression softened only the smallest amount as he held out his hand.

"Fitzwilliam Darcy."

Lizzy took it. In the corner of her vision, she saw Caroline smarting.

"Hello. I am Elizabeth Bennet."

It sounded plain when she said it out loud like that, but Lizzy had her dreams. One day, who knew what her life could be: playwright, novelist, woman of affairs? The possibilities were boundless. Lizzy felt a current in her hand where he had touched, and she pulled it away.

Caroline found her tongue. "Elizabeth is our neighbour. Her family owns the small estate, Longbourn. Awfully pretty, in its way. The Bennets have been there practically since the Conqueror, haven't they, Elizabeth dear? We also have Elizabeth's sister Jane here. She is over there speaking with Charles. But they also have three younger sisters, maybe a little too giddy for *this* gathering."

"Well," he said, seemingly struggling for further words, "I know myself enough of younger sisters."

"Not as much as Elizabeth! Good heavens, the Bennet girls are quite wild. Everyone says it."

"Everyone does," interjected Lizzy, "including themselves. In fact, I suspect they would be thrilled to know they were so discussed here this evening."

Caroline regarded her coolly and then looked back at the

gentleman called Fitzwilliam. Lizzy thought Fitzwilliam Darcy an odd, rather fusty name. It suited him well.

"Of course, they have quite thrown themselves into the women's suffrage movement. There isn't a day goes by when we do not see Kitty and Lydia parading about the village shops, wearing their purple sashes. And your other sister, Mary, called with a petition only yesterday. I must confess, I did not sign it, although, I think she may have softened my sister."

Darcy raised his eyebrows, and Lizzy just caught it, wondering what it meant.

"Good for Louisa. I must thank her later," said Lizzy. "I cannot see how one could be opposed to votes for women."

"Can you not? I say why change the old ways that work perfectly well. It is all the upheaval I cannot bear. All these dreadful incidents of young women who ought to know better, smashing things up and chaining themselves to railings and the like. Good gracious. The problem with young Mary's petition is not so much the petition itself. It is that the next step is taking a hammer to the post office window. And then where would we be?"

Lizzy took a sip of her sherry and shrugged almost imperceptibly. She was not cross with Caroline; she pitied her.

"Or the government could change the law. Give votes to women. Then there would be fairness all round and no broken post office windows."

Darcy looked at her steadily. He said, "I am afraid I call that rather unlikely."

Caroline nodded in an annoying fashion, but the man who had spoken was quite inscrutable.

"Unlikely?"

"Yes. Improbable, implausible, not—"

"I know what the word means. It's just an awfully strange remark, that's all."

"There is nothing strange about it."

Somewhere in his voice, there was a sneer. "A frank assessment of whether or not a proposition shall actually take place, or take place in a particular way, is fundamental to its overall evaluation."

"No, it isn't."

Caroline moved from appearing discomforted to being all-out alarmed.

"Now, now, Elizabeth."

But Lizzy was not listening to her. She was fixed on this Fitzwilliam person.

"It isn't. Would you have said that about slaving? Surely not. You either think a thing is right or wrong. One makes one's choice on that basis. We are moral actors, Mr. Darcy. Not cynics betting on horses."

She felt her cheeks redden. If she had been in her own home or a place she knew well, she may have acted differently. If she had been in a room full of friends, would she have said good evening and flounced off? As it was, something in the depths of his eyes kept her pinned down like a moth. They stood there, staring at each other. And it was somewhere between fire-hot and bone-chilling cold.

Beside them, Caroline was flustering.

"Horses! Yes indeed. The riding in this part of the country is wonderful, Fitzwilliam, really excellent. I hope you intend to stay long enough to enjoy it."

He remained silent but nodded, seemingly in assent.

"You'll come out with the hounds tomorrow, of course? Stirrup cup at eight?"

Darcy looked away from Lizzy's face, and it was as though they had both been released from an invisible net. Now they were fish flapping about on dry land. Caroline looked at him expectantly.

"Yes, thank you. Of course."

And so, the conversation between them went out with a whimper rather than a bang. A lady with an enormous diamond in her necklace approached Caroline and began speaking about Ireland. Two men approached Darcy with torrents of greetings. Lizzy saw her chance to get away and threaded back through the crowds to her sister with barely an "excuse me."

Soon, it was time for supper and the assembled company filed into a grand dining room. In the centre stood a colossal long table, polished to a shine and laden down with tall vases of flowers in all colours. Silver twinkled in the candlelight, and Lizzy watched as Jane's eyes widened with the glamour of it all. The proud man called Darcy was nowhere to be seen, and Lizzy began to think he had departed when he slipped into the room and was directed by a servant to sit beside Caroline. She appeared to be overjoyed about this development, and Lizzy observed him to smile politely and take his seat without complaint. Maybe there was a match brewing there. She upbraided herself for her interest in the man and resolved to end it. For why should she concern herself with such a pre-historic creature as could not support the obvious way in which the world must go? *No.*

Lizzy turned to her left where an unknown gentleman sat.

He nodded to her, smiling.

"Good evening, madam. Allow me to introduce myself. George Wickham."

He had light brown hair with a wave and a perfectly good face.

"Elizabeth Bennet."

They shook hands, although at the dinner table it was a slightly cumbersome endeavour.

He proved to be an excellent companion at dinner and, before long, they were laughing and quite thick with one another.

"How do you know the Bingleys, sir?"

"Not well at all. I would like to know them better. I am a friend of Mr. Hurst, who is the husband of Mr. Bingley's elder sister. I must admit"—he smiled at her, pausing over his soup—"I rather feared that the company might be a little too august for me. Breaking bread and drinking wine with the great and the good of fashionable society is hardly usual for me."

"Nor me."

Lizzy smiled back at him. He had a comfortable normality about him, a frank and open manner. She could talk to him with such ease.

"Now, now. You may not be the sort of girl one reads about in the gossip columns, but you are a lady of some distinction, anyone can see that. I myself am just a humble writer."

"A writer? How wonderful. What do you write?"

"I am working on my first novel, not without success. But I am sad to say that out of financial necessity, I write articles for the news sheets. But it is not my passion."

"But interesting, none the less."

"Well"—he looked up from his drink doubtfully—"it depends."

After that, he told tales of flogging up and down the country to pursue tales of woe and amusement. Of writing stories in train compartments and falling asleep during long court hearings. Of being bitten by dogs whilst interviewing their owners. Of having seen the King laughing in an unguarded moment on Horse Guards Parade. It all sounded impossibly colourful.

Just before pudding was served, Lizzy looked up and caught the Darcy man seeming to stare at her.

"I say, George. Do you happen to know that gentleman over there? With the dark hair and the stern face?"

"I do. But it is not a happy association I am afraid. That man is Fitzwilliam Darcy. I've known him all my life."

He paused, seeming to consider his words before flashing Lizzy a smile.

"And I've never had a smile out of the devil!"

Lizzy laughed, for she could well believe that to be true.

"Tell me about him."

"We knew each other as children actually. Our fathers were friends, in fact Darcy's father was an influential friend to me, in good times and bad. But the son was always an odd fish. Distant, proud, difficult. We were never really friends, just young boys thrown into one another's company. When I went up to Cambridge, he was there too, although fortunately we were in different colleges. I saw him infrequently which suited us both."

At that moment, on the opposite side of the table, Caroline Bingley laughed loudly, gesticulated, grasped at Mr. Darcy's arm. He simply appeared not to notice.

Wickham and Lizzy regarded the scene with interest.

"I have felt for many years that he is not really fitted for the modern age. He is the sort of man who would have been better off born in another century."

Nothing could have been more in accordance with Lizzy's own view. How gratifying to hear it expressed so well by another. Lizzy was just pondering that when Caroline stood to lead the ladies out of the room. As the second Bennet daughter rose to join them, George Wickham took her hand and, very elegantly, kissed it. Lizzy flushed.

PART 2: THE HUNT

THE NEXT MORNING, THE STABLES WERE TEEMING WITH PEOPLE AND horses and humming with noise. Boys ran about with saddles, footmen offered glasses of spirits to the riders from silver trays. Hot breath from the horses drew extravagant whorls in the cold air. Lizzy was one of few ladies. Most, including Jane and Mary King, had preferred to stay indoors. Louisa Hurst had suggested a morning of quiet reading and a walk in the maze if the weather permitted. But Lizzy was anxious to avoid that party. As it was, Bridges had walked her horse, Mrs. Wollstonecraft, from Longbourn to the Netherfield stables that morning. She mounted her horse in one movement and felt immediately at one with the world. Her gloved hand patted her affectionately, and she whispered: "Hello, old friend."

Lizzy pulled herself up straight and another horse and rider clicked up beside her.

"Not joining the ladies in the drawing room, eh?" George Wickham winked as he said it. "I should have guessed really."

"I am not one for indoor pursuits."

He smiled, admiringly.

"In any case, I love horses with a passion that overrides much else. Beautiful, wonderful beasts."

"Do you hunt regularly?"

"Yes. Everyone hereabout does."

"What about the races? Do you attend?"

Lizzy turned to regard him. He had a worldliness about him, edged with something else. Was it cruelty or verve? She could not say but discomfort shivered through her.

"I have never been taken to the races. Newmarket is rather far from here, and my parents have never made a habit of it."

She spoke curtly, primly. For she was not used to having handsome young writers circling about her assuming her to be more sophisticated than she was. At the edge of her vision, she saw that Darcy man atop his horse. He was speaking to another but then stopped and turned, seemingly to observe her. Lizzy ignored him. George Wickham moved his horse around her, boxing her in.

"That's a jolly shame. I can see you, in my mind's eye. Marking your race card, assessing the form. Squinting into the sun as your winner comes in."

He beamed as he spoke. The Darcy man continued to glare at them, and the rudeness of it annoyed her. Lizzy made a deliberate effort to laugh and encourage George Wickham's smiles. What he said next stopped her laughter like a thunderclap.

"I was there that day in the summer, you know. At Epsom. The day that poor woman died."

Lizzy felt the chill of the wind through her riding habit.

"How dreadful. I read about it in Father's *Times*."

She paused, fingering the reins of her horse, filling her lungs with cold air. Father was awfully free with his newspaper usually, but that morning he had called Lizzy into his library before breakfast. He wanted her to read it before her sisters, knowing how passionate they were about women's suffrage. It was a cause with which he agreed, and he had no difficulty in his daughters' activities. But when a young woman threw herself in front of the King's horse on Derby Day in the name of votes for all, that was a matter which required careful handling. Lizzy looked at the memory through a gauze in her mind. She was lucky to have Father, and she knew it.

Back in the present, George Wickham was staring at her. A flame of interest and meaning flickered in his eyes.

Lizzy was amazed to learn that he had been present at such a moment in history. "Emily Davison. I felt so wretched for her dying like that. But overwhelmed at her bravery too."

He smiled a half smile, but his eyes fixed her. Did he agree or disagree? She couldn't tell.

She did not have long to ponder it.

Within moments, the horns were sounding and the hunting party moving off. Lizzy put the conversation with George Wickham out of her mind. Walking along, she gathered a trot and shortly began a gentle canter, then a gallop. Ahead, the hounds ran as one, over fields, around hedgerows. Lizzy gathered pace, rising, leaning. The air in her nostrils was cold and sweet. The ground seemed to heave with the power of the horses, with the flow of the thing. And behind them, the house receded, its red-bricked, pillar-fronted facade shrinking moment by moment. Collectively, they skirted a patch of woodland and jumped a stream, crusted with ice. Gently, inexorably, the gradient changed; the ground beneath their feet rising to a hill. Lizzy whipped up it at speed, but many fell behind her. She had lost sight of George Wickham some time before, but now she saw the Darcy man in the corner of her vision. He always seemed to be on the edge of matters, near enough to see but too far away to know. There was no time to look at his face now, but she knew it was him. They rose to the top of the hill and having got there, slowed. The hunt entered a lull that hunts sometimes do, having run hell for leather, and they languished on a plateau. Darcy ventured Lizzy a glance, but it was such a fleeting connection that she could scarce keep it in her memory.

Shortly thereafter, George caught up with her. He appeared hot, and it was clear that his advancement had taken some degree of effort to achieve. He cried her a "hello" through the hubbub though, so he had some breath to spare. Lizzy felt a pang of pity, so she slowed for him. After that the speed gathered again. The party jumped a low hedge before taking another rise. Lizzy cleared the obstacle and thundered forth but, realising that she had lost George, slackened her pace. Most of the party were up ahead, screaming up the hill with renewed energy, but where was her friend? He had not come past her;

she was sure of that. She galloped a little way, but the hunt had lost her focus. She walked her horse about in a circle, and it was as she glanced back down the hill that she saw his coat, winking red through bracken. He had fallen at the hedge, that much was obvious. Lizzy galloped back to him with all speed. As she approached, she heard a groan.

"I say, are you hurt?"

His face was a contorted mess of blood and splattered earth, and he clutched at his arm, writhing. His horse was some distance away, seemingly indifferent. She dismounted and crouched down pleading with him to still his movements. He seemed unable to do so. Suddenly the ground around her shook with approaching hooves. She looked around to see the arrival of Fitzwilliam Darcy. His horse, which was a great black beast, halted with hardly a yard to spare but he did not immediately dismount. His eyes skirted the scene and flicked between Lizzy and George Wickham. He blinked and everything about him seemed to tense, to tighten like a coil. There was a moment of hesitation that was longer than it ought to have been. Then, he spoke.

"May I assist you, miss?"

His manner of speaking was awfully stiff, ludicrously so, in the circumstances.

"It is not I who needs assistance. It is Mr. Wickham." She turned back to him. "There is rather a lot of blood, but I think it only a surface wound to the face. Look." Lizzy glanced up to Mr. Darcy and found him staring stonily at the prostrate Wickham. He observed the man perfectly well but appeared unmoved by his plight.

"He is grabbing so at his arm." Lizzy gently ran her finger down the said arm and Wickham let out a groan. "I fear it may be broken. I say, do you think you can stand?"

She asked more in hope than expectation, and Wickham shook his head hopelessly.

"Oh, good heavens. Do you think we should move him?" asked Lizzy, looking up at Darcy, still mounted on his horse. "I am sure we could do it between us?"

"No."

Darcy slipped to the ground with no effort at all and stood beside her.

"We should not move him. He may have broken more than his arm. We should get help. He can be stretchered back to the house. It will be safer."

Darcy stepped closer to the patient, but he stopped short of crouching down to his level. His arm, he rose against the glare of winter sun that broke through the clouds in that moment. He studied the man but not with any affection.

"When I say 'we should get help,' I mean that I shall do it. You should rejoin the hunt. If you go now and cut across the field to the west, you shall find them again without any difficulty."

"I cannot possibly do that."

"Yes, you can. You have done enough, miss. This man is not your responsibility."

She stood up to face him. What a high-handed brute!

"If you are seeking to send me away, I shall not go. No, I cannot. One of us must ride for help, and the other stay."

"I would not want"—he paused. There was some manner of appeal in his eyes, but she could make neither head nor tail of it. "I—"

Lizzy grew impatient. She crouched back down.

"We cannot abandon him here, alone with his injuries. It would be unconscionable."

Darcy sighed.

"Well, we certainly do not have time to argue about it, so let it be as you say." With one movement, he slipped a hip flask out of his coat pocket and unscrewed it. Finally, he sank down to the muddy ground.

"George, can you sit up? No? All right. Well, I will leave Miss Bennet with this. Take some if you can."

Darcy passed the flask to Lizzy. His fingers brushed past hers and she felt a tingling, a burning inside her. Although Wickham should have been his focus, Darcy looked right at her and his gaze did not waver.

"Have some yourself if you need it. If you think he is passing out, put it under his nose. Keep talking to him. Take this."

He removed a handkerchief from his breast pocket and handed it to her. In her gloved hand, she stroked it with her thumb.

"You can press it against the wound on his face, if you think it necessary. But frankly, I suspect that the bleeding has already stopped. I will be no more than a quarter of an hour. You have my word."

And with that, he stood, turned on his heel, mounted his horse, and was gone in a thunder of hooves and turned earth. Lizzy watched the horse and its man gallop into the distance, leaving her with the moans and woes of Mr. Wickham. She found the dictates of Mr. Darcy most irritating and unnecessary but had to admit that keeping the patient talking was a good suggestion. So, she knelt on the ground and spoke aimlessly, chattering continuously, every now and then seeking an answer. Mr. Wickham, after a time, seemed to recover himself slightly, or maybe he just grew used to the pain. In any event, there was less in the way of crying out and more in the way of a few words. He said "thank you" rather a lot and said that he had a terrific pain in his side as well as his arm. Lizzy sympathised with the poor man.

It was in a lull in conversation that Lizzy heard the distant rumble of horses' hooves. *Thank goodness*, she thought as she observed Darcy and several others appear on the horizon and advance towards them.

There were three boys from the stables, two to carry the fallen Wickham and one to walk his horse back. It took no small effort to get him onto the stretcher and, thereafter, a slow procession back to the house began.

Fitzwilliam Darcy presided over matters with a grimace. He helped the men to heave the patient onto the stretcher and thanked them. It was a stony manner of thank you, but a thank you, nonetheless. Lizzy handed him his hip flask. As the rescue party advanced falteringly, the two of them were left behind.

More than a moment of silence crackled between them. Unspoken, they took the decision to follow back to the house. The day's hunting had been lost, and all Lizzy had to show for it was this odd, taciturn, handsome man by her side. To add to his other peculiarities, he appeared completely comfortable with silence. That was a trait not shared with his current companion.

"You made the journey to Netherfield and back with remarkable speed."

"I said that I would."

They both mounted their horses and settled atop them, surveying the landscape and each other.

"Why was that? It was not out of concern for George Wickham."

"No, it was not. I have no doubt that he shall be perfectly fine. He has a talent for survival, however undeserved."

There was a sudden gust of wind, and it upset their path slightly.

"That is harsh. And if you speak in that way of your fellow man, then one day you shall have cause to rue it."

He looked at her suddenly, and the brown of his eyes might have been an ocean deep.

"You are not the first person to say that to me, or words to that effect anyway. Fact is, I am less harsh on the man than I sound. He would have been fine on his own for a few minutes. But since you insisted on remaining with him, I endeavoured to be as speedy as possible."

"Why was that? Do you call him a danger, a threat?"

"Yes. I do. If you were a relation of mine, I would not have allowed it. But since I have no power over you, there was nothing I could do but reduce your time in the man's company through my own actions."

"If I were your relation, would you have power to keep me from my own free will?"

"I hope so."

"In that case, George Wickham was quite right about you. You are of the last century."

He did not answer it immediately, and Lizzy began to regret the length of journey they still had in one another's company. Ahead of them, the men had established a successful strategy for carrying Wickham and were doing so most effectively.

"Call it old-fashioned if you wish. It is not my view that blameless young women should be abandoned in the countryside with rogues, that is all."

"I call that most unfair."

"Do you deny your own innocence or seek to establish his?"

A flicker of a smile played across his face, but it did not linger long. Lizzy blinked, seeing it. But growing fury crowded out humour.

"I don't believe you know anything of me. We are perfect strangers. But that wounded man knows you, has known you for many years."

He looked straight ahead. The progress of the men carrying the stretcher was slow but steady.

"That is true enough."

"Forgive me, but I see no rogue. I see a gifted young man forced into commercial writing by cruel necessity."

Darcy blurted out an unfortunate noise. It was halfway between a cough and a cry of derision. Lizzy was undeterred.

"A true talent, who must write for newspapers because he does not have the private income that some benefit from. He has a place in society, but it is on the edges, not in the middle, not at the top. It is quite wrong to hold that against him. You must see that. And now, he is injured too. But still you cannot find him a kind word."

"No. I most certainly cannot!"

He spat the words out, flinging them like tiny weapons, and Lizzy could not carry on with the conversation. She knew that if they were to continue speaking, she would say more than she had already. For was there ever such a man as this one? She straightened her back and sat forward slightly, knowing herself to be observed.

"Well in that case, Mr. Darcy, let us say no more of it."

He did not answer, but a breath of energy whispered over her. The air was cold, but her cheeks were flushed, hot. Together, but apart, they ambled over the last hill before the house came into sight. What a mercy it was to see its familiar porticos, the folds of the fields around it. Even from a distance, one could see the lightly frosted maze and little figures gliding about it like swans on a lake. As they drew closer and closer still, Lizzy found that she did not wish to join the ladies, even Jane. She was fatigued from events, her riding habit splattered with mud and her hair had come free from its net on one side. The wind which had felt invigorating earlier in the morning, seemed to batter them now. All Lizzy wanted was to stable her horse and return to the privacy of her bedroom. After the most cursory of farewells to her silent companion, that is what she did.

Back in her room, Lizzy shed her soiled habit bodice and then her boots, their leather stiff and clammy with damp. She unfastened the top button on her skirt, exhaled, and fell upon the bed. It had been made beautifully in her absence and was soft and welcoming. In her mind, she lay upon a floating cloud, enveloped by comfort, suddenly free of cares. A wrap at the door interrupted her in these thoughts and jerkily, Lizzy looked up.

"Come in."

A small head of red curls and a furtive expression appeared as the door opened.

"I say, hello."

"Miss King. Mary, I mean. Sorry. I've just got in and I'm awfully disorientated." Lizzy sat up, somewhat surprised. "Do come in and shut the door."

She rose from the bed and smiled genially at the girl. She seemed to be a pleasant person, not quite at home in her surroundings but all the more charming for it. Mary claimed that she found Miss Bingley "rather terrifying," and since she did not ride to a standard good enough to hunt, she had been reading in her bedroom all morning. Hearing Lizzy's door and beginning to feel the sting of loneliness, she had come for a visit. Thus, the two ladies sat upon the chaise and chatted as they admired the view from the window.

From that very window, only the eve before, Lizzy had watched as Fitzwilliam Darcy arrived. How little time had passed since then, but how disrupted she felt.

"There was another reason for my visit, Elizabeth."

"Oh yes?"

"I'm quite ashamed of myself."

Lizzy turned to face her, doubting that she would find what Mary was about to say at all shameful.

"The thing is, those awfully nice biscuits that they put by the bed. Do you have them too?"

"Yes, Mary."

"Yes, I think everyone does. Aren't they scrumptious? Well, I think so. The thing is, I've eaten all of mine. Every last one. I feel a greedy beast saying it, but there it is. And I just did it without thinking. But it is so inelegant and unrefined, isn't it? Imagine how ill Miss Bingley shall think of me if she finds out? I mean, how very dreadful that would be. I bet she doesn't eat anything! And think of it. I might be spoken of. I may never get invited to a weekend house party again."

Poor Mary's face was quite creased up with worry.

"I have a full jar, Mary. Would you like it for your room? We could swap."

"Oh, I say that is so kind of you. I couldn't swap, but maybe if I could take some of yours, then Miss Bingley shan't think me such a shocking gannet as all that."

Lizzy stood, retrieved the jar and presented it to her friend, who thanked her again and giggled at the means of saving her reputation.

"You are such a dear, Elizabeth. I know how I shall repay you!" she said, seemingly struck by inspiration. "For not that I am one to gossip, but I have heard the most astonishing tale of our fellow guests. Do you want to hear it?"

Lizzy assented, expecting some story of no consequence about people of whom she knew nothing and cared less.

"Well, that young man who you were sitting next to at supper..."

"George Wickham?"

"Yes, that's the chap. Apparently, he's an awfully ruthless sort of journalist, you know. They say he'd do anything to get to the top, trample on anyone. He's had some jolly good stories, but his most recent has been all about the cat and mouse suffragists."

"You mean the women who've been in prison?"

"Yes. You must have read about it. These women who have been sent to prison for campaigning for votes and then gone on hunger strike and been packed off home because of it. Well, you know that they mostly go by assumed names, don't you? Those names in the newspapers are not their real names but ones that they give out. And the truth of it is that some of them are from the best families."

In Lizzy's mind, a bell started to sound. Quietly, in the distance, it began to be a constant, like wakefulness breaking through sleep.

"But this recent rash of stories in the newspapers in which the true identities of these women have been revealed…well! They are all written by George Wickham. He has been going about lifting masks left and right. Do you not think it scurrilous? And do you know the worst of it?"

"Go on."

"Well, one of his latest victims was a young woman called Georgiana Darcy who is only the niece of the *Earl* of Matlock! Yes, it's true. Apparently, she was arrested for her role in a protest in York but refused to eat in prison. She had a made-up name, but George Wickham knew her from old and ended all that. She was on the front page of the *Times* before she knew where she was. And do you know what? Her own brother is here, in this house! He is that awfully handsome, serious gentleman with the mysterious eyes. You must have seen him."

Lizzy nodded.

"I say he's being awfully gentlemanly not knocking that Wickham chap down, don't you?" Mary put her hand in the jar that sat between them and ate a biscuit. "It is all true. I had it from Lady Raffety."

Outside in the distance, the remnants of the hunt appeared, dishevelled and bedraggled. Noise gathered in the air above them. They advanced towards the house, the day's conquests over and buried. A dead weight of realisation and regret sank in Lizzy's belly.

PART 3: THE WALK BEFORE SUPPER

MARY KING HAD EVENTUALLY LEFT AND IN HER PLACE, JANE HAD appeared. She had, by her own report, enjoyed the day enormously.

There had been quiet reading and tea in the drawing room, followed by cards and a laughter riddled chase about the maze as the afternoon aged and died. Louisa was so friendly, she said, and such a turn on the piano. They had had a ripping day. Jane glowed.

"How was the hunt?"

Lizzy, who had been gazing out of the window at the weak sun setting across the fields, suddenly turned to her sister. She held a pencil in her hand, which she turned like a wand at a steady pace.

"Oh! It was…. It was fine. Thank you."

Lizzy felt a rush of heat to her face and a sense of otherness, but it passed just as quickly.

"Just think," said Jane, "tomorrow morning, we are off home. We shall have been here for two days, but the time has simply whipped past."

Lizzy continued to turn the pencil, and for a moment her sister's eyes lingered on it before she turned away in confusion. It was the first time in their lives that Jane had not known what to say to her, and she suddenly felt a stranger in her own family.

After that, Jane chattered about this and that while they dressed and pinned one another's hair. Lizzy neither saw nor heard her, for she was wrapped in the parcel of her own mind. Even as she dressed in her second-best gown, a charcoal and cream affair that had become too short for Lydia, an itching came to her body, a sense of unknown urgency pervaded her. It was a poor frame of mind for a supper party, but there it was.

The drawing room which Caroline used for drinks was at the back of the house, giving on to a terrace with the maze beyond. To the side of it was a gathering of thorny skeletons which Lizzy supposed to be a rose garden in summer. Inside the room, spirits were high and drinks in plentiful supply. Jane glided about the room on the arm of Charles Bingley, and Sir William, a neighbour who had known Lizzy since infancy, was just about to get going on Lloyd George, when something in the garden caught Lizzy's eye. By the maze, a flash of black, a whisper of smoke billowing into the air like a spirit. Lizzy took another sip of her drink and felt a sense of creeping energy. She looked at it for a moment, fizzing away and full of fruits and who knew what. She was certain that neither of her parents had ever seen, still less drank such a concoction. Just then the movement came again, and beside the maze, the back of a man's head appeared. A well-cut dinner jacket and a cigar held in the hand casually. He appeared to be alone.

"Sir William, would you excuse me? So kind."

Lizzy moved to the door, unlatched it, and slipped through. It made rather a noise as she clicked it shut, but he did not turn around even though he must have heard. She knew more than ever that she was right to approach him. The air was cold on her face, and the ground crunched under her slippered feet. As she got closer to him, his face turned to her and he smiled, cautiously.

Lizzy spoke:

"You told me a fibber. More than one actually."

"I did not."

"You could have said that your sister is a leading suffragette, instead of allowing me to think that you were a hopeless opponent. You said George Wickham was a danger, but you did not say why. So you allowed me to assume that you meant he is rather a lecher, a fact which is obvious to everyone. Rather than something even more treacherous."

He smoked his cigar and the sweet scent infused the air about her. Without seeming to hurry, he answered. "Both of those things are omissions rather than outright falsehoods. Allowing someone to fall into error is not the same as lying to them. I would not lie to you."

"Would you not?"

"No."

He fixed her suddenly with a liquid stare full of promise and meaning and things that she had no name for. It was he who broke the moment.

"I say, you must be cold." He glanced at her capped sleeves before holding his cigar in his mouth and shrugging off his jacket and draping it over her shoulders. How warm it was, how heavy.

"Should you like to walk?"

Lizzy glanced back at the house. Inside the glass of the terrace doors, the party was thronging. Dresses in all colours moved about, a low babble of noise came out, but it was all indeterminate sound. A maid struggled to move a table which had been somehow knocked over. For a moment Lizzy imagined herself watching a play on a stage, observing as characters came on and off, spoke lines one already knew. Standing right next to her, this Darcy man was a great height, but he was not overwhelming.

"Yes, I should. Shall we go this way?"

She gestured along the north side of the maze and so they went.

The hedge of the maze to their left grew taller and the uneven ground jostled them closer together like balls in a channel.

"I understand the other ladies played in the maze earlier. Might we attempt it?"

He looked at her sceptically. "If you wish to."

"That is not very enthusiastic."

"No. Well— Put it this way. There are some people in life who enjoy Shakespearian comedies. And there are those who—"

"Would rather a quick trip to purgatory?" she suggested.

"Yes. That's about it. At this time there is the added danger that we would get lost in it."

They glanced at each other as they moved swiftly through the gathering dusk. Soon it would be dark.

"And have to stay in there all night?" Lizzy laughed at the thought. "My parents would never let me out again."

"Which would be an appropriate reaction. I couldn't blame them," he added, smiling. But what did he mean?

"Fact is that mazes are not half as difficult as people say. Nobody but a fool would get lost in them for any time above fifteen minutes. The idea of the maze is a great courtly lie if you ask me."

They reached the darkened corner of the maze and stopped. Ahead a path curved into the rest of the garden, like a snake. It was that moment when dusk threaded itself into dark and the last streaks of daylight vanished. Beyond the carefully kept garden, rolled a patchwork of fields, villages, woods. He offered her his arm and she took it as they set out along the path.

"Well, we have something in common then, don't we?"

"Is that the only thing? A lack of admiration for mazes," she wondered aloud.

"I have a feeling it's not."

They walked a bit further. Lizzy glanced over her shoulder to the house and the drinks party continuing in the drawing room.

"Do you want to go back?" he asked. "I suppose we ought. Supper will be served soon. I do not believe that anyone observed you walking out with me if you are worrying about that."

"I am not worrying about it. Let us go a little further and then turn back." She lifted her arm from the warm blanket of his jacket and the moonlight lit it up, white, fine, soft. "Let's turn round there."

She pointed at the middle distance and he let out a laugh.

"It will take us all night to find the place. But yes. Why not?"

And they continued.

"How is your sister?"

"Recovering at our home in Derbyshire. I wish I could persuade her to be less extreme, to put less of herself and her health into what she believes in. But I'm afraid it is hopeless."

"I admire her, and women like her. My own views are at one with theirs, but I never do anything apart from sign petitions and wear a sash on market day!"

"That is not something to regret. If the women's movement are to win, which I believe they shall in the long run, then they must carry the generality of persons with them. Not just the extremists. Ordinary men and women of average values must be persuaded."

"You think they will be?"

"Yes. Eventually."

"But last night when we met, you said that the government would not simply change the law, do you recall that?"

"Yes. I meant that they will not change the law just like that. It will take time. I suspect more lives will be lost. I just hope that my sister's is not one of them."

"So do I."

They slowed; the air was still and although it was chilly, they were unconcerned.

"Elizabeth, we should turn back. You are cold. I can feel you shivering even though you try to hide it. And if we are both missing from supper, people will talk. About you, I mean. And I will not be responsible for that."

She knew he was right and nodded, although part of her regretted it. He let her arm go, and, in its place, clasped her hand with his.

"You don't mind?" He looked down at their interlinked hands as they walked.

"Not a bit of it. You know, when we met, I thought you an awful old stiff."

"Yes, I gathered that. If it is of any interest, I thought you were beautiful right from the start."

It was rare that Lizzy was lost for words. As it was, she tightened her grip on his hand and walked on.

"Beautiful, clever, thoughtful—when you were not being hasty. Unusual, in the best sort of way. Altogether, I found you rather appealing, which I am sure you now realise."

"I can be rather slow on occasion. But I believe I have caught up now," she said.

"Do you think you will let me see you again, away from this house party? Anything really. Will you see me?"

Lizzy stopped walking and looked him square in the face. She studied him unashamedly and in detail, and any person observing her might have thought her utterly fascinated. But then, he had been rather direct with her.

"Yes, I will see you."

At that moment, they reached the foot of the path, where it rejoined the north side of the maze. It was now quite dark, so dark, one could hardly see the gravel. The way was narrow and uneven and to their clasped hands was added further touches, contact that could not be undone. Their arms bumped and then, as Lizzy stumbled slightly, her leg brushed his. The lace overlay of her skirt caught on his trousers; neither party sought to separate them. His arm slipped about her, and the warmth that had been radiating gently, suddenly, enveloped her, blanketed her that she may never feel cold again. They reached the edge of the maze and paused. Lizzy shrugged off the jacket.

"You'd better have this back, or we shall look awfully guilty."

"We are awfully guilty, aren't we?" He took the jacket. "You go first, Elizabeth. No one will see you. I'll follow in a few minutes."

For a shave of a moment, she just stood there in the moonlight. In the distance, the party rumbled on and now there was music too. He was right. She could just slip back in. But her eyes lingered on his darkened form, his handsome face, and a great energy whizzed through her. It moved swiftly, disrupting ideas, changing things about entirely.

"Good"—and she leaned up on her toes to kiss him on the lips. A look of surprise danced in his eyes, but it did not last long. The feeling of his lips on hers was enough to melt her. Lest she should actually melt, she stopped.

His voice croaked somewhat when he found it.

"Go inside…before you are missed, dearest, loveliest Elizabeth."

JENETTA JAMES is a lawyer, writer, mother, and taker-on of too much. She grew up in Cambridge and read history at Oxford where she was a scholar and president of the Oxford History Society. After graduating, she took to the law and now practices full time as a barrister. Over the years, she has lived in France, Hungary, and Trinidad, as well as her native England. Jenetta currently lives in London with her husband and children where she enjoys reading, laughing, and playing with Lego. She is the author of *Suddenly Mrs. Darcy*, *The Elizabeth Papers*, and *Lover's Knot*.

Atmospheric
Disturbances

Christina Morland

*"My good qualities are under your protection, and you are to exaggerate
them as much as possible; and, in return, it belongs to me to find
occasions for teasing and quarrelling with you as often as may be..."*
—Chapter LX

ATMOSPHERIC DISTURBANCES
Christina Morland

LONGBOURN, DECEMBER 1812

*W*hen he met her gaze from across the room, she wondered that the others did not feel it: an electric charge, Mr. Franklin's kite and key, the brewing of a storm. This was not desire; she had become well practiced at recognizing that delicious swoop of the stomach when his fingers grazed hers or when he murmured "Elizabeth" so that only she could hear.

No, this was something else—something more dangerous.

Desire was part of it, just not the entirety. There was also a tinge of amusement (oh, to see him blush!), a smattering of anger (fie upon his abominable pride!), and yes, a good dose of yearning (ah, to kiss away that frown). Beneath all these simmering emotions: a thin, icy layer of fear.

Elizabeth Bennet and Fitzwilliam Darcy were on the brink of their very first quarrel.

Well, no. They had already quarreled more times than she could remember. But those disagreements had taken place *before* their engagement, when she had been trying to provoke him and he had been trying to—she supposed he had been trying to woo her, though she still found this difficult to comprehend. There were, in fact, a good many aspects of her betrothed she found difficult to comprehend, but she at least knew this: he took great pleasure in sparring with her.

So there was no reason to fear the approaching disagreement—yet her hands trembled with such intensity that she splattered the tea she had been tasked with pouring.

"Oh, Lizzy!" cried Mrs. Bennet, snatching away the very cup Elizabeth had been trying to fill. For two, perhaps three seconds, Elizabeth could do nothing but watch herself pour tea directly onto the drawing room table. Only when Jane came to her aid, gently prying the teapot from her still trembling hands, did she manage to regain her wits.

"Are you well?" her sister whispered as they frantically sopped up tea with the serviettes Mrs. Hill had just laundered for the fast-approaching wedding breakfast.

Elizabeth could say nothing to Jane; all her attention was focused on him. How would he look at her now, his future Mrs. Darcy? How did he feel, knowing he was on the verge of marrying a woman who could not even pour a cup of tea without—what had he accused her of, again? Oh, yes—*making a fuss*.

He met her gaze with what, to the others, must have seemed a neutral expression. But *she* saw how his mouth hardened, how his color deepened. Worst of all, he raised one eyebrow, mocking her. How dare he steal her tactic of laughing at life's absurdities?

At least he was the first to look away; Mrs. Bennet distracted him by rushing to his side and apologizing profusely—as if Elizabeth had just poured the contents of the teapot not on the table but on his head.

Now, there was a thought.

"She is not usually this clumsy!" assured Mrs. Bennet, holding out the half-empty teacup as a peace offering.

He shook his head, refusing her mother's gesture without a word —and all the amusement, embarrassment, and fear that had moderated Elizabeth's anger disappeared in an instant.

"Oh, but I *am* clumsy," she said in a tone that caused everyone else in the room—even Mr. Bingley, who had been steadfastly pretending to read the newspaper—to look over at her. She felt their curiosity, noted their stillness, yet kept her gaze pinned on *him*. Then, with careful enunciation, each word a jab: "Quite clumsy."

For Elizabeth, disparagement of her own person represented a radical new approach to winning arguments; she was much more likely to aim her wit at the foibles of her opponent. Yet she felt, almost instinctively, that to insult herself—the woman he loved—would prove an even greater challenge to Darcy's pride than any insult she could throw at him.

She was right—and wrong. His eyes flashed. His jaw twitched. His entire frame seemed to lengthen as he leaned forward onto his toes. He reminded her of a large cat, preparing to pounce. Had they been alone, he might very well have pounced (odd how her anger had obliterated all other feelings *except* desire). But they were not alone, and this had been her miscalculation. He may have enjoyed a good argument, but he absolutely hated having an audience.

With a curt bow, he muttered, "Excuse me," and exited the drawing room.

"We neither of us perform to strangers," he had said to her at Rosings, in that other life when she had not understood him.

Would she ever understand him?

"Oh, Lizzy! You have vexed him, and just days before your wedding, too!" someone called after her—her mother, most likely. Elizabeth could not be certain, for she was halfway to the door when the words reached her. She thought she heard other voices as well: a worried expression from Jane, a soothing comment from Bingley, a cynical chuckle from her father? Giggling from Kitty while Mary quoted Proverbs something or another?

Perhaps, or perhaps not. If she had learned anything in the year since she had met Fitzwilliam Darcy, it was that she was all too quick to make assumptions about those dearest to her.

Throwing open the front door, she hit a wall of wind so biting, so fierce, she nearly turned back. Then she saw him. He was turning the corner of the house, heading for the stables.

"Mr. Darcy!" she shouted, breaking into a run. She abhorred her total want of pride—to race after any man, even one she loved, represented a low point, for sure. Yet for all that she had dreaded their quarrel, she feared his silence more. Storms inflicted damage, but droughts choked the life out of everything.

He called out—but not to her. "John, my horse."

Everything in that moment conspired against her: the bitter chill in the air; his refusal to acknowledge her; the utter lack of distress in his voice, as if he were preparing for a leisurely ride across the grounds, rather than an escape from his quarrelsome betrothed. Still, she would have kept her tears at bay had it not been for one minor detail: he had addressed Longbourn's groom by name. Even Mr. Bingley, kind and affable Mr. Bingley, tended to fall back on "You there!" when calling for his horse.

Elizabeth swiped angrily at her eyes. She did not understand Fitzwilliam Darcy, not at all! He was, by turns, cold and warm, kind and aloof, reticent and garrulous. And then there were all those odd details that confounded categorization: he often turned his head just before smiling, as if worried that others might see; he could not sit for more than a quarter of an hour in idle conversation, yet could spend the entirety of a rainy afternoon teaching Kitty and Mary to play chess; he brought her no gifts, wrote her no love letters, and paid her few compliments, except the compliment of attention.

He also knew the name of every servant at Longbourn. Granted, there were only five, if one did not include the woman they hired on occasion to help with the laundry. ("Though I suppose you know *her* name, too," Elizabeth had teased after discovering he knew the names of all the others. "Tess," he had replied—correctly.)

There was nothing particularly laudable in his ability to recite these names. Indeed, she was tempted to interpret this knowledge as an extension of his pride, for as he himself had put it, "Longbourn, and all who live here, are now of great importance to me." The sentiment was at once romantic and ruthless: one either existed in the Darcy orbit—or was consigned to the invisibility of the ether.

As he followed John into the stables, Elizabeth knew, if she was ever to maintain her own center of gravity, that she could not allow him to take flight now.

He was just mounting his horse when she came striding in after him. Oh, why could they not have resolved their differences over a fragrant cup of tea, seated next to a crackling fire, instead of out of doors, where she could see her own breath and smell only horse manure?

At her arrival, he paused in his preparations but did not look down at her.

"John," she said, her gaze fixed on her betrothed, "I would speak to Mr. Darcy alone."

"The reins, John," said Darcy.

She saw, out of the corner of her eye, how the servant glanced between the two of them.

Had she possessed less self-restraint—had she been more like her mother or Lydia—she might have snapped at both men, reminding them that John had known her longer and therefore had no cause to consider Mr. Darcy's wishes over her own. Had she possessed more self-restraint—had she been more like Jane—she would have snapped at no one at all.

As it was, she was Elizabeth—and so possessed only enough self-restraint to keep from snapping at John.

"Oh, come down off your high horse, Fitzwilliam Darcy, and talk to me!"

Such a shameful outburst! At the very least, she ought to have avoided the pun. Still, it had the desired effect. After a brief pause, he dismounted and handed over the reins with a quiet, "Thank you, John."

Then he turned to face her.

Silence—and the fear returned, a shiver across her skin. Wrapping her arms tightly about her ribcage, she willed herself to hold his gaze —and good thing, too, for she saw how, with John's departure, Darcy's entire bearing changed. Gone was the proud gentleman, shoulders thrown back, chin held high; in his place stood a man so discomposed that he tugged at his cravat, as if it were too tight for him to breathe, and then threw aside his hat and gloves in order to run his fingers through his hair—a nervous habit she would never have attributed to him before their engagement.

He was going to apologize—either that, or offer his coat, for he must have seen her shivering.

Spinning on her heel, she called over her shoulder, "I do not want the horses to eavesdrop," and heard his reluctant laugh. They walked out into the open air, where a sudden gust reminded her, as she put a hand to her head, that she had forgotten her bonnet too. When he caught up to her, tucking a strand of errant hair behind her ear, she was tempted to lean into his touch and forget everything else.

Tempted, but not overcome. With a mighty yank, she pulled away from him (leaving several chestnut strands twisted about his fingers, if the stinging of her scalp was any indication). She was too angry to give in now.

Be honest, Elizabeth. You are not angry; you are afraid. Yes, she, the young lady whose courage never failed to rise, was afraid. Not of him, for he was too much a gentleman to lash out. Even when she had insulted him at Hunsford, he had possessed an admirable (if annoying) degree of self-control.

No, what truly frightened her was the epiphany he was bound to have, and soon: she was, and always would be, headstrong and obstinate. When he came to understand this unalterable aspect of her character, would he also come to regret his love?

So yes, she was afraid—deeply afraid. Still, she was no coward. She did not shrink back or attempt to delay the inevitable, but dove in, determined that if she must reap the whirlwind, let her at least be the one to sow the wind.

"You will be glad to know"—she lengthened her stride to outpace him, as if that could prevent a man some nine inches taller from keeping up—"that you are correct."

He was at her side in an instant. "As I endeavor to be correct whenever possible, I must ask you to be more precise."

Halting, she stared up at him, searching, *longing*, for any sign of humor in his countenance. But she saw only a scowl, and so resumed her onward march (realizing, with each step, that she had no destination in mind).

"You said, only minutes ago"—her teeth began to chatter as they entered the copse of trees just beyond the house—"that I was making a fuss."

"Elizabeth, for god's sake"—he was tugging off his coat—"I meant only—"

She quickened her pace, becoming almost too breathless to speak: "And you are right. I *was* making a fuss!"

"As you are now, too," he muttered, attempting to place the coat across her shoulders.

She dodged him by darting behind a tree. "Oh, but making a fuss is what I do best, sir!"

"So I have come to realize," he said, taking her by the hand and trying, none too delicately, to shove said hand into the arm of his coat.

"If you supposed from our previous encounters"—she tugged free of his hold—"that my impertinence was a mere ploy to attract difficult men"—then crossed her arms—"allow me to disabuse you of this notion!"

With what could have been a growl or a laugh, he threw his coat at her. Instinctively, she caught it. Each stared at the other, refusing to budge or blink.

Then, quietly: "Put on the coat, Elizabeth, and let us return to the house."

She was halfway to doing as he said before she experienced her own epiphany: he, too, was headstrong and obstinate. How easy it would be to slip on his coat, knowing he would offer her one of those rare smiles, the kind that made her feel as if she had just accomplished something marvelous. He would apologize for his abrupt departure, and she would forgive him without a word. Then he would say, stroking her wrist with his thumb, "I am only doing what I think best."

So she did what *she* thought best: she unfurled the coat like a flag and let it float to the ground. In a stroke of good luck (or perhaps it was just the wind), the coat landed at the base of a birch tree. Without stopping to think, she settled herself on his wrinkled garment, leaned back against the peeling bark, and looked up with one finely arched brow.

She nursed some small hope that her ridiculous behavior might make him laugh, but he appeared a little lost—and unmistakably sad. Had she gone too far, or not far enough? Would he turn on his heel and leave, or would he continue to stare down at her and frown?

With a heavy sigh, he lowered himself to the ground beside her.

"I am aware," she murmured into the breeze, "that my conduct today has been foolish in the extreme."

She had to bite back the words "will you forgive me?" She *was* treating him poorly, behaving with shocking incivility toward this man who deserved both her love and respect. He had, after all, committed no crime, broken no promise, done nothing that would, in the eyes of respectable society, seem untoward.

His only transgression had been acting like someone he was not—and this, to her, seemed the very worst of sins. This notion—that she knew him well enough to recognize when he was not himself—seemed nearly as absurd as her conduct. He remained an enigma she could not decipher. Still, she had once felt certain about a few core principles: he did not flaunt his wealth, and he did not suffer fools gladly.

Yet in the two months of their courtship, he had done both.

Another woman would not have complained. Her mother certainly had not. She had squealed with delight at the bolts of fabric, the pretty little serving dishes, and the silver slotted spoon that had appeared, one by one, at Longbourn: the first arriving a week after Mrs. Bennet had mentioned a need for new curtains; the second appearing on their table three days after her complaint about Longbourn's old, chipped china; and the third showing up in a tureen of potatoes the day after Mrs. Bennet had asserted the injustice of Lady Lucas owning a finer serving implement.

"You do realize," Elizabeth had told Darcy on the day of the serving spoon, "that even my mother is capable of recognizing a pattern, particularly when that pattern results in lavish gifts? Soon she will be decrying the state of our carriage."

"The gifts are hardly lavish" had been his only response.

For Mary, there was sheet music she was only barely qualified to play, while Kitty received a set of novels Miss Darcy had recommended during her short stay at Longbourn. Elizabeth supposed these gifts were not unreasonable—a considerate show of brotherly affection, perhaps? But then she had learned from her father that Darcy had also offered to pay for lessons with a master for Mary and tuition to a young lady's seminary for Kitty.

She found it notable that he had given Jane only a new quill pen and her father a single book from his own collection. For Elizabeth there had been no tangible presents at all. Had Lydia still been at Longbourn, she would surely have laughed at her sister: "He must not love you as much as he loves us, Lizzy!"

Elizabeth began to suspect the reverse was true: the less he liked a person, the more money he spent on his or her behalf. Indeed, by this measure, Lydia and Wickham were surely among his least favorite people in all of England. This theory, however, did not stand up to scrutiny, for she knew him to be a generous brother and landowner, and he by no means despised his sister or the people of Pemberley. Why then was he showering the Bennets with gifts when he so clearly did not enjoy their company?

And that was another thing: he willingly put himself in the way of her most tiresome relatives. He visited with her mother every day, and he never missed a card party at Aunt Philips's (though Elizabeth had tried, several times, to discourage him from attending). Had Mr. Collins resided nearby, she would not have been surprised to find Darcy dining with him every other evening.

She might have thought he was attempting to demonstrate his improved manners—but when in company, he behaved with all the cold civility Meryton residents had come to expect from him. She could not make sense of his behavior, except to fear that it signaled some deeper discontent with her. Yet when the two of them were alone (as they often were, thanks to the negligence of her parents and their own great willingness to walk out in almost any weather), he was everything she could have wished for in a husband: animated, affectionate, and the very best of listeners.

If only they could have spent the entirety of their courtship wandering the fields and woods of Hertfordshire, laughing at stories of each other's pasts, sharing their hopes for the future. For that matter, she wished they might pass the entirety of their marriage wandering through fields and woods. Instead, they would be expected to spend at least several months of the year in London, socializing with his more exalted friends; they would visit Lady Catherine, if ever that great lady forgave them; and they would, even in the quiet of the countryside, host dinners, balls, and card parties of their own. She would, in other words, have to share him with the world, and on those occasions, he would not be *her* Darcy, but that cold, austere, public Darcy she had first met at the Meryton assembly.

She glanced at him now, sitting uneasily with his legs crossed and his arms—well, he did not know what to do with his arms. He crossed them, uncrossed them, then planted the palms of his hands firmly on the ground to prop himself up. He looked nothing at all like public Darcy—but not quite like her Darcy either, for she had never thought to imagine him like this: knees at awkward angles, fingers pressed against dead leaves and cold earth. How many different men was he, this future husband of hers?

"I am also aware," she continued when he remained silent, "that another woman would thank you, rather than scold you. Surely that is what you are thinking—that I ought to express more appreciation for a man who would show such generosity to my most vexing relations, that I ought to be grateful for a man who would lower himself, quite literally, to be with me?"

He met her gaze. "That is what *you* are thinking, Elizabeth—not I."

Heat flooded her cheeks, and she had to blink away the sudden sting of tears. "Then what *are* you thinking?"

With a slight lift of his chin—"My thoughts are too varied and disorderly to give voice to them at the present time."

At such a statement, how could she do anything but laugh? He colored and turned away, obviously hurt, and she immediately checked her amusement.

"I laughed," she said, placing a tentative hand on his forearm, "only because that speech represented the most coherent explanation of incoherence I have ever heard."

He shot her a frown that was so clearly on the verge of becoming a smile that she could not help smiling herself. When he plucked up her hand and brought it to his lips, she felt that now-familiar, dearly-loved swoop of the stomach—as well as a deep sense relief. She had been wrong! This was not to be a long and tumultuous storm but a passing shower on an otherwise sunny day.

Then he dropped her hand, sighed, and looked at her in such a way that she knew they had only just passed under the eye of the storm.

"What I was thinking," he said wearily, as if every word cost him something to speak aloud, "is that I continue to misunderstand you, Elizabeth Bennet."

His eyelids fluttered closed, and in that brief moment of absence, she was reminded of how much vitality his eyes brought to the rest of his features. Had she really once believed that the dark gray of his irises held no warmth, no feeling? It was akin to believing the tempestuous sea or the deepening twilight were empty merely because one could not easily see through them.

Then his eyes snapped open, and she nearly flinched at the anger she saw there.

"In acting as I have toward your family, I have only been doing what I think best, Elizabeth!"

Ah, there it was, that phrase she had come to expect, for he had used it several times already during their engagement: *what I think best*. For all his inscrutability, she at least understood *this* aspect of Fitzwilliam Darcy.

Sitting up straight, she met his glare with one of her own. "You might have allowed yourself, in this particular instance, to be guided by one who possesses superior knowledge of the situation—say, perhaps, your betrothed? Then again, it must be *highly* unusual for you to meet with anyone who might claim superior knowledge on any matter, large or small."

He narrowed his eyes at her. "If you mean to say that I ought to have consulted you before engaging a residence for your family's visit to Town this spring, then I can only beg your forgiveness for my presumption. Yet even you must concede how such an arrangement would provide happiness for everyone concerned."

"Certainly for *you*! Tell me, have you measured, by map, the farthest one may go from Darcy House and still remain in Mayfair? For I suppose those must have been your two criteria: to place my family as far from you as possible, while providing an address less mortifying to your respectability than Cheapside!"

She regretted her words almost the moment they escaped her lips —and regretted them more when she saw the shadow of hurt cross his countenance. But he recovered quickly enough. With a grace she was coming to dislike—for he was never quite so elegant as when he was preparing to bolt—he rose and brushed the dried leaves from his breeches.

"Neither of us is in the proper frame of mind for discussing this matter."

She jumped to her feet just as he turned to leave. "Do not presume to tell me about *my* frame of mind!"

He went still, every muscle in his face taut, his shoulders a bundle of coiled tension. Even in her anger, she was tempted to reach out and touch him, to release that spring stretched almost to its breaking point.

Then he strode toward her, closing the distance between them. No part of him touched her, yet she could feel the heat of him, see the bobbing of his Adam's apple beneath his loosened cravat, hear the raggedness of his—or was it her?—breath.

Refusing to take a step back, she craned her neck to meet his gaze. "Pardon me, Mr. Darcy. Am I making too much of a fuss for you?"

He reached for her then, and she braced herself for something—a light shake of the shoulders, a rough kiss on the lips—but he halted, hands hovering inches from her shoulders.

"I suppose," he said, "you will add this to your list of phrases to hold against me?"

"I have no idea what you mean."

"First 'tolerable,' now 'fuss.' What are the other words I am sure to have thrown back at me, again and again, over the course of our marriage?"

This surprised a laugh out of her, and his entire frame relaxed. Ever so gently, he placed his hands on her shoulders and pulled her closer.

"I had rather hoped," he said, lips almost at her ear, "that we would give our attention to words such as 'ardent' and 'love.'"

Oh, she had to admire his technique. Distraction was a very fine method indeed—but certainly no match for her. Just as he leaned in to kiss her, she ducked her head, brushing her lips against his jaw. With a startled exhalation, he loosened his hold just enough for her to slip out of his arms.

Placing a good foot of space between them, she said, "We have more to discuss."

He rubbed a hand across his face. "I do not wish to quarrel with you, Elizabeth."

"Then perhaps you ought to listen to me instead."

He frowned, reddened, then opened his mouth to speak. But she held up a hand.

"You can be the very best of listeners, Fitzwilliam. Will you listen to me now?"

He gave a curt nod, yet before she could think how to begin, he retrieved his coat from the ground, holding it open for her.

"At least do me the favor of putting this on. You are shaking with cold, Elizabeth."

She hesitated, then gave a nod of her own; she could hardly deny that her arms and fingers were numb and stiff. Yet as soon as she slipped on the coat, she wished she had not. The wool smelled of him —there was that delicious swoop again—and his hands came to rest lightly on her arms. Unable to help herself, she leaned back against him, reveling in his warmth.

"Come," he said, taking her by the hand and leading her back to what she had decided was *their* tree. "Let us sit."

As they once again settled themselves on the ground—he had figured out what to do with his arms this time: one he slipped around her shoulders, the other he wrapped lightly about his knees—she asked, "Will it always be this way?"

"Do you mean, will I always give in to you so easily?"

"*You* give in to *me?*" She tried to shrug off his arm. "*I* have given in to *you*! Here I am, wearing your coat, wrapped in your arms, an obedient little wife-to-be—"

"Yes, terribly obedient," he muttered as she finally pulled out from beneath his arm.

They looked at each other, and she sighed. "Did I not pledge to tease and quarrel with you as often as I could?"

"You are as good as your word." Then, with a sigh of his own: "I know you are angry with me—and perhaps with some reason."

"Oh, thank you for that."

He scowled but continued doggedly: "Yes, I ought to have spoken with you first about leasing a London residence for your family, and no, I ought not to have accused you of making a fuss."

She closed her eyes, the hurt flooding back all at once. How awful, to be sitting all the way across the drawing room from him, watching as he stood with his back against the wall, arms crossed, all hauteur and disdain. How cold his voice had been when he had spoken those words to her—"It is just a house, Elizabeth; do stop making a fuss"—and in front of all her family and Mr. Bingley, too! True, she had been rather blunt in her rejection of his generosity—but only because he had failed to heed her previous, gentler refusals.

"I *was* making a fuss," she admitted. "I am beginning to wonder if it is the only way I may get you to listen to me."

"When do I *not* listen to you? Did you not just praise me for being the very best of listeners?" He shook his head. "This is why, at times, I can make no sense of you, Elizabeth. You contradict yourself!"

"You *are* the very best of listeners—when what I have to say does not inconvenience you."

He gaped at her. "What is that supposed to mean?"

"Just as I have said. You had decided already that it suited you more to tuck my family away in some respectable house not too far, and yet not too near, your own London residence."

"*Our* London residence, Elizabeth, and I was thinking of everyone involved. Bingley has no house of his own in Town, as you well know. To invite the Bingleys, as well as the Bennets…to have so many guests residing with us, all at once—"

"We Bennets have managed with tighter quarters each time we have visited the Gardiners."

"Which is precisely why I decided renting a separate residence would be for the best!"

"Would you ever allow such a liberty to be taken on *your* behalf, Fitzwilliam?"

"What has that to do with anything? And how is it a liberty to—"

"Are the Bennets, too, not allowed some pride? These past two months, you have patronized my mother, sisters, and even, at times, my father, in ways that I find difficult to—"

"Oh, I see. I am to show them kindness, yet do nothing at all for them? Perhaps you may advise me on how I am to act toward them, as I am apparently not meeting with your approval!"

"You might try talking with them, as you talk with me! Instead, you are cold and silent, throwing money at them—"

"Throwing money?"

"As if they are a leaky roof or unimproved acreage."

"Oh, for god's sake, Elizabeth—"

"To be frank—"

"Have you been anything else?"

"I am surprised that you would discuss matters of money with them."

"And yet, you just told me I ought to talk with them more."

"That is not what I mean!"

"No, I understand your meaning, Elizabeth. You suppose I have not changed, that I am capable only of arrogance, conceit, and a selfish disdain for the feelings of others—"

"Oh, so now you have decided to throw *my* ill-considered words back at me!"

She put her hands to her face, pressing the heels of her palms to her stinging eyes. Yet it mattered not; the tears fell, and fell hard—a downpour she could not control, only endure. Still she tried to outrun it, or at the very least hide; she scrambled to her feet and spun away from him, as if that might do any good. Surely the sight of her trembling shoulders would be just as painful to him as her tears.

When she managed to check her crying, she looked about and gasped: it was snowing. Softly, lightly—just enough to make the air sparkle and the earth appear fresh again. They were in no more danger of freezing to death than they had been a few minutes earlier —less so, since the wind had died down—yet she expected, any moment, that he would repeat his order to return to the house.

Instead, she felt his tentative pat on the back, a gesture so awkward, so tender that she began to laugh, as well as cry, into her hands.

"Elizabeth." His voice conveyed all the confusion, distress, and weariness she herself felt.

"Poor man," she managed, turning just enough to peek at him through her fingers. The snow had begun to turn his hair white. "I rather think *I* ought to comfort you."

"I would not be adverse"—he gently pried her hands from her face —"to a certain kind of consolation."

In a flash, her arms were about his neck, her face buried in the crook of his shoulder.

"I am ruining your fine attire," she said, even as she used the sleeve of his coat to wipe her nose. "What trouble I am making for you today!"

"No trouble," he murmured, kissing her hair. "Just a fuss."

She laughed against his chest, then leaned back to study him. Here was yet another variation on Fitzwilliam Darcy: eyes clear and wide and searching; hair wet from snow, curling about his ears and rumpled on top, as if he had run his hands through it one too many times during their argument. Had he ever been so handsome as he was in this moment?

She, on the other hand, must have looked a fright: red nose and tear-stained cheeks, hair sticking out every which way. Yet he gazed at her with that same intensity she had once mistaken for disapproval—an intensity that sent a jolt of heat through her now.

Still, she remained too contrary—and still too afraid—to tip her head back for the kiss they both wanted.

"This," she said, indicating her blotchy face, "is the woman you are marrying in three days."

"Thank god," he said, leaning in for a kiss that she stopped with an index finger against his lips.

"I know, I know," she murmured at his expression of dismay. "I am such a difficult creature. You are wishing you had caught someone more compliant—perhaps Miss Bingley?—when you had the chance."

He nipped the pad of her finger. "And you are angling for the compliment of my denial."

"I simply want to make certain," she continued, dodging another kiss, "before you regain the upper hand—"

"And here I thought *you* had taken that position—"

"That we have resolved our differences."

He raised his eyebrows.

"Or, at least the question of London—and my family."

With a sigh, he let his hands fall to his side. "This matters a great deal to you."

"Yes—or rather, no, not the house in London, not precisely. I appreciate your generosity, Fitzwilliam, truly. Yet it feels…" She hesitated, loath to start another round of quarreling.

"Cold," he said quietly. "Contemptuous."

She gazed up at him. "Yes, cold."

He let out a short, curt laugh. "These last few days, I suspected you were growing angry with me, but for an entirely different reason. I thought…" This time he hesitated.

She grabbed one of his hands and kissed it. "Do not fear to speak openly to me now; I am all fussed out for the day."

He smiled. "I thought perhaps you were angry at me for giving gifts to everyone in your family but you."

"What? You supposed me jealous?"

He raised his eyebrows at her tone.

"Yes, yes, I know—no more fusses. Allow me to state, quite calmly, that jealously is not among my many flaws. Indeed, I interpreted the lack of gifts as a sign of your respect—a rather unconventional sign of respect, to be sure, but a sincere one."

"Precisely! I hardly knew how to explain this behavior to myself, except to acknowledge that I had nothing to give you, besides my time, that did not feel like a cheap form of flattery."

"Nothing but your time?" She smiled. "Were you any other man, I might call such a speech arrogant."

"I am surprised to find myself excluded in this regard. I believe you once took great pleasure in attaching that word to my character."

"No, never pleasure. Besides, I have given up my old habits, or at least some of them. Now that you are to be my husband, only favorable adjectives will do for you."

"Except, I suppose, when you are angry with me."

Her smile slipped. "Not angry, at least not now. I only wish…" She bit her lip. "I wish you might show some small measure of warmth toward my family."

"I have made an attempt, Elizabeth. Have I not attended every one of the dinners and card parties your mother and aunt have arranged for us?"

"Yes, though as I have said to you before, if you are only to go so that you might stand about, silent and unhappy, I would have you decline every invitation!"

"You once exhorted me to practice, and so I have been."

"Have you? I suggested practicing conversation—not the purchasing of gifts that, by your own admission, serve as a cheap form of flattery."

He flushed, started to turn, then halted halfway. She was struck by the sight of him, staring down at his hands; here was yet another variant of this man she had once thought incapable of self-doubt or reflection.

"Forgive me," she said quietly. "I am not being fair."

"On the contrary, you have found me out—and made it impossible, I might add, for me to give you the wedding gift I had planned to present upon our arrival at Pemberley."

She laughed. "Oh, I suppose I might be persuaded to accept it." Then in a more serious tone: "I do not believe all forms of gift-giving are but cheap flattery to you. Your sister has told me of your generosity to her and to all who live at Pemberley—and I do not suppose you think so little of them."

"Yes, and yet—well, I do not know what to say to any of them, Elizabeth. Even with Georgiana, I sometimes have so little to say. The gifts, they…" He shook his head.

"They absolve you from the responsibility of talking when you feel you would rather not talk at all," she finished for him.

He looked so discomfited by this analysis of his character that she took pity on him and brushed her lips against his cheek.

"I hereby pledge," she murmured against his skin, so warm in spite of the cold, "to teach your sister all my quarrelsome ways, so that you may then find it easier to speak with her, too."

He laughed, and she felt all the heat of a sun that was not, on this wintry day, readily apparent. Given this sudden burst of happiness, she wished she could have swallowed the question that came tumbling from her lips.

"Why is your character so altered in general company? With me, with Mr. Bingley, and I suspect with a few others, you are yourself, and yet with most people, certainly with my family, you seem a different man."

For a long moment, he said nothing. Then, quietly: "My father used to present my mother with a different gift nearly every day during the last year of her life."

She stared up at him, hardly knowing how to respond to this statement that was, at once, a misdirection and a heartfelt response to her question.

"Most days, he gave her fresh-cut flowers," he continued, absently brushing the snow from his hair, then hers, "but also books she would never read, stationary she would never use, jewels she would not have time enough to wear."

Elizabeth was certain she had seen his parents' portraits at Pemberley, yet when she tried recalling their faces, she pictured her own parents. There was a time, long ago, when her father, too, had brought home trinkets for his wife. When had the gift-giving stopped?

"My mother was a very sickly woman," Darcy said after a long silence, "and I used to suppose my father gave her these gifts as a means of improving her spirits. I remember telling her, no more than a fortnight before her death, that she ought to be grateful for all he did for her."

"Oh, Fitzwilliam…"

"'I *am* grateful,' my mother told me, smiling—though I cannot think now how she could stand to smile at me after I had said such a thing to her."

The agony of his expression—guilt, regret, self-loathing—made Elizabeth swear she would bear without complaint every one of his cold spells, if only she never again had to see such suffering on his features.

"Only now, after your condemnation of my behavior, do I wonder…" He squeezed shut his eyes, then shook his head. "For all the gifts he gave her, I never once heard him offer her words of affection. He never, in my presence at least, said, 'I love you.'" He looked at her then, his gray eyes luminous—light and dark, sun and storm. "I love you, Elizabeth."

And oh, how she loved him! Had her throat not constricted, she would have told him so. As it was, she could only gaze up at him and hope he understood. He must have, for he smiled—not his stiff, public smile or a devilish, teasing grin. Those were surface smiles, reflecting the recipient rather than the bearer. No, this smile was pure incandescence, a fire lit from within, and she supposed herself the only person in the world fortunate enough to have witnessed it.

"Surely," she whispered, when she at last found her voice, "your father, even if he could not say the words—"

"Oh, he loved my mother. Of that, I have no doubt. He was not a cruel or heartless man. Indeed, he was all that was respectable and good. But he did not know how to speak of the things that truly mattered to him. He could go on for hours about ledgers or Napoleon or the best way to raise a horse, but to give voice to his feelings...no, a gentleman did not speak of such things."

She wrapped her arms about his waist and placed her ear against his chest, listening to his breath, to his heart—to those inner workings she so rarely heard.

"I do not mean to excuse myself, Elizabeth—to say it is because of my father that I sometimes behave as I do. Yet I am *something* like him; I do not find it easy to explain myself."

"Yes, and something like your mother, too." She placed a feather-light kiss just above his cravat, on the bare skin of his throat. "I will give you words of kindness and affection all the days we have together, Fitzwilliam."

He held her tightly, saying nothing.

"And other kinds of words, too," she added, "when the mood suits."

"Naturally." Then, after a pause: "You asked me why I am a different man with others, but what if I am not?"

She pulled back to look at him. "What do you mean?"

"For all that I have tried to change—for all the ways I will continue to live by your lesson, Elizabeth—I remain the man you accused me of being when I first proposed."

"No, I was wrong about you at Hunsford. I did not fully understand you then."

He raised a brow. "Do you fully understand me now? For I can say with certainty that I do not fully understand *you*."

"Very well, I do not *fully* understand you, but I know at least enough to say that those words I used—oh, I regret them, and always will! You are not arrogant, conceited, or selfish." She offered a crooked smile. "Just presumptuous enough to arrange my family's stay in London without consulting them—or me."

"Yes, I am that man—as well as the man who dreads your mother's chitchat."

"Oh, but we all dread that! Yet I have endured it for twenty years; I daresay you can manage for the month they will spend with us in Town. Oh, very well," she added, smiling at his expression of alarm, "we will leave the decision to my parents. If my mother can be persuaded to accept your generous offer, I will say nothing else on the matter."

He smiled his thanks—and then his countenance grew serious. "We may laugh about this now, but I remain, Elizabeth, the man you sometimes find disdainful and cold. There will come a day when all we have said and felt here will fade to distant memory, and we will argue again."

"Again and again, I am sure." She thought of her parents, of how she had never heard *them* argue. Carp and complain, mock and neglect—yes. But grapple with each other's true feelings? Confront each other's faults, loving each other all the while? No. "At least, I hope we will argue again and again."

He raised his brows.

"Oh, I do not truly enjoy quarreling with you, Fitzwilliam, but if it keeps you from turning your back on me—"

"I would never do that."

"If I had not chased after you and, as you put it, made a fuss, you would have left Longbourn today without a word to me. Tomorrow, you would have called on my family, cool and polite, pressing upon us both the pretense that neither of us was hurting."

He opened his mouth, presumably to disagree—then promptly closed it.

She saw then how his teeth chattered. How cold he must have been, giving up his coat for her! Shrugging out of it, she said (her own lips trembling), "Your turn now!"—but he refused to wear it, of course. And so, it was that they started back to the house, his coat slung across her shoulders, her arm wrapped about his waist—both of them thinking of other, more potent ways they might, in the days to come, keep each other warm.

Longbourn in sight, he said, "Knowing how much I have pained you, I wish I could promise never again to behave as I have today."

"And I wish I could promise never again to make such a fuss over small matters."

They stopped and stared at each other.

"It would be a falsehood," he said quietly.

"Yes."

With all the solemnity of a man headed to the gallows, he asked, "Can you still marry me, knowing that I cannot completely change for you?"

At last—a crack in the ice. It would never fully melt, this fear that he would one day fall out of love with her. But to know that he too dreaded the loss of her affections—well, she felt oddly grateful for his reciprocal fear. What a strange thing, this love! It thrived not on the absence of discord but from the sharing of it.

"So long as you can still marry me, knowing me for who I am—and always will be."

He kissed her hair. "Clever, beautiful, and exasperating?"

"Yes, of course, but also…" She grinned up at him, squinting at the sudden appearance of the sun. "Did I ever tell you how Lady Catherine described me during her unexpected visit to Longbourn?"

He made a face. "I do not think I want to know."

"She called me an obstinate, headstrong girl."

"How wrong she was!"

She arched a brow. "Resorting to cheap flattery, after all?"

"On the contrary. You are no *girl*, Elizabeth. Now, for god's sake, let me kiss you."

Obstinate, headstrong woman that she was, she did not.

She kissed him first.

CHRISTINA MORLAND spent the first two decades of her life with no knowledge whatsoever of *Pride and Prejudice*—or any Jane Austen novel, for that matter. She somehow overcame this childhood adversity to become a devoted fan of Austen's works. When not writing, Morland tries to keep up with her incredibly active daughter and maddeningly brilliant husband. She lives in a place not unlike Hogwarts (minus Harry, Dumbledore, magic, and Scotland), and likes to think of herself as an excellent walker. Morland is the author of two other short stories for The Quill Collective (find them in *Dangerous to Know* and *Rational Creatures*), as well as three Austenesque novels: *A Remedy Against Sin, This Disconcerting Happiness,* and *Seasons of Waiting.*

Elizabeth: Obstinate Headstrong Girl

Love in Limelight

Beau North

"There is stubbornness about me that never can bear to be frightened at the will of others. My courage always rises at every attempt to intimidate me." –Chapter XXXI

LOVE IN LIMELIGHT
Beau North

*Y*ou must allow me to tell you how ardently I admire and love you." My eyes met his, saw that he was serious. A peal of laughter burst from my lips.

"Oh, surely not."

His expression melted from hope to consternation, brows drawing down into one severe line.

"Are you…laughing at me?"

I shook my head. "Sir. You cannot think I would marry you. Not if you were the last man on earth, and I the last woman."

His stride—athletic, purposeful—had him across the room and at my side in an instant. I put my hand against the silken folds of his cravat. His hands were warm manacles on my arms.

"Do you mean to tell me that you don't love me? You've played me a fool?"

My mouth opened, breath catching somewhere behind my teeth. His chest rose and fell like the swelling of the ocean tide. I searched his eyes. Hurt, wounded eyes. I felt myself sliding into that gaze, swooning against my better judgement.

"I…I…"

And then his lips met mine. Warm, pliant, and completely still for approximately three seconds.

"Cut! That's a wrap!"

My co-star released me and stood back, beaming down at me. "That was incredible, Liz!" he said in his silky English voice. "Really, fantastic work."

I laughed, still a little shaky from the performance. I gave him an affectionate squeeze of the arm. "Thanks, darling, you too. I thought for sure I was going to miss my mark on that last take."

Our director, Charles Bingley, strode onto set with his usual flair. Charles was a natty dresser and always showed up on set in a masterfully tailored suit, complete with waistcoat and watch, and never wilted, no matter *how* hot it got. Between takes, we took bets on whether the sweltering heat in the studio would have Bingley doffing his suit jacket and rolling up his sleeves. So far, no one had won that bet. He was all smiles now, offering us each a handshake. To me, he gave an additional kiss on the cheek.

"Beautifully done, Liz. That'll show him," Bingley said with a wink, making me laugh. We both knew the *him* in question. "Now. She's waiting in your dressing room."

I groaned. "Charles, it's bad enough I got conned into doing this picture. Why on *earth* would you make me talk to a gossip rag?"

"Because the studio in its limited wisdom has given me a very little budget for promoting this film. Gossip rags are free publicity. You're a new face, with a living goddess of a sister. People want to know about you. And, you'll do it because I asked nicely, and you adore me."

"Well, I can't argue with that. But you owe me a cocktail. Hell, you owe me five."

He beamed and pointed a finger at me. "You got it, Lizzy."

In my dressing room, I found a tall, elegantly dressed woman peering closely at the framed photographs on my vanity. One was a photo of all four of my sisters back on our family farm in better times. I'd taken that picture myself, before leaving for England seven years ago. Next to that was a photo of my parents: my father with his sardonic smile, my mother who was still a beauty even in her golden years. My heart constricted at the thought of them.

The woman saw me enter and rose to her full height. She had a fine, willowy figure and a shimmering curtain of strawberry blonde hair, but only a lover would think her a beauty.

"Oh, hello. I'm Caroline Conway. You must be Eliza Bennet?" she asked, extending a hand. I took it with a tight smile. Oh, how I hated the *nom de scène* the studio had insisted I take when I'd agreed to do this film. I wasn't Eliza Bennet, starlet. I was Elizabeth Bennet, actress and professional wrench-in-the-works to one arrogant executive.

"Just Eliza is fine," I said, as I'd been instructed to do. *"Lizzy is a farmgirl. You will introduce yourself as Eliza."* I shoved the pompous voice of the studio head from my mind as quickly as I could. "Do you mind if I sit so I can get rid of this coif?" I pointed to my carefully arranged hair, which to me resembled nothing so much as a brown hydrangea. "The pins are killing me."

"Of course." Caroline took a seat on the little settee on the other side of the room where I occasionally napped between long takes. She was holding a small notepad in one hand and a pen in the other, seemingly conjuring them out of thin air as she hadn't had them a second ago.

"Do you mind if I begin while you do that?" she asked. I pulled out one of the pins keeping the heavy twist of my curls in place. Oh, it hurt, but it felt like heaven.

"Sure. Go ahead." I removed another pin. The hydrangea lost some of its shape.

Caroline Conway, premiere Hollywood columnist, was at present the most powerful woman in town, and clearly, she knew it. With a few lines on paper, she could destroy an actor's career or catapult nobodies like me into stardom. She didn't look down at her notebook as she wrote but kept her eyes forward, watching me, gauging my reactions…playing me the way a good actress plays a crowd.

"First, let me congratulate you on landing the lead of *The Head-strong Girl*. It's said to be the biggest production of 1934."

"Thank you. I'm delighted to be a part of it." What a load of horse apples! Months spent trussed up like a turkey in corsets and petticoats had been anything but a delight. Another pin fell on the pile.

"One would almost call your rise to stardom…meteoric."

I almost shrugged, then remembered the oh-so-careful grooming the studio had given me for just such an occasion and smiled brightly instead.

"I'd done some stage acting in London and New York, but when I saw the script, I just couldn't pass up the chance to audition. It's all been an absolute dream!"

Caroline's eyebrow, perfectly plucked, raised a fraction of an inch. *Maybe I wasn't as good as I thought.* "And some would say there's some favoritism from William Darcy, the head of the studio."

Favoritism? I could have laughed. William Darcy was an insufferable prig and an unrelenting thorn in my side. Since signing my contract for *The Headstrong Girl,* I'd made it my business to repay him in kind. Favoritism, my eye.

"Not at all," I assured her sweetly. "Mr. Darcy and I hardly know each other."

"Is it not true that you snatched this role from your sister, Jane Bennet?"

"No. Jane was never available for the role." Did I say that too quickly? I hoped not. "She was contractually obligated elsewhere." They could *exposé* me all they liked, but Jane deserved some privacy, by god. Caroline scribbled a few notes before looking up at me, my hair now free of its pins and making an enormous mane around my face. I took out the silver-plated brush they kept in my vanity, which was all but useless against my stubborn curls.

"And the rumors about you and your co-star in this picture, Rollo Fitz?"

I favored her with my most coquettish look. "I wouldn't *dream* of speaking to such rumors," I said, knowing it would be everywhere that Rollo and I were an item by this time tomorrow.

A smile spread slowly across her face. I forced myself to look away. Hers was a smile of knives, and it terrified me a little bit.

"He's a pip," she said with a wink, making me her conspirator.

I nodded, agreeing with a sigh. At least that part was true.

"Paint me a picture of Eliza Bennet," she said. "And how she came to be here in this moment."

I smiled, the first genuine smile I'd had since she'd introduced herself to me. "If this were a film, there would be a title card right here that says..."

ONE YEAR AGO

ELIZABETH BENNET STOOD ON THE DECK OF THE SHIP AS IT PULLED away from the dock, feeling as though she were leaving a piece of herself behind. The sky was a roiling, thunderous mix of dark grays and bruise-like purples. The rain would come, and soon, but she couldn't move as she watched the Southampton coast recede. She would miss England the way a lover misses a paramour. The museums, the cozy pubs, the bustle of people crowding on to an omnibus—it had become more a home to her than even the Oregon farm she'd grown up on. For seven years, she'd made her home there, from her years at the Royal Academy of Dramatic Arts to the smaller parts on Drury Lane and the Vaudeville, where her own mother had cut her teeth before coming to America and falling in love with an apple farmer.

"I'll never forgive you for this," a lilting, strangely familiar voice said from nearby. She turned her head slightly to see a young woman in a dark mink coat. The hat perched on her head threatened to go flying in the stiff wind; she held it in place with one gloved hand. The wind blew back the hat's birdcage veil, revealing the pretty, delicate features of the woman's profile.

Elizabeth looked away. She knew now where she'd seen the woman: on every other movie poster for Pinewood Studios for the last couple of years. It was Gigi Duvall, who'd been struggling to transition from former child star to full-fledged actress. Hollywood had not been as receptive to the poor woman's efforts as England had been, and her beauty and glamour made her one of the most sought-after guests for every party in London. Elizabeth herself had been at several of the same parties, but Elizabeth was strictly a stage actress and had not been particularly well known until she played Rosalind in *As You Like It* at the Old Vic. She and Gigi Duvall didn't exactly travel in the same circles.

She glanced back at the couple, readying herself to step in and diffuse the situation if things got rough. She didn't trust men as a rule; they were all either brutes or dopes in her eyes. Of course, she'd had her share of admirers and boyfriends, but she was as cautious with her heart as she had been with her checkbook. That had been a difficult lesson indeed.

Through her lashes, Elizabeth could see the man with Gigi, standing tall and ramrod-straight against the buffeting wind, as unaffected by the weather as he was by her anger. His hat remained firmly on his head, as if it would rather invoke the wrath of God than that of its owner. Despite the clenched jaw and furrowed brow, Elizabeth noticed he was remarkably good looking. Not classically handsome exactly, but compelling to look at. Still, a bully was a bully, and *this* man had bully written all over him. *Why do tall men always assume they can get away with everything?*

"It's for your own good," the man said in a deep, stern voice.

"And what would *you* know about what's good for me?" Gigi's lovely contralto voice shook with tears. "It's not as though you've ever been there when *I* needed you. You care more about the bottom line than you ever cared about me."

For a fraction of a second, Elizabeth saw the look of a wounded animal in his features. Was he a paramour, she wondered? A lot of powerful, rich men liked to keep beautiful actresses as their mistress. She could tell from the cut of his suit alone that he was richer than King Midas.

"I'm here *now*," he said, more gently than she thought such a large, somber man capable of. He folded her into an embrace. "We can start over."

Gigi turned her face into his coat, her shoulders shaking with sobs. He stroked her hair, her back. Such love, such tenderness.

He caught sight of her, and in an instant, all that softness vanished. His jaw could have been chiseled from granite. She'd been hasty, thinking him handsome. He was too stern, too severe. The look of pure malice he gave her froze the blood in her veins.

"Come on," the man said to the starlet. "Let's get out of here." Reluctant and miserable, Gigi allowed herself to be led away, leaving Elizabeth on the deck, her own troubles temporarily forgotten.

"IT WAS BETTER THAT TIME, BUT YOU'VE GOT TO LEARN HOW TO breathe and talk at the same time, darling."

Jane groaned and tossed the bound script onto the floor, pages fluttering as it sailed through the air.

Elizabeth smiled and set her own script aside. "I see you've already got the temperament of an actress."

"*You're* an actress," her sister said pointedly.

"A *theater* actress, Jane. We're a whole different animal."

Jane, the eldest of the five Bennet sisters, went to the large mirror that hung in her small apartment, wincing at her new reflection.

"It's hideous, isn't it?" she asked, looking at herself from different angles. "I never thought of myself as a blonde."

"On the contrary. I think it suits you," Elizabeth assured her. And it did. Secretly, Elizabeth was relieved that Jane's agent had made the suggestion that she go blonde. Jane's natural brown wasn't much lighter than Elizabeth's, and the two were always being mistaken for one another. Jane was the slightly taller of the two, but both women had fine features, high cheekbones, and upturned eyes of fiery green. Jane, who'd always had a fondness for sweets her sister didn't share, once bore a healthy figure some would have called plump. Since coming to Hollywood, she'd trimmed down a few sizes and could now merely be called *curvy*.

Jane flounced down on the worn sofa next to her sister. She closed her eyes and groaned.

"My god, I'd kill for a slice of cake right now. White cake with the fluffiest white frosting piled up to the ceiling."

"And you should have it."

"You're sweet, Lizzy, but I'm under strict instructions to maintain my figure. If I had cake now, it would be nothing but broth and soda crackers for a week."

Elizabeth's lip curled. *Hollywood.* Why should a place run by men tell women what was and wasn't good about their bodies?

"That's barbaric. What's wrong with a woman who looks like a woman? What's wrong with hips and tits?"

Jane laughed and took her sister's hand. "Oh, Lizzy. Have I thanked you for coming back all this way to help me?"

It wasn't as though Elizabeth had had much choice. After her last swain perfected her signature and made off with her checkbook and her jewelry, she didn't even have money for tea and biscuits. She had to sell everything she had left to book her passage back to New York, with no parts up for the taking right away. She'd boarded that boat with some clothes, a few photographs, and a handful of cards from her mystery admirer—one ardent fan of the theater who often sent flowers and notes praising her performance. She used to read them at night before going to sleep, grateful to that person, whoever they were. Those cards were never far out of reach now. The past six months, from that first awful discovery that she'd been chiseled down to nothing to living on her sister's sofa in Hollywood, had been some of the most humiliating times in her twenty-five years. She smiled and took her sister's hand. She *had* missed Jane.

"Only *you* could get me to come here. For you, I'd walk through hell. Or Hollywood."

Jane gave her a sidelong glance, her lips spreading into a smile. "Tonight, we'll walk through both."

Elizabeth held back a groan. "My first Hollywood party, I can't wait."

Jane laughed. "You might be a great actress, Lizzy, but you're a terrible liar."

"I'm going for *you*," she assured her sister.

"Charles Bingley is supposed to be there. It's important. He's a rising star at Pemberley Pictures. I need to impress him *now*, before I audition, and he sees I can't hit my cues to save my life."

"Well, we can't pass up the chance to meet the man directing"—she picked up the script and flipped to the title page—"*The Headstrong Girl?*" She made a face. "Who *writes* this stuff?"

CHARLES BINGLEY WAS NOT WHAT EITHER BENNET SISTER HAD BEEN expecting. He was young, handsome, and not an irredeemable letch.

Elizabeth wasn't worried about Jane's chances for the lead role in *The Headstrong Girl*. The man hadn't taken his eyes off her sister all night.

Granted, *most* of the men at the party hadn't been able to stop staring at Jane, who shone like a star in a thin gown of silver sequins that left most of her back bare. But it was Charles Bingley who kept Jane's glass filled, who put his palm on her elbow, rather than the exposed skin of her back as he led her around the room, introducing her to a whole host of whom Elizabeth assumed were Very Important People. He'd impressed Elizabeth as kind, polite, and a bit of a dandy in his elaborate suit.

With Jane securely in the company of Mr. Bingley, Elizabeth found herself languishing on the fringes of the party, listening to the gaggle of writers complain about executives and actors and producers. The air became thick with smoke from cigarettes and cigars and a few she was certain were not tobacco. She found her way upstairs and slipped out onto a balcony, into the glittering starlit night. She breathed deep the fresh air, feeling the warm breeze against her skin. The wide space was festooned with potted palms, hibiscus. Vines of fragrant night-blooming jasmine climbed the walls. And below her, in the garden, were rose bushes by the dozen, artfully arranged and adding their sweet perfume to the evening air. It was like stepping into Eden after choking on all that smoke.

"Hello." A contralto voice spoke from nearby. Elizabeth turned to see a familiar face looking back at her. Corn silk hair, bright blue eyes, long legs, and pretty hands. A diamond glittered on her left ring finger.

Gigi Duvall was sitting in one of the balcony chairs, looking back at her with open curiosity. She was dressed more conservatively than even Elizabeth in a black satin frock with long sleeves and an abundance of frills. *It doesn't quite suit her*, Elizabeth thought. It was as though she were trying to look like a child still, when she was at least twenty.

"Oh, hello there." Elizabeth smiled at the girl who she'd last seen on a boat bound for New York.

"Didn't I meet you at Sir William Lucas's party in Mayfair last September?"

Elizabeth *had* been at that party, heartbroken and brimming with mute fury over a row with Buster. She'd had more champagne than was wise and had been in rare form that night. She'd danced until her feet blistered and kissed a viscount in front of the whole damn crowd.

"That party...wasn't my finest moment," she said with a laugh.

"Oh, it was a terrific scandal. Poor Lord Dickey was absolutely heartbroken when you left without him."

"*That* was his name? I've got to learn how to choose my playmates better."

The girl giggled and held out her hand. "I'm Gigi."

Elizabeth took the girls hand and shook it. She looked so frail, but her grip was cool and firm. "I'm Elizabeth Bennet. Lizzy."

"I thought as much," she said, smiling as if she'd just heard a joke in church. "Is this your first time at the Garden of Allah?" Gigi gestured to all around her. The hotel was a famously glamorous venue for some of Hollywood's most notorious parties.

"It is. It's very beautiful."

"Yes. My family owns it now, not that they ever use it for anything but these ghastly parties. Did you know it was formerly owned by Alla Nazimova? She named it Garden of Allah as a little joke." Gigi sighed. "I saw her on stage when I was barely old enough to remember. It's burned into my memory. She was so strong, so passionate. I think she's the reason why I wanted to be in pictures. I wanted to get a head start on becoming the next Nazimova." She looked out at the city lights below, a lonesome expression on her features. "Perhaps children should only be indulged so much."

"Maybe," Elizabeth said. "Perhaps some little girls who saw your pictures decided they wanted to be in pictures themselves."

Gigi snorted. "You don't have to tell *me*. There's a room full of them in there. They all adore me, but they'll take a role from me in a hot minute."

Elizabeth wasn't sure what to say to that, so she said nothing.

"Gigi, what are you doing out here?"

The deep, masculine voice made both women turn in surprise. Elizabeth's heel caught in the groove of the stone tile and she felt herself slipping, falling...captured. Strong arms held her off the ground. She struggled to catch her breath, startled by the sensation of being lifted, set to rights. Her rescuer was tall, his face shadowed. She knew at once it was the man she'd seen with Gigi on the voyage from Southampton to New York, before the long train ride west. Warmth tingled on her skin where he'd touched her. She didn't like it.

"Watch where you're stepping," the man said, none too kindly.

"William, do be nice," Gigi said in a school mistress tone. "This is Lizzy, an acquaintance from England. Lizzy, this is William Darcy, head of Pemberley Pictures."

The man looked her up and down. She felt herself chafing under that gaze. If he was trying to spook her, he'd have to work a lot harder than that.

"You were on the boat," he said.

"You were?" Gigi's forehead wrinkled.

Elizabeth felt the corner of her mouth tugging into a crooked smile. "Nice to meet you too."

He sniffed. "You came here with Jane Bennet."

"My sister," she replied, her tone daring him to think carefully about how he spoke of Jane.

"Hmm," was all he said before turning to Gigi. "You'll catch your death out here. I thought you wanted this part."

"*You* want me to have the part. You know what *I* want."

"Out of the question."

Ooh, what a bully! If there was anything in the world Elizabeth despised, it was a bully. Why didn't Gigi just leave him?

Because he's the head of the studio. We don't get to leave them; they leave us.

"Your man here is a real piece of work," Elizabeth said before she could stop herself.

Both Gigi and Mr. Darcy looked up at her in surprise.

"He's not—" Gigi started.

"I hope you weren't planning to *work* in this town," Mr. Darcy said in a voice dripping with ice.

Elizabeth batted her eyelashes. "I wouldn't *dream* of it, Mr. Darcy."

A cold smile lifted his lips. They were full and soft-looking. *Why are you looking at his lips?*

"And your sister?"

Elizabeth's heart dropped to her stomach.

"William, *no,*" Gigi said, just as severe as he'd been a moment ago. "I'll go back inside if you stop that this instant."

"Of course, Gigi. If your *friend* apologizes to me first."

Elizabeth felt bile sting the back of her throat. This man was a monster. No...he was the devil himself. They'd only just met, and he already seemed to have a beef with her. She forced a smile through gritted teeth. *Jane. Think of Jane.*

"My apologies, Mr. Darcy."

The devil had the gall to *smirk* at her. He held out a hand to Gigi, who took it with some reluctance. She gave Elizabeth an apologetic look.

"Enjoy the rest of your evening," he said, still smirking, and led Gigi away, back into the crowded party. Elizabeth let out the breath she'd been holding, shaking with fury and vowing that one day it would be Mr. High-and-Mighty William Darcy apologizing to *her.*

"Hell, I'll make him crawl on his knees. He'll be *begging* for it," she muttered, having no earthly clue what "it" was.

"WHERE DID YOU GET OFF TO LAST NIGHT?" JANE ASKED THE NEXT morning, her blonde hair piled up in pink rollers.

"On the balcony for a bit, then I spent the rest of the night hiding. Did you know the Garden of Allah has a library?"

Jane rolled her eyes and poured herself a glass of orange juice. "You *would* be the one person to find the library at a party."

"Actually, there were a few others who found the library too," Elizabeth said, trying to keep her anger from quavering her voice. "Mr. Bingley, for one."

Jane blushed and looked down into her orange juice.

"I was surprised by how much I liked him, Lizzy."

"I think the feeling was more than mutual. I overheard him talking about you to the head of the studio."

Jane's eyes lit up. "With William Darcy? But...he's famous for never going to these parties! They say he can't be...*persuaded* into giving out roles like other studio executives can. They call him the most honest man in Hollywood."

Elizabeth snorted. "An honest *bore* is what he is." She hesitated a moment. "He was there with Gigi Duvall."

Jane's eyes lit with interest. "She *is* very beautiful."

"And apparently nobody wants child stars to be beautiful; they want them to stay children forever."

"Enough about that. What did Mr. Bingley say about me?"

"Did you see her, Darcy? She's an angel, the ginchiest girl I ever seen."

"Charles. I hope you aren't thinking of casting her for 'The Headstrong Girl'."

"Why wouldn't I?"

"She isn't right for this picture. She's too...sweet. Yes, she's pretty pure cheesecake but she smiles too much. You need someone with fire." His voice had sounded distant, contemplative. "A girl with grit."

"Darcy...she's an actress. Actresses act. I'm sure she'll be wonderful."

"No blondes, Charles. And if you're going to carry on like this, it's best you don't hire her. You'll be all over the gossip rags in no time; have that Conway woman breathing down our necks again."

"Mr. Bingley is hopelessly smitten with you, darling," Elizabeth said, choosing to omit the rest. *She* wasn't going to be the one to tell Jane the part was never going to be hers. Maybe Bingley would defy the studio and give Jane the role anyway. Stranger things had happened.

"You'll come with me today, won't you?"

Elizabeth groaned.

"Please Lizzy, pretty please. You're my coach. I need you to run the lines with me right to the last minute."

She sighed. "All right, doll. I'll go for you."

And that's how, a few hours later, Elizabeth found herself running headfirst into the brick wall that was William Darcy.

She'd been looking for the powder room while Jane went to face the gauntlet that was the casting call when she collided with something large, warm, and smelling faintly of cedar and citrus.

"Oh heavens, excuse me," she said, too embarrassed to look up. Had she accidentally opened the door to the men's restroom?

"Oh. You again."

Her stomach sank at the familiar sound of that voice. Deep, rich, and utterly infuriating. She looked up to see William Darcy, without his coat, his shirtsleeves rolled up in the afternoon heat.

Damn, she thought, seeing his forearms, which seemed to have been sculpted specifically to appeal to her. Too bad they were attached to such an unpleasant man.

"Mr. Darcy," she said coolly, forcing herself to look away from his forearms. Sure, he was a handsome beast of a man, but he had all the personality of an unripened avocado. She couldn't understand *what* Gigi Duvall saw in him.

"What are you doing here, Miss Bennet?"

The man had no sense of self preservation. He *would* provoke her.

Elizabeth batted her eyelashes. "Maybe I'm here to audition."

His eyes narrowed. "Is *that* why you came looking for me?"

She scoffed. "I was looking for a powder room."

He moved aside and she could see the gold lettering across the door he'd just opened.

WILLIAM DARCY, PRESIDENT

"Well, how was *I* supposed to know this was your office? I didn't stop to pick up a map at the front gate."

"So…are you?"

Was he *making conversation* with her?

"Am I what?"

"Auditioning."

"No, I'm here with my sister."

His left brow rose a fraction. "Too bad. I wanted to see if Elizabeth Bennet was going to storm the silver screen the way she did the London stage."

Elizabeth's mouth fell open. He'd *heard* of her?

"I wouldn't dream of it, really," she said, smiling sweetly.

He leaned back against the wall, stuffing his hands in his pockets. Elizabeth wanted to ask him to put his suit jacket back on, roll his sleeves down, anything. The sight of those muscled forearms was making her dizzy. There was tightly coiled energy in his expression that told her this man was not at ease but wanted her to think that he was.

"Why not?" he asked. Elizabeth had to retrace the conversation to recall what they'd been talking about. There was nothing biting in the question, just an open curiosity that Elizabeth suspected was more dangerous than any cutting remark he might have had prepared.

"Why not…oh! Why not audition? Well, as you said, I'm a stage actress. It's Jane who should have this role. Jane who wants it."

"But say Jane wasn't interested in *this* role. Say, she got another role entirely. Do you think you would audition?"

Elizabeth shook her head, feeling caught off guard by this softer, less severe William Darcy.

"This really isn't my world. When Jane gets her big breakout role, I'll go back to England, most likely. Or New York. I have a friend writing some…more experimental theater that I'd like to try."

"Why did you leave in the first place?"

"I just need a little scratch to tide me over." That voice called out to her from across the distance, the thousands of miles of land and ocean and months since she'd last heard it. She hated him, but she missed

him too. He had been like a drug to her, exhilarating, intoxicating. Well she'd learned her lesson. Elizabeth Bennet was on the wagon when it came to Buster, and men in general.

But "he" doesn't need to know that.

"I came to help Jane, of course. Give her some coaching. Help her land her first big role."

"Hmm." He seemed to mull this over, looking somewhere off in the distance. Elizabeth wanted to end this conversation. She needed space from his thoughtful silence and that careless lock of hair and those damnable forearms. There was a larger-than-life air about him, even while he stood so silent, so lost in thought; his presence filled up all the empty space around him, drawing her eye to him again and again. She reminded herself of how rude he'd been to her up until now. She reminded herself of what he'd said about Jane, and, much to her shame, she reminded herself that he was already taken up with a beautiful young woman who probably wouldn't appreciate the way Elizabeth was currently ogling her suitor.

"Your sister was in two pictures last year, if I recall, and didn't seem to need any coaching then," he said, looking at her now as if she owed him some kind of explanation.

As if he didn't believe her.

"They were smaller roles. No one needs coaching when all you're doing is looking at the camera and saying, 'Gee whiz,' you know?"

He chuckled. The sound was a caress, mink brushing against naked skin. Decadent. Tempting.

"I suppose you're right."

"Look. I should really get back. I don't know how long these things usually take." Why was she standing there playing Twenty Questions with the busiest man in Hollywood?

"Of course," he said, remaining propped up against the wall. She gave him a stiff nod and walked back the way she'd come, feeling his eyes on her back the entire time.

"Penny for your thoughts?" Jane sat on the other end of the

sofa, carefully painting her toenails while Elizabeth sat by the open window where the warm, dry breeze lifted the curtains. A book lay forgotten in her lap as she'd become lost in thought while watching the curtains lift and sway, lift and sway.

"I was thinking about William Darcy, actually."

Jane's brows rose. "I didn't think you liked him."

"I don't. I do think he's...unusual though. I think there's more to him than I got at first glance. That doesn't mean I like him. He's just got my curiosity going is all."

Jane smirked and capped the bottle of polish, a respectable pink, the color of conch shells.

"Poor Mr. Darcy. He's poked the bear that is Lizzy's unstoppable curiosity."

Elizabeth tossed her book aside and stood, stretching. She walked to the window and pushed the curtains aside, stopping their hypnotic dance.

"He's just...*odd*," she said, looking down into the courtyard below. Jane's apartment—now *their* apartment—was built in full Spanish Revival splendor, with stucco walls and a clay-tile roof. Down in the courtyard was a green space, lush with fragrant flowers and bristling plants. In the middle of it all sat a fountain, its blue-and-white-and-yellow tiles a splash of cool color in all the greenery.

Elizabeth liked the fountain best, liked the bubbling sound it made. She found it a soothing place to sit and think. And she *had* been thinking about her encounters with the head of Pemberley Pictures. He was stern, elusive, but there was a surprising warmth there too. The more she thought about him, the less she understood him.

"Odd, rich as King Midas, looks like all the best parts of Gary Cooper and Errol Flynn put together. Yes, I wonder why *any* sensible girl would ponder these mysteries," Jane said, smiling at her sister.

"Oh, don't crack wise with me or I'll—" Elizabeth's words were interrupted by the shrill ring of the telephone. Jane paled. They'd been waiting for days for any word on Jane's audition.

"Do you mind, Lizzy?" Jane asked, fanning her hands over her painted toes. "I'm still tacky."

Elizabeth raced to the phone and picked it up. "Hello?"

"That you, Lizzy?" The voice of her uncle Edward crackled in her ear.

"It's me, Uncle Ed! You want Jane?"

Edward Gardiner wasn't just their uncle, he was also Jane's agent. He'd come to Hollywood when it was still mostly orange groves as part of the family Vaudeville act and, unlike his sisters, had never left. He worked his way up from representing stunt workers in silent film to some of the biggest names in Hollywood.

"Sure, put her on, but I'll need to talk to you too."

Elizabeth handed the receiver to Jane, the cord stretching an almost perilous distance.

"Hello, Uncle Ed! Why, yes. Oh." Jane's face fell.

Elizabeth tried to calm herself. *So help me, if that William Darcy has done anything to hurt my sister's chances, I'll make his life a living hell.*

A moment later, Jane brightened, her eyes widening. "*Really? Oh, oh that's wonderful!* Yes, of *course,* I'll do it! Send the contracts and tell me where to sign!"

Elizabeth relaxed, relief flooding her. Obviously, the news was good if Jane was so happy.

"Yes, here she is!" Jane handed the receiver back to Elizabeth, her eyes wide and dancing with happiness.

"He wants to talk to you," she said, grinning.

Elizabeth put the receiver to her ear. "Hello, Uncle Ed?"

"You'll have to sign a contract too, Lizzy," he said without preamble. "Jane's been cast as the leading lady in the next Cagney picture."

Wait, *what?* "That...wasn't what she auditioned for."

"No, but this part is big. It could make her a huge star."

Elizabeth began to feel some of the weight of that sink into her. She thought of William Darcy, all false ease and temporary civility. *"What if she didn't want this role, would you audition?"*

"Uncle Ed, why would *I* need to sign anything?"

"Because Pemberley Pictures wants *you* for the lead in the Bingley film. The head of the studio saw you at the Old Vic in *The Admirable*

Basheville last year and nearly approached to sign you then but didn't. I don't know why."

Elizabeth's jaw worked as she processed this. "William Darcy?" was all she managed.

"The very same."

She didn't understand how he could offer her a role knowing she wanted to return to London sooner rather than later. *Who does he think he is?*

"Tell him I'm not interested."

Jane gasped. Her uncle grumbled. "Lizzy. You have to think about more than just yourself now. I know you sent money back when you were in London, and it was good of you, but you do this one picture and you'll never need to send another dime. Your mother and the girls can rebuild."

Elizabeth's eyes found the framed photos placed next to the sofa. Her parents in one, she and her sisters in the other, the peaks of the Oregon hills visible just behind them. Their family's apple orchard, like so many, had been ravaged by a blazing wildfire that consumed everything it touched. Orchards. Homes. Fathers. She felt a pang of guilt. She'd left for London just days after the funeral to attend RADA and hadn't been back since. While she corresponded with her mother and younger sisters as much as possible, she hadn't been able to return to the place that had been her first home, and her greatest heartbreak.

"*Fine.* I'll think about it."

"Don't think too long," her uncle warned her.

GARDINER GIRLS UPSET PEMBERLEY PICTURES
by Caroline Conway

Announced just this week, the role widely believed to be slated for Jean Harlow in the upcoming James Cagney picture has gone to Jane Bennet, who has had minor speaking roles in last year's *Ladies of Longbourn* from George Cukor and the Preston Sturges comedy, *In Want of a Wife*. This will be her first leading role for Pemberley Pictures.

This news comes as a surprise for most, as director Charles Bingley had tapped the ethereal Jane Bennet to star in his next film *The Headstrong Girl*. In a further surprise, the lead in that picture has gone to Bennet's sister, Elizabeth Bennet, who is well known on the London stage but, to date, has never appeared on screen. Elizabeth Bennet has signed an exclusive one-picture contract with the Studio. When asked for comment, the Bennet sisters' agent, Edward Gardiner, said, "It was a smart move for everyone involved. Audiences don't quite know what a treat they're in for. This might be Elizabeth's first picture, but I don't think it will be her last. Not by a long shot."

Most interesting is the rumour that the head of Pemberley Pictures, William Darcy, personally insisted on Elizabeth Bennet as the lead in *The Headstrong Girl*, which begins filming next month. Mr. Darcy, widely regarded as one of the more cautious executives, is not generally known for plucking up young unknowns for lead roles. Perhaps this news will see more undiscovered hopefuls flocking to Pemberley's doors?

HER FIRST DAY OF REHEARSALS HAD GONE TO HELL IN RECORD TIME. Everyone was so kind and welcoming. She'd immediately hit it off with her co-star, the gorgeous Rollo Fitz, and Mr. Bingley had seemed thrilled to have her there. He'd answered her questions with patience and thoughtful care, making the occasional note in her script in an unintelligible scrawl. Elizabeth appreciated the thought, anyway.

And then *he'd* walked onto set.

William Darcy was as forbidding—and fascinating—as ever, but he seemed distracted. Irritated. He was in the company of a lumpy young man in a wrinkled brown suit and a woman, dressed in trousers and a neat shirt-and-sweater-vest ensemble, complete with necktie. The woman, Elizabeth now knew, was Darcy's personal secretary, Cat. She'd been the one to give Elizabeth a tour of the lot where they'd be spending all their time while filming. Elizabeth had found Cat to be as odd a specimen as her boss. She liked to wear men's clothing, kept her hair in a blunt bob that had long gone out of fashion, and was rumored to live with a woman who she sometimes called "my wife." Elizabeth rather liked her.

"Who is that?" she whispered to Rollo, who made a face.

"The man in the ever-so-fashionable brown suit is Collins, one of the Breen goons from the PCA office. He's here to make sure that if we're dancing, we leave a little room for the Lord."

Elizabeth clapped a hand over her mouth to keep a giggle from escaping. She knew, of course, about the Hays Code and the Production Code Administration recent crackdown on what was "morally allowable" in Hollywood films. Collins, who seemed to be aware that they were talking about him, looked up at Elizabeth. He was undoubtably the palest man she'd seen since arriving in California. He straightened his jacket and made a beeline for them. Rollo groaned.

"Don't worry," Rollo assured her in a low voice. "He's harmless, mostly. I think."

"Very reassuring," she whispered back.

"You must be Miss Bennet." Collins didn't offer her a hand to shake or even give her a polite nod of greeting. He just took one long look at her, from head to toe. Elizabeth felt an uncomfortable pressure under that look, as if she were a sideshow act in a carnival. His beady black eyes homed in on the neckline of her dress; the bit of décolletage that had seemed flirty a few hours ago, she now desperately wanted to cover up. Her hands fluttered to her chest, her face turning crimson under his scrutiny. Collins opened his mouth to speak when a hand fell on his shoulder. Elizabeth, Collins, and Rollo all looked up to see Mr. Darcy standing there, wearing an icy smile.

"Mr. Collins," Darcy said, congenially enough. "I see you've met Mr. Fitz and Miss Bennet."

"Ah, yes, sir, Mr. Darcy."

"Mr. Collins, correct me if I'm wrong but it is your duty to review the script and the rushes, am I right?" The hand on Collins's shoulder squeezed. Elizabeth saw the little man wince. "Not to harass my actors."

"Mr. Darcy, hello." Elizabeth greeted him, trying to dispel the tension in the air. She was going to thank him for the opportunity, both for herself and Jane, but the look he gave her made her blood turn to ice. His so-called gallantry was a show, an excuse to flex his muscles and remind everyone who was in charge. Elizabeth took a step back, into Rollo's chest. Rollo put his hands on her arms to steady her.

"Will"—Cat tugged on his shirt sleeve. He looked at her without taking his hand off Collins's shoulder.

"Phone for you. From Gigi. It's urgent."

He swept the room with one last contemptuous glance before releasing Collins and following Cat from the room. Collins excused himself and went to speak to Bingley. Elizabeth wasn't sorry to see him go.

Rollo pulled her aside. "Are you all right? I thought he was going to throw you over his shoulder like a caveman."

Elizabeth nodded. "It's just Mr. Darcy. He's always like that."

Rollo looked confused. "You're talking about *William* Darcy, head of Pemberley Pictures?"

"Yes, yes, the man who was just in here."

Rollo shook his head and whistled. "I have a seven-year contract here, and this marks year four for me. I've dealt with Darcy a few times now, but I've never seen him lose his head like *that*." He leaned back, studying Elizabeth. "You've met him before?"

"A few times. The party at the Garden of Allah. Here at the studio when Jane came in for an audition." *Once, on a boat bound for New York.* She kept the last one to herself. There'd been something furtive about that voyage. And she wouldn't be the one to subject Gigi to more rumors.

"Hmm." Rollo gave her a considering look.

"Oh, stop that. There's nothing to *hmm* about."

"Actually, I was wondering if…if you might have dinner with me?"

Elizabeth blinked up at him in surprise. Of course, Rollo *was* handsome as a dream. His wavy hair was the color of caramel, his eyes a tawny brown that seemed lit from within. His build was tall and slender with broad shoulders and narrow hips. He was deeply tanned, and his smile so bright and white it could have lit the room if the power went out. The thing was, she didn't get the impression that Rollo was at all interested in her, at least not romantically. She'd always prided herself on being a good judge of character until she'd let herself get hoodwinked by Buster. But still…a woman *knew* if there was any spark of attraction.

Maybe today hasn't gone to hell after all.

She blinked up at him. "Why, Mr. Fitz. I'd be delighted."

ARCHERY WAS GOING TO BE THE DEATH OF HER.

The arrows weren't real, only a soft balsa wood painted to look like metal, but trying to pull back a bow in the ridiculous costume they'd stuffed her into was proving to be more than a challenge.

"You need to pull the string back more," Rollo whispered urgently.

Elizabeth wanted to snap back at him that *he* should pull the string back, seeing as how *he* was wearing a sensible coat rather than sleeves the size of a timpani drum. Instead she smiled, thought, *Make it look effortless*, and pulled the string back. The arrow flew in a sad little spiral, clattering to the floor a few feet away. That was fine; it wasn't meant to fly. The stunt department would film the arrow hitting the target some other time, and those scenes would be spliced in after this one. In the weeks since filming began, she'd learned so much about how pictures were made that she found the process an endless source of fascination. She wanted to see *all* aspects of film: from the writers' room to the storyboards, right down to the editing floor.

Bingley called cut and Elizabeth relaxed as much as she could in a forty-pound dress.

"You did it." Rollo smiled down at her. "Well done."

"Thanks, Fitz."

Another source of confusion and irritation for her: Rollo had asked her on several dates, all of which had been nice. Not extraordinary or particularly exciting, but nice. They'd had dinner and talked, about London and New York, about stage acting versus film acting, even about the weather. But he still ended every date with a chaste peck on the cheek. Elizabeth liked Rollo just fine, but she wasn't sure they were anything more than pals. And yet, he kept taking her to nightclubs and fashionable restaurants, ending each date with the same dry peck.

Cat entered the set and tiptoed over to where Bingley sat in his director's chair. The two women had taken a liking to each other, and Elizabeth had even taken a taxi out to the neat little house in Laurelwood that Cat shared with her partner, Louise. She'd learned that Cat and Darcy were actually second cousins and that he was one of the few members of the family who'd have anything to do with her.

Today, Elizabeth noted, she seemed to be dressed like a woman about to lead a safari, with blousy pants tucked into tall leather boots, a matching jacket, and a silk scarf. Elizabeth had to admit, Cat had flair. She knelt down and whispered something in Bingley's ear. Bingley asked her something in return, and when Cat nodded, he frowned.

"Lizzy!" Bingley called out to her. She excused herself and went to him, holding up the heavy velvet skirt and layers of taffeta pinafore underneath. She could feel sweat soaking into the dress and felt sorry for the unfortunate wardrobe assistant that would have to unlace her from it later.

"Yes, Charles? Hello, Cat."

"Lizzy, go with Cat," Bingley said, somewhat irritably. "Boss wants a word."

Elizabeth blinked at Cat. "All right. How long will this take?"

Cat gave her a crooked grin. "Depends. Come on. Follow me."

Elizabeth followed dutifully, thinking back to the costume she'd worn for the RADA production of *Hamlet.* It had been a modern dress production, set in the Roaring Twenties. Her gown had been a low waisted silk affair so thin in the right light it was translucent. What she wouldn't give to wear that again after all the layers of velvet and silk and whalebone corsets that dug into her ribs.

Luckily, Cat didn't lead her all the way to the main offices—nearly a quarter mile from the set—but to a tiny trailer that looked more like a shed on wheels than anything. Inside was a desk covered almost entirely with tools, bits of wire, tape, miles of electrical cord coiled like snakes in the corner. And William Darcy, making the small space feel impossibly cramped with his overwhelming *Darcyness*. He was pinching the bridge of his nose like a man with a headache but looked up when she came stumbling in after Cat.

"Miss Bennet, good. Thank you, Cat. That'll be all for now."

Elizabeth looked around the strange space. "What is this place?"

"It's the gaffer's trailer. He wanted to talk about retirement before going back to set." He sighed. "He'll be a hard man to replace. Been here with us since the beginning."

"And you needed me here because..."

"Because of *this*." Darcy pointed to something on the desk. Elizabeth came forward to see what he pointed to, feeling unnerved by his nearness. It was a newspaper.

"Co-stars Canoodle at Musso and Franks," the headline read with a byline from Caroline Conway. The picture was one of Elizabeth and Rollo, stepping out of a restaurant arm-in-arm dressed in their fine evening wear. She scanned the article. "This is hardly the scandal sheets," she declared.

"Is it true?"

He was standing very close. He smelled faintly of something tart and delicious. Grapefruit? *She* smelled like an alley on Skid Row.

"Rollo and I have gone to dinner a few times, yes." It was the truth.

"And did you...canoodle?"

Elizabeth laughed. It was the most ridiculous thing she'd ever heard him say.

"Mr. Darcy, that's really none of your business."

"I don't like fraternizing on my sets," he said.

She looked up at him, a challenge in her eyes. "What about Gigi?"

His face shuttered, the edge of his clenched jaw like granite. "What *about* her?"

"The rules don't apply to her?"

His body, big and strong, came even closer to her, making her step back against the desk. He was so unlike the other powerful men in Hollywood, the studio executives whose physiques could best be described as collapsed souffles. William Darcy's power wasn't just in his wealth or his success; it was written into every atom of his being. He was a force of nature; his authority, an unspoken law that everyone in his orbit was compelled to obey. Even Elizabeth, who'd made it a point to defy and harass him at every opportunity, felt a giddy sort of need to put herself in his power. In his control. She felt pinpricks of heat all over her body at the thought.

Darcy put a hand on the desk on either side of her, trapping her. Elizabeth's pulse started to race.

"What do you know about Gigi?" he asked in a silken voice. She didn't trust it, that voice.

"I know how much you care about her," she said. It was the truth. Since she'd first seen him on the boat, it was the first thing that had been obvious to her. He truly cared about Gigi Duvall.

He inhaled, looking down at her through hooded eyes. Elizabeth swallowed. If this was a movie, this would be where he'd lean down and kiss her. His face was close enough she could feel his breath tickling her skin, his eyes fastened on her lips. What would it be like, she wondered, to lean forward just a little bit, to feel those lips on hers? He took her chin in his hand, the pad of his thumb rubbing the spot just under her bottom lip.

"End it with Fitz," he said in a low voice.

Elizabeth pulled out of his grip. "Excuse me?"

"You heard me, Elizabeth."

Heat coiled in her belly at the way he said her name. *Good lord.* This thought was immediately followed by a cooler one. *Who the hell does this turkey think he is?*

"No, I don't think I will, Mr. Darcy. I *like* Rollo. And it's not stated in my contract I can't date co-stars."

He growled and pressed himself closer. Elizabeth found herself now sitting on the gaffer's desk. Out of instinct, she reached up, putting a hand on his chest. Heat radiated through his shirt into her palm. She could feel the line of his undershirt, and under that, the hair on his chest. It was a shock, the intimacy of it, and she removed her hand as quickly as she'd placed it there. The *spark* was there, all right.

"Mr. Darcy...I've heard people say you're the most honest man in Hollywood."

He froze.

"I would hate to be the one that ruins your reputation." His eyes narrowed. They were blue, his eyes, ringed in a darker blue that was almost black. His lashes were long and dark, curling at the ends. Very pretty, all told.

"Are you *threatening* me, Miss Bennet?"

"While you have me in such an undignified position? I wouldn't dream of it, Mr. Darcy."

She could see the shock of it hit him like a splash of cold water. He quickly stood to his full height, putting much-needed space between them. "Miss Bennet, I apologize," he said, not looking at her. "That was..."

The most exciting minute and a half of my life.

"Unforgivable," he finished. While it stung somewhat, she felt a palpable relief. It was obvious that there was an attraction there, but equally clear was the fact that he didn't actually *like* her.

And the feeling is mutual.

"Please excuse me." He fled the trailer without a backward glance. With a shaking hand, Elizabeth reached up and touched the spot just under her bottom lip.

Isn't it?

STARS DESCEND ON AMBASSADOR FOR ACADEMY AWARDS
by Caroline Conway

All of Hollywood came out for the 6th Annual Academy of Motion Picture Arts and Sciences award—and while some walked away with gold statuettes, others took their prizes home on their arms.

Director Charles Bingley was in attendance with starlet Jane Bennet, star of the upcoming film *Toledo Red*, while her sister Elizabeth Bennet arrived on the arm of leading man Rollo Fitz. The two have been seen dining around Hollywood since filming began on their picture, *The Headstrong Girl.* Don't they make a handsome couple?

After the ceremony, the impressive roster of stars in Pemberley's stables were invited to the home of William Darcy, the elusive head of the studio, for the most exclusive after-party in Hollywood. What this reporter wouldn't have given to be a fly on the wall at *that* shindig...

ASHWOOD MANOR WAS AS IMPOSING AS ITS OWNER. TO ELIZABETH, IT seemed to take up her entire view. The house itself wasn't ash or wood but a cream-colored stone, with rows of peaked gables that brushed the treetops. The massive property was nestled on a hillside overlooking Los Angeles, all on its own. It was so quiet up there, away from the bustle of the city.

"It's really something, isn't it?" Rollo said as their driver was waved in through the scrolled gate at the guardhouse.

"It's astonishing," she said, taking it all in. There was a long strip of green lawn in the front, but otherwise it seemed Mr. Darcy had allowed the natural vegetation of the area to flourish. Palm and palmetto, acacia, and row upon row of tall, thin cedars. She rolled down the window and breathed deeply. The night air was heavy with the perfumes of jasmine and rose. Music floated in through the open window, someone singing "Love is the Sweetest Thing" accompanied by the murmur of voices and tinkling peals of laughter. Elizabeth smoothed her dress, a slinky affair of gold lamé that glittered in the evening torchlight.

"You look beautiful," Rollo assured her. Elizabeth smiled and took his arm. There was no particular heat in his remark, just as bland a statement as if he was saying, "Very pleasant weather we're having." She'd begun to suspect that Rollo's preferences lay outside the fairer sex, and a few weeks of close observation had all but confirmed her suspicions. She didn't mind; she'd gone on several dates with closeted men in London. They'd been a bit more frank about themselves than poor Rollo, but the London stage was a far cry from the Hollywood press. She thought about bringing the topic up but decided to let him tell her on his own terms. In the meantime, he'd become a good friend, and she enjoyed spending time with him.

Not as much as you'd enjoy being trapped on a desk under William Darcy.

She shushed that voice as she let Rollo take her hand and help her up the low, wide steps leading to the mansion's entrance.

She'd not spoken to William Darcy since their charged encounter in the gaffer's trailer, but that didn't mean he was any less on her mind. He hovered on the edge of her awareness at all times, his looming presence seen just out of the corners of her eye while visiting the set or storming across the lot, Cat hot on his heels. It was for the best, she told herself.

The inside of the mansion was tastefully decorated; every piece of furniture and hanging masterpiece positioned just so. Everything was expensive and elegant, but too orderly, too precise. The word that came to Elizabeth's mind was *restrained*. Every room seemed to lack the wild edge that would breathe life into the space, but she could feel it, the potential of what the place could be with a little more chaos in the mix.

And then, like a sudden crack of summer lightning, there he was in all his after-six glory. The tuxedo jacket was deep black, the shirt brilliant white. It was no different from what every man in the room was wearing, but it was entirely his own. He was a man of stark contrasts, the self-righteous executive who'd demanded her apology, the carnal creature who'd nearly had her at his mercy.

As if sensing her stare, he looked up, locking eyes with her. How could there be so much fire and so much ice in one look?

"He's at it again," Rollo said in a low voice for her alone. "Undressing you with his eyes."

"He is *not*," she said, looking up at her date. "Does it bother you?"

Rollo smiled, but it was the tired smile of a man still in the trenches. "I wouldn't want you to be uncomfortable, if that's what you're asking," he said, leading her away into a more secluded corner of the party. A waiter in a white jacket stopped and offered them champagne in crystal flutes from the tray he carried. Rollo took two, handing one to Elizabeth.

"It makes me uncomfortable...but not in the way you'd think."

"Because you might feel something for him?"

"Perhaps. But it would just be physical. I don't actually *like* him."

"Hear, hear." Rollo raised his glass in a little salute and drank.

"There isn't...any *other* reason why it might bother you? Him looking at me like that?"

Rollo leaned down and gave her an affectionate peck on the cheek. *The Usual Fitz.* Elizabeth had described such kisses to Jane.

"I think you've figured out by now that there isn't," he said, so quietly she had to lean close to hear him.

She embraced him, carefully so as to not spill her drink. "You could have told me," she whispered in his ear. "It doesn't matter. I adore you, Rollo, and I'll always adore you no matter what."

He chuckled and returned her embrace. "Don't look now," he murmured. "But here comes trouble."

"Good evening, Fitz. Miss Bennet."

Elizabeth slid out of Rollo's arms to see William Darcy standing there. *Looming.* Her skin bristled at his nearness.

"Mr. Darcy"—Fitz nodded—"wonderful party."

"Yes." Darcy looked down into her eyes. "Welcome to my home."

She felt herself flush and looked away.

"Can I have a word in private, Miss Bennet?"

He held out a hand, a clear invitation. Elizabeth looked at it for a long moment, her thoughts muddled.

"What about Gigi?"

To her surprise, he smiled, turning her insides to mush. "Gigi won't mind. Why would she?"

Darcy looked at Rollo. "I'll have her back to you in two shakes, Fitz. Just a quick bit of business."

Rollo nudged her from behind, and she felt herself taking Darcy's hand, letting him loop her arm through his. Somehow, she kept her spine straight as he marched her past partygoers, waiters, and stern-faced security guards into a high-ceilinged room that smelled of books, leather, and orange oil. A room that smelled of *him*. She stopped in her tracks.

"You have a library."

"I like to read. It simplifies things to have my own."

He directed her to a deep-seated leather chair in the Chesterfield style. She sank into it. The leather was buttery soft and supple with frequent use. This was *his* chair, she realized.

"Miss Bennet, I won't beat around the bush. I've been reviewing the rushes for *The Headstrong Girl* and I like what I'm seeing. You've got talent, maybe a bit raw, but with more work, it can be refined. I'll be speaking with your agent tomorrow, but for tonight, I wanted to know what you would say to a seven-year contract with Pemberley Pictures? We can talk percentages if you like. I'm not as extravagant as other studios, but I'm fair. And unlike Paramount or RKO or any of the humps down on Poverty Row, when I say seven years, I do mean calendar years."

Elizabeth was stunned. Gooseflesh raised on her skin, making her shiver.

"*This* is what you wanted to talk to me about?"

He looked confused for a moment, but Elizabeth detected falsehood in his confusion. He might have known good acting when he saw it, but William Darcy couldn't act his way out of a wet paper sack.

"What else would we discuss?"

Her face turned hot. She wondered if there might be steam coming out of her ears.

"You *know* what."

She looked up at him. He took a deep breath. A stubborn lock of hair fell out of place, kissing his brow. She realized, with not *much* surprise, that she liked him. Not just the way he looked, but the way he cared for the people who depended on him for their livelihood. The way he'd taken in Cat and given her work—important work— after her family had rejected her. He'd found Jane a part that was worthy of her. He was a man who rolled his sleeves up (*thank heavens!*) and went to work with the rest of them. Yes, he could be cold. But he was also *good*.

"Elizabeth." There it was again, that toe-curling way his lips caressed her name. "I can't…"

"Shhh. Come here, William." She held out a hand to him. She wouldn't take what wasn't hers. He was with Gigi, and she wouldn't interfere. But she needed to have this moment, this one memory to lock up in her heart forever.

He put his hand in hers, kneeling down beside her. He brought her hand to his lips, kissed it. Rather than letting go, he continued trailing slow, methodical kisses from her hand all the way up the crook of her elbow. Each kiss sizzled her goosefleshed skin. Her breath came hard and heavy, chest rising and falling like a marathon runner.

"Elizabeth," he said, thumbs caressing the sensitive skin on the inside of her wrist. "Elizabeth. Elizabeth." Each repetition of her name was punctuated by another tender kiss on her arm. Elizabeth thought she might turn into a puddle if this went on much longer.

A sharp rap at the door made them both jump. She laughed, trembling now with a nervous sort of energy.

"What?" he barked. The door opened and there was Cat, wearing a tux of her own and looking rather dapper in it. A stone-faced security guard stood behind her.

"Will, you'd better come. George has been spotted trying to get in."

Elizabeth didn't know who George was, but she could tell from Darcy's expression that this news was far from welcome. "*Here?* Where's Gigi?"

"She's in the party, with the other Miss Bennet and Mr. Bingley for now. Should I fetch her, bring her here?"

"No," he said firmly. "Let's try to track him down *before* he gets inside." He turned to Elizabeth, gave her an imploring look. "Will you wait here? There are things I should probably say. Not related to your future with the studio." This last was said with a smile…small, hopeful, but definitely a smile. She smiled back at him, breathless and dizzy and strangely hopeful.

"Sure. Jane tells me I have a talent for finding libraries at parties."

He nodded, all business again. "Good, wait here."

And with that he was gone, following Cat and her escort out and shutting the door behind him.

"Oh thank god. I thought he'd *never* leave."

Elizabeth's stomach dropped. Down, down, right down to her shoes. *You aren't hearing that voice. There was something in the champagne and now you're hallucinating.*

A figure stepped out of the shadows. He'd been hidden behind the heavy green velvet drapes. Elizabeth knew this was no hallucination. If she was dreaming him up, he wouldn't be wearing threadbare tails. His hair would be unkempt, the ever-present bandana sticking out of his back pocket.

"Buster? What the hell are *you* doing here?"

He smiled, that easy grin that had charmed her so easily in London. He wasn't handsome like Rollo or compelling like Darcy. Buster had a face like a boxer's, his nose crooked from being broken more than once. A scar stood out in sharp relief against his top lip, a living reminder of a stunt gone wrong. But what he lacked in beauty, he more than made up for in easy charm. It was him, all right.

"I could ask you the same thing." He looked her up and down and whistled. "Nice dress, kid."

"Don't call me that."

"A seven-year contract from the big guy himself, huh? You're moving up in the world. Of course, it looks like you've got him wrapped around your little finger. Might as well go whole hog, am I right, Lizzy?"

"What. Are. You. *Doing*. Here?"

He waved a hand in dismissal. "Family business. Not that it isn't great to see you, kid, but your being here *does* complicate things."

She'd forgotten his habit for fast talking. She'd thought him so clever at first, but now she saw him for what he really was. A swindler and a fraud.

"I don't suppose you'd have any of the money you took from me? Or should I just call the coppers now?"

He raised his hands. "Who, me? If I *did* do anything to you, which you can't prove, it was on British soil and wouldn't fall under the jurisdiction of the LAPD."

"I don't have to listen to this," she said in sudden fury, launching herself out of the chair. He reached out, grabbed her arm as she was walking past him, pulled her back to him. She tried to wriggle out of his grip, but he only pulled her closer.

"Not so fast, kid." He seemed to consider her anew. "Whoever you're thinking about running to tell that I'm here, how about don't. I'd hate to embarrass you in front of all your fancy new friends."

"You're the one they're looking for, aren't you? Your name isn't really Buster... It's George, isn't it?"

He smirked and tipped an invisible hat. Her stomach churned. How could she have ever fallen for such a wretch? She thought he was her drug but really, he was poison. At that moment the doors burst open and in walked the antidote.

Darcy's gaze was one of pure loathing. He looked at Buster's hand on her arm, saw her struggling to free herself.

"Let go of her," he growled.

"Oh, hello, Will. Sorry, was this one yours?"

"Lizzy?" A small voice from behind Darcy called her name. Gigi was there, despite Darcy's best efforts to block her from the room. She saw George holding her.

"What are you doing with my husband?"

Elizabeth's mouth fell open. "*Your* husband? I thought you were with..." She glanced at Darcy, who paled. Buster laughed, finally letting go of her arm.

"Hell, don't you have *eyes* in your head, kid? She's not his woman. She's his sister!"

Is that the floor falling out from under me, or is my head spinning? This news certainly explained a few things...and changed other things. She looked at Gigi.

"How long have you two been married?"

"Since I was seventeen," she said. "And we're *not* married anymore. I divorced him after he took up with some floozy back in London!"

"Ah." Darcy looked back and forth, wild-eyed.

Elizabeth's stomach dropped. "His...his woman in London?"

Darcy started for her. "Lizzy..."

"That wasn't some floozy. That was *me!*"

Gigi looked like she'd slapped her across the face. "Is this true, Lizzy?"

Elizabeth turned to Buster, her palm cracking against his face. His eyes widened, hand flying to the reddening palmprint on his cheek.

"I suppose it's not enough that you took every penny I had, forcing me to leave a place I loved and come *here*, but you had to do all of that without telling me you were *married?*"

"She didn't know, Gigi," Darcy said, putting his arm around his weeping sister.

"But *you* did!" Elizabeth said, wheeling on him. She felt as if someone were dropping hot stones down her throat. "Didn't you? That's why you didn't like me! Why did you hire me? To keep an eye on me?"

He looked back at her, face blank of all expression.

"How *could* you!" Then, another sickening thought occurred to her. "That's why...that day...you thought...you thought, what? That I was just some easy bit of fun?"

"Elizabeth, I—"

"No. No, no, no, no, *no.* To hell with your bozo contract, your offer, your studio, your parties! When we wrap this movie, I'm on the first train back to New York, the first boat back to England. I don't care if I have to ride across the Atlantic in a pickle barrel!"

She turned to Buster, poking a sharp finger in the middle of his chest. "And *you.* George, Buster...whatever your name is! So help me, if you come near me again, I'll throw you to the sharks myself."

She spun on her heel, storming from the room. How strange to leave that scene and discover a party happening just on the other side of the door. She felt dizzy, disoriented. Someone grabbed her elbow.

"Lizzy, wait." It was Darcy. "Let me explain."

"You don't have to explain anything to me, Mr. Darcy. I know I'm on the up and up, even if you don't."

"Please, can we—"

She pulled her arm from his grip. "Don't. Don't ever speak to me again." And with that, she disappeared into the crowd, searching for Jane, for Bingley, for Rollo.

For any friendly face.

CAROLINE CONWAY PAUSED HER NOTETAKING AND LOOKED UP AT ME. "I heard it was quite the party last week."

"I'm not much one for parties, myself," I said, folding my hands in my lap. The perfect young lady, who sometimes fantasized about throttling a certain executive with those small, manicured hands.

"There are rumors linking you to former stuntman George 'Buster' Wickham. Care to comment?"

"I know Buster," I said, trying to sound as vague and casual as possible. "I knew him when I was working in London and he was under contract with Pinewood. But we were...acquaintances at best." Jane had already informed me—through Mr. Bingley's intel—that Buster had been offered a long-term contract with a Canadian film studio and would be gone for good. All he'd had to do was sign a half-dozen gag orders and agree never to contact Gigi ever again.

"I see." Caroline made a few more notes before looking back up at me with a bright, completely untrustworthy smile.

"So. What's next for Eliza Bennet? Will you be continuing your work for Pemberley Pictures?"

"I don't like to plan too far ahead," I said, which sounded better than *I'd rather eat glass.* "I suppose it will all depend on how well *The Headstrong Girl* does, but I like to keep my options open whenever possible."

"Well. This has been...illuminating." She stood and gathered her things. I rose and held out my hand, relieved the interview was behind me. If I could just get past this, the wrap party, the premiere, I could put this town, this studio...and everything else in my rearview.

Caroline shook my hand and excused herself. I watched her go, feeling some trepidation. Not for myself, but for Jane and Bingley, for Rollo, and for Gigi, especially Gigi. The guilt I felt over Buster had kept me awake every night since the disastrous party. Of course, I hadn't *known* he was married. He'd happened to meet me on a night when I was feeling particularly homesick, and the rest was history. Months of my life spent going out on the town with another woman's husband.

"Excuse me." I stuck my head out the door and called out to one of the production assistants running around the set. "Could you let Edith know I'm ready to be cut out of this dress for the last time?" The young man, looking harried, nodded and scampered off. I went back into my dressing room and put my hands against the wall so that the costume director could undo the seam without damaging the gown. I had literally been sewn into this last costume every day for a week, and I was aching to get out of it, to shed the corset and pinafores and slip into my silk trousers.

The door opened and closed. I heard the lock click into place and turned around.

"You're not Edith."

"Not last I checked."

It was difficult to breathe with him so near. He was dressed down again today, no jacket, tie loose, shirtsleeves rolled up. I wondered for a second if that was for my benefit. He leaned against the door, looking back at me with soft eyes. I'd never seen such an expression on his face before. It made him look boyish. Lovable.

"What are you doing here?"

"You won't return my calls. You sent my flowers back."

"Well that should tell you something." I started cleaning pins and brushes off the dressing table, anything to avoid looking at him.

"I saw Caroline Conway just outside."

I froze, hairbrush in hand.

"I told her I was madly in love with you."

I whipped around, pointing my makeshift weapon at him. "You did *what?*"

He shrugged. "It's true, Elizabeth. I told her I first fell in love with you when I saw you play Ophelia on the West End. I was visiting Gigi at the time. I think I went to every performance. Every time I came to see my sister those four years she was in London, I would find out if you were acting, and where and in what. Gigi used to make fun of me for it."

He pushed himself off the door, coming nearer to me.

"When she told me she suspected George had another woman, I hired an investigator."

"And he found me."

Darcy nodded. "At first I thought the two of you were working together. Grifters often work in teams, and Gigi has a fortune of her own outside the family money. Gigi Duvall is her stage name. Her real name is Georgiana Darcy. We didn't get where we are by being reckless, with our hearts or our checkbooks. And being the good, responsible Darcy that I am, I told her to cut him off when she first suspected."

"And that's why he robbed me blind." I nodded. "Thanks for that."

"I can repay—"

"I don't want your *money*! I want my dignity back!" I shook my head. "Taking up with a married man. Your own sister's husband. No wonder you treated me like the worst kind of gold digger when we met. Even the first time you saw me on the boat to New York, you looked at me like you would have been just as happy to throw me over the railing."

He paled visibly at that. "I know. And I was an ass at that party, too. But if it's worth anything, it didn't take me long to suspect that you were as much a victim as Gigi. When I hired you…"

My head snapped up. His face flushed a splotchy red, and he *still* managed to look divine. How did he do that?

"When I hired you, it allowed us to do what's called a risk assessment…"

"Oh, so you snooped around and figured out I didn't have two nickels to rub together? Well, that's aces."

"Lizzy…I know you don't have any reason to trust me. And part of why I acted so badly when we first met…I was…it was *you!*"

He put his hands on my shoulders. I had to resist the urge to arch up into that touch, to rub my face against his arm and purr.

"You and George…it broke my heart. Because for years, *you* were the only star in my sky."

"Why didn't you ever come back and speak to me? Introduce yourself?"

"I sent you roses every time. Did you ever get them? My notes?"

I blinked in surprise. "That was *you?*" I turned and grabbed my purse. In the inside pocket was a stack of small cardboard notes, worn thin with age and frequent use. I looked at the first one.

"From an admirer." I tossed it over my shoulder.

"Your performance defies description." That one joined the last on the floor.

I read the next one. "Wishing you all the best this season."

I tapped my finger against his chest. "No signature. Nothing personal. If this is how you woo a woman, it's no wonder you're still single."

He shrugged. "You awed me a bit. You still do."

No, no, *no.* I would *not* let myself soften towards him.

"When you started seeing Fitz, I thought the jealousy would eat me alive."

"Rollo and I are just friends, you chowderhead."

"I know that," he assured me. "I mean, I know that *now.* You don't have to worry. Rollo raked me over the coals after the party. We…had a long chat."

"I hope the coals were extra hot."

Just then, when I thought he'd reached the limits of his apologies, he did the most unexpected thing. He sank to his knees. One of the most powerful men in Hollywood brought to his knees by a scrappy little actress. "What in the Sam Hill are you *doing?*" I cried.

"I'm groveling. Let me grovel, Liz. Let me be the chowderhead you claim that I am."

I fought against the smile that tugged at my lips. It was a heroic battle, one day poets will write epics about it, but I'm not ashamed to say my efforts to appear severe were thoroughly routed. I reached out, my fingers toying with the lock of dark hair that fell across his brow.

"Did you *really* tell Caroline you were in love with me?"

"I did. This time tomorrow, I'm going to be all over the scandal sheets. 'Millionaire Mogul Heart Broken by Obstinate, Headstrong Girl.'"

God help me, I loved him too.

"Say, that's not bad. You could have a career writing headlines."

He stood and took me into his arms. It was everything I knew it would be. Wild and beautiful, like lightning in a bottle. And the bottle was *mine*.

"I'd prefer making headlines," he said. "As long as it's with you." And then he kissed me.

And *that* kiss was no three-second movie kiss. Or the one after. Or the one after that.

"I don't know what will happen next," he said, pulling back a little while still keeping me firmly in his arms. "I only know that when I'm near you, I don't feel horribly bored with the world. You make me feel wonderfully, tremendously alive."

I smiled and put my arms around his neck. "Too many adverbs, darling."

He grinned. "Guess I've got a lot to learn."

I pulled him down for another kiss. "Better start now."

BENNET SISTERS SNATCH PRIZES
by Caroline Conway

The 7th Annual Academy Awards not only saw Jane Bennet winning best actress for her role in *Toledo Red* but also her sister Eliza Darcy née Bennet walking in on the arm of her new husband, the uncatchable catch, William Darcy. Eliza Darcy was nominated for her role in *The Headstrong Girl*, but it was ultimately Jane Bennet's star-making turn as Cagney's doll that wowed the Academy this year.

Jane Bennet's next project will be the romantic jewel heist comedy *To Encourage Affection*, to be directed by her fiancé, Charles Bingley.

When Mrs. Darcy was asked what was in store next for *her*, she indicated a turn in the director's seat might not be outside of her grasp in the future. "I'd like to see if I can step into the shoes of Dorothy Arzner or Mabel Normand, try my hand at making my own pictures. We've all got stories to tell, if audiences are willing to listen."

When asked for comment, William Darcy said, "I would be surprised if she stopped there. I could see my wife running Pemberley Pictures one day. It'll be me riding her coattails, all the way." And this reporter suspects there's no place he'd rather be.

BEAU NORTH is the author of five books and contributor to multiple anthologies. Beau hails from South Carolina but now resides in Portland, Oregon with her husband. In her spare time, Beau is the co-host of the podcasts *Excessively Diverted: Modern Classics On-Screen* and *Let's Get Weirding: A Dune Podcast.*

Elizabeth: Obstinate Headstrong Girl

The
Uncommonly
Busy Lane
to
Longbourn

Joana Starnes

"But vanity, not love, has been my folly... Till this moment, I never knew myself." —Chapter XXXVI

THE UNCOMMONLY BUSY LANE TO LONGBOURN
Joana Starnes

*T*he wind picks up and sends the branches swaying above my head as I sit in one of my favourite spots. One of my hiding places, I should say. I pause here often at the end of my walks when I feel unequal to returning to the house. The odd bulge of the vast tree-trunk makes for an uncomfortable seat but, at least, 'tis a dry one. Another gust of wind, stronger than the last, tugs at my bonnet and whistles in the leaves. I look up as many fall around me to add to the amber carpet at my feet. On impulse, I reach down to gather two fistfuls and throw them in the air, much as my sister Kitty and I used to do when we were little, when romps in piles of autumn leaves held great appeal. Papa laughed. Mama scolded.

Some things never change. Mama scolded me this morning, too, for dashing out of the breakfast parlour as soon as I possibly could, rather than listening with rapt attention to our cousin Mr. Collins's tales of his parish in Kent and his bountiful patroness, Lady Catherine de Bourgh.

"I expect you to make up for it and pay him every courtesy at dinner, young lady," she had admonished me, "for he has been most attentive to *you*."

Sadly, that is true. Mr. Collins insists on lavishing me with his singular brand of attentions, ever since Mama had less than tactfully pointed out that my sister Jane would be very soon engaged.

"A proposal is imminent," Mama assured him.

For once, she might be in the right. I hope she is. Dearest Jane! There is not a kinder soul in the world, and she deserves to be blissfully happy. As a rule, I have little patience for the platitudes voiced about a courting couple: that it would be an excellent match; that they seem to have been made for each other. The hackneyed phrases ring true this time, even to a confirmed sceptic like me. I have yet to meet a gentleman better suited to Jane's disposition. If only Mr. Bingley would follow his heart and propose soon. He certainly gets little encouragement from his supercilious sisters or his vastly arrogant friend.

"She is tolerable; but not handsome enough to tempt *me*," I mimic the judgement he had brazenly passed upon my person, and I throw another fistful of leaves into the air.

The register is far too low, the vowels long and exaggerated, yet I snort with laughter at my own performance. The impudence of the man! Not that the insult still rankles. It does not. If anything, I am highly diverted by Mr. Darcy's sullen temper, his lack of manners, and his excessive pride. What amuses me less is my temporary lack of discernment. To think that my interest was piqued when I first laid eyes on him at the Meryton assembly! I even thought him remarkably handsome. That is, before he opened his lips to speak. Thank goodness that he did, upon reflection, otherwise I might have still found him appealing.

I shrug. What folly, to be swayed by first impressions! Handsome is as handsome does—and I am not merely thinking of his shocking incivility to me. That is a trifling matter. But his abominable conduct to poor Mr. Wickham shows him to be the very worst of men.

I shake crumpled leaves off my gloves and rise to my feet, although I am still not ready to head home; the stupidest of men is waiting for me there to regale me with more accounts of Lady Catherine and her opulent abode.

Why did Mama not encourage him towards my sister Mary? Only the other day, Mary sent Lydia into a fit of giggles by praising the solidity of Mr. Collins's reflections. *She* might be willing to accept his suit and, in due course, make the fourth at Lady Catherine's quadrille table as Mrs. Collins. But I cannot. Not even if he were the last man in the world!

The notion comes to me as I resume my walk. Of course! Why did

I not think of this sooner? I should ask Jane to drop a few words in Mama's ear about turning Mr. Collins's attention towards Mary. Mama never pays heed to what I have to say, but she *would* listen to Jane—and all the more readily if Jane were to fulfil Mama's best hopes and become engaged to Mr. Bingley.

Naturally, then the threat of the entail would lose its sting, but this is a selfish thought and I dismiss it. I wish Jane to marry the gentleman she loves so that she can be happy and not because this marriage would preserve the rest of us from want.

The delightful prospect of my dear sister settled in wedded bliss no further than three miles away, at Netherfield, puts a spring in my step. So does my choice of path—I am heading home the long way around. My skipping turns into a run, and I giggle like a mad thing as I scamper down the slope, imagining the look on Mr. Collins's face if he should see me thus. Ah, the solemn horror! *"Cousin Elizabeth, for shame! What would Lady Catherine say?"*

I can easily imagine Her Ladyship's response, seeing as she is Mr. Darcy's relation. His aunt on his mother's side, Mr. Wickham told me. I laugh as I picture an older and female version of Mr. Darcy, grey-haired, stony-faced, and wearing a heavily trimmed bonnet.

And then I hear a loud snort and dart my eyes that way—only to spot the gentleman himself! The snort was equine, not human, but I catch a diverted look on his habitually stern countenance. The confounded man has the effrontery to laugh at me? I grimace and toss my head back as I slow down. Heaven forbid that I should entertain him further by losing my footing and tumbling downhill.

I feel the urge to tell him he is trespassing. He has no business to ride over my father's land unless he is coming to call. Clearly, he is not on his way to visit us, which would be a pleasing notion if I had not the ill-fortune of coming across him on my walk.

I nod in greeting—I must, there is nothing for it—and he tips his hat with a quiet "good morning," but he does not ride off. To my dismay, he dismounts and approaches me on foot, leading his black horse.

"A fine morning for a walk," he observes. "Or for a run," he adds, increasing my vexation. He *is* laughing at me, I know, even before I catch the twitch of his lips. I raise my chin in defiance. Let him. I care not one jot for his good opinion.

"Indeed," I say curtly. Then the mischievous devils that sometimes prod me into speech get the better of me and I ask, "Do you often indulge in that particular amusement, too, sir?"

The mental image of the impeccably attired Mr. Darcy running through the dell is almost as diverting as my picturing his aunt, but I forbear to smile. Oddly, today he has no such reservations. In fact, he grins widely as he answers, "Not often, no. Although I can see the attraction. Myself, I prefer a good gallop. 'Tis far more satisfying, you will agree."

Will I indeed? I suppress a frown at the man's choice of words and the arrogance of his assumptions and reply flatly, "Is it? I cannot say."

"How so? I rather thought you possessed decided opinions on everything."

That answers it. He *is* determined to provoke me.

"Not without sound information, I do not. So, I shall not comment on the pleasures of a good gallop, seeing as I do not ride."

"Why not?"

I make no answer. 'Tis none of his affair. The brashness of the man! Does he expect me to own that Papa cannot afford to keep riding horses for each and every one of us? Or that I prefer to roam on foot at my leisure, rather than sit in the saddle and parade down the lanes, puffed up with my own dignity like Miss Bingley? Or indeed like his sainted sister who, Mr. Wickham told me, has no time for old acquaintances and childhood friends but grew up to discard them, just like her haughty brother?

"Enjoy your ride, sir" is all I say with a frosty nod, so that he might leave me to my own devices, only to find that he does not take the hint, for he asks:

"May I escort you to Longbourn?"

I purse my lips. He is uncommonly obtuse for one who prides himself on his understanding. It seems I shall have to put it plainly—so I do.

"I thank you, no. That will not be necessary. The path I have in mind is not a bridleway. Nor is the one that brought you hither," I point out. I will not be quite so uncivil as to say he is trespassing. This is the nearest I am prepared to come to that. "You should keep to the main thoroughfares. Good day, Mr. Darcy."

"Oh. Good day then, Miss Bennet."

He is not best-pleased, which does not surprise me. Not the sort to take kindly to being told he is in the wrong. This is often the case with those who would most benefit from the experience. But be that as it may...I am not in the least disposed to task myself with educating Mr. Darcy—nor am I inclined to wait and wave him off. I curtsy and leave him, so glad to have only my own company again that I break into a run before the path turns, to take me out of sight. I could not care less if he is still watching.

MY SCHEME MET WITH SUCCESS. I SPOKE TO JANE ABOUT MAKING MAMA see the merit of guiding Mr. Collins's interest from me to Mary, and she consented. Between us, we agreed that Jane should speak to Mama of my obvious faults. I listed them myself; I am wilful, hoyden-ish, wild and not in the least biddable, which would be a disadvantage for both Mr. Collins and Mama. Mary would make a much more amenable mistress of Longbourn. She is not averse to taking Mama's advice. Moreover, unlike me, Mary is sensible of Mr. Collins's good qualities, such as they are, and would not refuse him if he offered, whereas—most selfishly—I would.

"Oh, Lizzy, no," my sweet Jane had protested. "I cannot say that. Selfish indeed! I love you too much to blacken you so."

"Jane, you must! Precisely because you love me. Can you see me wedded to that man? Besides, you would only voice the truth. I love you all dearly, but I *am* too selfish to tie my fate to his."

"And you would be in the right to reject him, dearest, come what may. Our cousin is Papa's heir and of good character, I know, but not the sort of man that would make you happy. I shall try, Lizzy," Jane had undertaken with a sigh. "For your sake and Mama's and

Mary's, I shall try. But it goes sorely against the grain to speak ill of you."

I have no notion what she told Mama, but it carried weight. Especially as the advice came from one who was known to love me the most. If Jane declared me unable to recommend myself to Mr. Collins's attentions and affections, Mama was far more likely to take note than if I said so myself.

Suffice to say that, when Mr. Bingley delivers the invitations to the Netherfield ball in person—a compliment to Jane, of course—my sister Mary receives a similar compliment from Mr. Collins, who applies for the honour of her hand for the first set. Verily glowing, she accepts. I am delighted, both for her and for myself. Now I can happily envisage reserving *my* first set for Mr. Wickham.

MY SCHEME COULD NOT HAVE BACKFIRED MORE DISASTROUSLY. TRUE, I saved myself from the discomfort of standing up with Mr. Collins, only to fare a great deal worse: lest I be forced to sit with the wallflowers for the entire evening, I had to accept the first gentleman who asked. And that was Mr. Darcy.

I seethe as I move along the dance with him as my partner. I have reasons aplenty to be cross. Firstly, because *he* is to blame for Mr. Wickham's absence. Lieutenant Chamberlayne as good as said that outright when he came to greet us and apply for Lydia's hand for the first set. He said that Mr. Wickham charged him with conveying his regrets for having to travel to Town on an urgent matter of business, but the lieutenant did not scruple to voice his own suspicions: namely, that Mr. Wickham's business might have been less pressing had he not wished to avoid a certain gentleman here.

I knew whom he meant even before Mr. Chamberlayne cast a meaningful glance towards the spot where Mr. Darcy was standing, looking as severe as ever. The lieutenant could not say more. Lydia all but dragged him away, the foolish girl. I had scarce begun to conquer my vexation at her exposing our family to ridicule with her unguarded and flirtatious conduct, when I turned around to find Mr.

Darcy standing directly before me. He offered a cursory greeting and a stiff bow, then applied for my hand.

So here we are, dancing—the least likely couple. I see my neighbours' astonishment at the great honour thus bestowed upon me, but I try to ignore their covert looks. I strive to ignore my companion, too, until it strikes me that he would deem it a great punishment if forced to talk, so I make some slight observation on the dance. He obliges me with a very brief reply, then falls silent.

"It is your turn to say something now, Mr. Darcy," I chide. "I talked about the dance. You ought to make some kind of remark on the size of the room or the number of couples."

He does no such thing. He only assures me that whatever I wish him to say will be said.

"Very well," I concede. "That reply will do for the present. Perhaps by and by I may observe that private balls are much pleasanter than public ones. But now we may be silent."

"Do you talk by rule then, while you are dancing?"

"Sometimes. One must speak a little, you know. It would look odd to be entirely silent for half an hour together."

"Not necessarily," he crisply disagrees.

I sigh, ready to give up my game. His society is so tedious that even teasing him fails to divert me. However, after a period of silence, he asks:

"Do you and your sisters often walk to Meryton?"

This is too great a temptation, and I am unwilling to resist it. I *shall* avenge myself for this evening's disappointments.

"We do. When you met us there the other day, we had just been forming a new acquaintance."

The effect is immediate. A deeper shade of hauteur overspreads his features, so much so that his mien is quite as forbidding as it had been on the day I had alluded to, when he laid eyes on Mr. Wickham on the main road in Meryton and treated him with supreme contempt, as if they had not been brought up together. They were inseparable companions, Mr. Wickham told me on the following evening when I encountered him at my aunt Philips. Inseparable—until driven apart by Mr. Darcy's jealousy, once that gentleman's father had begun to treat Mr. Wickham as a particular favourite.

I long to tell Mr. Darcy that discarding one's boyhood companion and forcing him to make his own way in the world by exploiting an ambiguity in an imperfect law, and thus withholding his rightful inheritance, was reprehensible. But I am not supposed to know these particulars. Mr. Wickham trusted me with his confidence, and I will not betray him, as others had done.

His lips so stiff that I wonder how he is able to speak, Mr. Darcy replies, "Mr. Wickham is blessed with such happy manners as may ensure his making friends. Whether he may be equally capable of retaining them is less certain."

I am astounded at his audacity. Mightily provoked, too. So, I heatedly retort, "He has been so unlucky as to lose *your* friendship—and in a manner which he is likely to suffer from all his life."

Mr. Darcy makes to speak, as do I. I have a great deal more to say. But I am denied the opportunity thanks to my infernal cousin, who has been stumbling along the dance nearby, hand in hand with Mary.

"The other way, Mr. Collins!" I hear my sister urge him but to no avail. The buffoon does not heed her. He careers into me and his clumsy foot lands heavily on mine. I try to not yelp in pain—and fail abysmally.

"MY DEEPEST APOLOGIES, SIR!" MR. COLLINS SAYS TO MY DISAGREEABLE partner for the fourth time, as if it had been Mr. Darcy's foot that he had crushed. I dart my eyes heavenward. Some wretched neighbour, whom I cannot detest enough, must have informed my cousin of Mr. Darcy's connection to Mr. Collins's revered patroness, and he is now paying more assiduous court to Lady Catherine's nephew than to Mary. "Pray allow me, sir," my cousin pleads, seeking to spare Mr. Darcy the tedious task of supporting me as I hobble ignominiously from the set.

"I would say you have done enough," Mr. Darcy verily growls, refusing to be supplanted, and for once I am almost glad. I would rather lean on his arm than my cousin's. Mr. Collins would be so concerned with gaining Mr. Darcy's pardon that he might steer me into the potted plants or forget about me altogether. "Return to the set, sir, and your partner," Mr. Darcy orders him, not deigning to acknowledge Mary's look of gratitude at that suggestion. Nor does he acknowledge Mr. Collins's fifth apology—or was it the sixth?—as he guides me towards the nearest armchair. He turns it at a better angle, and I lower myself into it—ungainly, I fear, but most gratefully.

I glance up at Mr. Darcy and thank him for his assistance, but he cuts me off with a perfunctory, "Not at all," then asks, "How badly are you hurt?"

He does not wait for my reply but drops down on one knee for a closer look. I gape. The man has lost his senses! But my discomfort flares into utter horror when he reaches out, as if aiming to raise the hem of my dress and see the damage for himself—along with half the ballroom.

"Stand, sir!" I hiss as I tuck my injured foot under the chair, which only serves to send worse pain shooting through it. I bite my lip and hiss again, "Pray stand and leave be. You are making a scene. Desist, for goodness' sake!"

"I rather thought that the blame for making a scene lies with Mr. Collins," he resentfully shoots back.

"And do you imagine *this* is helping matters?" I fulminate in a fierce whisper with a gesture of anger and frustration towards his unchanged posture.

Finally, he rises to his feet.

"Forgive me for thinking of your welfare and not the impertinent curiosity of busybodies," he says testily, then asks, "Is there anything you wish me to do? Fetch your mother, perhaps?"

"Heavens, no!" I reply without thinking. If Mr. Collins's blunder and Mr. Darcy kneeling at my feet had not quite managed to attract everyone's attention, Mama's ill-judged effusions would surely do the trick. I look around, hoping against hope that the incident escaped her notice, but a familiar cry of "Oh, Lizzy!" puts paid to such foolish notions. I cringe, waiting for the onslaught, and make no reply to Mr. Darcy as he takes his leave.

AT LONG LAST, PAPA COMES TO MY RESCUE. WHAT TOOK HIM SO LONG? Peevishly, I refuse to oblige him with a conspiratorial smirk of shared amusement when he quips that one can have too much of a good thing and leads Mama away, urging her to spare some maternal attention for my sisters.

Jane tears herself from Mr. Bingley to inquire about my welfare, but I bid her leave me and make the most of the evening.

Not much hope for me, I fear. I seek to stand after a while and test my injured foot but shooting pain forces me to sit down again. That should be a fine to-do if some bone should be broken. I will surely go distracted if this confines me to the house. 'Tis bad enough to find myself confined to a chair for now, instead of skipping on this merry tune with the others. My unimpaired foot is tapping in time under my skirts, and I make no attempt to deprive myself of this modest pleasure. Nor do I seek to stop myself from directing some very uncharitable thoughts towards Mr. Collins, who gracelessly bounds along with a resigned-looking Pen Harrington, nattering all the while to her as if he does not have a care in the world.

"MAY I JOIN YOU?"

The sound of Mr. Darcy's voice catches me unawares. I did not notice his return until now, when he is standing beside me, a cup of punch in each hand.

I am tempted to observe that, as he can see, I am currently devoid of company and beggars cannot be choosers. But that would be uncivil even as a jest, so I only say, "Pray do."

He offers me one of the cups, for which I am grateful, as no one else had thought of bringing me refreshments. Not even Jane. I thank him as he pulls himself a chair.

"My pleasure," he says, then falls silent. This time, I cannot give myself the trouble of forcing him to converse. I sip my drink and shrug. He may do as he pleases.

The fortunate souls with full command over their unharmed limbs are lining up for another set. As I sit watching them with undiminished envy, my companion decides to break his vow of silence.

"My apologies for the earlier display of temper. I should have grasped that you had no wish to draw further notice to your predicament," he says, much to my surprise. I rather thought him incapable of acknowledging himself at fault.

"Ah, yes, my predicament," I say, choosing to make light of it.

"Are you still in pain?"

"Only if I attempt to stand," I answer truthfully, which makes him glower at my cousin. To my unholy satisfaction, the glare has the power to arrest Mr. Collins's capers. He blanches and nearly stumbles into my friend Charlotte's back.

"That man should be tethered to a chair," Mr. Darcy mutters between his teeth, and I cannot help laughing. He is not wrong there.

"Mr. Bingley's ballroom would certainly be a safer place should Mr. Collins be thus confined." And gagged, for good measure! But I keep the latter preference to myself.

Mr. Darcy turns towards me, no hint of amusement in his eyes.

"I would like to finish what I had to say before we were interrupted," he solemnly announces.

"And that is?"

"A word of warning: Mr. Wickham is not a man to be trusted."

I bristle, as much at the tone as at the implications.

"And I should believe you without question?"

"Yes."

"Why?"

"Why should you believe *him*?"

Because his very countenance vouches for his open and amiable temper, which is more than I can say of yours, I would very much like to snap. But, unlike Mr. Darcy, I am mindful of my manners. So, I merely ask, "What makes you think I do?"

"You spoke of his lifelong suffering."

"Which, of course, is not of your infliction," I scoff.

His left brow arches in the most provoking manner.

"Precisely," he says. Just that, and nothing more.

I frown and refrain from informing him that, much as it will shock him, not everyone alive is eager to take his word as the gospel truth. I only say, "I thank you for your warning. I shall bear it in mind."

Had I purposely set out to rile Mr. Darcy, now I might have rejoiced in my success, for he looks well on his way to losing his temper as he tersely says, "It is particularly incumbent on those who cling to their opinions to be secure of judging properly at first."

I give a dismissive shrug. "Naturally."

He verily scowls. "Has anyone told you that you can be awfully headstrong?"

"No. To my good fortune, most of those in my circle are well-mannered."

I am rather proud of my aptly coined set-down. Sadly, its effect is ruined by Lydia, who could not have chosen a worse time to rush past us, chasing after Kitty and seeking to pull the ribbons from her hair.

"So I see," says Mr. Darcy and takes his leave with a stiff bow.

To my chagrin, the evening does not improve. Quite the opposite. When the dances are at an end, Jane comes to help me walk into the supper room. By now, I can just about walk without hobbling, but I might as well have spared myself the effort, for all that awaits me therein is the opportunity to see my relations making an exhibition of themselves. All except Jane, of course. But as for the others, I am convinced that, had they made an actual agreement to expose themselves to ridicule as much as they could during the course of one evening, it would have been impossible for them to play their respective parts with more spirit or finer success.

As always, Mama's talents in that regard are unsurpassed. Throughout supper, she enumerates to Lady Lucas the advantages of the excellent match she expects Jane to make with Mr. Bingley, and my efforts to check her enthusiasm on the subject—or at least her loudness—meet with no success at all. I can scarce eat a bite but blush and blush again with shame and vexation, as it is clear to me that Mr. Darcy and Miss Bingley, who are sitting too close to Mama for my comfort, can hear every single ill-judged word.

When at long last Mama's attention veers towards the excellent fare, I begin to revive a little. It does not last long. After supper, Mary hastens to oblige the company with a song. If only she could restrict herself to *one*! But no, she overstays her welcome at the pianoforte, playing one ill-chosen piece after another in a dreadfully affected manner. When Papa catches my anxious glances entreating his intervention and finally takes the hint, 'tis only to make me wish that he did not. I love him dearly, but his wit can be cruel at times, and this is one of the occasions. He teases Mary for her efforts in everybody's hearing and assures her that she has delighted the company for long enough. She is deeply mortified, and I cannot blame her. Papa's ill-applied sarcasm mortifies me, too. That, sadly, is nothing to my cousin's lengthy speeches, which he proceeds to deliver with pompous solemnity and with repeated bows to Mr. Darcy who, Mr. Collins says, is due all the proper manifestations of his respect towards anybody connected to his most gracious patroness.

Mama puts the finishing touches on the wretched performance when she praises the unmitigated nincompoop for his cleverness and common sense, then goes on to say that Mr. Collins would make almost as wonderful an addition to our immediate circle as Mr. Bingley, and the day when she will have two daughters so advantageously married will be the happiest day of her life.

I am not one to dwell on vexations, but now I wish the ground would open and swallow me whole. My only joy is that Jane and Mr. Bingley seem to be spending their entire time conversing with each other, so they catch little of the mortifying spectacle. I do my best to meditate on that sole happy thought.

I AM RELIEVED TO FIND THAT, BY MORNING, MY FOOT IS AS GOOD AS new. I can go down for breakfast without any discomfort, so I assure

Papa there is no need to send for Mr. Jones, the surgeon-apothecary. In fact, I am well enough to agree to escort Kitty, Lydia, and Jane on their walk to Meryton, to call upon our aunt Philips.

Mary does not wish to come. I take it as a good sign that Mr. Collins does not offer to accompany us either.

The walk is pleasant, and my foot behaves. Kitty and Lydia saunter ahead, chatting merrily as they are wont to do, leaving me and Jane to our private conversation. I do not bring up any of the mortifying scenes I witnessed yesterday. They cannot be too soon forgotten. Instead, I urge Jane to speak of her own recollections of the ball. Fortunately, they are happier than mine. Mr. Bingley is everything that is charming—except Jane's declared betrothed. We do not speak of this either, but we both hope he *will* declare himself on his return from Town. He aimed to leave at dawn this morning, Jane says, and return by the week's end. Good. Jane's happiness cannot come soon enough to my way of thinking.

My own hopes for a felicity of a similar kind, such as they may be, are bolstered as soon as our call at Aunt Philips' comes to an end and we leave her house—for who should we encounter but Mr. Wickham!

I am secretly thrilled that he returned so promptly and cannot help thinking I may have served as inducement, especially as I witness his unconcealed delight at our meeting. He asks permission to escort us home and 'tis readily granted.

The walk back is even more enjoyable than the stroll into Meryton, as one might imagine. Thoughtful as ever, Jane prevails upon Kitty and Lydia to walk ahead with her, despite their disinclination to deprive themselves of Mr. Wickham's genial conversation, and I am left to chat to him without interruption. And we do chat freely, I am pleased to say. True to his unreserved temper, he loses no time in openly acknowledging that his business in Town was somewhat of a subterfuge.

"'Tis not for me to avoid a certain gentleman of our acquaintance," he says, a meaningful twinkle in his eye. "If he wishes to avoid me, *he* must go. But as the event drew nearer, I came to see that scenes might arise which would cause discomfort to blameless parties. Mr. Bingley might have been inconvenienced, and through him, your sister. I hope you will not blame me for choosing to stay away."

"Blame you? Oh, no," I reply swiftly. He is in the right and, with hindsight, well I know it. If Mr. Darcy did not hesitate to blacken Mr. Wickham's name to me, there is no telling what other mischief he would have wantonly caused. And truth be told, I should only be glad that Mr. Wickham was spared my family's mortifying exhibitions.

The recollection of Mr. Darcy's gratuitous interference angers me afresh. Perhaps I should warn Mr. Wickham of the damage to his good name, wilfully perpetrated. But he speaks first:

"I am pleased to see you are recovered," he smilingly observes, and I chuckle.

"News travels fast."

"It does. My friend Chamberlayne informed me you were incapacitated during the first dance. I do hope you have not suffered excessively. In fact, seeing as you are as sprightly as ever, I almost dare hope you used Mr. Collins's gaffe to your advantage to escape an unwelcome partner."

I am blushing, I expect, but I choose not to disabuse him of that notion. Mr. Wickham slows his pace till we come to a standstill.

"Dare I also be quite as ungentlemanly as to hope you missed me?"

I do not disabuse him of that notion either but cast him an arch glance.

"Hope springs eternal, as they say," I quip, and his handsome countenance brightens into a wide smile.

And then he tries to kiss me! For the life of me, I cannot say why I avert my face and dip my head. My first kiss, this might have been. And why not? I cannot say. Perhaps I was hoping for something different—something better than a furtive affair on the lane to Longbourn. I start to walk, my face still averted, and only look up when he reaches for my hand. I find a silent apology in his eyes when they meet mine. I am rather pleased to discover he is not backward in also voicing it.

"Pray allow me to beg your pardon for my presumption, Miss Bennet. I fear I was too forward and overstepped the mark."

I am unsure as to what I should say, but I do not have the chance to ponder further. I whip around, in equal measure vexed and startled, when a too-well-known voice drawls behind us:

"Indeed, why break the habit of a lifetime?"

Lips pursed, I stare as Mr. Darcy dismounts. I have not heard the hoofbeats. The grass that grows freely on the lane used by no other carriage than ours must have muffled them. Or I had better things to do than paying heed.

"I see you took my advice and kept to the well-established lanes," I acidly observe.

Mr. Darcy's tone is every bit as caustic when he retorts, "I am not averse to taking good advice, Miss Bennet. I only wish you could say the same."

I refuse to dignify his blatantly malicious comment with an answer. I will not make the moment more disagreeable than it already is. Sadly, Mr. Darcy does not share my scruples.

"A word, Wickham," he demands with an almighty scowl.

Better-bred by far, Mr. Wickham bows. "I would be happy to oblige but, as you can see, I have a more pressing duty to attend to," he says, offering me his arm.

I do not hesitate to take it and make my allegiance clear. I would not have imagined that Mr. Darcy's scowl could grow any darker, but I am proven wrong as he indicates the road ahead with a jerky nod and snaps, "You take too much upon yourself. Miss Bennet can walk home with her sister."

Whoever has charged *him* with deciding whom I can and cannot walk with? I fume as I glare up the road and spot Lydia, who is just rounding the bend, as much of an interfering nuisance as ever.

"Come along, you two!" she calls. "What is—?"

I expect she was about to ask what was keeping me and Mr. Wickham. But, upon noticing Mr. Darcy, she breaks off with a giggle and stands there grinning, as if in anticipation of a diverting spectacle. I flinch. What have I done to deserve such a sister? And what is Jane up to? She was supposed to keep Lydia in check.

As if on cue, Jane comes into view as well, urging Lydia to leave me be, only to pause in her tracks when she discovers that Mr. Wickham and I are plagued with unexpected company.

"Be not alarmed, madam," my tormentor scoffs at me. "I will only detain your most attentive escort for a moment. Then I shall be *pleased* to return him to you," he adds with sufficient emphasis on one word as to leave me in no doubt that he means the opposite. "We are going the same way, after all. I must speak to Mr. Bennet."

I roll my eyes. What now? And then I see his game. He aims to blacken Mr. Wickham's character to Papa as well.

"Must you, now!" I glower.

"Oh, yes. You may depend upon it."

Predictably, Mr. Wickham comes to my rescue. "You may remember me speaking of scenes unpleasant to more than myself," he tactfully observes, then entreats: "Pray go, Miss Elizabeth. I shall follow directly."

YET HE DOES NOT. WE ARE ALMOST HOME, JANE AND I, AND HE HAS NOT caught up with us yet. Lydia and Kitty are long gone. I slowed my pace considerably, and they lost patience. I keep darting glances over my shoulder, yet I am denied the reassurance of seeing Mr. Wickham approach—even if he should be forced to come with that wretched man in tow.

Suddenly, my mind is made up.

"Jane, I must return," I declare.

"Why? Surely you do not fear for Mr. Wickham's safety?"

"But I do," I retort. "I never should have left them."

I make an about-turn and hasten back.

"Wait!" Jane calls after me. "Let us send someone. A maid. Or John. Or Papa. You should not go yourself, if you are expecting conflict."

"No need. Mr. Darcy would not dare harm Mr. Wickham in my presence. Not if he is unwilling to be exposed for a cruel and vicious blackguard," I say and break into a run. My ankle protests, but I ignore it. I must. This is not the time for self-indulgence.

"Lizzy, wait!" Jane calls again. "Wait for me. I will come with you."

I wish she would not, grateful as I am for her sweet concern. My eldest sister is the epitome of kindness, but she is not an active sort. She slows me down, and I do not like it. I wish she would let me go by myself. I would reach the dreaded spot much sooner.

"Hurry!" I urge, and she can only nod, panting from the exertion. She cannot run any faster. In the end, I give up trying to tailor my pace to hers and dash ahead, only to have my worst fears confirmed when I discover a pair of riding boots protruding from the undergrowth. There is no sign of the black stallion, nor its cowardly rider.

"Get help!" I cry towards Jane as I point at the stark justification of my fears.

But she does not turn back.

"Jane, go! Go and fetch—" I plead, but my entreaties abruptly end in a gasp as I come closer and notice that the gentleman is not in regimentals. The recumbent form is Mr. Darcy's.

"Oh." Jane gasps, too, when she catches up with me. I am struck dumb as I step closer. What is *he* doing there, lying on one side as if asleep?

I am kneeling down before I know it and touch his shoulder, then try to raise his head.

"Mr. Darcy?"

He makes no answer. 'Tis Jane who chokes out a strangled whisper:

"Good god!"

She points at something, but I cannot bring myself to look that way to see what she is trying to show me. I stare at my hand as I draw it back to explore the sticky wetness I found under Mr. Darcy's head. I gape as vivid-red droplets trickle down my fingers. Blood!

I CALL HIS NAME—ONCE, TWICE. IT MAKES LITTLE DIFFERENCE. HIS eyelids flutter open, but his stare is vacant as he looks at me. I doubt that he can see me.

"We should get help," Jane repeats what I have argued all the while, albeit for a different reason. "You go," she sensibly urges. "You will get home much sooner than me."

I nod. She is in the right. I scramble to my feet, pick up my skirts and break into a run, oblivious to the pain in my ankle. I do not think I had run faster in my life.

Assistance is soon summoned, and we are on our way—Papa, our manservant, John, and I—in the cart that is normally destined for the farm. 'Tis maddeningly slow, but Papa said it would serve better than the carriage.

"We do not know his injuries. He had better be fetched back lying flat."

I do not argue the point. Papa knows best. Little as he is willing to exert himself in ordinary circumstances, in times of crisis, he always rises to the challenge.

We trundle along, only to hear the noisy clatter of another vehicle behind us.

"Pull aside and make way, John," Papa instructs, once he had cast a brief glance over his shoulder. "We do not need another misadventure down this lane."

John obeys, and timely, too. No sooner does he steer the cart out of the way than our own carriage flies past at breakneck speed. I gape as I spot Mr. Collins in the coachman's seat, his hair ruffled by the wind, urging the team onward with strangled cries of "Yah!" and mad flicks of the ribbons.

"I would not have missed the man's acquaintance for the world," Papa dryly remarks, gesturing towards John to carry on. "Who would have thought that my staid cousin should be quite so worthy of joining the exclusive Four-in-Hand?"

I purse my lips, not altogether pleased with his ill-timed levity. But then, such is Papa—a man of parts. As for Mr. Collins, he is only apt to follow his own advice. While we were preparing to leave the house, I heard him insisting that he should be the one to fetch Mr. Jones. I thought he meant he wished to accompany our coachman, not that he would drive the carriage himself. Still, I told him that the errand was needless. Mr. Jones should be on his way already. Mr. Wickham must have gone to fetch him—borrowed Mr. Darcy's horse to ride into Meryton.

I still have no notion as to what passed between them. Judging by the bruise I eventually spotted on Mr. Darcy's chin, I can only imagine there was some scuffle of sorts, during which he fell and hit his head against a stone. That was what Jane had pointed at, when we came upon him: there was a bloodstained stone by his head, where he lay. But no matter. I shall learn the details later. Now the material point is to ensure that Mr. Darcy will survive.

I shudder. It does not bear thinking that poor Mr. Wickham should hang for murder. He could so easily be blamed! Everyone in Meryton knows there is no love lost between them. Lieutenant Denny must have spoken unpardonably freely and shared the tale with all and sundry, for surely the information could not have come from Mr. Wickham. He so earnestly said that, while he gratefully remembered the goodness of the father, he could not expose the wrongdoings of the son.

If anything should befall Mr. Darcy, *I* will know it for what it was: a tragic accident, not murder. But it would carry no weight. I was not there to witness the events. All I have to offer is my firm belief in Mr. Wickham's goodness. Yet I know full well that circumstances might condemn him.

I wring my hands in my lap. Why, oh why, did I not stay behind? If I did, they would have had the decency to not brawl in my presence like a pair of hot-headed fools. Then none of this would have happened, and neither of them would be in mortal danger. I flinch and my face crumples. I sit up on the hard bench with a start when Papa puts an arm around me.

"There, now, Lizzy. You are not going to be missish, are you? All will turn out well, my dear girl. Take heart."

I appreciate his attempt to reassure me. Nevertheless, the phrase sounds meaningless and empty. All will be well. How does he know that? I clasp my hands together and silently pray he will be proven right. Mr. Darcy *must* survive. Not just so that Mr. Wickham should be safe from the hangman's noose. Even if poor Mr. Wickham were not involved in this nightmare, I would not wish any man to come to harm. Not even one as haughty and prideful as Mr. Darcy, bent on causing mischief. Aye, he would have done well to stay at Netherfield this morning or follow Mr. Bingley into Town or goodness knows what else. Instead, it had pleased him to come to Longbourn, pick a quarrel with Mr. Wickham, and thus be the architect of his own misfortune. Even so, he does not deserve to die for that.

THANKFULLY, WE FIND HIM ALIVE, BUT HE STILL APPEARS TO BE BLEEDING from his injury. The kerchief that Jane had pressed to his head as I went for assistance is soaked with blood.

"Did he awake at all while I was away?"

Jane mournfully shakes her head. He remains unconscious as Papa and John lift him onto the cart. He is still unconscious when our carriage catches up with us mere yards away from the gates of Longbourn. Mr. Collins pulls up alongside to inquire after him, and also to allow Mr. Jones to scramble out and come to do his duty.

I leave the surgeon-apothecary to it and forget to ask what kept him so long. When we arrive at the house, there is much commotion as Mr. Darcy is brought in. Predictably, Mama's voice is the loudest, but Mr. Collins will not be put to shame. He is well-nigh as vociferous as Mama when he offers his own chamber for Mr. Darcy's use.

"'Twould be wrong—nay, unnatural—for me to luxuriate therein while Lady Catherine's nephew is forced to make do with the other guest room. Why, 'tis so small and cramped and wholly inadequate for one of his station. Indeed, the very best that can be found at Longbourn is still not good enough for Her Ladyship's kin. Not even my cousin Bennet's chamber. But there we are. Nothing we can do about it but settle him in the most presentable bedchamber available for visitors. Unless you would be so kind, Cousin, to cede your bed to our illustrious guest?"

Papa makes a face. "I thank you, sir, for taking the trouble to assess our modest chambers with such diligence. Still, I fear that some details escaped your notice. Why, my windows are full west. My bedchamber would be too brightly lit for one who suffers from a head injury. I am quite certain Mr. Jones will agree."

"Oh, yes, naturally. Excessive sunlight should be avoided for now and the curtains drawn," the surgeon-apothecary says, nodding with energy, while Mr. Collins seems struck by the wisdom of Papa's remark.

"My dear sir, how right you are! Of course, of course. I should have thought of that myself. I am most grateful for your perspicacity and your kind concern for Mr. Darcy's welfare. Why, I…" He mutters as he stumbles up the stairs at the end of the procession: John and Papa's man, who are carrying Mr. Darcy, then Papa, Mama, Mr. Jones, our maid Sarah—and a panting Mr. Collins, bringing up the rear.

I heave a long sigh and walk into the drawing room.

"Sit, Lizzy," Jane entreats me. "Let me go ask Mrs. Hill to fetch us a cup of tea. And refreshments for Mr. Jones, when he returns. Oh, yes, I also think I should send word to Netherfield. I should not leave Miss Bingley and her relations to wonder what has become of Mr. Darcy."

I take a seat and gladly allow my sensible sister to take charge. Before long, our trusted housekeeper comes with a fresh pot of tea and assures Jane that the requested refreshments are well in hand as well. I do not feel like eating. I doubt I could touch a bite. But the cup of tea that Jane places in my hands is welcome.

This is how Mama and Mary find us when they walk in. Mama lowers herself into a seat with a weary sigh, and Mary goes to pour cups of tea for the both of them. She brings one to Mama, who takes it and reaches up to affectionately pinch Mary's cheek.

"Such a sweet, steady girl! What wretched luck that the confounded man should have stolen your thunder in this fashion. How very like him, too. This morning should have been all about you, my dearest child, and your sterling achievement in securing Mr. Collins. Yet there he is, that Mr. Darcy, causing all this fuss and claiming everyone's attention for himself."

It must have been the first time in living memory for Mary to receive such fulsome praise from Mama and be called sweet, steady, and her dearest child. Yet, to her vast credit, Mary would not bask in it. Her tone is as censorious as mine and Jane's as the three of us chorus, "Mama!"

"You should not say that," Mary adds, shaking her head.

But Mama shrugs.

"And why not?" she scoffs. "What has Mr. Darcy ever done to deserve all of us running around in circles for his benefit? If any gentleman should have been brought injured and bleeding to our door, it ought to have been Mr. Bingley."

This is also the first time in living memory that my dear, good-natured Jane loses her temper and her gentle manners. She glares at our mother and snaps, "For goodness' sake, Mama! Of all the dreadful notions!"

HALF AN HOUR LATER, THE DRAWING ROOM IS THE VERY OPPOSITE OF quiet. Kitty and Lydia have joined us, too. So has Papa, and then Mr. Jones, who comes to say that Mr. Darcy's condition appears stable enough, and that the bleeding was stemmed, and the wound attended.

"Nevertheless, I am much concerned that he has not regained consciousness as yet. I sent word to my wife to bring some draughts that might revive him. And she is an excellent nurse. I daresay she will serve much better than Mr. Collins, for all his eagerness to exert himself on the patient's behalf."

"Is he still in Mr. Darcy's chamber?" Mary asks.

The apothecary sighs. "Aye. He will not be dissuaded. He is adamant that no one is better suited than he to nurse the gentleman back to health. He has vast experience, he claims, for his father suffered in like manner from a severe blow to his head. Regardless, this does not qualify Mr. Collins for the purpose. Apparently, his sire died from that injury. Passed away in his son's arms."

"Not the best recommendation, then," Papa remarks, and I am sorry to say but I cannot help glaring at him. Today I cannot abide his archness.

I am of a mind to say something, beg him to see the seriousness of the matter, when Mrs. Hill enters.

"Lieutenants Denny and Hazelgrove, ma'am," she says to Mama as she bobs a curtsy.

I straighten in my seat and reserve my daggers for the newcomers. For Lieutenant Denny, to be precise, who is the first to walk into the drawing room. He bows and addresses himself to Mama:

"My dear madam, Hazelgrove and I came to offer our assistance at Colonel Forster's behest. The post of regimental surgeon has not been filled as yet, seeing as we are not likely to see any real action in your peaceable environs, but Hazelgrove here knows a thing or two. His maternal uncle is an army surgeon, you see."

Mr. Jones does not look best pleased at the prospect of being supplanted by one whose credentials are nothing more than a family connection to an army surgeon. I agree that this is not much of a recommendation either. Perhaps 'tis Papa's place to speak, not mine. But such considerations rarely stop me.

"Have you apprenticed with your uncle in the treatment of head injuries, Mr. Hazelgrove?" I ask.

"Not as such, ma'am," he mumbles. Mr. Hazelgrove has a dreadful stutter and, not surprisingly, being put on the spot is not helping matters.

I do feel for him in his discomfort, yet I still press him:

"Then why does Colonel Forster deem you—?"

I do not get to finish. Lieutenant Denny intervenes, keen to come to his friend's aid. I might have appreciated his loyalty to Mr. Hazelgrove had I not held him responsible for landing Mr. Wickham in deep water by sharing secrets that were not his to tell.

Over and above my existing resentment, Lieutenant Denny angers me all the more for he says, "The colonel must have thought this was the least he could do under the circumstances. He feels responsible for not smelling a rat in the first place. Naturally, I hastened to assure him that he could not have known. None of us could. Even I, who had my suspicions, only put two and two together when the rogue fled on a better horse than his sorry purse could afford—Mr. Darcy's mount, I would wager—"

'Tis all I can do to not jump to my feet in indignation as I cut him off:

"Enough, sir! You are accusing a gentleman who is not here to defend himself."

"Which is as good a proof of guilt as any. Why should he flee if he is blameless?" Lieutenant Denny counters.

"Perchance because he knew full well he would be blamed, once his *friends* had freely told the whole of Meryton of his longstanding feud with Mr. Darcy?" I retaliate with harsh emphasis on one word in particular.

Papa calls my name, a clear warning in his tone, but I do not turn towards him. Nor do I look at Jane when she reaches out across the narrow space between us to hold my hand and firmly clasp it, as if to caution silence.

If I do keep silent, 'tis not because of her injunction, nor my father's. 'Tis because Lieutenant Denny looks upon me with nothing short of pity as he says quietly and without rancour, "Miss Elizabeth, it was Mr. Wickham himself who spread the tale in the officers' mess with new embellishments at every repetition. He likewise shared it in my hearing with many of those who showed themselves disposed to listen and give him succour—not so much in the polite salons where Mr. Darcy would be welcomed as in the taverns Mr. Wickham so eagerly frequented. I beg your pardon, that is more than you needed to know," he adds, his contrite glance darting from me to my parents in turn, then my sisters, as if to apologise for his lateness in grasping that such disclosures belong in a military camp, not my mother's drawing room.

Colour rises in my cheeks, and I can scarce tell if I blush in shame or anger at the implication that he thinks me as worthy of his compassion as some deceived wench in one of Meryton's disreputable taverns. Even I, with my sheltered upbringing, know that our little town boasts a couple of those—taverns—that is to say, not wenches; the number of wenches must be considerably greater.

"Are you saying that all this time we have been nursing a depraved horse-thief in our bosom?" Mary asks, fired up with righteousness.

My hands are shaking even as Mary's jumbled metaphor moves me towards nervous laughter. Yet I do not laugh. I stare at Mr. Denny who solemnly nods, wholly unaffected by my sister's ludicrous phrasing. He either has a very good ability to keep himself in check or he is not blessed with a sense of humour.

"Goodness me, such tales of poor Mr. Wickham," Mama cries. "Not a horse-thief, surely! Lizzy, did you not say he only borrowed Mr. Darcy's stallion to ride for Mr. Jones and notify him that much sooner?"

I dart my eyes to Mr. Jones, waiting for the vindication. But all he has to offer is a fresh indictment:

"No one came to my house this morning, ma'am, except for Mr. Collins."

I RISE TO MY FEET AND RETREAT TO THE TABLE TO FEIGN INTEREST IN pouring a fresh cup of tea. But my hands are still trembling and dear Jane, who came to join me, softly intervenes.

"Allow me."

I shake my head. "No matter. I do not need it," I own in a very low whisper. "I only wished to walk away."

"Then come," she says, setting the teapot down.

We excuse ourselves and I follow her out of the drawing room, across the corridor, then into the morning room.

"Sit, Lizzy," Jane urges me, and I obey.

She lowers herself onto the same sofa and reaches for my hand. I sigh.

"I did not behave well just now, did I? As unguarded as Lydia, and with as little regard for propriety. I as good as accused Lieutenant Denny to his face."

Jane gives a little sympathetic grimace. "You are distraught. Too much has happened this morning."

"Yes, but—" I push the hair out of my face and whisper, "This is in every way horrible. I cannot believe Mr. Wickham capable of such acts…saying one thing to me and doing another…or purposely inflicting harm on Mr. Darcy…"

"Perhaps it was an accident. It could easily have been. But he *should* have fetched help instead of vanishing and leaving Mr. Darcy to his fate," she says with a frown that is almost severe—not a customary turn of countenance for my kind and all-abiding sister.

"The shock of it…The fear that he would be blamed…He must have lost his head…"

Jane squeezes my hand. "Lizzy dear, are you quite certain you are not in danger of losing yours?"

"What do you mean?"

"'Tis not like you to keep seeking excuses for questionable conduct, nor insist on thinking well of someone at all cost. I thought that was my province," she adds, trying to jest, but I cannot smile. Eventually, she sobers, too. "I should be sorry to think ill of anyone, especially Mr. Wickham, whom you favour, but it would grieve me a great deal more to see you deceived. Or worse still, seeing you deceive yourself with determination."

I make to speak, but she will not let me.

"We do not know what passed between them, either in their boyhood or today. But no man with a clear conscience would leave another to lie injured and unattended. Least of all half-hidden in the undergrowth by the side of a remote country road."

This is the most unforgiving speech I have ever heard my sister utter. It strikes me all the more forcibly because it comes from her.

DEAREST JANE BIDS ME STAY WHEN SHE RETURNS TO THE DRAWING ROOM to do her duty as the eldest daughter of the house. I remain seated for a while to make the most of the quiet, even though there is no peace to be had. I seek to order my thoughts, but this is soon shown to be a thankless task. In the end, I give up and make my way back to the drawing room.

The military gentlemen are no longer here.

"Has Mr. Hazelgrove gone up?" I ask.

"No," says Mr. Jones. "I thanked him all the same, but I would rather he did not try his hand on my patient."

The sentiment is commendable, but I still long to ask whether Mr. Jones should not be with his patient rather than sitting here with his refreshments. However, I say nothing of the sort. I have already been outspoken one time too many today. I take a seat and look for some employment in the workbasket.

I have barely been sitting thus for ten minutes when Lydia snickers from her chair—the closest to the window:

"La! I never thought they could walk so fast."

With such encouragement, Kitty is prompt in leaping from her seat to see what has amused Lydia so. I should know better than to follow their example, but my gaze is involuntarily drawn towards the window, too, in time to see that my youngest sister is right: never before had I seen Miss Bingley and Mrs. Hurst move with such celerity.

In a matter of seconds, they are shown into the drawing room.

"How is he?" Miss Bingley blurts out in lieu of a greeting.

Vaguely more civil—or less dependent on Mr. Darcy for her felicity—Mrs. Hurst bids us good morning before inquiring into the gentleman's condition. For once, Mama holds her peace and allows Mr. Jones to have his say. He does so but receives little by way of thanks from Miss Bingley who announces:

"I sent a rider after my brother to charge him with fetching Mr. Darcy's physician with the utmost haste. He must receive the best care possible. And I have come to take him to Netherfield."

"Did you bring a cart, ma'am?" Papa asks with an air of perfect civility, and this time I find his penchant for sport less aggravating, particularly when Miss Bingley sneers:

"Of course not. Why would I? Do you imagine, sir, that I am the sort who travels in a cart?"

"A pity, then," Papa replies, "for Mr. Darcy can only be moved in such a vehicle. He must be kept supine, Mr. Jones tells me, or his condition might worsen."

"Nonsense," Miss Bingley splutters, but she looks less sure of herself. Little store as she sets by Mr. Jones's opinion, she is reluctant to gainsay him on medical matters. She heaves a dramatic sigh. "Oh, well. Then a cart must be found—"

"I still would advise against moving him," the surgeon-apothecary interjects. "He has been made comfortable and is now kept warm. Taking him over a distance of three miles at the speed of a cart will do him no favours."

"I will not countenance leaving him here, of all places," Miss Bingley venomously declares but, unperturbed, Mr. Jones shrugs.

"I fear you must learn to brook it, ma'am, if you have a care for his safety."

Miss Bingley makes to speak, but before she can say a word, the door is flung open and Mr. Collins bursts into the room.

"Mr. Jones, you must come at once. He is worse! Far worse than we expected."

Miss Bingley's hand flies to her chest. I would have called the gesture theatrical, but her distress looks genuine.

"What happened? Speak, man!" she orders Mr. Collins.

But he is too affected to even acknowledge her with a bow. His pleading eyes rest on Mr. Jones as he stammers, "The Lord have mercy, but I fear his mind is affected. I was tending to him, you know, running a wet cloth over his brow, when he seemed to awaken and spoke to me—"

"A good sign," Mr. Jones intervenes, but Mr. Collins frantically shakes his head.

"Nay, sir, not at all! For his gaze was unfocused and he spoke naught but gibberish. Except at first, when he thanked me for my kindness and said he was grateful for my assistance. But then he beseeched me to promise to stay away from Mr. Wickham. 'He is no good... not safe...' he said. 'You should have believed me.' I most fervently assured him I believed him wholeheartedly, of course. How could I not believe that man to be a scoundrel and a villain, seeing as he has injured Lady Catherine's nephew? For a moment, I hoped that my earnest expressions did their office, for Mr. Darcy quietened a little and smiled. But then… Oh, sir, do come up and assist him, for he is not himself!" Mr. Collins entreats and his voice breaks into a squeak. "He said… He said I was the most beautiful creature he had ever beheld!"

Incorrigible, Papa chortles, but I ignore him as my head spins with the implications. No, Mr. Darcy was clearly not himself if he did not realise that he spoke to Mr. Collins. The astounding declaration that had so unsettled my cousin might have led me to believe that Mr. Darcy had been aware of Jane watching over him while he lay injured by the side of the road and agreed with Mr. Bingley as regards my sister's beauty. But the rest of Mr. Collins's report showed that the disjointed speech was not meant for my sister's ears any more than for his. It was not Jane whom Mr. Darcy had warned against Mr. Wickham and who ought to have heeded the words of caution in the first place.

I am still reeling from the shock and scarce comprehend what I have just heard: Mr. Darcy's first thought upon regaining a semblance of consciousness was to repeat that warning and that I was the most beautiful creature he had ever beheld!

I am not given the opportunity to gather my wits. When Mr. Jones scrambles to his feet to rush to his patient, Miss Bingley hastens to the door ahead of him.

"Take me to Mr. Darcy," she orders my cousin. "I must see him at once and nurse him back to health!"

"Preposterous," Mr. Collins splutters. "An unmarried young woman in Mr. Darcy's chamber? Lady Catherine de Bourgh would never permit something so unseemly. She would rightfully say that no young woman except her esteemed daughter should be allowed at Mr. Darcy's bedside. In Her Ladyship's absence, and Miss de Bourgh's, *I* should be the one to tend him as Lady Catherine's parson and the one most closely connected to the family."

"That is ludicrous," Miss Bingley scoffs with a dismissive gesture. "He needs a woman's gentle care."

"Pray do not imply that I cannot be gentle," Mr. Collins heatedly counters, to Papa's growing amusement. "And as I said, a young unmarried woman—"

"What of me?" Mrs. Hurst intervenes. "I am a married woman and one of Mr. Darcy's closest friends. I will attend him in my sister's stead," she declares, but Mr. Collins will not have it.

"Madam, I must protest—!"

"And so must I," Mr. Jones cuts in, his tone severe. "There is too much confusion here, and far too many eager nurses. As of this moment, *no one* is allowed at Mr. Darcy's bedside except myself, a maid of my choosing, and my wife, when she arrives."

"What of Mr. Darcy's highly respected and exceedingly skilled physician?" Miss Bingley sneers. "Will you presume to bar him from Mr. Darcy's presence, too?"

"No, madam, I will not," Mr. Jones evenly replies. "But until such time as he reaches Longbourn, I shall brook no further interference!"

THE NEXT HOURS TURN OUT TO BE INSUPPORTABLE. I OCCASIONALLY make my escape from the drawing room, but I need a great deal more than a few snatched minutes to gather my thoughts.

Recollections intrude, a jumbled assortment. Was I supposed to read attraction in Mr. Darcy's long stares and in all our perplexing interactions? They never had the clear markings of attraction—yet what other explanation is there for the recent sequence of events?

I shake my head as niggling thoughts buzz within like a swarm of unsettled bees. And if there was attraction—what of it? He would never step out of his sphere and offer for me. But... if he does, what should my answer be?

What, indeed? I dislike him, do I not? Am I so shallow as to change my mind simply because he thinks me beautiful? I grimace. I *was* sufficiently shallow to trust Mr. Wickham implicitly because he flattered me, and Mr. Darcy did not. I, who had always prided myself on my good judgement, had shown no common sense at all! I believed the flatterer and shunned the other. How is that for discernment, Elizabeth Bennet?

Had I been in love with Mr. Wickham, I could not have been more wretchedly blind. But vanity, not love, had been my folly. Pleased with his overt preference, I closed my mind to reason and to all manner of salient points. Such as the fact that I knew nothing of him except what he had told me himself. Or the impropriety—glaringly obvious now—of his disclosures after only one day's acquaintance. Or the other glaringly obvious matter: the enduring friendship between Mr. Bingley and Mr. Darcy. It surely meant something that Mr. Bingley, who was kindness and probity personified, should know Mr. Darcy for upwards of a decade and still regard him as his closest friend. If Mr. Darcy were quite so unprincipled as Mr. Wickham had painted him, his friendship with Mr. Bingley would have been incomprehensible.

Thoughts of Mr. Bingley awake me to my duty. I should not leave Jane to host his sisters without assistance. She is unlikely to get much help in that regard from Mama, Lydia, or Kitty.

I return to the drawing room to discover that playing host to Miss Bingley and Mrs. Hurst is as taxing as I expected. There is no sign of them returning to Netherfield, despite the promise to notify them of any developments.

So far, there are none. Mrs. Jones had arrived with the draughts that her husband had requested, but he comes down after a while to tell us they failed to have the desired effect. Mr. Darcy is still slipping in and out of consciousness and alternates between stupor and agitation.

I am not surprised that Miss Bingley is alarmed by this report. But if she continues to pace up and down the room as she vocally disparages Mr. Jones's skill, I fear that, much like Mama, I shall begin to beg compassion for my poor nerves.

"MR. BINGLEY AND HIS PARTY, MA'AM," MRS. HILL ANNOUNCES AT LONG last.

The four, whom I have already espied through the window, are shown into the overcrowded drawing room. One of them must be the medical man—his manner and the telltale bag he carries are sufficient indications. The other gentleman seems to be about Mr. Darcy's age and has the same bearing. He is escorting a fashionably dressed young lady. Very young. She cannot be much older than sixteen. Her strong resemblance to Mr. Darcy leaves me in no doubt of her identity.

I am proven right when Mr. Bingley introduces the newcomers. She *is* Mr. Darcy's sister. The tall gentleman is their cousin, a Colonel Fitzwilliam. The fourth is indeed the physician, and he promptly requests permission to go and attend his patient.

Likewise, as soon as she has greeted us, Miss Darcy wishes to see her brother.

"Goodness knows if you will be allowed into his chamber, my dear Georgiana," Miss Bingley says with the air of a martyr. "That self-appointed Cerberus, the apothecary, forbade me from attending your brother."

I see something akin to relief fleetingly cross Miss Darcy's features. Despite what Mr. Wickham had to say of her, I am disposed to like her already.

I am being facetious, of course. I am such a hypocrite. I inwardly grumble about Papa's archness, but I am just as bad. Nonetheless, in short order, I discover there is nothing unlikeable about Miss Darcy. Mr. Wickham's description of her was a shocking falsehood. He said she was very, very proud and far from amiable. Yet there is not a shade of hauteur in her. She is not proud. She is excessively timid. And also deeply attached to her brother. And extremely anxious about his injuries.

Word is sent up and the maid comes back to let Miss Darcy know that, naturally, the physician and Mr. Jones have no objections to her sitting with Mr. Darcy. She goes up and remains with him for a long time.

Eventually, the physician escorts her back to the drawing room. 'Tis far less crowded now. Thank goodness, Mr. Bingley had prevailed upon his sisters to return to Netherfield, once he had assured himself that his friend was in no imminent danger.

"But Charles, we cannot leave without him!" Miss Bingley had predictably whined.

"Regrettably, we must. We cannot impose upon Mrs. Bennet's kindness, Caroline, you must see that. My man will stay behind to carry frequent reports, and I will return first thing in the morning," he said with a steady look at Jane.

Despite Mrs. Hurst's and Miss Bingley's protestation, he carried the day. His newfound air of authority is as remarkable as it is pleasing.

The colonel, Mr. Darcy's cousin, also left with them. Mr. Bingley offered to take him as far as Meryton in his carriage, for Colonel Fitzwilliam wished to see Colonel Forster and find out what progress was made in apprehending Mr. Wickham.

When Miss Darcy had briefly come down to see him off, he had embraced her and fiercely declared, "He will not get away with it, Georgy. You have my word. Not this time!"

Not this time? What else had Mr. Wickham got away with in the past? I cannot help but wonder.

Miss Darcy seemed reassured by her cousin's manner. If I were Mr. Wickham, I should be terrified.

Yet, as Mr. Darcy's physician guides Miss Darcy to her seat, she looks a great deal less reassured.

"Will you come down to let me know if there is any change?" she pleads.

"Of course, you may depend upon it. But I expect none. He is sleeping now. I venture to hope he will feel better when he awakens."

"God willing," Miss Darcy fervently whispers.

"Yes. But you should have a care for yourself as well. A little rest perhaps, or a walk in the fresh air?"

"A very good notion," I say and rise to my feet, while Miss Darcy firmly declares that she could not possibly rest. But the suggestion of a walk seems welcome.

We walk out together and head towards the little wilderness on the side of our garden. 'Tis not a very big place, but we go along the same paths again and again. In silence. I will not press her to make small talk. She clearly does not need that. I leave her to her thoughts, and I attend to mine. Not that I have any success in ordering them. They are still jumbled when Miss Darcy finally speaks:

"I thank you. You are unfailingly kind and considerate. Just as my brother said you were," she says—a fresh surprise.

"He did?"

"Oh, yes. I dearly wished to meet you. He never gives glowing praise to the ladies of his acquaintance in his letters."

I stare. *Glowing praise? He wrote to his sister about me?*

The second question passes my lips without my notice.

"Repeatedly," she replies with a wistful smile which turns into a pain-filled grimace. "I only wish we met in happier circumstances," she whispers and, to my dismay, bursts into tears.

I am too affected to keep a civil distance. Instead, I reach out and put my arms around her. I hope she will be comforted rather than offended.

She does not recoil but returns my embrace. I am not as tall as she, yet she somehow nestles against me, her head on my shoulder. She clings to me as she weeps pitifully with loud, racking sobs.

"All will be well," I whisper. "He *will* get well." Platitudes are all I have to offer, just like Papa when he sought to comfort me with the very same words. "All will be well," I repeat although, much like Papa, I cannot vouch for that. But I pray I am right as Miss Darcy is still weeping into my shoulder.

And then she whispers brokenly, "My fault. This is all my fault. Oh, why did he have to confront Mr. Wickham for my sake? He promised he would not. He promised!"

Her fault? Why should she say that? I know not, but I do know she is wrong. I sigh. I must tell her she should not reproach herself. I must own the truth, even if she will hate me for it.

"It is not your fault, Miss Darcy. 'Tis mine. I am to blame for their confrontation. Your brother sought to warn me against Mr. Wickham, and I foolishly refused to pay heed. He came to Longbourn this morning to share his concern with Papa, since I would not listen. So, you see, *I* am to blame. I hope you can forgive me. I pray he will recover and that he will grant his forgiveness, too." I sigh and force myself to continue. "You say he wrote of me with glowing praise. I cannot imagine why. I do not deserve it. I am sickened by my folly, to trust a man only because he is plausible and charming."

"You must not be so severe upon yourself," Miss Darcy whispers. She has stopped sobbing to listen to my confession, but tears are still running down her face when she pulls away from my embrace to look at me. "This...what you told me...it explains a great many things that have puzzled me of late. Not least his extended stay at Netherfield, although he said he would only be away from Town for a se'nnight." She draws a deep breath. "He *would* have persuaded you in a se'nnight that Mr. Wickham is a reprobate—persuaded you in a matter of minutes—had he shared everything he knows. But he would not. He is too honourable and too attached to me to reveal that I, too, was taken in by Mr. Wickham's appearance of goodness. My brother would never disclose the true reason for the bad blood between them, but I think *you* should know it. I can only hope you will not despise me when you do."

Haltingly, and with vast difficulty, she begins to speak.

By the time she is quite finished, and I learn the villainous manner in which Mr. Wickham had abused the trust of Mr. Darcy's father and tried to deceive his benefactor's daughter into consenting to an elopement so that he could lay hands on her dowry, I am beside myself with anger. I hope Mr. Wickham is apprehended and made to pay for all the anguish he had caused. 'Tis a vast pity that we live in a more civilised age than our ancestors. Hanging is too merciful; he deserves to be drawn and quartered.

DINNER IS ANNOUNCED—QUITE LATE, GIVEN THE CIRCUMSTANCES—AND we gather round the table, although most of us lack the appetite. Only Mama and the younger girls do full justice to the fare.

We return to the drawing room for more tea—I do believe that today I have ingested a gallon—and a short while later we espy a very large and imposing carriage advancing at a stately pace along the drive.

"Heaven help us, who is coming now?" Mama grumbles, setting her cup down. "I am as fond of company as anybody, but this is beyond the pale. Are we to have no peace at all today?"

"I fear not," Miss Darcy whispers with something like a wince.

Yet the sight of the approaching carriage has a very different effect on Mr. Collins. He is verily glowing as he leaps to his feet.

"The greatest honour is to be bestowed upon this house. This is the equipage of Lady Catherine de Bourgh," he informs us and excitably darts out of the drawing room.

"I should not care if she is the Queen of Sheba," Mama scoffs. "Can she not lodge in Meryton at the Red Lion? Enough is enough. This is a gentleman's house, not a busy hostelry."

LADY CATHERINE DE BOURGH MAKES HER GRAND ENTRANCE INTO OUR home, escorted by Mr. Collins who bows so low that I fear he might break in half, whereupon I can see I have been uncannily accurate in my guess: she does look like an older version of Mr. Darcy in a bonnet. But while his countenance is handsome, hers is haughty and hard.

She barely deigns to acknowledge us but demands that Mr. Collins take her to her nephew. Miss Darcy has something to say in that regard. With astounding firmness for one so diffident, she requests that her brother is left undisturbed. Seemingly, when the peace of a loved one is at stake, even a lamb can become a lion.

Sadly, Miss Darcy is not fierce enough, and thus no match for Lady Catherine. Her Ladyship royally proceeds to climb the stairs in search of her nephew.

As it turns out, there is one thing I should say in her favour: she achieves what the reviving draughts had not. She brings Mr. Darcy from his stupor or his sleep or whatever it was. No one could fail to be jolted into alertness when Her Ladyship is present.

I am not party to their conversation, seeing as it takes place in a gentleman's sick-chamber. But in less than a half-hour, I can hear Lady Catherine returning downstairs in far worse humour than when she had climbed up. I doubt she is aiming to come into the drawing room and exchange pleasantries with us even before I hear her fulminating at Mr. Collins:

"And *that* is the thanks I get for quitting my brother's townhouse as soon as I received your express and hastening thither to come to his aid! He refuses to honour his mother's dearest wish and mine. Point-blank refuses to oblige me!"

"It must be the head injury, Your Ladyship," my cousin stammers. "He has not been himself ever since he awakened, I can vouch for—"

"No, Mr. Collins, I will not be satisfied with paltry excuses. Not himself indeed! I say he is very much what he has always been, an obstinate, headstrong boy, and I wash my hands of him. Anne has other cousins. Let him do as he chooses. I will not be placated any more than I will suffer to be contradicted. I have always been celebrated for my frankness, and he might as well know that he has gone too far this time. I am most seriously displeased!" Her Ladyship declares as she storms out.

I wonder if I will ever learn what all this is about. Not that I give it much thought. 'Tis Lady Catherine's affair and perhaps Mr. Darcy's, but most certainly not mine.

THE HOUSE GROWS QUIET ONCE LADY CATHERINE IS GONE. MISS DARCY comes down eventually to convey her brother's gratitude for our hospitality and assistance, as well as his apologies for the disruption.

"He most particularly wished to come down and thank you himself, but I persuaded him that there is always tomorrow, and he would be better advised to return to his rest."

We all follow his example in a while. Mary cedes her chamber to Miss Darcy. Mr. Collins has to countenance making do with the imperfect guest chamber and also with sharing quarters with the physician. Our cousin is not best pleased, but short of relocating to the Red Lion, he has no other option. Longbourn is a small house after all, and Mama is in the right: it *has* begun to resemble a busy hostelry.

"Let us hope that no one else appears on our doorstep tonight," Mama mutters as we retire to our chambers.

She is in luck and her hope is fulfilled. The night passes peacefully, and no one comes knocking upon our door. At least not until the morning, at an unconscionably early hour.

"HE IS COME! I TELL YOU, HE IS COME! GRACIOUS, JANE, AND YOU NOT even out of bed," Mama cries as she bursts into the room.

For the briefest moment, before I am fully awake, I wonder what she can be about. I yawn and stretch, but I am not allowed to luxuriate under the counterpane. Mama pulls it aside and tugs at Jane's arm.

"Wake up, dear. Come now, do wake up! Make haste and dress. Did you not hear me? He is come."

"Who is come?" Jane mumbles sleepily.

"Mr. Bingley, of course. Who else? I should be very cross with him for turning up at such an ungodly hour, but I shall not fault his keenness. 'Tis a good sign. So is the look on his face. I had a peek at him when Hill showed him in and mark my words, that look spoke of a proposal. Come, child, let us not keep him waiting. I will send Sarah to help you dress. Make haste!"

I receive no such injunctions, but I do not dally either. Jane might need me as a complacent chaperone. But that post is filled by the time I come down. Kitty was more advanced than me, so Mama brooked no delays and sent *her* to accompany Mr. Bingley and Jane on their walk.

Mama cannot tell me where they went, but they must be further afield, because I do not come across them when I walk out into the garden. Instead, I find Miss Darcy—and with her—her brother!

"Oh! Good morning," I greet them, pleasantly surprised. "I am happy to find you are recovered, sir. But should you be up and about? I see your head is still bandaged."

He chuckles. "Vanity, Miss Bennet. Mere vanity."

I fail to grasp his meaning, and likewise the cause of his good humour.

"Vanity, sir?"

"Indeed. The gauze covers the spot Mr. Jones had to shave to do his stitching."

I wince at the recollection of the freely bleeding wound that had required stitches, but before I can ask about it, he airily adds, "I trust the hair will grow back before a certain desirable event takes place."

"Which event might that be?"

"It did not escape my notice that my friend came to call upon your sister at a suspiciously early hour. I should not wonder if he came to ask a most particular question," he says, offering me his free arm.

I take it and, as the three of us fall into step together, I cannot help owning, "You puzzle me exceedingly, Mr. Darcy."

"Do I? How so?"

"I thought you would find that event less than desirable."

"You judge me rightly. I did, at one time. It was presumptuous of me and, moreover, misguided. But I have learned a number of valuable lessons of late."

"Such as?"

"That life is short and offers few certainties, if any, and only fools would squander its best gifts or cavil when Lady Fortune has the goodness to smile upon them."

"You speak in riddles, sir."

"My apologies. I know. I shall endeavour to speak more plainly, by and by."

"And so should I," I say, my air growing solemn, as befits the apology I have to make. I feel uncomfortable in the extreme, but it must be done, and there is no time like the present. "I must tell you how deeply I regret not heeding your advice regarding Mr. Wickham. I am distraught to—"

"Pray, do not make yourself uneasy over that. 'Tis too fine a morning to waste it speaking of Mr. Wickham."

"You are very forbearing, considering his infamy." Then, lest Miss Darcy think I spoke out of turn and hinted at his sins against her, I add swiftly, "He attacked you and left you, without any attempt to lend assistance."

"The vanishing act is very much in character," Mr. Darcy nonchalantly replies. "As for the attack, in all fairness, I threw the first punch. It just so happened that, once he reciprocated, the stone I hit finished his work rather more promptly than either of us would have chosen."

"I see. Am I to take it that you are a proponent of fisticuffs?"

"Not since my boyhood. Still, this episode in particular was long overdue. And highly invigorating."

"So is the country air, sir, and a vast deal more healthful."

Mr. Darcy chortles. "True, I will give you that."

His sister squeezes his arm and beams at me. "I have grown quite partial to the air of Hertfordshire. A most refreshing country. Can we stay for a while longer, brother, if Mr. Bingley will have us?"

"Oh, I do not doubt he will. To my good fortune, he is an exceedingly obliging sort. I intend to avail myself of his welcome and stay for as long as it takes."

Miss Darcy does not ask "For as long as *what* takes?" but I very nearly do. And then I catch myself and hold my peace. I believe I know the answer. A blush creeps into my cheeks and I smile.

JOANA STARNES lives in the south of England with her family. Over the years, she has swapped several hats—physician, lecturer, clinical data analyst—but feels most comfortable in a bonnet. She has been living in Georgian England for decades in her imagination and plans to continue in that vein till she lays hands on a time machine. She is the author of nine Austen-inspired novels: *From This Day Forward —The Darcys of Pemberley, The Subsequent Proposal, The Second Chance, The Falmouth Connection, The Unthinkable Triangle, Miss Darcy's Companion, Mr. Bennet's Dutiful Daughter, The Darcy Legacy,* and *The Journey Home to Pemberley,* and one of the contributing authors to *The Darcy Monologues, Dangerous to Know: Jane Austen's Rakes & Gentleman Rogues, Rational Creatures,* and *Yuletide: A Jane Austen-inspired Collections of Stories.*

Elizabeth: Obstinate Headstrong Girl

Resistive
Currents

Karen M Cox

"And your defect is a propensity to hate everybody."
"And yours," he replied with a smile, "is willfully to misunderstand
them." —Chapter XI

RESISTIVE CURRENTS
Karen M Cox

AUGUST 1980

*A*lmighty God, into your hands we commend your daughter, Elizabeth, in sure and certain hope of resurrection to eternal life through Jesus Christ our Lord."

Beth Bennet peeked out from under lowered eyes she was pretending to keep shut, discreetly watching her Grandma Alice. Nestled between Beth's parents, poor Grandma clutched Beth's dad's arm for support. Under a tent that shunted away the heat of the midday Colorado sun, stood the gathering of close friends and family of Elizabeth Alton Gardiner, aged ninety-five, whose life had ended four days previous while she sat in her chair watching *The Guiding Light*. Grandma Alice had come in from the kitchen with Great-Nana's afternoon tea (she always took it with a shot of whiskey) and found her mother slumped over in her chair, while Fitzy, their fat little Chihuahua, paced back and forth, barking like mad.

Funerals for people of advanced age had a different vibe than those for younger people, Beth decided. She had only been to one other funeral, when her friend's father passed away suddenly in their junior year of high school. The man's family and friends had been in a terrible state of shock and grief, and agony seeped out of the funeral home curtains and into the stale air of the room where the service was held.

However, Great-Nana's send-off ended in the bright sunshine of a weekday afternoon and had a cycle-of-life aura, an undercurrent of gentle acceptance. Earlier, children's voices were heard around the perimeters of the funeral home during visitation, and now here at the graveside, the young ones' voices traveled on the air as they played under the trees and stooped to pick up dandelions. People gave each other hugs and shook hands as they relayed their fond memories of Miss Lizzy, as they all called her.

Very different, indeed.

"In the name of the Father, and the Son, and the Holy Spirit, amen."

"Amen," Beth murmured, along with the others gathered around the casket.

She took a deep breath, pulling herself up to her full height, a respectable five foot eight. A trickle of sweat ran down her back, making her question her decision to wear a long-sleeved navy dress, even as she congratulated herself on her choice of comfortable, low-heeled pumps. Friends and family filed by, expressing some last words of sympathy before dispersing to the cars lined along the cemetery drive. Slowly, the family made their way toward the car, speaking to people as they went.

A matched pair standing with their arms crossed, Beth and her father simultaneously leaned against his harvest-gold LTD, waiting for Grandma Alice to finish speaking with her friend Myrna.

A man, maybe in his late forties, approached and shook Mr. Bennet's hand. "Sad day."

"Yes. Grandmother led a long and happy life, but we will certainly miss her, won't we?" said her father.

"We will."

Tom Bennet paused and placed a hand at Beth's elbow. "Do you remember my daughter?"

"Yes, but I haven't seen her recently. Probably not since she was a little girl."

"Beth, this is my cousin Bob Carter."

Beth held out her hand. "Nice to see you."

Tom beamed with pride. "Beth is studying engineering at Fordyce

University." He turned to her. "Bob got his degree back in...when was it, Bob?"

Bob struggled to school his expression and cover his surprise. "Uh...'62. University of Colorado."

Tom winked at his daughter.

Bob kept his eyes on Beth, like she was a human anomaly, or a train wreck he couldn't turn away from. "Wow, engineering school is quite an undertaking. Fordyce has a good reputation too. Will this be your first year, Beth?"

"Third, actually. I'll be heading back next week."

"Oh," he said, more surprise coloring his voice. "Engineering's tough," he repeated.

"That's what they tell me."

"Well, I guess you really must mean it—you're through all the pre-rec courses now."

"Soldiering onward." She smiled sweetly.

"I had a lady classmate in civil engineering. Sometimes the ladies went into chem-E. How about you? What's your area of concentration?"

"I'm electrical, actually."

"Electrical engineering?"

"Yes, with the advance of computers, lasers, and robotics, it's an up and coming field. I like to learn new things."

"Electrical work can be kind of dangerous sometimes, can't it?"

"Yeah, gotta make sure not to cross those wires the wrong way." She paused and purposefully pitched her voice higher and sweeter. "Or get my fancy scarves caught in the machinery. I can't wear my dangly gold earrings in the lab either. It's a sacrifice sometimes."

Bob laughed a bit nervously. Mr. Bennet smirked at his cousin's discomfort.

"If you'll excuse me? I think Grandma Alice needs a hand." As she left the men in her wake, Beth was sure she heard Mr. Class of '62 call her "a spunky little gal" while her father laughed. She rolled her eyes and made her way to her grandmother's side.

Beth linked arms with Grandma Alice, and they began a slow

progression to the car. Mr. Bennet opened the door and helped settle his mother in the passenger seat, across from his wife; then he slid in the back behind his mother and next to Beth.

"Dad," she whispered. "Shame on you. You enjoyed that."

"I'm sure I don't know what you mean," he answered, all innocence.

"That bit with your cousin. It's like you're baiting someone and bragging at the same time."

He chuckled. "Kills two birds with one stone—confronts the male chauvinism and lets him know how smart my daughter is—all at once."

She shook her head, amused in spite of the ambivalence she felt at being the spark for her father's mischievous verbal pranks.

He patted her hand. "For what do we live but to be sport for our neighbors and laugh at them in our turn?"

"Whatever you say, Daddy."

"Now, don't be prissy about me teasing Bob. You know I'm proud of you."

"I do know it." He *was* proud, but she wondered if she would spend her college years and beyond merely carrying out her father's penchant for challenging the status quo. Being the instrument of his conversational antics could get pretty tiresome.

She just wanted to do her own thing.

ALICE SAT IN THE RECLINER AT THE BENNET'S HOUSE, A CUP OF TEA—sans whiskey—in her lap, staring into space.

"You doin' okay, Grandma?" Beth asked.

"Yes, dear. I'm all right. Awful tired though."

"Are you staying here tonight?"

"No, I'm going back home. I don't want to be a burden on your mother."

Beth suppressed a laugh. That was Grandma Alice code for "I want to limit my time with your mother."

"You sure you want to stay at your house by yourself?"

"Oh yes. I'll be fine, just fine. Mama was ninety-five—it's not like we didn't expect this, and I've prepared myself for it. I'll miss her dreadfully, though. She was one tough woman, your Great-Nana. Funny, too."

"I remember she always said, 'I dearly love to laugh.'"

"And laugh she did, even when life was uncertain. Times were hard when she came out here from back East."

Beth settled on the sofa and leaned her head on Grandma Alice's shoulder, ready to hear this Great-Nana story for the umpteenth time. Beth took Alice's papery, spotted hand in her own young-looking one.

"Mama's own parents were gone, died of diphtheria while she was away at school. No brothers or sisters. She was all alone in the world and looking for adventure, so she answered a newspaper advertisement for a school teacher up at Apple Creek, way back in 1906."

"That was brave to travel to Denver all by herself. It must have been lonely too."

"I think it was easier for her after that first winter."

"After she met Great-Grandpa Gardiner?"

"My mama always told me the loneliness was the hardest part that first year. Harder than the wood stove cooking. Harder than making her own fire every morning. Harder than the two feet of snow. You know, there was a mighty blizzard that October after she moved here."

"I remember."

"Once she and my father found each other, though, they helped each other along. She told me, 'Everything was easier with two, especially back then.'"

"I wish I'd met him," Beth said. "All your stories make him seem larger than life."

"He was a wonderful man, a good husband and father. He ended up being sheriff for thirty years. He was a rancher too, and, before that, a cattle wrangler. What you might call a *man's man*."

Beth wrinkled her nose. "My university is full of *men's men*. If Great-Grandpa was like them, maybe I wouldn't have cared for him so much after all."

"Well, I can't tell you what young men are like today, but I do know Lizzy Alton wasn't too fond of Stephen Gardiner at first."

"I happen to think I can tell a lot about a person the first time I meet him, if I pay attention."

"Sometimes, I suppose you can. But it depends on the situation too. You need to give people some grace. That's what Mama always told me, and my lifetime of experience bears it out."

"You are too nice, Grandma."

"It pays to judge slowly, sweet girl. You mark my words."

Out of respect, Beth didn't disagree, but in her soul—in her very being—she *knew* Beth Bennet's first impressions were damn near infallible.

FORDYCE UNIVERSITY, NEBRASKA
SEPTEMBER 1980

TOP PERKS WAS, BY FAR, THE BEST COFFEE SHOP IN LINCOLN. IT WAS A couple blocks off campus, hidden in plain sight, an old red brick building with a few ironwork tables on the sidewalk during the warmer months. Beth discovered it sophomore year, after a particularly bad experience with burnt student center coffee. Commiserating with a classmate, she learned what apparently all the upperclassmen knew—Top Perks was the go-to place for a caffeine fix. It was worth it to splurge, not only on the coffee, but on their famous cinnamon rolls with cream cheese icing.

She chose a table outside so she could alternate people-watching with reading her current spy novel. About halfway through her cinnamon roll, she picked up her coffee to take a sip and stopped cold, holding her cup in mid-air.

He strode down the street, like a man on a mission, pausing only to look up at the signs on the buildings. He was tall, but not too tall, just the right height to be appealing. He was lean, but not skinny, like so many of the guys who hadn't quite left the over-grown puppy stage of late adolescence with their annoying exuberance and disproportionately large feet and hands. His shoulders were broad like a swimmer's, and his hair was a wavy, rich brown that almost brushed his collar.

He caught her staring, which was mortifying, but still, it took her a full five seconds after he smiled in acknowledgment to remember herself. Her mug clattered on the iron table, and she snatched up her book and opened it to…well…somewhere in the middle. She surreptitiously watched him slow his steps as he approached the coffee shop.

He gestured toward her table. "Ah, is that any good?"

A baritone voice poured over her like warm honey, with a twang that added just a spicy, exotic hint of "other." What *was* that delicious accent? Now that he was close enough, she could see his eyes were almost the same dark, rich brown as his hair, and his lower lip had settled into a pout that gave off an aura of Byronic mystery.

The jolt in her veins felt exactly like she had just touched a hot wire.

"Pardon?" she said, lamely. "Oh. Oh, this?" She held up the book. "It's okay. I mean, the main character is a little unbelievable, and I'd like more description of all the exotic locales, but it's entertaining, I guess." She shifted in her chair. "It's okay."

"That's good to know, but I was talking about the sweet roll."

Beth laughed. How could she not? Her reaction was a stereotypical farce, straight out of a bad sitcom. She collected herself and grinned at him.

"They are amazing. You really should try one. The coffee's good, too."

He hitched his backpack more firmly on his shoulder. "Guess I'll have to give it a try. Thanks for the recommendation."

As he walked toward the door, she gave in to the urge to watch him go. He looked just as good retreating as he did on the approach, she decided. Hoping he might come back outside, she lingered over her coffee, but Hot Mystery Student never returned. Under the guise of getting a refill, she went back inside, scanning the room with feigned nonchalance. He sat in the corner by the window, an empty plate in front of him. Frowning in concentration, he reached in his bag and pulled out a pair of glasses, put them on, and Beth nearly sighed. Some people might think sexy nerd was an oxymoron, but here was the living proof that those two ideas were absolutely compatible. He took a sip of coffee and continued writing in a spiral-bound notebook. Was he a journalism major? An historian? A poet?

He glanced up, settled his eyes on her, and lifted his cup in salute.

She saluted back and stepped up to the counter to get the unwanted refill. Part of her wanted to go over, start a conversation, but he had returned to his work. Feeling atypically shy, she decided to let the moment be.

The doorbell chimed as she left the coffee shop, a giddy smile on her face.

BETH STEPPED ONTO THE MEZZANINE THAT OVERLOOKED THE COMPUTER lab. Work stations spread out before her like bees in a human hive, lining the walls of the vast room. Because it was early evening, almost every terminal was occupied. Standing above them gave her the best vantage point for finding an open station, but it also heightened the attention she garnered for being the incongruity in the room, also known as "girl engineer."

Beth should have been used to the surprised looks by this point. She was starting her third year, and she wasn't the only female student in the program. Her own classmates had grown accustomed to her, most even liked her, but the incoming freshmen and new grad students always did a double take. Somehow, the amazement that she could be a woman and still want to work with electronics never seemed to fade.

She couldn't help it; all things electrical and technical were in her soul. Her father had taken her to see the mainframe at his university in Denver when she was about fourteen. It was a huge monstrosity that took up an entire room.

"This is just the beginning," Dr. Singh, her father's friend in the budding computer science department had told her. "The better the technology gets, the more computers will take over every mundane chore that humans do now, freeing up people to do more important and creative things. Computers will make everyone's lives easier. That's how they will change the world."

Beth was fascinated by the whir of the machinery, whispering its promises of speed and efficiency, and the blinking lights, winking at her in deceptively random patterns. The strange, cryptic language of math and science that Dr. Singh had scrawled all over his blackboard (derivatives, circuits, and equations that looked like paragraphs) lured Beth like a siren's song. She knew she'd found her niche.

Now if she could only get everyone else to believe it too.

The only other woman in the computer lab drew Beth's attention, and she lifted her hand in greeting. Her friend Charlotte waved back and indicated the empty terminal next to her.

Beth swung her backpack on her shoulder and descended the stairs into the pit, ignoring the swiveled heads and eyes following her through the room.

"Hey, how are you?" she asked, giving Charlotte a quick hug.

"Good. How was your summer with the family?"

"It was okay. My great-grandma died while I was home."

"Oh, gosh, Beth. I'm sorry."

"It's fine. I mean, she was in her nineties."

"Still…"

"Yeah, my grandma lived with her, so she'll really miss her a lot." Beth set her backpack on the floor beside an empty chair and sat down. "Have you started the homework for circuits yet?"

"Just now." Charlotte nodded her head toward her screen. "Have you been to the electronics lab?"

"No. I had to sign up for a Wednesday section, so my first lab is tomorrow. Why?"

"Let me know what you think about the T.A."

"What's wrong with him?"

"Let's just say he seems to be following in Dr. De Bourgh's footsteps."

"Wonderful."

Dr. De Bourgh taught their Circuits 2 course last spring. At first,

Beth expected some solidarity from the department's only tenured female professor, but that proved to be an unwarranted hope. De Bourgh was cranky, difficult to follow, and obtuse whenever she was asked a question. That in itself wasn't unusual, but De Bourgh lacked the mischievous charm of, say, Dr. Kasani, who, at the beginning of every semester, said in his heavily-accented English, "I university's biggest weed-eater," followed by a wicked grin as he mimicked felling students in the way one might trim a hedge.

"Hi, ladies! Long time no see." The women turned at the sound of familiar voices.

"Hey, guys!" Beth brightened at the sight of Rene and Charles, friends from the study group formed second semester, freshman year —the semester that seemed to kick everyone's ass. They survived by banding together and bonding over midnight study sessions and bad student center coffee.

"You been to electronics lab yet, Queen Bee?" Rene asked Beth, using the moniker they gave her that first semester they became a team.

"No. Why does everyone keep asking me that?"

Charles laughed and shook his head. "The guy doesn't seem all that bad to me. Kind of stiff, but he's new. Maybe he's nervous."

"I know better than to listen to you, Charles. We all know you're too easy-going," Beth said, shaking her head.

He shrugged his shoulders. "I just think you ought to give people a chance, that's all."

"And we love you for it." Beth retrieved a mechanical pencil and a notebook from her backpack. "I haven't been to class yet, but I'll know by the end of the first lab if he's going to be a decent guy or a prick. Woman's intuition."

"Whatever you say, Bennet. But, hey, wasn't it you and your woman's intuition who came up to me after that first Calc 1 roll call and tried to greet me in French?" asked Rene.

"Are you ever going to let me live that down, Fournier?"

"Nope. I'm from Pittsburgh, not Paris. You know more French than I do."

"I thought maybe you were from Quebec. It was an honest mistake," she grumbled.

"And reminding you of it never gets old." Rene grinned at her and turned to the screen in the row behind Charlotte. "Let's get down to business. I've got to be at work by five."

ON WEDNESDAY, BETH SAT ON THE PLEATHER BENCH RIGHT OUTSIDE OF room 126 and opened her pre-lab report, glancing over the procedures. She heard voices within and assumed the last lab had some lingerers but stopped cold when she heard her name in the strident, smoker's tones of Dr. De Bourgh.

"Despite her charming exterior, Miss Bennet can be difficult at times. Obstinate. Headstrong."

Beth's hackles raised. Geez, the woman was a piece of work!

A deep and smooth voice with the drawn-out vowels of a barely concealed Southern accent responded.

"An ECE education seems like a pretty difficult route to take in order to get an MRS Degree or to please a daddy who wanted a son."

Her cheeks aflame, Beth stood up and abruptly walked into the room. De Bourgh ignored her, as was typical, but the guy was facing the door. Beth froze. It was Hot Mystery Student from the coffee shop, right down to the wavy hair and glasses. His eyebrows rose; perhaps he recognized her too, and yet he just stood there, as if he couldn't believe what he was seeing or that he had been overheard.

"But, um, yes. I—I'll keep that in mind." Apparently, the Southern accent became stronger in the presence of awkward embarrassment.

"Just watch yourself," De Bourgh said, striding out of the room without a look back.

Beth took her seat, folded her arms over her chest, and stared at the man who'd insulted her before even meeting her.

He nodded curtly, then walked behind his desk, shuffling papers and intermittently looking up as other students filed in. She shot him dagger-looks and vilified him repeatedly in her mind, shoring up her anger for when he would inevitably spurn her. She couldn't decide whether to fume or pout. Why couldn't he have been a journalism student or a poet? Instead he was the new T.A. her friends had been buzzing about. Another rigid, aspiring academician to whom she had to prove herself; the ever-present chauvinism was already exhausting, and the semester had barely even started. She wished Charlotte, or one of her other friends, was in this lab. Being alone always made it that much harder.

THE T.A.'S NAME WAS WILLIAM DARCY, AND HE WAS A FIRST-YEAR graduate student from Louisiana. New grads didn't usually teach the upper division labs, so Beth figured he was a strong student. De Bourgh wouldn't have taken him otherwise. The old battle-axe liked to have T.A.'s run her courses as much as possible so she didn't have to sully her mind dealing with undergrads.

Although Darcy was nice to look at, and that subtle Southern accent was kinda sexy, Beth tried to forget their first encounter at Top Perks. She spent each lab on edge, waiting for the day he made some misogynistic comment about "lady engineers," used sports as an example, and then, as an afterthought, singled her out and asked if she got it, or told a ribald joke that left half the men laughing and the other half uncomfortable that he'd told the joke in front of her.

But as the weeks went by, none of those things happened. Darcy didn't joke *at all* with anyone. He never called on her, even when she raised her hand. Never even looked at her.

And he was quickly becoming the bane of the students' existence because he graded harder than any T.A. they'd ever had.

DARCY HANDED OUT THE LAB REPORTS IN ALPHABETICAL ORDER AND, like always, handed Beth hers without making eye contact.

She sighed at the 14/20 circled in red at the top.

"If there are any questions, please see me after class. We have too much material to cover today. This lab is one of the longer ones."

Beth had gotten a reputation over the last several weeks for having a steady hand and exacting attention to detail. The other two guys in her group disliked doing the actual wiring, so it often fell to her. Sean liked to read the instructions to her, step-by-step, panicking whenever something didn't go exactly as planned. Mark did little but fiddle with the pieces in the kit until Beth snapped at him to knock it off. The three of them were studying a bunch of wires on a breadboard when she felt Darcy's presence towering over her.

"Problem?"

"Well…" Sean began.

"We'll get it," Beth interrupted.

"Here." Darcy pointed to the board. "Move this…and here…" He fiddled with the O-scope settings. "And there you go."

She frowned up at him, feeling defensive. "Thanks."

"Nice wiring, Ms. Bennet."

He walked off.

"Does he call you all by your last names?"

Sean and Mark looked at each other, then at her. They both shrugged.

"I dunno," said Mark.

"Maybe it's a Southern thing," Sean answered.

Beth sighed, psyching herself up for a mini showdown. It was time to have a little conversation with Mr. Darcy.

AFTER THEY FINISHED THE LAB, SHE APPROACHED THE FRONT OF THE room. "Excuse me?"

"Yes, Ms. Bennet?"

"Could you please explain the answer for number four?" She held up her lab report.

"Certainly." He went on to guide her through the steps of the problem and point out her errors.

"You know, I tried to ask this question in class."

"When? Today?"

"No. I raised my hand twice when we went over the pre-lab and tried again last week when we built the circuit. You never called on me. I gave up."

"Your board looked good. I…didn't realize you had a question."

"How could you possibly realize it? You never look my way."

"I think that's an overgeneralization."

"You ignore me."

"I do not." He looked uncomfortably at Steve, who was the only student left in the room. Steve packed up and raced out the door, pretending he hadn't heard the interchange. Darcy took off his glasses and leaned forward, putting his elbows on the desk. His voice was solemn. "You could cut me a small break, Ms. Bennet."

"Cut you a break? Why do you need me to cut you a break?"

"Because I'm trying to find my way—at a new university, with a new job, and frankly, with a new kind of student."

"What does that mean?"

"You're my first female student."

"What about Charlotte?"

"Who?"

"Charlotte Lucas, in your Monday section."

"Ah, yes. I forgot about her."

"Lovely. You ignore me and forget about her."

"I'm not…" He pinched the bridge of his nose. "You are attributing intentions to my actions that are not accurate."

"You are not intending to ignore me in class?"

"Of course not."

"Well, I think unintentionally ignoring me is worse."

"It's not unintentional."

Her eyes widened. "You're *trying* to ignore me?"

"Yes. I mean, no. Not the way…" He sighed in exasperation. "You're willfully misunderstanding me. This is…it's…uncharted territory. For me."

"Because I'm a female student."

"Well, to be honest, yes. The first I've met. Ever. In engineering, that is. Of course. I have met other female students. In—in anthropology. Or English.

"Welcome to the twentieth century."

"Thank you." His lips twitched, and her heart jumped, betraying her and her righteous indignation.

"You're welcome."

"It's not like I'm afraid of you, you know," he said.

"I don't want you to be."

"What do you want then?"

No one had ever asked her that, just point blank, without some caveat. It gave her a moment's pause, but old habits kept her guard up. After only a brief hesitation, she answered:

"I want to be treated like everyone else."

"Are you sure about that? Just like everyone else? A freshman student? A poorer student? A lazy one?"

She thought a moment. "Okay, good point. I suppose I want the same shot, the same chance to earn my place."

"I believe you receive that in this course."

Beth nodded. "Okay then. So, why don't you call on me?"

"I guess, I don't want you to think I'm picking on you. Singling you out."

"But that means you're not giving me the chance to show my stuff."

"Wait…what?"

"To show you what I know. To get the same feedback on my answers that other students get. By 'not singling me out,' you change the whole dynamic. You're not doing me any favors. The others think you're ignoring me because I'm a woman. It reinforces the idea that I don't know what I'm talking about. It's a vicious cycle."

He frowned, his lower lip sliding into a thoughtful pout. "I hadn't considered that."

"Of course you didn't." Beth put her books on the desk and leaned forward slightly to make eye contact. The conversation had made her bold, bolder than she ever had been with an instructor. It was strange; the most recalcitrant and stiff teacher she had ever known had now become the most approachable. She repeated, "I want the same chance as everyone else in the room."

"Point taken."

"I don't need your so-called help to get through this class."

"That much is obvious."

She drew back, studied his face. His eyes were dark, his expression somber and reserved, but unlike in every other interaction before, this time those eyes didn't look away.

"Thank you." She shouldered her backpack. She knew he would watch her as she walked out, but…she didn't mind.

ENGINEERING DAY WAS THE DEPARTMENT'S BIGGEST PR EVENT OF THE year. Many of the students avoided it like the plague, but Beth always enjoyed seeing the kids from the Lincoln area middle schools gawk and point at the contraptions on display. Plus, De Bourgh's syllabus said she would offer extra credit for participating, so Beth jumped at the chance and talked Rene, Charlotte, and Charles into joining her.

"I think we should do something different. No rockets or batteries or robot arms. It's all been done before." Beth sat forward on the orange couch, pencil poised over a legal pad to take notes. The others surrounded her in the student center lounge.

"Yeah," said Charlotte. "We need something sexy."

Charles looked shocked. "Sexy? For Engineering Day? With kids?"

"Well, maybe cool is a better word. Something cool that will appeal to kids."

"Music." Rene gestured with his hands, mimicking a conductor.

Charlotte, her voice rising with excitement asked, "You mean like an electric guitar?"

"Yeah. Except"—Rene's shoulders slumped—"I can't play a guitar. Can anyone else?" He looked around the group.

Charles raised his hand. "I can. Well, a little. And I can play electronic keyboard. See, I'm in this band…"

Charlotte playfully punched his arm. "You're kidding me! Really?"

"Yeah, really."

"Why didn't you tell us?"

"We just started playing together about a month ago."

"Okay," said Rene. "So, we've got a little guitar demonstration, some keyboard. What else?"

Charles rubbed his chin, thinking. "I bet the music department will let us borrow a Moog synthesizer. Like a mini one that would be easy to transport. Moog synthesizers have a keyboard, so I can fiddle with that too, if no one else wants to."

"I took five months of piano lessons," said Charlotte. "I wanna learn the Moog!"

Charles laughed.

"Okay." Rene rubbed his hands together. "Now we're cooking with gas. No suggestions, Queen Bee? What can you do? Plug the synthesizer into the wall?"

"I can play the Theremin," Beth said in a small voice.

"The What-a-min?" Rene asked.

"The Theremin," Charles answered for her, standing up to demonstrate. "It's an electronic instrument invented in the twenties by some Soviet guy. Current goes into a box with two antennas, one that points up, like this"—he demonstrated with his right hand—"and the other is a loop down here"—he indicated with his left hand. "The musician forms a capacitor between his hand and the antenna, which creates an oscillator. The oscillator's output mixes with a fixed oscillator's output. The difference between the two outputs is converted to a signal that controls loudness here"—he indicated the volume antenna —"and pitch here on the right. It's unique because—"

"You play it without actually touching it," Rene interrupted.

"Yep." Charles dropped his hands to his hips and turned to Beth. "It's extremely difficult to play."

"Damn, Queen Bee." Rene goggled at her.

Charles grinned. "I didn't know you could play a Theremin, Beth."

"I'm not really skilled at it. My dad bought me one when I was a teenager. I just kind of knock around on it sometimes. I mean, I have it here in my apartment, but I don't play, because it…well, neighbors, you know."

"Could you learn something for Engineering Day?"

"Maybe if it was short. We could have like a 'collage' of electronic instruments. Charles could play the keyboard and the Moog synthesizer. I'll play the Theremin—"

"I'll corral the kids and answer questions." Charlotte raised her hand.

"Okay. Who's going to present the idea to Darcy? De Bourgh says any demonstrations have to be approved ahead of time." Beth was jotting down notes to put into a written proposal. When no one answered, she looked up.

"I nominate you, Queen Bee," Rene said, amused.

"Oh, geez. Why?"

"Because Darcy li-i-i-kes you," Charlotte said, laughing.

"He does not!"

"Mark Collins is in your lab, and he says Darcy watches you walk in"—Charlotte walked her fingers in the air—"and he watches you walk out. And, he looks your way first when he asks a question."

"It's overcompensation—from the time I told him to quit ignoring me in class."

"*And,* whenever Darcy sees us in here talking, he makes a point to come over and join the conversation. He doesn't do that when you aren't around."

"I'm not interested in *any* conversation that comes from Darcy. No way."

Charlotte's eyes widened. "Oops," she squeaked, pursing her lips together.

Beth grimaced, realizing about two seconds too late who was behind her. Rene and Charles looked down at their books, pretending to read.

"Um…hello. How's it going?" Out of the corner of her eye, Beth saw Darcy put a hand on the back of her couch. To his credit, Darcy gave no clue that he'd heard her. Maybe he hadn't. She could only hope.

"Good," she answered, waiting for one of the others to chime in. They looked anywhere but at her.

"Cowards!" she mouthed at them and turned around.

"Hey listen, Mr. Darcy. We have an idea for Engineering Day. We need to sketch out the details first, and then it'll be ready for your approval," she said, false bravado firmly in place.

"That's great, Ms. Bennet. Why don't you come by my office hours when you get the specifics lined out?"

"Sure. It will probably be early next week."

"That will work."

"Okay, thanks."

He frowned at the top of the others' heads. "Well, I'll see you around."

"Okay."

A weak chorus of "bye," "see ya," and "later" followed Darcy out of the lounge.

After he left, they all sat looking at each other. Rene intoned in a deep voice, mimicking the accent, "Why don't you come by my office hours, Sugar?" The other two laughed.

Beth threw her pencil at him.

BETH WIPED DAMP PALMS ON THE SIDES OF HER JEANS AND TOOK A DEEP breath. She heard the swell of young voices outside the door, heard Rene trying to shout over them as he briefly explained their demonstration. Then, about thirty kids filed into the classroom lined with chairs. She and Charles were set up at one end. The plan was to start with the electric guitar, followed by the Moog synthesizer demonstration, followed by her demonstration of the Theremin—a verse of "Out Here on My Own," with her singing the rest of the song, accompanied by Charles on the electronic keyboard. They would finish with him playing a couple of other popular songs to pique the kids' interest.

Playing the Theremin required steady hands; minuscule changes in fingering affected pitch and volume. Beth was worried about her nerves but channeling the shakiness into a vibrato for the opening notes gave the song an emotional twang that actually fit quite well. The more she played, the stronger she sounded, and by the time she got to the singing part, her hesitation was gone.

Somewhere in the middle of the second verse, her attention was drawn to the doorway by movement. Standing there, leaning against the doorframe, arms crossed, was Darcy. He didn't look how Darcy usually appeared, however. Gone was his scowl and cool mask of indifference. In its place was a transfixed Darcy, the shadow of a smile trying to fight its way into the open. They locked gazes as the chorus swelled along with Charles's keyboard accompaniment. Darcy's expression coaxed a happy grin from her, and as it bloomed full on her features, Beth turned back to the students and finished the last phrase, reveling in the rapt faces, especially those of the little girls in the room.

"Thank you," she said, after the applause ended. "Okay, we're going to end the demonstration with some more electronic keyboard playing from Charles. Rene, Charlotte, and I will be milling around so feel free to stop us and ask questions, sing along, or dance if you like."

The sweet intro to "Dancing in the Moonlight" floated over the air, and Beth laughed as she joined a group of three girls who were twirling each other under their hands and bebopping to the music. She saw their eyebrows raise in surprise, heard their giggles, and she froze as a strong hand caught hers.

Darcy pulled her into a dancing embrace, leading her to and fro, under his arm, finishing with a little dip at the end. Charlotte's eyes nearly popped out of her head, Charles missed a note, and Rene stared.

"You can dance," Beth said stupidly.

"You look shocked," he said, laughing. "My mama forced cotillion classes on me when I was thirteen."

She wanted to say she was more shocked that he would exhibit in front of his undergrads and unknown middle schoolers, but she held her tongue. Instead, she faked a little curtsy, and he followed suit with a gallant bow. He kissed her hand, turned, and walked out.

"Nice exit," she murmured.

One of the girls tugged on her arm. "Beth, can we try that instrument you played?"

"What? Oh, sure. Right this way."

She watched the doorway, but Darcy didn't return, and soon her attention was consumed with a hoard of middle schoolers and the screech of the Theremin.

THE DAY BEFORE THANKSGIVING DAWNED GRAY AND COLD. CLOUDS loomed low as Beth trudged the sidewalks through campus, trying not to shiver as the dampness seeped into her bones. She had spent all weekend in bed with a fever, some kind of stupid cold that resulted in a trip to Student Health on Monday. The doctor's examination indicated strep throat—easily treated with erythromycin—but she still felt crappy. She thought the twenty-minute hot shower would help, but it hadn't—although it had made her late—and now she was walking with a wet head, making the cold feel even worse.

Darcy greeted her when she entered the lab. Of course. She could never slip in under the radar like the other students. "Good afternoon."

"Sorry I'm late."

"Glad you could make it."

She didn't dare tell him she'd been sick. No excuses. Show no weakness. She plunked down in her chair and pulled out the lab procedures.

Twenty minutes into the lab, she thought she might scream in frustration.

"I thought you said you could do the wiring, Sean."

"I can. I mean, I need to. You've wired every lab, and Darcy's starting to notice. The semester's almost over, and I need to wire at least one."

Beth shut her eyes and leaned back in her chair. Her head hurt like hell, and her stomach felt like it was on its own roller coaster ride. "Go ahead then."

It was just her luck Sean decided to dig in his heels the day she most wanted to hurry through. Student Health had told her to expect a few days' recovery, but two days' worth of antibiotics had seemed to do nothing except alleviate the sore throat.

The sickly smell of something akin to burnt hair permeated the room.

"Dammit," Sean muttered to himself. Then to Beth, he said, "What does step four say again?"

"For Pete's sake! Let me see it." Beth stood up and leaned over the table, inspecting the board. "You shorted out the transistor." She squinted at the board and handed him a new one.

"Thanks."

"Anytime. Just read…" She had stood up, too fast she supposed, as everything tilted forty-five degrees and black crept in at the edges of her vision. The world became a tunnel and voices echoed, shouting her name, before they were silent, and all went dark.

BETH OPENED HER EYES TO A GLARING FLUORESCENT LIGHT. SHE squeezed them shut again and turned her head to the side—a big mistake, as the movement sparked an overwhelming wave of nausea. No tunnel vision now; instead, a red miasma swarmed across the inside of her eyelids.

"Ms. Bennet?"

"Yeah. Where am I?"

"You're in the university hospital ER. Can you tell me your birthday?"

"I brought her bag." Was that Darcy's voice? What was he doing here? "It probably has her ID in it."

The other voice said, "I'm trying to ascertain if she's oriented. Where do you go to school, Beth?"

"Fordyce."

"Who's the president of the United States?"

"What?"

"The president. Who's the president?"

She tried to think. "Uh, at the moment, it's Jimmy Carter. But not for long, right? Reagan takes office in January." Her stomach pitched and rolled, and her head pounded. She still couldn't bring herself to open her eyes.

The doctor's voice addressed Darcy. "You her boyfriend?"

"Uh…no. No. T.A. For her lab. She—she fainted in class. I brought her in."

"She have a roommate? Family? Someone to call?"

"My roommate went home for Thanksgiving. My family's out of state."

"Uh, I'll just step out," Darcy said. "Get some coffee. Or something."

Beth lay in blissful silence except for the scratching of pen against paper, the doctor writing notes. Slowly, she became aware of the beeping machines and other voices in the ER, muffled by a curtain drawn around her gurney. "God, I feel awful."

"There's an emesis basin right here, if you have to be sick," he said. "You're not pregnant, are you? Sorry, but I have to ask."

"No. Not pregnant." She grimaced. "Unless a star has risen in the East."

She heard a soft chuckle coming from behind the doctor, followed by the smell of coffee.

"I don't get it. They said it was just strep throat," she said.

"You had strep?"

"Yes."

"Treated at Student Health?"

"Yes."

"When?" asked the doctor.

"Monday."

"We'll get those records. In the meantime, we're going to do a CT scan and keep you for observation, okay? According to your friend here, you hit your head pretty good when you fainted."

"I fainted?" She opened her eyes and looked straight into William Darcy's handsome face, as he sat down right beside her bed.

"Yes." Darcy leaned forward, a concerned frown moving over his features. "And hit the table on the way down."

"So, we'll treat the head injury," the doctor went on. "You've got a big knot there, and we want to make sure it's nothing serious. But then we have to figure out why you fainted in the first place. My guess is you had some kind of reaction to the antibiotic."

"I'm allergic to erythromycin?" Her head was starting to clear as she held Darcy's gaze.

"Ah, if that's what they gave you, it may not be an allergy per se, but that your stomach couldn't take it. I'll be back in a few minutes."

The silence stretched out a minute or so, before Beth spoke. "You brought me here?"

"Well, I called an ambulance."

"Oh, geez."

"Would you like me to phone someone? Your mother perhaps?"

"Please, for the love of all that is holy, don't call my mother. She'll make my head hurt worse, if that's possible."

"A friend then?"

"I'm supposed to eat Thanksgiving dinner with Charlotte's family tomorrow. They're local. I really need to call her." Beth tried to sit up.

"No, lie back down. You still look a little green." Darcy got up and guided her back, so she rested on her side and put the emesis basin next to her. "I'll call her. Don't worry about a thing."

"What about your Thanksgiving plans?"

"No big deal," he said.

"Were you going home?"

"Planned to." He glanced at his watch. "Flight's gone now."

"I'm sorry, Mr. Darcy."

"It's okay."

"But still…"

"On the bright side, I hear they have turkey dinner right here at the hospital."

"You should call the airport. Maybe there's a later flight."

"There might be. I don't think you should be alone, though."

"They'll probably send me home tonight. Charlotte can help me."

"When she gets here, and when everything's all right, then I'll go. It's not a problem, really. I wasn't looking forward to family Thanksgiving anyway."

"Why not?"

"Every time I go home, my mother tries to introduce me to some Tulane or LSU debutante."

"Your mother and mine should compare notes."

"My mother needs no encouragement in that department, thank you."

Beth chuckled.

An orderly pushing a wheelchair opened the curtain. "Hi, there! I'm Rosemary, and I'm going to take you down for a CT of your noggin." She turned to Darcy. "You the boyfriend?"

"A friend," he repeated. "I'll wait, if that's okay. I can watch her stuff."

"Sure. The doctor's probably going to keep her overnight for observation, so when a room opens up, we'll let you know where she is. I'll show you to the waiting room."

"Good morning, Ms. Bennet."

Beth stirred and opened her eyes. A nurse was checking her blood pressure, but the voice came from yet another young doctor standing beside the bed.

"Good morning."

"I'm Dr. Hill. I'm a resident here at the hospital. How are you feeling this morning?"

"A little better. My head hurts."

"I imagine it does. You have a mild concussion. We've got you on a different antibiotic"—he indicated the nurse, who held up a horse pill and a glass of water—"and I think we can send you home if there's someone to help you out this weekend."

"That nice young man who brought your bag up last night while you were sleeping, perhaps? The night nurse said he stayed until visiting hours were over. Can we call him for you?"

"He's not...I mean, he's my T.A. Besides, it's Thanksgiving, and he probably went home. I'll call my friend. Maybe she can come pick me up."

"Can she watch over you for a few days?"

"Yeah, we'll figure something out."

"I think I can help with that." Darcy knocked on the doorframe.

"May I come in?"

Beth started to nod, then clutched her forehead. "Nodding is bad."

The doctor pushed at his glasses and put his pen in the pocket of his white coat. "Okay. So, we'll call your friend...?"

"Charlotte Lucas. Her number's in my bag. Where is it again?"

"I stuck it in the closet last night." Darcy went over and retrieved the backpack, handed it to Beth.

"Thanks."

Dr. Hill nodded. "We'll get your discharge instructions and a follow-up appointment. You should be good to go by about four o'clock, maybe in time for some Thanksgiving dinner."

After the doctor left, Darcy took the chair beside the bed.

"You look better today."

"Thanks."

"So, was it an allergic reaction to erythromycin?" Darcy said.

"They say it's a 'gastric intolerance' not an allergy."

"I stand corrected."

"It still messed me up but good." She squinted at him and considered. "You didn't catch a later flight home?"

"Couldn't find one. Called my parents last night and told them I had a friend in the hospital, so I was going to stay over Thanksgiving. I needed to get some work done in De Bourgh's lab anyway."

Beth sat, pondering what to say next. She had never been particularly good at hiding what was on her mind, though, and this situation was no different.

"Mr. Darcy?"

"Will. I think we can be on a first-name basis now, don't you?"

"Maybe. I'm not sure."

"Or if not 'Will,' maybe just Darcy. The 'mister' makes me feel ancient. And I'm not that much older than you."

"Okay."

"Good."

"Will?"

"Beth...?"

"Why are you being so nice to me?"

"I shouldn't be nice to you?"

"I really haven't given you any reason to...to go above and beyond like this."

He shrugged. "It's not like I could leave you sprawled on the lab floor."

"Now, that sounds exactly like something you'd say."

Darcy reached over and fiddled with the hospital bracelet around her wrist, then laid his hand over hers. "No, I couldn't leave you sprawled on the lab floor, that's for sure." He glanced at her with a smile she thought she might have seen when he saw her across the room on Engineering Day.

He cleared his throat and looked up at the bag hanging from her IV pole, then his eyes followed the tubing down to her wrist. "I'm nice to you because I like you." He drew back his hand. "In fact, I like you a lot."

Beth stared at him as if he had just sprouted seven heads. She was speechless.

"Although, I'm pretty sure you're not too fond of me. Just from certain things you've said."

"Mr. Darcy. I mean, Darcy...Will, I—"

"Ah, that's much better than stuffy, old-fashioned 'Mr. Darcy.' I hope you don't mind or think I'm overstepping, but I called Charlotte last night and left a message. I couldn't get a hold of her though."

"She wasn't home? That's odd."

"I also got your home phone number from the university mainframe and called your parents. I figured you were kidding about your mother, and I thought they should know."

"Yes... No...what I mean is, yes, thank you. And no, you're not overstepping."

"I told your dad I'd check in on you today. He said they would be here by four."

"Bennet Descent is imminent. I hope the hospital is prepared."

Darcy's serious expression broke into a wide smile that became him quite well.

"Well, I guess I should go," he said.

"Thank you for your help. Really."

Darcy patted his knees as if to give himself the jumpstart to leave. "Get well soon. Beth."

"Bye," she whispered softly. Then, louder, as he approached the door, "Hey, Darcy."

"Yes?"

"Does Chinese take-out sound good for Thanksgiving? I bet Shanghai Shack is open."

"Sure thing."

"Why don't you grab us some sweet and sour chicken, and we'll have Thanksgiving dinner here while I wait for my parents. It will be better than eating alone, right?"

"Most definitely. I'll be back in an hour."

Surprisingly pleased with herself, Beth leaned back and closed her eyes.

"I NEVER WOULD HAVE PUT THOSE TWO PEOPLE TOGETHER," BETH SAID. "I couldn't believe it when she called here. Charlotte and Mark Collins, of all people! I mean, he stomps on everyone's last nerve, hers included. At least, I thought he did. She must have felt sorry for him. That's the only thing I can figure."

"She went out with Collins last night?"

"Not out. In. That's even worse. She'll never get rid of him now. They went to his place and watched some Star Trek marathon on cable. He's always bragging about having cable." Beth nibbled on a carrot. "She woke up on his couch this morning at five a.m., which is why you could only get the answering machine last night. Talk about waking up in a panic."

"Maybe she likes him."

Beth stared at him as he deftly lifted a piece of chicken with his chopsticks. "Collins?"

Darcy shrugged. "Sometimes people realize there's a connection they hadn't noticed before—like Collins and Charlotte and Star Trek." His calm, brown-eyed gaze settled on her. "Beth, I…"

He was interrupted by a flurry of activity at the door.

"Oh, my baby!" Mrs. Bennet wailed as she rushed in, arms outstretched. "Are you okay? I just knew something awful like this would happen if you went so far from home! I knew it! I told your father..." She faltered and took in the young man sitting beside the bed. "Oh! Well hello there." She looked expectantly at Beth, who inwardly groaned at her mother's blatant interest in Darcy.

"Mom, this is William Darcy. He brought me in after I fainted in class."

"Oh, Mr. Darcy! William—may I call you William? Thank you so much for taking care of our Beth. You're a hero."

"Mom, please."

"No, truly you are. Like a knight on a white horse. I'm Franny, by the way."

Darcy stood, setting his take-out box on the bedside table. "Nice to meet you."

Mrs. Bennet giggled and looked at Beth. "He's so tall!"

Beth shut her eyes in mortification.

"Are you an engineering student too?"

"No. Well, yes. I'm a grad student. I'm the T.A."

Mrs. Bennet's long pause conveyed her confusion perfectly.

"I'm the teaching assistant. For Beth's electronics lab."

"Oh, I see! Well, we are so grateful to you—"

"How are you feeling, Beth honey?"

"Grandma?" Beth's eyes popped open.

"I rode along with your mama. Wanted to see for myself that you were really all right."

Beth looked around her. "Where's Dad?"

Mrs. Bennet frowned. "He's at home, waiting for his sister to call and tell him his Thanksgiving dinner is ready. Good thing we planned to go over to her place, or I'd have had a refrigerator of food go to waste."

"Dad didn't come?"

"He said driving six hours to an out-of-state hospital was a mother's...what did he call it again, Alice?"

"A mother's prerogative." Alice reached over and hugged Beth.

"Well, I'll be going." Darcy backed away from the bed.

"Oh, don't leave on our account," Mrs. Bennet said. "You haven't finished your lunch." She pointed to his take-out.

He took the chopsticks out and closed the box. "No, it's okay. I'll get out of the way."

"Oh honey, you're not in the way at all!"

He cleared his throat. "Um. Beth. I guess I'll see you Wednesday?"

"Yes. Wednesday."

"Last lab."

She smiled. "Yes, last lab. Thank you. For—for all your help. And for Thanksgiving dinner."

"You're welcome." He turned to the others. "Nice to meet you."

They replied in kind, and with a final nod to Beth, he left.

Mrs. Bennet raised her eyebrows and nodded her head. "He's cute!"

"Oh, for heaven's sake, Franny! The poor girl has a concussion. She doesn't want to discuss her handsome instructor right now. Why don't you go see if you can find the nurse and ask when we can take her home?"

Grandma Alice sat down in the chair beside the bed. "How are you really, sweetheart?"

"I'm okay. Noise and light still hurt my head some."

"I persuaded your mama to get a hotel room near campus. That should help maintain the peace."

"Thank you for coming all this way. You didn't need to do that."

"Oh, I think we did. After young Mr. Darcy called and said the doctors didn't want you to go home alone, Franny wouldn't rest until she saw you."

"I would have been fine."

"Most likely. But we'll stay close through the weekend—and longer if you need us."

"You'll spend the whole weekend with my mom for my sake?"

Alice grinned. "I must love you a whole lot." She patted Beth's hand. "Your mama loves you a whole lot too."

"I know."

"Good thing Mr. Darcy was around when you fainted."

"I hate that word 'fainted.'"

"Why?"

"It sounds so...wimpy."

Alice laughed. "You always want to put up that brave front. Beth honey, you were ill. No shame in getting help when you're ill. Don't be stubborn. Sometimes, you're just like my mama was."

A quiet settled between them with Alice lost in her memories and Beth not knowing what to say.

"That reminds me." Alice brightened and leaned forward in her chair. "Did you ever have a chance to read her journals? The ones we found in the attic last summer?"

"I haven't," Beth said, feeling a little guilty. "There's been so much to do this fall. I—"

"Oh, my dear, don't apologize. I know you're busy. I just thought you might get a kick out of them. One is from her first year in Denver."

"Do you want to take them back with you? I won't be able to read them while I'm recovering."

Alice considered. "No, I don't think so. Your dad had the university library put them on microfiche to preserve the text. And I think—no, I know—that my mother would want you to have them. They really tell a young woman's story. You'll get to them when you get to them."

"I do want to read them. They're sitting on my bookshelf."

Franny bustled back in. "The nurse said you could go home as long as I drove you. You'd think she was just glad to get rid of us."

"Imagine that," Alice said, smiling at her granddaughter.

THE BENNETS LEFT FOR DENVER ON SUNDAY MORNING, ASSURED THAT Beth was on the mend. The new antibiotic made her feel like a new woman, and although she tired easily, her other concussion symptoms were all but gone.

She reveled in the solitary quiet left in her mother's wake and was wondering what to do with herself when her gaze landed on one of Great-Nana's black, leather-bound journals.

"Surely a few minutes won't hurt," she said to herself.

Beth made a cup of tea and settled on the couch, journal in hand. Gingerly, she opened the yellowed pages of the diary, but before she could get past "*July 1906, Denver, Colorado,*" a knock at the door interrupted her.

She was shocked to see William Darcy on the other side of the peephole. "What in the world—?" She opened the door with a surprised, "Hi."

"Hi. I wasn't expecting you to be up and around."

"Then why did you knock?"

"I expected your mom to answer."

"Why would you willingly subject yourself to my mom?"

"It might have been your grandmother who answered." He pursed his lips, trying to hide his amusement. "And your mom is not that bad. I've known a few like her in my time."

An awkward silence ensued.

"Oh," Beth said, stepping back and opening the door. "Won't you come in?"

"Sure, for a minute. I just stopped in to check on you."

"Well, I'm fine, as you can see." She stood up straighter and smiled at him, trying not to feel awkward.

"Mm-hmm." Darcy looked doubtful. His eyes traveled down to assess her for himself, and Beth felt their progress in little sparks all along her skin.

His gaze stopped at the book in her hand. "And what is that?"

She tore her eyes from his face and looked down. "A book."

"I know it's a book! You're not supposed to be reading."

"How do you know I'm not supposed to be reading?"

"*Everyone* knows you're not supposed to read right after a concussion."

"I didn't think a few minutes would matter."

He scowled at her. "Dr. De Bourgh was right about you. You are obstinate." He reached down and snagged the book from her hand.

"Be careful with that! It was my great-grandmother's."

"What is it?"

"Her journal. She took the train out to Colorado in 1906, all by herself, to teach school. Grandma Alice thought I'd like to read it, so I brought it with me in September. This is the first chance I've had to think about it."

"Well, you shouldn't be reading it. Yet."

"I'm frustrated. I can't do anything I need to do, and I'm a little stir crazy, and I can only listen to the radio for so long before I want to pitch it out the window. It's been a long weekend."

"I can imagine. Where's Charlotte?"

"She had to work this afternoon. She'll be here later this evening."

Darcy looked down at the book in his hand. "I could read it to you. If you want."

Beth stared at him.

"Unless you think it's too personal."

"You continually surprise me, Darcy."

"Do I?"

"You do." She turned toward the couch. "Okay then. Read away. Great-Nana is no longer around to protest. Not that she would anyway. She was not a shy or retiring sort of woman."

"Sounds familiar."

Beth grinned over her shoulder. "I've been told I'm a lot like her. Maybe it's because I was named Elizabeth too."

Darcy shed his coat and hat and sat in the living room chair. "Feel free to lie down if your head hurts."

"Don't mind if I do." She fluffed the pillow and laid her head opposite his chair so she could see him. He *was* pretty easy on the eyes.

He began in his accent-tinged baritone:

"I don't know what I'll find in this wilderness, uncharted for a woman on her own, but I know I have no choice other than to forge ahead"—and soon Elizabeth slipped into a lovely place between asleep and awake, carried by the lull of his voice.

JULY 1906
DENVER, COLORADO

ELIZABETH ALTON STOOD ON THE TRAIN PLATFORM, SHIELDING HER EYES
from the midday Colorado sun. A trickle of sweat ran down her back,
making her wish she could have worn something besides a long sleeve
blouse with a high neck collar. She was looking for the sheriff of her
new home in Apple Creek, a small town several miles from Denver
proper. According to the letter written by Dr. Bingley, this Sheriff
Gardiner would meet her train, holding a sign with her name.

Well, it was almost her name.

Lizzy had applied for the position using her initials, E.M. Alton.
She listed every other fact on her application with painstaking accuracy—her schooling, her class rank, her area of concentration in
mathematics from Longbourn College—but Dr. Bingley's advertisement had also mentioned the resiliency and stamina needed for a
teaching position on the frontier. He didn't specify that only male
applicants would be accepted, but Lizzy thought her sex might be a
detail best unknown until he met her. If he had reservations, she knew
she could change his mind. She needed this position. Besides, it wasn't
like she truly misrepresented herself. She *was* resilient; she had been
on her own since her parents had passed the previous year and had
done quite well, thank you very much.

Still, she knew she would be a surprise to Dr. Bingley, the man
who the town's parents had chosen to recruit a teacher for their
children.

"All will be well," she whispered to herself, hoping the words
would buoy her confidence. She brushed at the wrinkles in her skirt, a
respectable navy weatherproof foulard, and retrieved her wide-
brimmed hat from its box on top of her luggage. She needed to look
like a woman in charge, not a bedraggled, wrung-out traveler when
she met this Sheriff Gardiner, who would drive her to Apple Creek, to
her new school, and her boarding house accommodations.

She turned to the right and saw him. Well, at first her attention
was caught by the sign bearing her name, but it was quickly diverted

to the gentleman holding the sign. He was tall, one of the tallest men she had ever seen, with piercing blue eyes and tanned, weathered skin suggesting a life led outdoors. He was watching her, open admiration in his gaze as he smiled and tipped his hat.

His acknowledgment jolted her back to reality. Lizzy tied her hat box to her valise, and with a deep breath, approached him.

"May I help you, miss?" he asked.

"Yes, I'm Miss Alton."

"Pardon?"

She indicated the sign. "I'm Miss Alton. The schoolteacher. Dr. Bingley hired me. You're here to drive me to Apple Creek, I presume? Sheriff Gardiner?"

The smile dropped from his face, as he looked in bewilderment from her to the sign and back again. "*You're* E.M. Alton?"

"I am."

His brows drew together in an angry frown. "I was expecting a fellow, not a lady."

"Yes, I can see that. Nevertheless, I am Miss Alton, and I am bound for Apple Creek. I have a trunk over by the ticket office. If you could help me with it, I'd be grateful. It's quite heavy."

"Young woman, this is no joke."

"It certainly is not."

"You have misrepresented yourself to Dr. Bingley." His scowl was formidable, but Lizzy had the courage of a desperate woman with nowhere else to go, and she met his glare head on.

"I have not misrepresented myself. I have my college diploma right there in my trunk, and I assure you, sir, I am a willing and capable teacher."

"You did not tell him you were a *female* schoolteacher."

"He did not ask. Sir."

"Bingley," he muttered under his breath. "You careless, absent-minded sap."

Lizzy folded her hands in front of her. "Sheriff Gardiner," she said patiently, "I understand now that I am not who you were expecting. But your town needs a teacher, and I need a position."

"You *need* to go back home to your family."

"I have no family living and nothing to go back to." She paused, took another deep breath, annoyed at its shakiness and at the tears she felt beginning to form. She blinked them back. "And I am depending on you to deliver me to the boarding house on Brook Street in Apple Creek, Colorado. So, if we could please get on, I understand it is a good half-day's ride. I am exhausted and would like to get to my room before nightfall so I can wash up and rest."

"...and then the rude sheriff squints at me, studies me up and down, and says, 'Well, I guess you're Bingley's problem, not mine. The wagon's over there. I'll get your trunk.'

It turns out the Brook Street boarding house is for men only, and completely inappropriate for a teacher, even a male one, as it is a cluster of rooms above a saloon. (I myself begin to wonder about Dr. Bingley's logic.)

So, Sheriff Gardiner deposits me at the Bingleys' home on Pine Street, and I'm lodged in their guest room until appropriate accommodations can be found. Jane Bingley, the doctor's young wife, is pleasant and compassionate, thank goodness, and Dr. Bingley is also polite, although he looks at me every so often, completely baffled. Then he chuckles and shakes his head.

I overheard the men's voices through the open window of the guest room as I put my things away. Dr. Bingley asked the sheriff if he thought I'd really stay here in Apple Creek. The disdain in the sheriff's voice was unmistakable as he said, 'Unfortunately for you, Bingley, I do think she'll stay. And it's unfortunate for me as well.'

'Why is that?'

'If you can't find other lodgings for her and go through with your plan to rent that little house next to the school, I will have to protect a single woman, living alone on the outskirts of town, whom everybody in town knows is living alone. More work for me. And a distraction from upholding the law— one that I don't need right now.'

I had to stifle a disbelieving laugh at his rudeness. Honestly, Sheriff Gardiner is a horrid, crude sort of man."

Beth's eyes opened when she heard Darcy chuckle. "What?"

"She's made her mind up about him already, hasn't she?"

"About the sheriff? Yeah, I guess she kind of jumped the gun, so to speak."

"Are you tired of listening yet? You looked like you were asleep."

"No. Just in that pleasant in-between." She shifted onto her side, pleased to find his eyes resting on her. "Unless you have to go."

"I don't want to go," he said in a gentle voice that sent shivers over her skin.

Beth smiled at him. Darcy carefully turned the page and read on…

"October 22, 1906

The snow continues unabated for the third day in a row. No one, even here, could possibly have anticipated this kind of storm in October. I ordered boots, trying to be prepared for my first winter, but they have not arrived. I certainly didn't think I would need them so soon. Snow happens here, of course, but blizzards are relatively uncommon, or so I've been told.

I have plenty of water, given the snowfall, but my food supply is dwindling rather low. I have no idea when I will be able to get to the general store for dry goods. The local townsfolk tell awful tales of people trying to get from their barns to their homes during these storms up in the mountains, and then freezing to death mere steps from their front doors. I dare not try getting to town or to the neighbors' some quarter of a mile away.

Then again, although the food supply is a worry, even more pressing is the need for firewood. I am down to my last few logs. Eating is the lesser of my worries—it shan't matter if anything is in my pantry if I freeze to death! The woodpile is not far, just around the other side of the schoolhouse. I must think of some way to mark my path back to my little dwelling and try to find the stash of logs…"

Lizzy stood just inside her door, wrapped head to toe in as many layers as she could find, taking extra care to cover her head, hands, and feet. Bending down, she gathered up strips of fabric torn from the new bolt, bought to make her spring skirts. She sighed, wishing she could have thought of another way, but the fabric was a sturdy, dark green, visible in the snow. The wind still whistled against the window frames, but she was afraid to wait much longer to get firewood. She had no idea how long the storm might last. The strips were tied together, she figured about thirty yards long and six inches wide. She closed her eyes and tried to recall which way was the most direct path to the wood pile.

The wind bit into her feet and fingers as she ventured out into the swirling snow. The heavy cloud cover nearly blocked the daylight, giving a gray cast to everything. She glanced back and saw her green tether, visible just a few feet behind her. Lizzy trudged on, trying to gauge if she had taken the correct number of steps to reach the schoolhouse.

"I should be there by now." She retraced her steps, using the green lifeline until she reached her own door, noting the change in the sound of the wind as she approached the house. After warming up, she tried again, venturing out into the gray and white abyss, stopping each step to close her eyes and focus on the wind.

The third trip out, a combination of luck and listening helped Lizzy find the schoolhouse. It was a simple matter at that point to find the wood she had stacked beside it. Wrapping as many logs as she could carry in a blanket, she tied the green rope to the school building and found her way back home. Now exhausted, she collapsed into a fitful slumber.

Lizzy woke to the sounds of someone pounding on her door, accompanied by panicked shouting. She shivered; the fire was very low and the room cold. Sitting up, she tried to call out, but her voice, hoarse from disuse, came out cracked and weak. A louder sound, definitely not the pounding of human hands, rattled the door in its frame. She jumped up, wrapping a blanket around her.

"Miss Alton! Are you in there? Open up! Miss Alton!" This was followed by another bang against the door. It shimmied on its hinges.

"Stop! Stop!" Her voice finally came back in full force. "You're going to break my door down! I'm in here! I'm fine!" She waited for a pause in the blows and then called out. "I'm coming to the door. Don't break it down." Then as an afterthought, she asked, "Who is it?"

"It's Sheriff Gardiner."

She should have recognized the deep, booming voice. He had certainly made no bones about using it to criticize her at every turn. The sheriff then proceeded to barge into the room, seize her hand, and started inspecting her fingers, one by one. He studied her facial features carefully and then *demanded* to see her toes.

"I beg your pardon!" Lizzy yanked back her hand and stepped away from him.

"Stop being so prissy." The sheriff shrugged off Lizzy's shock. "Do you have frost bite? I saw that rope you tried to make tied to the back door. I half-expected to find your body huddled in a snow drift. What in the Sam Hill were you thinking?"

"I didn't *try* to make a rope. I *made* one. And I used it to get firewood when I ran out..." She thought back, but she had no concept of time. Her clock hadn't been wound since the storm began. "Whenever it was that I ran out."

"Well, Lord saved you, that's for certain."

"Saved myself, thank you."

His lips twitched in amusement. "Lord helped."

Lizzy sank down onto a kitchen chair, suddenly teary. The sheriff sat down too. "Thank the Lord," he said softly.

"I do. I do thank Him." Sobs choked her, and Lizzy put her head on her arms and gave herself over to the wave of emotion that appeared in the blink of an eye. After a moment, she felt a large calloused hand on hers. He scooted his chair close and moved his hand to gently cover her hair, still in a messy braid that hung over her shoulder.

"It's all right," he said, stroking her hair. "It's all right now. You're safe. We'll get you to town. Let Doc Bingley have a look at you."

Lizzy raised her head. "I can't get to town. It's..." She looked out the window. The gray clouds were still there, but the snowfall had slowed to a gentle swirl of flurries.

"The storm is winding down. I came as soon as I found out you were here alone." He leaned his chair on its back legs. "It was quite an ordeal. There's about two and a half feet of snow out there."

"Two and a half *feet*?"

"Yep. Worst storm I can remember. At least hereabouts. Worse blizzards in the mountains, of course." He stood up, towering over her, but she didn't feel uneasy this time. "Get your things. I'm taking you to Bingleys' for the duration. Don't argue," he said as she started to reply. "No child is coming to school in this weather, and anyway, you need warm food, fussing over by Jane Bingley, and a once over from the doc."

"I'm fine," Lizzy grumbled. "I'm not a hothouse flower from back East that needs to be coddled. Not anymore."

"Nevertheless. I'm taking you to Bingleys'." He turned toward the door. "Pack light. I want the horse to make it back. And, Miss Alton?"

"Yes?"

"I'm not coddling you. I'm taking care of you." He put his hat on his head. Smiling, he said, "Welcome to the West."

"WELL, I LIKE HIM," DARCY SAID.

Beth's eyes opened. "He was a good man, a good husband and father," she said sleepily.

"What do you mean?"

"He was a *man's man*, Grandma said. He was her father, you know."

"I like her, too. Miss Alton, the schoolteacher, is pretty much my idea of the perfect woman: smart, brave, determined, resourceful."

"She was all those things. There's a picture of her in there too. Taken about 1912."

He thumbed through the pages and pulled out a vintage photograph. "Lovely. She was tall, like you are."

Beth yawned. "Mm-hmm."

"More? Or do you want me to stop? Am I keeping you from resting?"

"Oh no, please keep reading. I want to hear what happened."

Darcy read on into the afternoon, and Beth discovered how her great-grandfather's face transformed when he smiled, learned about the time the sheriff shocked everyone at the county fair by asking the schoolteacher to dance, and how they eavesdropped on his straightforward marriage proposal—when he asked her to be his "helpmeet" and share his life.

When she awoke, Darcy was gone, an afghan was tucked around her, and the journal was lying open to the last page he read, right after the sheriff's proposal. Beth's eyes wandered the page and caught the last few lines Darcy must have read before he stopped.

...as proposals go, it might have sounded awkward. But, to me, it was terribly romantic, mostly because I knew it came straight from his heart. To have the admiration of such a man is something to treasure. And to think, if I had continued to judge him based on that disdainful scowl and those abrupt words at the train station, how much would I have missed?

How much, indeed.

DECEMBER 1980

BETH HAD ALREADY FINISHED THE FINAL QUIZ BUT SPENT EXTRA TIME checking her answers, trying to be the last one out. The room was filled with angsty silence as students squirmed in their chairs. Every once in a while, she heard an exasperated sigh. Beth let out a couple of those herself, forming a desperate resolution—to talk to Darcy. Since Thanksgiving, he had been all business with her. It was appropriate, she supposed, he *was* still her instructor, but it felt...wrong, somehow. She wanted to thank him again. She wanted to know what his plans were for winter break. She wanted to ask him what he meant when he said he liked her.

Yes, her feelings were starting to get in the way, but she wasn't quite sure what to do about it. If only he could catch more than a glimpse of the real Beth—not the girl engineer always on her guard. The Beth who loved her friends and family and liked her work. The girl who maybe liked him a little bit too. It was as if they had started down the road to being friends—maybe friends with the potential for more—and it felt like it had all come to an abrupt halt.

Finally, the last student turned in his final, shaking his head as he walked out. She and Darcy were alone.

He was sitting at the desk, frowning at some papers in his hand, and apparently ignoring that she was the only one left in the room.

Beth stood and began slowly putting away her pencils and calculator. She approached the desk, her final in her hand.

"Question?" he asked.

"No. No questions." She laid the paper on top of the stack and hitched her backpack onto her shoulder. "Well, I guess this is it."

Darcy looked up at her, and in a very business-like way, he said, "Yes." He cleared his throat. "Um, I—I've enjoyed having you in class this semester."

"Thanks. You were a good instructor." She grinned. "Tough, but good. I learned a lot."

"It's kind of you to say that."

"I learned more than just electronics though." She gathered her courage. "I just wanted to thank you again for helping me out when I was sick. I promised my mother I would convey her thanks too and tell you if you're ever in Denver at Thanksgiving, she owes you a turkey dinner."

Darcy chuckled softly. "Well, I appreciate it, but she owes me nothing. I was happy to do it. For you." Those brown eyes scanned her face, as if memorizing it.

"You know, I misjudged you."

"Oh?"

"At the beginning of the semester, I thought you were just another arrogant jerk who thought girls belonged in the home ec department and out of engineering."

"But you don't think that anymore?"

"No, I don't. You listened to me when I came to you, and you changed. You gave me the shot I wanted. The shot I deserved. It's more than some would do, including some women. I know it wasn't always comfortable for you." She laughed. "There were days you hardly said a word, even to the class as a whole."

"I wasn't trying to be unapproachable. I tend not to talk a lot in new situations. Some of that's my own personality, but some of it's a line of defense."

"What do you mean?"

"You think you're the only one who builds a wall against the status quo?" He shook his head. "I have found that some people here think Southerners sound stupid. I've tried to neutralize my accent, but I'm not always successful, so I tend to be tight-lipped until I get to know people."

"And then you use words of four syllables to keep them at bay?" She paused. "Sorry, I can't seem to help teasing you a little."

"S'okay. I don't mind it so much when it comes from you. And yes, that's probably where the four syllable words come from."

"For what it's worth, I don't think the accent makes you sound stupid."

"No?"

"Not at all. I find it..." She felt a blush creep into her cheeks. "Rather charming, I guess."

"Oh. That's good to know." He sat back in his chair, looking at her thoughtfully.

The tide of awkwardness washed over her, and she fought to put herself back on even ground. "Well"—she held out her hand—"thanks again. For everything."

Darcy stepped around in front of the desk and took her hand in his. The faint scent of aftershave weaved its way to her, making her lean toward him without conscious thought. They stood there, together, frozen in the moment—a crossroads of sorts. Possibilities ran through her like a current, waiting for one spark to dismantle her resistance.

"I'll see you around." She couldn't look away.

Darcy didn't shake her hand with his typical business-like brusqueness. Instead he held it, as if it were a precious thing to protect. "Yes, see you around, Beth."

She stepped back. "Merry Christmas."

"You too."

JANUARY 1981

BETH OPENED THE DOOR TO HER APARTMENT, STRUGGLING TO MANAGE her suitcases. She flipped on the lights and went straight to the thermostat, cranking the heat up.

It had been a sort of melancholy winter break. To begin with, it was the first Christmas without Great-Nana, which left a bigger hole than Beth had anticipated. Her aging great-grandmother usually just sat around, laughing at the shenanigans of the young people and telling stories about the old days. But she had been a fixture at the family Christmas gatherings, and she was missed. Beth had a sense of life shifting and passing without the matriarch's presence, so, during those weeks at home, she turned to the rest of Great-Nana's diaries to fill the void.

She realized the journals served another purpose too. Reading about her great-grandfather Gardiner put her more and more in mind of William Darcy. And Beth liked thinking about William Darcy—that enticing, provoking man! No matter how many times she promised herself she would think no more about him, he still entered her thoughts at odd times—his rare, beautiful smiles, the barely constrained drawl that captivated her, serious brown eyes that seemed to look inside her soul like no one else's.

And here she was, back from winter break and still, he was invading her thoughts.

"Stop it, Beth," she muttered to herself. "You're infatuated, that's all this is." *You were from that very first moment outside the coffee shop. Get on with your life. This semester is the hardest, and you'd better stay focused.*

She made herself a cup of hot chocolate, covered in marshmallows, just the way she liked it, and stared out the window at the gentle snowfall, replaying Great-Nana's story of the Blizzard of '06 in her imagination.

A knock at the door startled her. She set down her cup and looked out the peephole. Her heart lurched.

"Will!"

He stood in her doorway, looking rather grave. "You're back."

"What are you doing here?"

"Ah…" He rubbed the back of his neck, then chuckled.

"I mean, it's good to see you."

He dropped his hand to his side and looked up at her, hopeful. "It's good to see you too. Beth."

"It's freezing out here. Do you want to come in?"

"Yes. Yes, I do." He shut the door behind him with a soft click.

She tilted her head in question while he stared at her.

"I—I'm not your instructor anymore."

"No."

"You don't dislike me anymore."

"No, I don't dislike you. Of course not," she said.

"I'm running down a list. It's the logical thing to do."

She clamped her lips shut to keep from spewing a giddy laugh.

He continued, almost as if he was looking past her. "But this isn't logical, is it?"

"It's not?"

"No."

"Hmm." She raised an eyebrow, waiting.

"So, I'm not your instructor, you don't dislike me, and this isn't logical."

"What is this about?"

"This." He took one of her hands, interlaced their fingers. "What I've been thinking about since October. When I started making the list."

"What list?"

"The list of all the reasons why I want to kiss you. Then I started adding all the reasons I *couldn't* kiss you. Moving them from the negative column to the positive column, as they worked themselves out."

Beth's smile bloomed over her features. "How scientific of you."

"Yes." He paused. "Can I? I mean, may I? Kiss you, now, that is?"

She nodded.

He drew her in, one hand behind her head, the other around the small of her back. He hesitated, and the last thing she saw before her eyes fluttered closed was his questioning gaze. She leaned in and rejoiced when he pressed his lips to hers.

After he pulled back to gauge her reaction, she put her arms around his shoulders. "No words of four syllables?"

"Not this time." He kissed her again.

BETH SLID TWO PIECES OF PIZZA INTO A TAKE-OUT BOX. "I'M ALMOST afraid to ask, but what changed your mind? About me, I mean."

"I don't know that I ever changed my mind. It wasn't like that," Will said, laying his napkin beside his plate. "You snuck up on me."

"Like you said happened with Charlotte and Collins? Who are still dating, by the way."

"You forget nothing. I'll have to keep that in mind."

She shrugged. "I have a mind for minutiae."

"One of the things that makes you good at electronics."

"I know I'm sort of an odd duck." She closed the pizza box and rested her chin in her hand.

"I wouldn't call you odd."

"You wouldn't?" she said with a warm smile.

"I'd call you unique."

"That sounds much better."

"I've never met a woman quite like you before. I'm sure I noticed you from the beginning of the semester."

"Girl engineer." She pointed at herself. "Hard to miss."

"But after that conversation we had about me ignoring you in class, you made me think."

"I was blunt. You don't have to sugarcoat it. But perhaps you liked that."

"Maybe I did. At first, I figured De Bourgh was right, that you were difficult." He toyed with the napkin in front of him. "But then I started paying attention. I saw you pull more than your fair share in the lab, week after week. I saw you with the kids at Engineering Day. Watched you playing that bizarre instrument."

"Me and my Theremin—nothing odd about that." She couldn't stop looking at him, at every plane and angle of his face, his wavy hair, his competent hands.

"I heard you sing. You surprised me at every turn, and I found myself wondering how you would dazzle me next."

Beth wondered if she had ever heard anything quite so romantic.

He ran his finger over her wrist, as if touching her would keep this new electric current flowing between them.

"I was raised to think of women as…different, foreign, if you will. But you"—he stopped as if to gather his thoughts—"you are 'other' and yet, at the same time, not 'other.' How could that *not* intrigue me? Getting to know you would be an adventure. And once I realized *that*, the real question became how much might I miss if I walked away without finding out more."

"Great-Nana thought the same about her sheriff."

He nodded, then leveled his serious gaze at her. "So, obstinate, headstrong girl, what do you say?"

"I say, we find out more."

KAREN M COX is an award-winning author of five novels accented with romance and history: *1932, Find Wonder in All Things, Undeceived, I Could Write a Book,* and *Son of a Preacher Man,* as well as an e-book novella companion to *1932, The Journey Home.* She also contributed short stories for several Austen-inspired anthologies. Originally from Everett, Washington, Karen now lives in Central Kentucky with her husband, works as a pediatric speech pathologist, encourages her children, and spoils her granddaughter.

Something Like Regret

Elizabeth Adams

She began now to comprehend that he was exactly the man, who, in disposition and talents, would most suit her. –Chapter L

SOMETHING LIKE REGRET
Elizabeth Adams

*T*his was a bad idea. This was an awful, horrible idea.

As I walked from one room to the next, surrounded by elegant brocade and rich tapestries, all I could think was that I should never have come. Every praise uttered by Mrs. Reynolds, each tasteful piece of art or comfortable furniture, reminded me of what I had given up. What I had refused. What I had thrown away as if it were poison.

Of this elegant home, I might have been mistress. I might have had regular meetings with this competent housekeeper, going over menus and discussing household accounts. There would be no screaming that there was no fish to be had, and no panicking at the slightest change to the expected. Pemberley was clearly not the sort of home where the mistress retired to her bed demanding salts and the attendance of her housekeeper. Mrs. Reynolds would be appalled by the very idea.

Pemberley was all that is charming and elegant, a house fit for a dream, inhabited by angels and tended by fairies. I followed the housekeeper up the stairs silently, but my mind was screaming, "Foolish girl, foolish girl, foolish girl!" until my thoughts kept rhythm with my heels on the cool marble steps.

This does not come without a price, I reminded myself. *You would have to marry Mr. Darcy if you wished to be mistress of this magical place. You would have to sit across from him at every meal, entertain him on the pianoforte whenever he wished, and abide his glowering while you did so. You would have to suffer his intimate company, and eventually rear children with him. You would have to converse with and entertain him daily, and knowing his fastidious nature, it is unlikely you would ever truly please such a man.*

I have seen many marriages and watched closely those of my relations with all their various missteps and victories. A wife who cannot please her husband is in a precarious position indeed. I did not wish to be such a one. I would never wish my husband to find me silly or unworthy of his time.

After our quarrel, Mr. Darcy likely viewed me as worse than silly —as blind, gullible, and stupid. My vain and prejudiced behavior last autumn cannot be excused, not even by the most liberal of judges, but perhaps my natural candor will explain why I did not immediately suspect Mr. Wickham of lies and manipulation when he first shared his disturbing history with me. I possess a curious nature and an open disposition that my sister Jane tells me allows my companions a certain level of ease. They share information they otherwise would not with a neighbor, or a relation, or a near-stranger as sometimes happens.

I have learned better, and now view every confidence with more suspicion and less sanguinity than before. But I digress.

As I peered out yet another large window at yet another fine prospect, I could not help but wonder what sort of husband Mr. Darcy would make. His cousin seemed to believe he would do the position justice, but what could he base such an assumption on? Mr. Darcy had never been married before. Each time I saw him in Kent or in Hertfordshire, he wore a frown or a blank expression, displaying his taciturn nature for the world as if it should not bother anyone as it clearly did not bother him. His fastidiousness and utter refusal to concern himself with others' feelings or comfort made every gathering awkward and would surely make him a less than agreeable companion.

In short, Mr. Darcy would be devilishly hard to please and, though he comes with a truly magnificent estate, living with him would be exhausting and fretful. No, I made the right decision; I simply should have made it more civilly.

I do feel terrible for how I refused Mr. Darcy. I have never been so embarrassed over anything in my life! If the opportunity to apologize were to present itself, I would take it and gladly. But I cannot regret my decision to refuse him.

Pemberley may be a splendid estate, but without the freedom to invite my family and friends, or to visit them as I choose, it would quickly become a cage. A beautiful cage, but a cage, nonetheless. This reminder kept me from feeling something like regret amidst these wondrous views and tasteful décor. *Remember it is a cage, Elizabeth. Do not forget.*

I followed my aunt and uncle up a flight of stairs so wide they could hold two passing carriages, but I managed to maintain my composure until my uncle began peppering Mrs. Reynolds with questions of her master. My uncle is a gregarious man, always willing to talk and ready to find amusement wherever it might present itself. In this way, he is an odd combination of my parents, though, thankfully, in reduced measure. His eyes twinkled with mischief when he glanced over his shoulder and smirked at me. I only shook my head at his antics. I would not be able to avoid hearing of Mr. Darcy this day—best to get it over with.

I had tried not to think of the quiet man from Derbyshire lately. After our quarrel in Kent, I could think of little but Mr. Darcy. Realizing I was foolish where I had thought myself clever was a blow to my pride as well as my vanity. Jane has long owned the title of *Most Beautiful Bennet Sister*, but I had claimed *Cleverest Bennet Sister* as my own years ago and I was loath to relinquish it. Alas, I would be a simpleton indeed if I could not recognize what was right before me.

Mr. Wickham was a charming cad and Mr. Darcy was a taciturn gentleman. If only one could mix them together to make just the right sort of man. But that is a silly fancy and best not imagined.

After castigating myself and receiving succor from my dear Jane, I resolved to think on it no longer. It was unlikely I would ever see Mr. Darcy again, and I was certain of nothing more than the belief that he would not seek me out. I was doing well in my plan to forget him and our tumultuous past, until my aunt suggested we visit Pemberley.

Mr. Darcy's Pemberley. Perfect Pemberley. The estate *I-might-*

have-been-mistress-of Pemberley. I realized she would not be dissuaded and so I came along, if not entirely willingly, at least civilly. At least he was from home. It would be mortifying to be caught touring his estate four months after I spurned him so furiously.

"I never had a cross word from him, and I've known him since he was four years old." Mrs. Reynolds was speaking about her master again, and I tried to cover my surprise. I believe I was successful, for she continued on without remarking on my incredulity.

But incredulous I was. Mr. Darcy, a pleasant man! Mr. Darcy, kind and generous? The best brother, the best master, the best landlord. Could it be true?

Mrs. Reynolds was intelligent, observant, and competent. I could not discount her word without proving myself to be without those qualities.

I thought about what she said, about what I knew of the dark man from Derbyshire. He was intelligent. In fact, he made most men seem silly by comparison. *Much like my father.* As I considered our interactions in Hertfordshire, without the lens of prejudice I had so gleefully donned last autumn, I began to think he was not always bad. He had made witty comments (admire us better from his seat by the fire, indeed!) and argued intelligently. Had he been arguing? Or had he been debating, as my father was wont to do when in need of mental stimulation? I have often thought my father would have done better as a professor at Cambridge or Oxford, but his lot was to be born first and inherit an estate, as was Mr. Darcy's.

Was it possible Mr. Darcy had not been arguing with me but had in fact been seeking intelligent discourse? Mr. Bingley did not like disputes; he would certainly never willingly argue with his friend. Mr. Hurst seemed as unlikely a candidate as his wife and her many bracelets. Caroline Bingley had the necessary intelligence, but with her constant agreement with everything any rich gentleman said, she would not make a willing debate partner, nor an exciting one.

I stopped in the middle of the room in shock. Did Mr. Darcy admire my mind? Is that why he was constantly engaging me in arguments? And why he believed himself in love with me? I felt my skin heat and tingle as the blood rushed up my neck. I do believe I was rather flattered. *Oh, dear.*

The tour continued and we found ourselves in a gallery. There were portraits of long-lost Darcys and their various hounds and steeds. I could not keep my mind from wandering to the idea that this could have been part of my legacy, had I accepted him in April. These people, with their powdered wigs and fashionable hats, could have been my children's ancestors.

It was a disconcerting idea, indeed. I shook off my morbid thoughts and focused on Mrs. Reynolds. She stood before a painting of a young man in Georgian attire. He was tall, like many of the other Darcy men on display, and he stood beside a magnificent horse. His countenance was familiar. He had the same jaw and nose of the younger Mr. Darcy, and the same strong brow and confident stance—Mr. Darcy's father.

Next to him was a portrait of a woman with fair hair and bright blue eyes. She looked aristocratic and delicate, but there was a kindness in her expression. She must be Mr. Darcy's mother, Lady Anne Darcy.

And then he was before me—Mr. Fitzwilliam Darcy. He had his mother's eyes, but otherwise he was the image of his father. He wore a small smile, one that I had seen when he looked at me occasionally. Before I could inquire, my aunt asked how old Mr. Darcy was when it was painted.

"Twenty-two, ma'am. Not long before his father died."

So that was the difference. I supposed the severity and constant frowning began after he inherited. I had never thought on it before, but he had been only a year older than myself when he had inherited all of this. All these people who relied on him, the servants and tenants and even the nearby villagers whose security was directly tied to Pemberley's prosperity. And his young sister! She must have been ten or eleven years old when her father passed.

I doubted I could do it. I barely tolerated chaperoning Lydia on a walk, let alone being her sole guardian. Yet he had taken it all on, and by the look of things, he had succeeded marvelously. I felt a strange sensation in my chest, a sort of swelling of emotion. With more than a little surprise, I realized I felt proud of Mr. Darcy. Proud that he had accomplished all that he had, proud to know such a man, and proud to have once been thought well of by him. So well that he was willing to fracture his own family in order to marry me.

I swallowed thickly and continued to gaze at his portrait. My relations and Mrs. Reynolds moved down the room, but I stood rooted to the spot, staring.

"I cannot make out your character," I whispered. "But I begin to think I do not know you at all."

The remainder of the tour passed by in a blur. My aunt recognized a miniature of Mr. Wickham and when the housekeeper told her he had turned out quite wild, my aunt turned questioning eyes on me. I whispered that Mr. Wickham had proven to be very different from how he presented himself. Her expression told me I would be explaining later, and I nodded, too caught up in the present to worry about future conversations.

Why did Mr. Darcy leave the miniature hanging? Mrs. Reynolds said he had left the room exactly as it had been when it was his father's favorite. How it must have galled him to have a painting of Wickham hung next to his own, as if they were brothers, when he knew that man's true character. How painful his father's admiration of such a man must have been. And how magnanimous Mr. Darcy was, to not wish to ruin Wickham in his father's eyes. Had he done it to protect his father's feelings? Or had he retained some affection for Wickham himself? After all, they had grown up together. They had been boyhood friends. Such ties were not easily thrown off.

How much worse Wickham's betrayal now appeared—and how wretched I felt for my former preference. He had not tried to seduce just any heiress, but the sister of his old friend, knowing it would be the worst possible thing he could do to Mr. Darcy. How it must have hurt! It was one thing to know a former friend had slid into dissipation and made unsavory choices. It was quite another to be betrayed in such a blatant and personal way. I had thought Wickham could sink no lower in my estimation but seeing the position in the Darcy family he had once occupied hardened my heart irrevocably. How could he do it? To Darcy, to Georgiana! A fifteen-year-old girl! The daughter of his benefactor!

My thoughts were flying faster than I could sort them. I had thought Mr. Darcy resentful. Demanding. Impossible to live with. But he had left the painting of the man who tried to ruin his sister's life, and by extension his own, hanging in his father's favorite room. He was either incredibly sentimental or loyal to a fault. I imagined it was the latter.

The thought crossed my mind that had I become mistress of this house, one of my first orders of business would have been to smash the miniature to smithereens. I could claim it as an accident later. Surely the Darcy siblings could not desire to see the face of someone who had hurt them so deeply; they should be able to remember their father in peace.

I looked up when the bright sunshine crossed my face. The great door was open, and my aunt was leading me outside while my uncle tipped the housekeeper. My aunt said something about viewing the formal gardens, and I nodded absently.

We began with the rose garden. A gnarled, old gardener guided us, pointing out the different varieties; he was knowledgeable and kind. I should have given him more of my attention, but my mind was too full to pay heed to which were Lady Anne's favorites and which were Miss Darcy's. We were to explore the park next, and I anticipated having some time on my own to sort my thoughts. I left the rose garden before my relations, as my aunt had a pebble in her shoe. I walked around the hedge, enjoying the fine day and trying not to think myself into a hole, as my father would say.

Mr. Darcy seemed a different creature here. Mrs. Reynolds had nothing but praise for him, and the success of his estate could only be in his favor. The gardener had commended his attention to his sister's preferences. If the animals could talk, I am certain they would have burst into song about his love and care for them. It did not match with the Mr. Darcy I had known before, but then I realized after I read his letter that I had not taken the time to know him. I had allowed his early rudeness to prejudice my every perception—my vanity had taken me for a wild ride. I thought I had corrected this after reading his letter, but had I really?

I thought I had learned after Hunsford. I thought I had come to know myself better. But had I truly reconsidered Mr. Darcy's character or merely felt guilty for abusing him so dreadfully and being so gullible to Mr. Wickham's lies? As I walked along the path, I could not help but wonder if I had learnt as much as I thought I had.

I had been so certain Mr. Darcy was a bad-tempered man. My belief in his cruelty had been built on lies and misinformation, but my impression of his nature had been colored by nothing but his own behavior—had it not?

I was now questioning even that. The reports I received of Mr. Darcy here were so different from how I viewed him. I began to think my understanding of human nature to be hopelessly flawed.

"Miss Bennet!"

"Mr. Darcy!" My face instantly flamed. Had I conjured him here with my thoughts?

"What brings you to Pemberley?" he asked, coming close enough I could see that he appeared a bit thinner than when I saw him last, and his hair was lightened by the sun.

"I am traveling through Derbyshire with my aunt and uncle. She spent her childhood in Lambton and wished to visit."

"Ah." He looked down at the hat he was gripping tightly, then glanced back up at me. "Are you enjoying your trip?"

"Yes, we're having a lovely time." I twisted my hands, not knowing what to say but unwilling to leave an awkward silence. "I thought you were away from home." He mumbled something about business with his steward as I rambled over him. "We never would have come had I known you would be here. I would never presume to intrude so." I looked down, and to the right, and beyond him, but I could not bring myself to look at his face. *Oh, what he must think of me!*

"It is no intrusion. You are most welcome," he said.

The surprise must have shown on my face for I believe I stared at him for a full minute before responding. "Thank you."

He finally spoke again. "Are your family well?"

"Yes, they are all well. And you? Are you well?"

"Quite well, thank you."

"The gardens are beautiful," I said, trying to dispel the awkwardness but hoping to not give him the impression I was pining after his estate. Though it was spectacular...

"Thank you. They are the work of many generations."

"Like the library?"

He smiled wistfully. "Yes, much like the library." He twisted his hat in his hands. "Is your family well? Are they at Longbourn?"

I grinned at his repetition. There was some solace in knowing I was not the only one made nervous by our surprise meeting. "Yes, they are all well. My sisters are all at Longbourn but Lydia, the youngest. She is in Brighton with a friend."

"Right. Well, I should," he hesitated and gestured to his attire, which I belatedly realized was coated in dust. "Please excuse me, Miss Bennet." He turned toward the house and strode rapidly away.

Relief flooded me as I watched his retreating back. It was over, and I had survived it unscathed.

"Lizzy, who was that?" asked my uncle.

I turned to see they had caught up to me. "That was Mr. Darcy."

"It was kind of him to stop and greet you," said my aunt.

You have no idea, Aunt. After our last conversation, not hurling insults at one another was kindness itself.

I nodded and they continued to speak, of what I know not, and I followed them along the path the gardener had pointed out to us. As we were approaching a wood, I realized I had had the perfect opportunity to apologize and I had not taken it. *Foolish girl, indeed.*

WE WERE EXAMINING SOME PLANT MY AUNT FOUND FASCINATING, BUT no one could identify, when she peered beyond my shoulder and said, "Is that Mr. Darcy?"

I whipped my head so quickly I felt my bonnet shift. Indeed it was he, coming up the path in great, long strides and what looked like a determined expression on his face.

"Miss Bennet, would you introduce me to your friends?"

"Yes, of course. This is my uncle, Mr. Edward Gardiner, and his wife. Aunt, Uncle, this is Mr. Darcy."

"I am pleased to meet you."

He spoke evenly and bowed respectfully, leaving me to wonder if he realized these were my relations in trade. Surely he must know? I had no uncles on my father's side. Did he not know that?

I could not help but notice that his hair was damp at the ends and he was now wearing a clean jacket, though his cravat looked as if it had been tied in haste. While I was woolgathering, my relations greeted him and complimented his estate, thanked him for allowing them to tour it, and asked him the identity of the plant we had been discussing for the last five minutes. Her question answered, my aunt smiled happily and took my arm, leading us ahead while the men followed behind, discussing fishing.

What was happening? Mr. Darcy was telling my uncle where to find perch nearby. He was being kind. And personable. And friendly. Who was this man?

After more than half an hour had passed, and my aunt had sent me more than one expressive look, she said she was tired and requested her husband's arm for support. I did not believe it for a minute. She rarely tired after only an hour or two of leisurely strolling through evenly graveled gardens.

"Miss Bennet," Mr. Darcy said quietly as he stepped beside me.

"Mr. Darcy."

We neither of us knew what to say to the other and the silence was nearly painful. Finally, after gathering my courage and taking a deep breath, I spoke.

"Mr. Darcy, there is something I have been meaning to say to you for some time."

"Oh?"

How could one little word inspire such unease?

"Yes. I want to apologize for my behavior the last time we spoke in

Kent. Well, the time before the last time." I lowered my eyes. I was bungling this horribly. "You know what I refer to. I was intemperate and unkind and the furthest from ladylike I have ever been. I am deeply sorry for speaking to you the way I did, and for believing that man's lies, and for throwing them in your face so viciously."

I shook my head and looked away. I could feel his gaze on me. He had been watching me since I began speaking, but I did not want him to see my flushed cheeks or the shame in my eyes.

All was silent between us, no sounds but my aunt and uncle's indistinct chatter and our steps on the path.

"What did you say of me that was not true?" he finally said. His voice was quiet, as if the words pained him. "Though your accusations were ill founded, my behavior to you at the time merited the severest reproof. I *was* arrogant, conceited, and disdainful of others' feelings."

"Please do not remind me of what I said! I have never been more ashamed of my words or my faulty judgment."

Seeing we had far outstripped my relatives and were rounding a bend that would hide us from their sight for some time, he stopped and faced me.

"Miss Bennet, I beg you would not blame yourself. Wickham is a practiced deceiver and suspicion is not in your nature. How could you know what he was? My own father was deceived by him, and he had much greater experience in the world."

His expression was earnest, and I was surprised by the realization that he truly meant to exonerate me. "Mr. Darcy, I cannot allow you to take all the blame for that evening. It is gentlemanly of you to attempt it, but I hope I am not so selfish as to allow it."

He shook his head, and I realized my words were almost the reverse of one of the many insults I hurled at him that fateful evening.

"You do not know how your words have haunted me."

We were walking again, more slowly this time, and he spoke haltingly, as if the words were being dragged from him, but he refused to stop. I could sympathize with the feeling.

"*Had you behaved in a more gentlemanlike manner.* I have always prided myself on being a gentleman. On being a credit to the Darcy name, to Pemberley." He shook his head and grimaced slightly. "By you, I was properly humbled."

"I certainly had no notion of my words making so strong an impression! I didn't think you'd consider them beyond a passing thought."

"Of course not! You thought me devoid of every proper feeling."

This time it was I who stopped and turned to face him. "That was wrong of me. I should not have spoken to you as I did."

He startled, and I realized I had placed my hand on his arm. I flushed and brought my errant hand back to my side, but I would not allow myself to look away. He had admitted his faults; I could admit mine.

"You were not the only one filled with pride," I said as we resumed our pace. "I had thought myself so clever by taking an instant dislike of you. Of course, I was doomed to be proven wrong in the bitterest possible way. That is what happens when one charges ahead recklessly with no guide but one's own vanity."

"I cannot argue with that."

We were silent for some time, listening to the birds and walking side by side, easier in each other's company than I had ever felt with him before. I wished he had been this kind in Hertfordshire. I might have enjoyed coming to know him, and who knows what might have happened then.

"I beg your pardon?"

Oh, dear. Had I said that aloud? "Hmm?"

"You said you wished something."

"Oh!" I plucked a leaf off a bush and twirled it while I tried to think of something to say. I eventually decided there had been enough confusion between us. "I was wondering why we could never be this easy before." I peeked up at him, hoping I had not opened a box I could not close should its contents prove disturbing.

To my surprise, he raised a brow and said, "I believe we both know the answer to that."

I laughed. It leapt out of me before I could stop it and I tried to subdue it, but it would not be quieted. Mr. Darcy was laughing too, his shoulders shaking slightly and his eyes gleaming. "Touché, Mr. Darcy."

We rounded the next curve and the house was in view. The path went down an incline and he offered me his arm, without much confidence I thought, but he seemed pleased when I accepted it. He led me to the front of the drive near my uncle's carriage and we stopped to wait for my relations there, turning back to where the path crested the hill and wended its way down. The Gardiners were nowhere in sight, and judging by the pace they had been going, they would not arrive for another ten minutes.

"Would you like to come in for some refreshment?" he asked politely.

"I cannot. We are due for dinner at an old friend of my aunt's and we must return to Lambton if we wish to be on time."

He nodded. "I understand. Perhaps another time."

I tried to smile and show him that I meant no disrespect. I was quite surprised by our talk together and I no longer dreaded his company as I once had. In fact, I would own to a certain amount of curiosity about Mr. Darcy. I had been so wrong about him, and he had been so unexpected. How could I not long to know more? Another few minutes passed before he spoke again. "I am expecting a party tomorrow, some of whom are known to you. Mr. Bingley and his sisters, and my sister, Georgiana."

"Ah." I did not know what he expected me to say to that. Why would he bring up Bingley when we had been getting along so well?

"May I introduce my sister to you while you are here? Or do I ask too much?"

Apparently, it was a day for surprises. "I would be honored to meet your sister," I said.

I glimpsed my aunt and uncle halfway down the hill; they would be upon us in a matter of minutes.

"We are staying at the Red Lion." That was as far as my boldness would take me, but I could not deny I wanted to meet Miss Darcy. If reports of her brother had been contradictory, those relating to Miss Darcy had been no less so.

"I will call on you there." He said it with such assurance and solemnity that I felt myself blushing, though I could not imagine why I should blush. He was only being agreeable. He was not the sort of man I was interested in romantically. I wanted someone more garrulous, more sociable, more like myself.

Didn't I?

THE NEXT DAY, I ACCOMPANIED MY AUNT ON A SOCIAL CALL IN THE village after breakfast and we returned to the inn to meet my uncle before going out again. I wondered if Mr. Darcy would call. His sister was due that morning, and she would likely be tired from her journey. Mr. Darcy could hardly run out of the house so shortly after his guests arrived.

Suddenly it occurred to me that he might bring the Bingleys with him when he called. What would I say to Miss Bingley? I will tell you, dear reader, that I worried for my reaction. Jane is my most beloved sister, and Miss Bingley was a primary instrument in hurting her dreadfully. How could I not wish to avenge Jane, at least in some small way? Fear not. Though the idea is tempting, I would not do anything rash—but I have contemplated it.

We were preparing for our outing when the maid informed us that we had callers: Mr. and Miss Darcy. She seemed quite impressed and regarded us in a new light.

My aunt told her to show them in and I stood by the window fidgeting, wondering how I should greet them, and what Miss Darcy would be like, and whether Mr. Darcy would be as pleasant as yesterday or if he would revert to the Mr. Darcy I had known in Hertfordshire and Kent. Before I could work myself up too much, the maid opened the door, and there they were.

Mr. Darcy seemed even taller than I remembered; he could easily reach up and flatten his palm against the ceiling. He greeted my aunt and uncle, then turned his gaze to me. His expression was tentative, but warm, and I responded politely. At least I think I responded politely. I was horribly nervous, and it's possible I was only mildly coherent, but he did not seem to mind.

Miss Darcy was introduced, and it was immediately clear that not only had Wickham lied about Mr. Darcy, he had told an egregious falsehood when he called Miss Darcy proud. She was nothing of the sort. She was so shy it was almost crippling her, and she could barely whisper a greeting to us. She managed to raise her eyes from the floor during the introductions, but she wore a nervous, wary sort of expression. I immediately decided to do everything in my power to put her at ease. My affability ought to be good for something, after all.

My aunt had just offered to ring for tea when Mr. Darcy said Mr. Bingley was waiting in the carriage and would we mind if he came up? My aunt agreed and soon we were sitting around a small table, drinking tea with the Darcys and Mr. Bingley. The latter clearly wished for information of Jane. I considered taunting him a little in exchange for breaking my sister's heart, but he was so guileless I could not bring myself to do it. I told him Jane was well and still at Longbourn, but I could think of nothing clever to say that would induce him to return there.

I turned my attention to Georgiana, who became more talkative when we began speaking of music. I chanced a glance at Mr. Darcy and saw him watching us with a gentle expression, his eyes soft and happy. Why had I thought him so inscrutable before? Had I become more perceptive than I had been? Was I simply paying more attention to him? Or was he the one who had changed?

The call ended before anyone tired of the others' company, as all calls should, and Miss Darcy summoned up her courage to invite us to dinner two days hence. My aunt and uncle glanced at each other for only a moment before accepting and I could not help but notice the flutter of something, I could almost call it anticipation, that welled up inside me.

THE NEXT MORNING, I WAS PREPARING TO WALK WITH MY AUNT TO THE local haberdashers when a letter from Jane arrived. I had not heard from her in a week and I was eager to read it, so I stayed behind.

The letter was as I expected, filled with news of the local parties and calls and the pig who had escaped and trampled Mrs. Goulding's roses again. At the end, she mentioned receiving a letter from Lydia in Brighton, which I thought very odd, but Jane thought only right as she had sent our youngest sister three missives without a response.

Anyhow, Lydia was full of nothingness as she always was, but she did mention something about Mr. Wickham which Jane thought she should pass on to me.

Apparently, he had been playing cards each night (unsurprisingly) and had had a stroke of luck. He had done rather well one night, then to be a good sport had gone back to allow the gentlemen to win their money back. Shockingly, he had won again, and rather a lot, too. He had been so lucky, he decided to quit the regiment! He did it in a rather irregular way, quickly after the card game and without much word to anyone but Lieutenant Denny, who only knew that Wickham had packed a bag and said a quick farewell, but Jane was certain he intended to resign properly and must have had some urgent business to take care of.

I rolled my eyes. I was quite certain I knew what urgent business he had to take care of. Himself. What other explanation could there be for a man who had suddenly come into money? He must have owed his fellow officers, and I assumed the local shops, and after hearing of his victory, everyone would expect to be paid. The greedy braggart wanted to keep it for himself, so he left. Hopefully on a ship bound for the Americas, but even they did not deserve such a plague.

Jane went on to describe our young cousins' antics and our mother's reactions to them, usually involving smelling salts and hartshorn, and I was again reminded that Longbourn was a decidedly different place than Pemberley.

No wonder Mr. Darcy had been so worried about connecting himself to my family.

I put the letter away and prepared for our outing. My aunt and I decided to return Miss Darcy's call while my uncle met Mr. Darcy and the other gentlemen for a fishing excursion that they had arranged the day before.

Pemberley was as grand as it had been two days earlier but being received as a guest was a slightly different experience. I noticed the butler who greeted us watching me with interest, though it was well concealed. It may have been my imagination, but the two footmen we passed also looked our way, then quickly returned their attention to their duties.

I suppose it was to be expected. If the master returned home from a journey, bathed and changed quickly only to return outside to meet a group of tourists on the path, it would be noticed. If he then took his sister into the village only hours after she arrived to meet those same tourists, it would be even more odd.

I am certain Mr. Darcy did not make a habit of greeting strangers and giving them personal tours. The staff were naturally curious. In fact, when I thought about it, it was rather peculiar. His initial greeting was kind enough. It had not been necessary to seek us out again, or visit us in Lambton, and he certainly did not need to introduce his sister to me.

Could he still care for me? Examining the evidence impartially, I must conclude that his heart was still engaged, but I could not deny my incredulity. I had been abominable to him! I had told him he was the last man in the world I could ever be prevailed upon to marry! An amiable man would not forget such an insult. How much less so would the resentful Mr. Darcy?

Yet he was being kindness itself. He was attentive, and generous, and gentle with his sister—and with me. He was solicitous of my feelings. He sought out my company. He apologized and accepted my apology in return. Could it be he had misunderstood his own nature and he is, in fact, *not* resentful? Or could it be for my sake? I hesitated…but my heart whispered it was for me. I could scarce believe it. How could his love survive the insult I had dealt his pride?

I could only conclude, upon fair and reasonable reflection, that Mr. Darcy still cared for me and that his care was stronger than his pride. What I could not decide was whether he would act, or if he simply could not bear me thinking ill of him and had sought to change my opinion—without renewing his addresses. I instantly knew that not to be the case, despite my own doubts to the contrary. Mr. Darcy had been honor itself. He would not give me any attention if he did not intend to act upon it.

The thought hit me with full force: Mr. Darcy would ask me to marry him again.

"Mrs. Gardiner and Miss Bennet."

I heard our names being announced and forced myself to turn my attention to the room. We had been shown to a parlor that had not been on the tour yesterday.

Miss Darcy stood and greeted us, and I gave her my best smile, remembering her shyness and wanting to put her at ease. Miss Bingley merely nodded, as if she were the queen receiving visitors at court. I refrained from smirking at her, though it was a near thing.

I took the chair nearest Miss Darcy, and my aunt sat next to me. The next fifteen minutes were some of the most awkward of my life. I tried to speak to Miss Darcy more than once, but each time I broached a topic, music, travel, or otherwise, Miss Bingley would interrupt and turn the conversation toward their mutual acquaintance whom I did not know. I could see Miss Darcy's discomfort, and Mrs. Annesley had a pinched look about her lips, but without being overtly rude, it was difficult to manage the situation.

Finally, my aunt and Mrs. Annesley began their own lively discourse and they drew in Mrs. Hurst and eventually Miss Bingley, too, allowing me a few minutes to speak to Miss Darcy. She truly was a sweet girl and I thought we might become friends if we were given more than five minutes to converse.

Ten minutes later I had made her laugh twice with tales of growing up in a house with four sisters. Miss Bingley was not pleased at my accomplishment, but each time she turned to speak to us, my aunt would ask her a question to maintain her engagement in their conversation. Bless my aunt Gardiner!

Tea was eventually called for and Miss Darcy poured while the most sumptuous fruit was brought in. It was all laid out on a table to the side of the room and I stood over it long after the others had made their selections, trying to choose what to put on my delicate china plate. If I had been at Longbourn, I would have returned to the buffet more than once, as it was a well-known fact that fruit is my personal weakness.

"Find anything to tempt you, Miss Bennet?"

I jumped a little and nearly dropped my plate. "Mr. Darcy!"

Standing just behind me, he had leaned over to speak in my ear. He was wearing a devilish grin, clearly pleased with himself for having surprised me.

"The berries are particularly good," he said. "They are grown here on the estate, and likely picked this morning."

I nodded and placed a spoonful on my plate. "I thought you were fishing with the gentlemen?"

"I was, but I wanted to greet you. And your aunt."

I smiled. Such an admission deserved one after all. "Well met, Mr. Darcy."

He smiled back at me, and I could not help but think how friendly he appeared when he did so, and how much I liked him when he was like this.

"Will you have some?" I asked, gesturing to the table.

"Of course. I can never resist fresh fruit."

We both heaped our plates enormously high, making a sort of game of how many grapes we could pile on top of the blackberries without any spilling off the side.

Miss Darcy broke free of Miss Bingley's clutches to greet her brother. When she sat back down, it was in my previous chair, leaving her place on the divan next to Mrs. Annesley. I chose to sit in the empty divan across from her. Mr. Darcy sat next to me rather quickly —I assume to avoid any machinations of Miss Bingley who was glaring at me with daggers in her eyes. He seemed moderately pleased with himself, and I hid my smirk. It felt as if Mr. Darcy and I were working in concert to foil Miss Bingley's plots. I did not dislike the feeling.

I wondered what it would be like to have a partner in all things, someone to support me in social situations such as this and to share private concerns. I will confess, but only to you, dear reader, that I had not given it much thought before. I had thought of marrying Mr. Darcy, and it had seemed a daunting prospect. I had liked other gentlemen, and flirted a bit, but they had never been in a position to marry me or I had not been interested enough to truly contemplate marrying them. Thus my daydreams, such as they were, had not gone beyond a dance or a pleasing countenance. Faced with a legitimate option for a marriage partner, the idea of what the marriage itself would be was somewhat hazy to me.

I knew what I did not want. I did not want a marriage like my parents'. I wanted mutual respect and esteem. I wanted strong affection. I wanted to *like* my husband. I had wanted all these things for some time, but what did I want our interactions to be like? What did I wish for in my daily life? I did not want someone like Mr. Collins, fawning over anyone of consequence and embarrassing me constantly. I wanted a husband with his own pursuits. I did not want to be constantly tripping over him and redirecting him as Charlotte must.

I wanted an intelligent man, one I did not need to be embarrassed for, and one who could eat at table without making my stomach turn. I slid my glance to the left and peeked at Mr. Darcy. I had never particularly noticed his eating habits before, which must mean they were unobtrusive, and I was well acquainted with his intelligence. Surely he had ways to occupy his time? He seemed willing to be available for social duties when needed. He was polite, and I felt sure he would not know how to *fawn* if the fate of Pemberley depended on it. He was not charming, but I began to find his quiet presence pleasing and dignified, not needing to fill every moment with his own voice, like Mr. Wickham had done.

I cringed at the reminder of my folly. Truly, what had I been thinking? Thankfully, my heart had not been touched. I pity the woman who loves a man like Wickham.

As this thought crossed my mind, I glanced at Miss Darcy. Had she always been this withdrawn? Or like most shy people, did she have certain persons she was comfortable being voluble with and only timid in greater company? My sister Mary was similar. Even Jane could be bashful at times. I wondered if Miss Darcy was still wounded from her misadventure with Wickham last summer, and if it had made her more withdrawn. Poor girl!

I felt relief I had not fallen into a similar trap. Oh, I never would have agreed to an elopement, but had I a little money, or had he, would I have agreed to marry Wickham? I shuddered at the thought and could only hope I would have seen sense in the end.

"Are you well, Miss Bennet?" Mr. Darcy whispered. Everyone was speaking of the seaside, and I hoped his words went unnoticed. "You are quiet today."

"I am merely thoughtful, that is all."

"Dare I ask what you are thinking of?"

Wickham, your sister, marriage—possibly to you. No, I could not say that! "Decisions, the future, inconsequential things like that." I gave him what I hoped was a winsome smile, and he quirked an inquisitive brow at me.

"Is that so? And have you come to any conclusions?"

I knew we were speaking in riddles, but did he mean what I thought he meant? Did I *want* him to mean that? "I believe the subject requires further study," I said slowly.

He nodded; a light flashed in his eyes that I was certain I was not imagining. "Then I hope you find such an opportunity."

I stared into his too-green-to-be-blue eyes, trying to understand what I saw there, but I was a muddle of confusion. "I hope so, too."

He seemed pleased with this answer and grinned at me before turning back to the group. I could feel my cheeks heating and took the opportunity to return my plate to the sideboard. I stood near a window and gazed out, thinking I was doing a passable imitation of Mr. Darcy. When I felt I would not disgrace myself, I returned to the small divan I shared with the master of the house and participated in the conversation, all the while wondering if I was glimpsing my future, in this house, beside this man.

THE NEXT DAY, MY AUNT HAD YET MORE CALLS TO MAKE, AND MY UNCLE had planned to spend some time visiting the local vicar, whom he had become friendly with during another call. I had thought to accompany my aunt, or perhaps to stay behind and catch up on my correspondence, but before I had chosen, a note arrived from Pemberley. Mr. Darcy requested my company on a ride in his curricle if I was not otherwise engaged.

My aunt read the invitation with a triumphant smile, which I tried to ignore, and she quickly penned the reply that I would be happy to accompany Mr. Darcy on a ride about the countryside. My aunt left with a kiss to my forehead and a pat to my hand, though I know she was restraining herself. My uncle stayed with me until Mr. Darcy arrived. I tied my bonnet ribbons, slipped on my gloves, and gathered my shawl. My uncle greeted Mr. Darcy and said something about keeping me safe, and then Mr. Darcy was handing me up into the high curricle. I had never ridden in such a conveyance, though I had seen them often enough, and the view from such a vantage point was grand.

He climbed up beside me and we shared a tentative smile, and with a flick of his wrist, we were off.

I wanted to be light and charming, but I knew all too well what this meant. Such a pointed gesture would not go unnoticed. Such attention could only mean one thing. I was painfully aware of it, as I knew he was. The thought of what it must have taken for him to try again, to attempt to earn my favor after such a harsh rejection, inspired compassion in me and I found myself relaxing, knowing that whatever nerves I was feeling, he must be feeling threefold.

We left the village and drove along the main road until it forked just past a small river. We took the less busy lane and he slowed our pace, pausing to show me a tree he had fallen out of as a boy while playing with the son of the owner of said tree.

"What estate does it belong to?" I asked.

"It is a farm, owned by Callum MacGregor."

I could not hide my surprise that Mr. Darcy would willingly play with the child of a farmer.

"Surely you do not think children care for such things?" he asked.

"Children do not, no. But did young Master Darcy? I am not certain."

He laughed. "Did young Miss Elizabeth care for such things?"

"She did not. Young Miss Lizzy was friends with many tenants' and farmers' children and did many unladylike things."

"Such as?"

"Such as climbing trees, and splashing in the stream, and catching frogs. And chasing the boys who stole our dolls."

He laughed again, and I was struck with how different he appeared, here in Derbyshire, away from drawing room protocols and guests no sane person would enjoy.

"You're thoughtful again."

"Forgive me."

"Not at all. May I ask what stole your thoughts away?"

"I was thinking that you seem different here. More at ease." He looked at me quizzically and I continued, "In Derbyshire, and at Pemberley, especially."

"It is my home."

"Of course." I was not more at ease at home than anywhere else, but I could certainly see why he was. I shot him a teasing look. "You seem happy."

"I am always happy when I'm with you."

My tease was turned around neatly, and I could not but admire him for it. And for the slightly wicked gleam in his eye that told me he was flirting and knew it and enjoying every second of it.

I knew he had not always been happy in my presence, but I chose not to think of our tumultuous past. He was being quite charming, and I was determined to enjoy it, though I suspected I would spend most of the day with crimson cheeks. I turned away, then glanced back at him, then back to the trees we were passing. I could not help the smile I wore, or the warm feeling his words had given me. To affect such a man!

We crossed a small bridge, and he told me the stream originated in the Peaks, and I asked him to tell me more about the area. He was remarkably knowledgeable; I felt that I could listen to him for hours. He told me about the plants and trees, the local wildlife, the crops and animals raised on low or high ground. I asked him questions about the people who lived on the land and his relationship to them. To my surprise, he knew most everyone we passed and the owners or tenants of every farm and estate. He knew what they grew, how long they had held the land, and who would inherit it.

This is it, Elizabeth. This is what it would be like to be married to him.

The thought struck me so forcibly, I nearly lost my breath. I had been torturing myself, wondering what life would be like with such a man—hoping it was better than I feared and fearing it was not as good as I hoped.

Here was something solid I could depend upon. Two hours in his company and not a cross word between us. A good, kind, generous man. Beloved by his friends and family, respected by his neighbors. In disposition and talents, he was perfectly suited to me. I half wanted him to make his proposals right then only to spare me the anxiety.

He touched my hand, and I startled.

"You were far away again. Have I vexed you?"

"Not at all!" I answered brightly. "I don't remember when I've been so well entertained." His smile was so brilliant I wanted to encourage him. If we had been walking, I would have taken his arm. As it was, I had only words at my disposal. "I could quite happily spend many hours in such a manner."

His eyes widened, and I beamed at him, hoping he understood my encouragement as it was intended. He opened his mouth, then closed it, then opened it again. I imagined I had an inkling of what it would cost him to lay his heart before me again. How daunting a prospect!

I held his gaze, hoping I communicated my receptiveness in my eyes, though I likely appeared only anxious.

"Miss Bennet, you are too generous to trifle with me. If your feelings are the same as they were last April, tell me so at once."

I began to shake my head, unable to find the words to say I no longer hated him and in fact liked him rather well.

"If your feelings are *not* the same, if you will allow me to court you anew, to court you properly, it would make me very happy." I smiled as he looked at me, his heart in his almost-blue eyes. "Very happy indeed."

"Yes, I mean no." I paused to take a breath and gripped his hand in both of mine. "I mean my feelings are utterly different from what they have been, and I would be pleased to be courted by you." He stared at me in wonder, as if he had never seen a lady before. "I truly would." I watched him anxiously, finally realizing the ridiculousness of our situation and laughing at him. "I thought you said you would be happy, sir!"

"I am happy. So happy I cannot believe my good luck."

"It has nothing to do with luck," I said seriously. "It has everything to do with you."

I knew I would remember the next moment for the rest of my life. He was so joyful, his grin wide and his eyes alight. He raised both my hands to his lips and kissed them fervently, then held them to his chest.

"Elizabeth."

I FLOATED BACK INTO THE INN WITH A SILLY GRIN ON MY FACE AND humming a tuneless song. My uncle and aunt immediately suspected what had occurred and demanded every detail, though I could not oblige them entirely. I told them what was most important, but I kept for myself how he had kissed my hands more times than I could count, and how he had become so distracted by an errant petal that had flown into my hair that the carriage nearly toppled while he tried to retrieve it. We had laughed and flirted and teased, and I had held his left hand in both of mine while he drove with his right. We had spoken of everything and nothing, and only returned to the inn when we feared my uncle would come searching for me if we stayed away any later. Before we entered the village, he asked if he might see me again tomorrow, and I assured him I had no other plans. He promised to think of something lovely for us to do, and I had left him, feeling as light as a feather on the breeze.

Who knew courting was so enjoyable?

WHEN WE ENTERED PEMBERLEY FOR DINNER THAT EVENING, MR. DARCY immediately asked my uncle if he could speak with him privately. They were gone only a few minutes and when they returned, both looked at me in such a way it was impossible not to know what had occurred.

Mr. Darcy paid me particular attention, despite Miss Bingley's constant interference, and I sat to his left at dinner, directly across from my aunt. He was making his preference known, in no uncertain terms, and no one present could be blind to it. I was almost entirely happy, but one thing stood in the way of my complete contentment.

Jane.

Dear, sweet, heartbroken Jane. I deflated slightly at the thought. Miss Bingley's constant haranguing when the ladies withdrew after dinner did nothing to improve my mood. Any simpleton could see that she was distressing Georgiana and making herself appear shrewish and bitter, but angry people are not always wise. I finally separated myself from the group and sat in a corner near a window, hoping my absence would force a change of topic.

When the gentlemen returned, Mr. Darcy immediately came to my side. "What troubles you, my dear?"

I smiled wanly at him. It was strange how I had so immediately come to trust him. How I wished to tell him all my troubles in the hope that we might solve them together. Had he always inspired such feelings or was it a result of our recent understanding?

I squeezed his hand and stared out the darkened window. "I worry for Jane, that is all. I feel guilty for being so happy here while she is home alone. She is so good, and she did not deserve to be jilted."

He sighed. "That is my doing, I'm afraid. I should have told Bingley long ago that I was mistaken. I thought that so much time had passed, and I did not wish to interfere again, but..." He sighed again and joined me in peering into the night.

"You take too much on yourself. Mr. Bingley is his own man. You did not force him to leave, nor stop him from returning. If he was persuaded, he allowed himself to be."

I do not know where my boldness came from, but the past days had shown me that Mr. Darcy was a man of honor, but still only a man. If Mr. Bingley had trusted him over his own heart, that was his choice. He was not a child to be taken hither and yon without any say.

"I cannot overlook it so easily. Bingley is modest, and his trust in me is complete. I did him a great disservice." I shook my head and he twisted his lips bitterly. "If someone had tried to convince me against you, if they had lied about your presence, say here in Lambton, I would not forgive them easily."

"You also would not have listened," I added quietly, knowing it to be true.

He smiled at me so tenderly it ached. "No, I would not have. Nothing could keep me from you."

"And *that* is the difference between you and Mr. Bingley."

He smiled again. "I will speak with Bingley tonight."

I eyed him narrowly. "Because of me, or because you wish to?"

"Because it is past time I corrected my error."

He spoke with such surety that my pride in him swelled alongside my attraction, but his dread was so evident that my heart ached for him. It would be a difficult conversation, and their friendship might suffer as a result.

I turned so our hands were hidden by my skirts and squeezed his hand. "All will be well, Fitzwilliam. I am certain of it."

He was surprised to hear his given name on my lips, then he gripped my hand tightly and said, "Thank you, Elizabeth. Your support means a great deal to me."

Caroline Bingley's voice crashed into our peaceful moment. "Mr. Darcy, you must join us. I am certain you can settle the debate."

I had no idea what she was talking of, but it was clear she wished to separate Mr. Darcy from myself. I squeezed his hand once again and told him to go. I would stay by the window a while longer. Miss Bingley was easier to manage when I did not join in the company, and this day had been so lovely, I did not want it marred by her petulance. I was much happier staring at the stars and reliving our lovely ride through the countryside and thinking of the future and how very bright it seemed.

THE NEXT MORNING, I WOKE AS HAPPY AS WHEN I FELL ASLEEP. I WAS loath to leave Lambton in two days' time after we had so recently reached an understanding, but I did not think I could ask my relations to delay on my account. We were to stop in two other towns on our way home and would reach Longbourn within the week.

Mr. Darcy asked if I would correspond with Georgiana, and I agreed. She seemed happy at the notion. She had invited me to go riding with her this morning as her other guests preferred to sleep until midday, and I told her I would love to but that I was no horsewoman. I suggested a walk instead, and it was agreed she would send a carriage for me and I would spend the morning at Pemberley with Miss Darcy.

I saw my aunt and uncle off on their excursion and waited for the Darcy carriage to collect me. I was pleasantly surprised when I saw Mr. Darcy coming down the village road in his curricle. I skipped out the front of the inn just as he leapt down.

"Miss Bennet, I hope you do not mind that I decided to collect you myself?"

"Why would I mind? What a lovely way to spend the morning."

He grinned boyishly and handed me up, and then we were off. I waited until we were out of the village, and then I could wait no longer.

"Will you tell me of your conversation with Mr. Bingley last evening?"

He grimaced. "It was not unexpected. He was rightfully angry, but

Bingley is never cruel, even in his anger. We had words, and I apologized; he forgave me, and he is now making plans to return to Netherfield."

"Truly?"

"Yes. Does that please you?"

I beamed at him. "Of course! I am very pleased. Jane will be so happy. Thank you, Fitzwilliam!" I impulsively reached up and kissed his cheek, as I would do for my father or uncle when they did something kind for me. His response was nothing like theirs, though. He flushed crimson, and the reins went slack in his hands as he turned his face to me.

He stared at me until I was certain my complexion matched his and then he said, "Shall I expect such a reward each time I please you?"

I had thought I could not become any redder, but I felt myself flush down to my waist, if such a thing is possible.

Feeling my courage rise, I said, "Perhaps. If you do something particularly kind, your reward might be even greater."

His eyes flared, and I wondered if I had gone too far. After a short eternity, he said, "I shall hold you to that, Miss Bennet."

I smiled tremulously, and he drove on.

We eventually spoke of Pemberley and his sister, and he recommended a path for our walk. Before I knew it, we were pulling up the drive and he was handing me down, kissing my hand before he released it—right in front of the footman!

Georgiana was waiting, and we made our way to the lake. It was beautiful and idyllic, and her company was pleasant and sweet. More and more each day, I could see myself living here. In this place, with these people. I felt as if I belonged, as if it was where I was meant to be. If I were to accept another gentleman and make my home on another estate, I would find a measure of happiness, but I somehow felt that I would never be as happy as I could have been here. I felt silly as I thought it, knowing it was not how the world worked and that my life was not a fairy tale, regardless of how fantastical it had seemed lately. But I felt it, nonetheless.

Georgiana was taking up her place in my heart as my sister, and Fitzwilliam as my husband. I could not tell you how it began, I only knew that it was happening, and that this place, this *Pemberley*, was coming to be as dear to me as my beloved Longbourn.

By the end of our walk, Georgiana was calling me Elizabeth, though I told her she could call me Eliza if we were being sophisticated and Lizzy when we were being childish, as my sisters still did. She giggled and told me I could call her Georgiana, or Georgia as her family had called her when she was smaller. Her eldest cousin called her G, but she had never liked it. We walked into the house arm in arm, thirsty but refreshed, and headed to a small sitting room at the back. She told me her brother had had it redone for her as a surprise. It was her favorite room because of its views of the rose garden. If the windows were opened in summer, the scents were delicious.

We had tea and chatted amiably and yet another piece of the future fell into place. I was surprised at the rapidity of my feelings, but then I supposed it was only fair. After all, I had chosen to hate him before we were even properly introduced. Coming to care for him in a week did not seem so strange when compared to my earlier behavior.

I did not see Miss Bingley or Mrs. Hurst as I left, but I did think Georgiana hurried me past a set of doors that I thought led to the breakfast room. I heard low voices inside and hid my amusement at her mischief.

Mr. Darcy met us on the front steps and I happily climbed into the curricle, pleased to end a splendid morning with a delightful ride.

"Would you mind if we drove for a while before returning to Lambton? There is someplace I wish to show you."

I agreed and he led us up the drive, onto a rise with a beautiful view of the house and park.

"Oh! How lovely!" I cried.

"This is one of my favorite places. I always stop here when I return from a long journey."

"I see why. How could you ever tire of this view?" I smiled at him, wondering if he would think me forward if I took his hand. We Bennet sisters are an affectionate lot, always hugging one another and bussing cheeks and walking with our arms linked; we show affection with kisses and show support with a touch on the arm or holding hands.

Mr. Darcy was not my relation, but I wanted to touch him, quite desperately. Just to hold his hand, perhaps rest my head on his shoulder. Would he be appalled? Offended? Would he think less of me? Find me uncouth? I felt a tug on my hair.

"You are doing it again. Where have you gone now?" he asked me, his voice gentle and indulgent.

"I was wondering if you would be distressed if I took your hand."

His eyes darkened in a manner I was beginning to recognize, and he leaned toward me. "Not at all." He took my hand and laced his fingers through mine. "I find this the furthest thing from distressing."

The relief must have shown on my face, for a surprised laugh leapt from him, and he touched the tip of my nose with his finger.

"You may be as affectionate as you wish whenever you wish. I promise I shall not be offended or scandalized."

I sighed. "That is a relief to hear." I gave into my impulse then and rested my head on his shoulder. He stiffened, but I believe I had only taken him by surprise, for he then reached his arm around my shoulders and pulled me closer and I laid my right hand on his chest, my left still holding his and resting on his knee. I sighed in contentment and snuggled a little closer, and he squeezed me tight before placing a kiss on the top of my head.

We sat there, in the curricle on the rise overlooking Pemberley, for so long I lost all sense of time.

"I am thinking of following Bingley to Netherfield," he finally said, his voice deep and lazy, like a slow-moving stream.

"You are? When would you arrive?"

"He will escort his sisters to Scarborough then head to Hertfordshire from there."

"Can Mr. Hurst not escort them?"

"Impatient, are we?" I could feel his laugh reverberate through his chest.

"Jane has been suffering so long, Fitzwilliam. Of course, I wish Bingley restored to her as soon as possible."

"Of course, you are right. Forgive me, my love."

I nestled a little deeper at the endearment, and he toyed with a curl hanging over my shoulder.

"I have some business here, but I could be there in a month, perhaps less."

"A month." My voice sounded flat and pathetic, but I could not bring myself to care.

"Parting from you feels insupportable after seeing you every day like this. I had hoped…" He stopped and I waited for him to continue. When he did not, I prompted him.

"You hoped?"

He continued in a soft voice, "I had hoped to show you Pemberley in the autumn."

It was August now. If he did not arrive until September, and we continued courting and eventually became engaged, it would be difficult to return before late November, and it would be cold and dreary by then. He must mean…

"It sounds beautiful," I said, just as softly. "Perhaps I will see it." I heard the question in my voice, but I did not want to force him into a declaration if he was not yet ready to make it. However, if he was only uncertain of *me*, I was more than willing to give him the assurance he required.

"Would you like to?"

"I would like that very much." We were whispering now, avoiding each other's eyes as we sat embraced at the overlook.

He pulled his arm away from my shoulders and turned me to face him. "Elizabeth, if you are not ready, stop me now."

My eyes met his as steadily as I could. I did not think I was breathing, but I was not stopping him either.

"Elizabeth, holder of my heart, would you do me the very great honor of becoming my wife?"

He was so solemn, so earnest, so very *mine*, that I could do naught but cry, "Yes!"

His face broke into the widest smile I had ever seen on him and I followed my impulse and threw myself into his arms, landing on his chest with a thud. He laughed and held me close, leaning back onto the cushion and holding me so tight it was difficult to breathe.

I will not abuse your patience, gentle reader, with tales of how we sealed our agreement or our whispered words of affection that can mean nothing to anyone but us. I will tell you that I was grateful we were quite alone, and that Fitzwilliam drove me back to Lambton at a snail's pace, stopping to show me his favorite views and how pleased he was by my acceptance.

THE REST SEEMED TO HAPPEN IN A WHIRL. FITZWILLIAM SENT A LETTER with me to give my father, asking for his blessing and consent. I knew I would have some work to do with convincing my family of the merits of the match, but my aunt Gardiner had promised to assist me, and I was so happy I could not truly care.

Fitzwilliam rode into Lambton the morning of our departure to see me off, and he placed two letters in my hand, the second of which he made me promise not to open until the third day of our journey. I was beyond curious, but I agreed and slipped the letter I had written him the night before into his pocket.

We had decided between us that we did not wish to wait through a long engagement, and we did wish to spend the autumn at Pemberley. He would come to Hertfordshire by the tenth of September, and we would marry the fifteenth. My aunt agreed on the timeline, saying there was no reason to wait when we had already known each other a year, and that five weeks was ample time to plan the simple wedding we both desired.

I knew my mother would dislike a simple wedding, but I also knew she would wish to make such an advantageous match official as soon as possible and would not protest the date. I only hoped Mr. Bingley would take Darcy's advice and allow his brother Hurst to escort his sisters so that he might get to Jane that much sooner. My last evening at Pemberley, Mr. Bingley told me had written to his housekeeper at Netherfield to begin preparing the house. He had also sent a letter to my father, advising him of his return and saying he hoped to visit Longbourn soon after entering the county.

I applauded his efforts and wished him safe travels.

Our journey home was uneventful, and I reread Fitzwilliam's letter more times than I can remember. One passage in particular made me blush in embarrassment, but I will admit, I read it more than any other.

I can hardly believe you will be my wife in little more than a month—more importantly, I will be your husband. Mine will be the privilege of sharing a life, a home, and a bed with you. Your kisses will be mine alone, your affection my reward—for what I know not, but I am grateful, nonetheless. My dearest, loveliest Elizabeth, you are all that I could ever wish for and more than I ever dreamed of. Speed time for me, my love. Five weeks now feels interminable...

I could do naught but reply.

My Dear Fitzwilliam,

How shocking it is to refer to you as such, and yet, how delightful. I have never written a love letter before. I am certain I will improve with practice, if you do not mind being the recipient of my fledgling efforts.

I have not opened your second letter, as requested (it really is quite cruel of you to leave me in suspense, teasing man), but your first has brought on more blushes than the whole of my life. I too look forward to our life together with eager anticipation. Was it only yesterday that I left Pemberley? It feels ages ago.

I watched the forest through the window as we left, wishing the trees and paths and animals a silent farewell. Is it strange that I feel Pemberley is already my home? Perhaps I feel that way because you love it so dearly and I love you so dearly.

I have never been one to wax poetic on my feelings toward others, but if I am all you could wish for, you have far surpassed my wildest dreams. I never dared to hope that such a man would be my husband. That he would love me, and want me with him forever, and hold me in such tender regard.

You honor me with your affection, Fitzwilliam, and you have mine in its fullest measure. All my heart has to give, I give to you. All my affection, my kisses, my embraces, my love, it is all yours. It is my privilege to be your wife and a source of great joy to have such a husband.

Have I made you blush yet? It is only fair as I was the color of a beet root while reading your letter and my aunt sat across the room, smirking behind her needlepoint as I did so. Have I told you how happy I am that you have become friends with the Gardiners? They are my dearest relations next to Jane and it pleases me greatly that you see their value.

I am quite a pathetic creature as I miss you already and I saw you only yesterday morning in Lambton. How ever will I maintain my equanimity for five long weeks? Hurry to Hertfordshire, my love. You will be greeted with open arms and warm affection.

Your Elizabeth

I followed instructions and waited until the third day of our journey to open his second letter. I was rather surprised to see practical suggestions of places to visit and a detailed travel guide. It wasn't until I reached the end that I understood his game.

If you should visit Ravenswood Hall, explore the maze and pay special attention to the fountain in the northwest corner. It occurs to me that it would be an excellent place to steal a kiss, or three, when next we visit my friend John. He has recently married, and he and his wife will return to Ravenswood by the time I bring you home to Pemberley. (I do not think I shall ever tire of thinking of Pemberley as your home.) We can test the maze ourselves. You may tell me then if you approve my plan.

If you are not pleased with the maze, there is a ruin near Bellamy that has a very fine prospect; there is also the river at Peagram, with its secluded willows...

He went on, telling me of secluded glades and hidden follies he knew of. Truly, he was practicality itself.

LONGBOURN WAS IN UPROAR WHEN I RETURNED. MR. BINGLEY'S letter had been received, and my mother was beside herself with excitement. I immediately went to my father and told him my news, followed by Fitzwilliam's letter to him. I do not believe I have ever seen him more shocked, but after much persuasion and convincing him that I really did like my betrothed, he relented and gave his consent. I made further nuisance of myself by refusing to leave him until he promised to answer Fitzwilliam's letter immediately. I next went to my mother and Jane and their responses were all you could imagine, though Jane was so distracted with thoughts of Mr. Bingley that she expressed mild surprise, then agreed with everything I said without question.

Within ten days, the settlement arrived, and my father signed and sent it on its way. Now that everything was official, I felt relief settle over me like a warm shawl. The bans were being read, my gown was ordered, and the wedding clothes were well under way.

Lydia had returned from Brighton without having done worse than being caught kissing Lieutenant Denny behind Colonel Forster's house. The lieutenant had been punished with extra duties and Lydia had been confined to her room by the good colonel for four dreadfully long days, according to her. Fortunately, my father was appalled enough when he heard the story to limit her unchaperoned excursions into Meryton.

Mr. Bingley returned and came to call the very next day. He wasted little time, and within a fortnight, he had proposed to Jane. Now that my dear sister had her own love, my happiness was complete. I needed only Fitzwilliam by my side, and I would be content.

He wrote faithfully, a full letter every two to three days. My mother was convinced he must be terribly in love with me to write so much. She asked me to read the letters aloud more than once, but I refused, keeping them as my own delightful secret.

The tenth of September finally arrived, but Mr. Darcy did not. Neither did he on the eleventh. Finally, though I worried he would never come, he rode up the drive on the twelfth, smart and confident and devilishly handsome. I ran out to the drive to greet him, not caring if the servants saw me, and before he had handed the reins to the groom, I flew into his arms, nearly knocking him over.

He laughed and held me tightly, lifting my feet off the ground.

"You came!"

"Of course, I came. Did you think I would not?"

I leaned back to see his face but remained in his arms. "I knew you would, but I feared it would be only a few hours before the wedding."

"I was held up by business in London, but everything is finished now, and I am at your disposal for the next fortnight."

"I think you mean for the rest of my life," I said gaily. He always managed to bring out the impertinence in me, though I think he rather liked it.

"You are right, of course, my love. I am yours always."

I smiled and rested my forehead against his. "As I am yours, Fitzwilliam."

ELIZABETH ADAMS is a book-loving, tango-dancing, Austen enthusiast. She loves old houses and thinks birthdays should be celebrated with trips—as should most occasions. She can often be found by a sunny window with a cup of hot tea and a book in her hand. She writes romantic comedy and comedic drama in both historical and modern settings and occasionally puts her sociology degree to use in nonfiction. You can find more information, short stories, and outtakes at www.eadamswrites.com.

Elizabeth: Obstinate Headstrong Girl

The Last
Blind
Date

Leigh Dreyer

"I could easily forgive his pride, if he had not mortified mine."
–Chapter V

THE LAST BLIND DATE
Leigh Dreyer

SEPTEMBER 2019

A blind date? How desperate did her friends think she was? Was she twenty-three and single with no current prospects? Yes. But was she content? Also, yes. When Jane had told her during their break between tables, she had been so stunned she had not argued properly. She would swipe left on this whole situation before it got out of hand. She would just say no…like D.A.R.E. Week—but with a man involved.

"Thank you, Nancy Reagan," she muttered while refilling the Coke for the fourth time for the woman at table five. *How much could one woman drink?*

Charlotte shoved between them to grab some ice for a pitcher. "Why are we thanking Nancy Reagan?"

"Never mind." Elizabeth groaned and walked back to table five.

"Those mozzarella sticks should be right out," she said, placing the Coke on the table and pivoting around to table seven. "Did you all decide on whether you would try some pie tonight? Our special is the blueberry, but I was always a cherry girl myself."

The couple shook their heads and she smiled, pulling the check from her apron and placing it on the table. "Thank you for coming in tonight. Go ahead and pay up at the front whenever you're ready."

She hustled back to the kitchen to check on her orders.

Another waitress moved past Elizabeth with a large tray propped on one shoulder. "Charlie said his friend is heading to the game at six.

He'll pick you up a little earlier. You know you can never find parking at those things."

"Jane, I'm rethinking this whole thing. I don't know why I agreed in the first place. And football? I'm likely to embarrass the poor man. He knows I'm a huge fan, right?"

"Oh, no—you aren't squirming your way out of this one."

With that, her blonde friend pushed through the silver kitchen doors back into the dining room, glistening smile in place.

Elizabeth rolled her eyes and stepped up to the warming station, peeking through to the cook. "Billy, do you have table five's app ready? They've been waiting like ten minutes."

Billy Collins searched through several receipts.

"Charlotte took those out for you a minute ago. Where were you?"

"Me? Oh, I stepped out for a smoke and a chat with an old boyfriend," Elizabeth deadpanned, leaning against the counter. "Where were you?"

"Nowhere! Just here cooking."

If there was one thing Billy Collins did not understand, it was sarcasm. He was a bit of an odd duck, but a great cook, once you got him to focus and attend to the task. However, he liked to hear himself talk and consequently, the wait staff at Bennet's had learned not to address him unless there was a real need.

Billy turned away from her and flipped a burger on the grill. "I heard you have a date tomorrow night with some guy—a real hot shot."

Elizabeth let out a sardonic chuckle. "We'll see…"

"Well, I'd love to take you somewhere." He snapped his fingers as if he had a brilliant idea. "The circus is—"

"Thanks, but you know I make it a policy never to date people I work with."

"I know, you've said as much to me two or three times before. But I think you are—"

"I appreciate the compliment but I'm completely serious. I don't want you to think I'm even warming to the idea. Let me be perfectly clear. This is me—just saying no." *Thanks again, Nancy.* She pivoted on her heel and headed back into the dining room. She would never go on a date with Billy Collins!

The shift continued as it always did. Elizabeth served, took orders, refilled drinks, and gave out checks until her feet hurt and her back ached. At eleven, the last table left, ringing the bell on the door, before Charlotte locked it behind them. Elizabeth grabbed a gray bucket of silverware and a stack of napkins before letting herself collapse in a booth. Jane slid into the seat across from her and started rolling her own bucket of silverware.

"Will Darcy is handsome—like seriously gorgeous—and you will have fun. Besides, you love football. I don't know why you're making such a huge mountain out of a molehill."

"Jane…" Elizabeth sighed as she gathered her thoughts and placed a rolled place setting on the stack in the middle of the table. "I'm happy." She emphasized her happiness with a fake grin and a shrug at the bucket in front of her. "I don't need some guy to *make* me happy."

"This isn't about happiness, Lizzy. It's about going out and having a good time in the company of an attractive male specimen."

"But I don't *need* a date, Jane."

"No one said you did."

"That's not what it sounds like. Charlie spent an hour talking the guy up yesterday."

"Only because you seem anti-dating all of the sudden." Jane stopped rolling and looked directly at Elizabeth. "Will Darcy happens to be hot and to be on the fast-track to being one of the youngest CEOs in the country. He's going places, Lizzy. He's Charlie's best friend from boarding school, and *you*, my neurotic soul sister, are my best friend, so naturally it would be completely amazing if you two could get together. Obviously, if it doesn't work out, Charlie will have to cry himself to sleep for a few days—"

"You'll be there to comfort him."

A few minutes passed as the friends tackled their side work so they could finally go home. *Maybe it would be fun.* Elizabeth had not been to a good football game in a while. As a grad student at University of Oklahoma, her classes took up the majority of her time, and when she wasn't studying, she was working thirty hours a week at the restaurant. Paying her way through OU had not been easy, but with scholarships, some help from her parents, and tips, she had thus far avoided student loans. Tickets to football games were too expensive and so hard to get anyway; mostly she had to settle for watching the games on the diner TVs and wearing her Sooners shirt on Friday. She wondered if Charlie had told Will Darcy how big a fan she was.

"He probably doesn't even know who Nancy Reagan is," Elizabeth blurted out while giggling at the absurdity of her statement. *I have* got *to stop talking about Nancy Reagan!*

Jane dropped her half-rolled utensils and slammed her hands on the table. "Who? Will Darcy?"

Elizabeth laughed. "Never mind!"

"Anyway. Look. Charlie sent me this picture of your date. See… handsome. So amazing. Lizzy, you have to trust me."

The first description that flashed in her mind was tall, dark, and handsome. *Cliché.* Studying the handsome man on Jane's phone, Elizabeth narrowed her eyes. "I've known you too long to trust you. He's probably a player."

"Listen, just make it through half-time tomorrow. If you are miserable, Charlie and I will come get you."

She laughed, then Jane's words hit her. "Wait, do you guys have tickets too?"

"We're in a whole different section. Your tickets are…well…*better.*"

"Okay. I will be on my best behavior. For Charlie. For you. For great tickets…" she said, laughing.

"Oh Lizzy, Charlie makes me feel so blessed. And, we just want all our favorite people to feel the same."

"Ha! If there were forty Charlies, I still couldn't be as happy as you!"

"Seriously, Lizzy. Take a chance. Tell me you'll try to have a good time."

Elizabeth shook her head. "Fine. I will try to enjoy free stadium food and the ambiance of a great American sport in the company of a good-looking man."

"That's all I ever ask."

"But I swear, Jane. This is the last blind date I go on."

A MORNING SHIFT HAD NEVER PASSED SO SLOWLY. IT SEEMED THAT FOR every breakfast burrito and sweet tea ordered, years melted away. Every second passed like an hour, and by two o'clock, when she made her way home, she was ready for a shower and a nap. Unfortunately for Elizabeth, instead of a nap, she got to spend an hour working on her technical writing essay and statistics homework. She would be glad when the year was over.

Jane had told her the mysterious Will Darcy would pick her up at six, so Elizabeth showered and stood in her underwear looking through drawers at all of her possible "first date" clothing options. Boots, jeans, shorts, dresses, t-shirts, and jerseys—all of which seemed wholly inadequate. Jane said they had good seats, so what was she *supposed to* wear? This would all be much less pressure if she was going with Jane and Charlotte.

She grabbed her phone and dialed Jane furiously. Jane picked up with a cheery, "I was wondering when you were going to call me! I'll be right there!" Jane hung up and Elizabeth let out a groan of frustration, threw her phone on the bed, and collapsed on the pillows. *Why me?* Minutes later, she got up to a frantic ringing of her doorbell.

"I brought Charlotte," Jane said as she pushed past Elizabeth carrying a garment bag and pulling a disheveled Charlotte into the room.

Charlotte shrugged apologetically. "I just got off work."

Elizabeth sat on the couch, resigned to her fate as a human Barbie doll (and maybe a little relieved) for the next hour.

"I'm grateful you at least showered and put on mascara," Jane said, running her fingers through Elizabeth's hair and sizing her up in her comfy should-never-be-seen-outside-of-home tank top and leggings.

"This particular ensemble"—Jane pointed at the clothes—"wasn't your plan, right?"

Elizabeth rolled her eyes. "Of course not. I wasn't sure what to wear. I was thinking my Bradford jersey and some skinny jeans."

"Were you going to paint half your face crimson too?" Jane asked.

Charlotte chuckled.

"Traitor," Elizabeth said out of the corner of her mouth.

"Hey, I'm just here for the show. Don't blame me for laughing," said Charlotte.

Crossing her arms, Elizabeth said, "I am not planning on painting my face, though, now that you mentioned it, it seems like a good idea. Thank you for the suggestion."

Jane looked aghast. "You aren't serious."

Elizabeth shook her head.

"Thank god because I have the perfect thing!" Jane rummaged in the garment bag and extricated a strapless sundress with a cream top and flirty, crimson skirt. "You can wear it with your Oklahoma boots."

"I'm going to look like a sorority girl!"

"No," Jane said patiently, "you are going to look like a put together young woman who is a speech pathology grad student with plans to work in the medical field as a pediatric dysphagia expert."

"You know, Jane, you may be the only one who has ever listened to Lizzy's life plans," said Charlotte. "My favorite part of any group date we've been on together is when the guy's eyes glaze over when she starts explaining that a speech pathologist does more than teach kids how to say their *r* sounds and launches into a fifteen-minute diatribe on the reduction of female contribution in the workplace."

"Thank you. I pride myself on attending to my friend's ambitions and helping them seek their dreams." Jane smiled sweetly at Charlotte before pointing an accusatory finger at Elizabeth. "Which is why you will wear this cute dress and let Charlotte and I curl your hair, so you make a good impression for once...or so help me."

Charlotte began to dissolve into laughter while Elizabeth changed into the dress. "Remember that time we were all going out to lunch with, oh gosh, what was his name? Rod? Ryan?"

"Richard," Elizabeth said glumly.

"And she showed up after a Tough Mudder 5K, absolutely filthy? Mud splatters all over, and her legs coated in gunk."

"How could I forget?" Jane exclaimed, plugging in a curling iron in the bathroom. "And that was with someone she knew ahead of time. Imagine what she might do on a blind date without someone to help her along."

"Hey! I had told him that I would be coming straight from a race, and he didn't seem to mind," said Elizabeth, defending herself.

"Whatever happened to him?" asked Charlotte.

"He was an engineering student and left for an internship at Caterpillar the next semester. Last I heard, he works for Tesla now."

"Ah," said Charlotte, "so it was doomed from the beginning. Guess it worked out okay in the end. Now you have the elusive Will Darcy, esquire, to escort you to football games. Have you told her where she's sitting, Jane?"

"Don't you dare ruin the surprise!" Jane said, storming back in the room and holding three different tubes of lip gloss. "Which one?"

"Middle," said Charlotte, pointing. "It will go better with the red and her dark hair."

"Come in the bathroom and sit down, Lizzy," Jane commanded. "Charlotte, pull that kitchen chair in here for me."

Charlotte sat on the edge of the bathtub while Jane worked her way through Elizabeth's hair, curling strands and offering random pieces of advice.

"Now, I've only met him the one time—he's always so busy with work, like someone else we know." Jane winked at Elizabeth in the mirror.

Elizabeth folded her arms across her chest. "And what does the fabulous Mr. Darcy do that keeps him so busy?"

Jane met Charlotte's eyes and Charlotte shrugged and motioned as if to say, "Might as well."

Jane turned back to Elizabeth's hair and carefully curled a strand. "He's training throughout his family business to take over as CEO eventually."

"And his family business is…what? Is it like the mafia, where if you tell me, you have to kill me?"

"Pember Oil."

"Fitzwilliam Darcy? *That* Will Darcy?" Elizabeth stared disbelievingly at Jane in the mirror. "Jane. Pember Oil isn't a company. They're practically the largest landowners in the state!"

"I think they're sixth in the nation actually," Charlotte said nonchalantly, looking at her fingernails.

Elizabeth's jaw dropped and she looked between her friends for reassurance. "What do I even do on a date with someone like that? Where does he live? New York? LA?"

"Just moved back to Oklahoma City, actually, but he does travel extensively to inspect various refineries and other assets. To be honest, I'm not positive of everything he does. He might come off as a bit standoffish."

"What does that mean, exactly?" asked Elizabeth.

"I mean. I'm just giving you a heads up because you can be a bit… obstinate, and Charlie says Will Darcy has never been great at expressing his feelings."

"Lovely," said Elizabeth. "Just what I always wanted—an emotionally stunted man child of my own."

"See what I mean?"—looking at Charlotte—"Headstrong!"

"She's just saying, you're no emotional expert either, Lizzy," said Charlotte coolly, picking up a shampoo bottle from the tub and reading the contents on the back.

"I just meant… All he really does is work. I'm not sure he has much of a social life here," Jane continued.

Elizabeth stared at Jane in the mirror, unable to turn her head without experiencing third degree ear burns from the curling iron.

Charlotte shrugged. "And all I'm saying is that sometimes people can't fall in love without proper encouragement. You convince yourself at the start of any relationship that the guy is an idiot, treat him like he's an idiot the whole time, and refuse to even consider a second date. Why won't you even give this guy a chance? You don't even know him. Charlie is friends with him so he can't be all bad."

Elizabeth wanted to crack back with a witty remark, something about how Charlie would be friends with anyone, but instead she took what Charlotte said to heart. *Maybe she's right. Maybe I do end things before giving them a chance to begin.*

Unwilling to take any comment too seriously, lest she begin to explore her own painful inadequacies, she decided to lighten the mood. "Well, you two have me convinced I'll be satisfied with him." As intended, her friends snickered at the little joke, but Elizabeth continued: "Laugh as much as you want but you won't laugh me out of my opinion. Especially since it's a blind date and they never turn out. It's more likely that we'll never meet again."

Charlotte rolled her eyes.

"Done," said Jane with a final flourish of Elizabeth's hair.

Elizabeth studied herself in the mirror with Jane and Charlotte on either side of her. She was pretty. If she was honest with herself, it was the best she had looked in months. Between work and school, the messy bun had been her best friend. She turned, considering her whole reflection, a woman who seemed confident…and feminine.

"You're going to have a blast," said Jane, kissing her cheek.

"I wish you were sitting with us." Elizabeth realized she couldn't help but smile at her. "I'd be a little less trepidatious about this whole thing if I knew you were there."

"We'll meet up after."

"Okay." Elizabeth took a breath and gave her friends a look. *"What? I'm going to have a good time!"*

Charlotte and Jane grabbed Elizabeth in an embrace.

Okay. I'm going to have a good time.

THANKS TO JANE AND CHARLOTTE, ELIZABETH HAD BEEN READY FIFTEEN whole minutes before she expected a knock at her door. Before leaving, Jane had pointedly looked around the apartment and, without saying a word, told Elizabeth all she needed to hear. Like a whirling dervish, Elizabeth straightened her schoolbooks on the side table, shoved the clothes strewn on the couch into her bedroom closet, and wiped the kitchen counters of jelly globs and breadcrumbs. When she threw the paper towel into the overflowing trashcan, she decided she'd better take it out before her date arrived too.

She pulled the trash bag from the can and walked down the stairs to the dumpster. Jane's dress was cute but shorter than what Elizabeth was used to. She was grateful no one was around when she heaved the heavy trash bag into the dumpster in an unladylike hurling motion, causing her dress to hike up to uncomfortable levels of immodesty.

"Are you sure about this girl?"

Elizabeth ducked back around the corner, hoping the masculine voice had not just seen her panties on display.

"I can't believe you fixed me up with a college student. ... Yeah, at least it's grad school. ... And football, Charlie. You know how I feel about it." At hearing Charlie's name, Elizabeth froze. "Hell no, I didn't wear boots! ... I know it's *Oklahoma*."

Elizabeth looked down at her boots and frowned.

"I looked at her Instagram photos. If that's any indication of my blind date, maybe you think me blind too. ... Do you think I can bail at half-time?"

What. A. Creep! She stepped around the corner of the building to face the ass who must be her date. She was going to tell him exactly who wears the boots—but was met instead with the back of a tall man (nicely filling out a pair of khakis!) walking to the parking lot.

Hmph! Did he just ditch our date? Livid, she marched up to her apartment to call Jane and tell her just what she thought of Charlie's best friend. He had all but called her an ugly hillbilly! Slamming the apartment door, she dialed Jane and listened to the phone ring. She started at the doorbell.

Elizabeth swung the door open, ready to give this guy a piece of her mind and found herself facing the most attractive man she had ever seen. *Tall, dark, and handsome. Definitely cliché.* Despite herself, she admitted she liked his thick, dark chocolate locks and his smooth-shaven, chiseled jaw. And his collared Polo shirt fit his shoulders and broad chest to perfection. *It really is unfair that someone so gorgeous is such a jerk.* He seemed almost surprised to see her but his piercing eyes—long lashes framing a center of light gray—quickly masked any emotion.

"E-Elizabeth?"

Elizabeth nodded. "Will?" she asked, proud that her voice did not quaver.

"Darcy."

"What?"

"My dad. He's Will, too. My friends usually call me Darcy."

Hmph. Sounds pretentious.

"Are you ready to go, or do you need a minute?"

"Just let me grab my clutch."

She picked up her keys and phone too. "Ready."

"You look nice." She blushed at the unexpected compliment as he took in her appearance and noted his lopsided smile at her boots. *Yeah, I know what you're thinking, but you're in boot country now, partner.*

"I stole your roommate's parking spot. Charlie told me she's gone for the summer. I hope that's all right."

"Of course. She decided to work back home and stay with her parents."

"Yeah, when I was younger, I would come back here for summer break with my dad." Darcy's eyes darted to her. "After the d-divorce."

"I'm sorry," said Elizabeth and was stunned at how much she meant it. "And not just because you had to spend your summers sweltering in the Oklahoma heat. Where did you grow up?"

"Manhattan. But I went to boarding school in England—that's where I met Charlie."

"Ah, that's right. But your dad is here?"

"Oklahoma City. The company—that's why I've moved here," Darcy said. Elizabeth noticed his eyes took on a bit of a distant look. He met her gaze and crooked a smile. His eyes changed in an instant from cloudy and concerned to a blank, inoffensive glance. "He wants me to take over as CEO eventually. I've already taken on a fair amount."

Darcy held the door for Elizabeth as they stepped into the sunny parking lot. He led her to a BMW. *Preppy. Unpretentious but not a Toyota either.*

Unlocking the car doors, he opened the passenger door. Elizabeth slid into the front seat, annoyed again at the shortness of Jane's dress. Almost at once, she was distracted by the delicious scent of *him* wafting through the car. She inhaled deeply and relaxed into the seat. *He may be a jerk, but at least he smells amazing.*

The car was impeccable; the seats and carpet pristine, the dash free of even a speck of dust. In contrast, Elizabeth's car was practically a second apartment. She was relieved she had wiped her boots so as not to leave hillbilly dust in the interior. *He probably has a maid who cleans it for him.* Then the driver's door opened and the man himself got in the car.

"I figured we would eat at the stadium. Charlie said you and Jane wanted to meet up after the game."

Elizabeth smiled. "That sounds great. I'm, uh, not much of a drinker so maybe we can find an ice cream parlor or some place that has really great dessert." Her cheeks flushed.

"I don't drink, so that works for me." He looked over at her face and then eyed her bare legs so quickly she was not sure it had really happened. *I guess I'm not quite a bridge troll, eh, Darcy?* She felt her face soften into a smile to match his own before remembering that he was, in fact, the worst. He thought she was a country bumpkin at best and was probably toying with her. She bit her lip, cleared her throat, and turned back to face the windshield; he put the car in reverse, and they were on their way.

Nearing the stadium, Elizabeth had expected to walk a while through crowds of tailgaters, frat boys covered in crimson and white paint, giggling coeds, and alumni. Instead, he pulled down Lindsey Street.

"Students aren't allowed to park here." Elizabeth pointed back in the direction of the larger parking lots they had passed to get here.

"Well, I'm not a student. I did my undergrad at Princeton and grad school at Cornell."

"That's impressive. Still, security gets really cranky about parking on game day."

"I think we'll be okay." Darcy chuckled as he showed security his ticket, found a spot, and parked the car, and Elizabeth sighed. Men never listened. Several friends from her year in the dorms had their cars towed on game day. Sooners did not mess with their football and that included the comfort of the rich alumni walking to their fancy, shaded seats while everyone else hiked three miles in the heat to the nosebleed section. She was glad she brought her phone in case she needed to Uber home after his car was impounded.

After scanning her ticket and walking into the stadium, she took in the scene.

"The student section is on the other side," Elizabeth said, observing the passing signs for the Santee Lounge, sprawling areas filled with comfy couches, chairs, and tables in perfect view of the game, and restrooms with no lines.

"We're in section five."

At that moment, the stadium opened up to a view of the field.

"You have got to be kidding!"

He turned abruptly to the sound of her crazed voice. "Are you okay? Did something happen?"

"We're centerfield on the Oklahoma sidelines," she shout-whispered. Elizabeth did not want to alert the other fans to the fact that she was in complete shock over their seats, but at the same time, these tickets must have cost an absolute fortune.

"Yes, I know," he said. "I got my tickets through old family friends. They are out of town for this game and were nice enough to let me use their seats."

She nodded and sensed his hand burn down her arm until it caught hers. "Come on," he said, and she followed him into the best football seats she had ever seen.

The stadium teemed with activity though they were still early. She had only been to "the palace on the prairie" stadium a few times, but football had been part of her life since she was young; and being from Oklahoma, *football was life* in high school. With a homey thrill in her chest, Elizabeth settled into the stadium hum of excitement as she listened to cowbells, people finding their seats, and the student section already beginning to cheer. At that moment, she felt to be an alumna in these particular seats might be something!

She stole a peek at Darcy, who looked at home in these luxury seats; his correct posture seemed almost cocky, and she remembered his callous remark from earlier. This was a lucky reminder as it saved her from feeling something like regret. Yet after a few minutes of no conversation, Elizabeth felt an awkward silence between them. On closer observation, she noticed his shoulders were tense and he was clenching his jaw, his eyes darting around the stadium.

"Are you okay?" she asked.

Suddenly his face altered to a practiced expression of nonchalance. "Of course."

"You just don't look comfortable, is all. We don't have to stay, you know. We could catch a movie or something."

Darcy's eyes met hers and he took a moment searching before he spoke. "Charlie told me you like f-football."

She smiled. "I do. I love it. Thank you for bringing me. I've never seen a game from seats like this. And I'm really excited for this game. Tech has a good team for once, so it won't be the complete slaughter it usually is." She reached across the arm of the seat to put her hand on his. "But I don't want you to have a bad time if you are really hating all this."

He bit his cheek. *How does someone do that and look completely tempting?* "Can I tell you a secret?" He leaned close to her, his other hand covering hers.

She swallowed. "Yes." She was almost embarrassed by how husky her voice had become; she cleared her throat.

"I know almost nothing about football."

Spell broken. "What?"

"I barely know how the game works. It's basically rugby, right? I mean the huddling and the tackling."

"Are you American?"

He scrunched his brow.

"Are. You. American?"

"I told you I grew up in New York. Summers in Oklahoma. What else would I be?"

"British?"

"Ha, ha. I just went to prep school there. I don't have an accent."

"That people tell you about," she said under her breath.

"Pardon?"

"Nothing. I just don't understand how an insanely attractive red-blooded American male doesn't know a thing about America's sport."

"I thought baseball was America's sport?" Darcy held up a finger and then slowly pointed it at her, grinning. "And did you say I was attractive?"

Elizabeth's face instantly flushed bright red. She took a deep breath. "Okay, I *might* have said something of the sort, but didn't you play a sport in school?"

"Rowed crew."

"That sounds...posh."

"I'll have you know it's physically taxing and requires a lot of strategy and teamwork. The coxswain—"

Elizabeth snorted. "The what?"

"Ugh, never mind, Oklahoma." Darcy leaned back and rolled his eyes.

Did he just call me "Oklahoma"? Well if I have to carry the banner for the Sooner State, don't mind if I do. Whatever, J. Crew! And she propped her boots up so he could not miss them.

After a few minutes of her pouting and his sulking, Elizabeth started to feel guilty about her boorish behavior. Charlotte and Jane had been right. She turned people away from her long before they turned away themselves. If there was something to be said in Elizabeth's favor it was that her stubbornness and pride never lasted long when she saw someone pained by her opinions. She wanted to relieve that pain faster than she had caused it and was always quick to apologize and admit her own faults.

"Listen, I'm sorry. I shouldn't tease. I know nothing about rowing. That was immature." His face was still turned away from her and it was impossible for her to see any hint of his reaction to her apologetic overture. After a moment, she tried again. "Would you forgive me? I'm frankly mortified and, well, I'd like to start again."

Darcy looked down at her, as if he was sizing her up. "If you want the truth, my dad was a huge football fan, but since I was always with my mom during the school year—before boarding school anyway—I never learned to play. Charlie has always given me a tough time about it." Eventually, his shoulders relaxed, and his eyes lit up. "In the UK, football is soccer. And rowing gave me some valuable alumni connections to help me get into Princeton."

"Okay, okay. I sat through thousands of games with my dad. I can teach you if you want."

"You went to games with your dad?"

"Don't sound so surprised. If it's sports related, he'll talk about it. I can't tell you the hours spent watching ESPN with him explaining rules and regulations or yelling strategy at the TV."

"That sounds like most guys."

"He's brilliant for strategy and knows every rule. My mom's on disability for anxiety and depression; and escaping into *any* ballgame was my dad's coping mechanism."

"I'm sorry. That sounds awful." Darcy reached out and placed his hand over hers in a comforting gesture. Even through her own embarrassment at her confession, she recognized the sparks rushing through her leg where their hands rested. These sparks were becoming her old friends, and from the light in Darcy's eyes, she doubted she was the only one noticing their electric connection.

"When I think about the past, I try to only remember the happy times."

"A good way to be. I wish I did the same."

"Football was always a great time, so...." She smiled at him as his thumb brushed against the back of her hand. "So, there's two teams...."

His eyes rolled, and he laughed, a deep rumble as his shoulders shook. "Thanks. I was under the impression there were three."

"Very easy mistake to make."

"And our team is red?" Her heart raced when his lips curved upwards and the light playfully lit up his gray eyes.

"Yes, for this game, the Sooners are in the red jerseys. Texas Tech will be in white."

"Excellent."

"So, absolute basics. One team has the ball and has four chances, or downs, to get the ball ten yards *down* the field toward their end zone. After four downs, the ball goes to the other team and they start the same process. The little guy down there with the orange number sign shows what 'down' or what 'try' that team is on."

"Each touchdown is six points, a field goal is another one, and the team can also go for two, right?"

Tossing her hair over her shoulder, she said, "I thought you said you knew nothing about football."

"I thought you recognized I was an attractive red-blooded American male?"

"Okay, okay, too basic. What questions do you have then?"

"I'm sure they'll come up as we watch," he said. He gave her an appraising look and she felt her cheeks glow under his inspection. She applauded herself for facing him directly—a lesser woman would have looked away or melted under the scrutiny of his discerning—and striking—eyes.

"You've told me about football and a little about your family. Tell me about you. What do you do for fun?"

She could think of a lot of things she would *like* to do for fun, especially with this gorgeous man looking at her so intently. She pushed that thought from her mind.

"Mostly just work and school. I don't have time for much else, honestly." *I sound so incredibly lame.* Before she could properly think through something that did not make her sound dull, he spoke again.

"Did you meet Jane before the diner?"

"We grew up together. We're practically sisters. I met her the first day of preschool."

"She seems nice. Charlie's a lucky guy."

"Yeah, and she's crazy about him. They fit each other like a glove."

"I only met her once, but she seemed quiet."

"She said something like that about you."

"Oh, did she now?"

Elizabeth shook her head and continued. "She isn't at all quiet once you get to know her. Jane's modest. She won't tell everyone she meets that she's getting her masters in O-chem with a 4.0, but she's bright and beautiful and the nicest person I've met in my life."

"That's quite the recommendation."

She nodded and smiled. He returned the smile, but said nothing, turning his attention back to the game. Then there was a lull. A lull which metamorphosed into another uncomfortable silence.

"I was thinking"—he clenched his hands open and closed—"we'd go grab some dinner before kick-off, so we don't miss too much of the game. I hear the fried green tomatoes, steak bites, and the seared duck breast are the best."

Elizabeth's mouth gaped.

Darcy stuttered and sat up quickly. "I-I'm sorry. Are you a vegetarian? I didn't mean to offend you. Charlie didn't say."

Elizabeth shook her head. "No, no. I'm surprised. I expected hot dogs or tacos or something from a regular food stand."

"Would you rather have tacos? I like tacos." Darcy shifted in his seat. Elizabeth felt a nervous tension radiating from the way his shoulders stiffened to the way his eyes darted from her to the lounge door, and finally to the floor, waiting for her answer.

She rested her hand on his shoulder, the muscles below her touch tensed suddenly, then relaxed.

"We can have whatever you'd like. The steak bites sound delicious —honestly. I'm not used to guys spending so much, you know, on a date. I'm used to paying my own way, so this"—she gestured between them— "is a little new and slightly embarrassing to me." Darcy looked as if he wanted to argue with her, but she shook her head and stood up, sliding her hand down his arm to grab his own. "Now, lead me to this fancy-pants dinner place."

They moved into the lounge and Elizabeth prepared herself for a dinner menu using words she had only seen on *Food Network*, words like *deconstructed* or *roulade* or *puddings* that were not a dessert. They sat at a four-top and she regarded the waitress as she moved around them.

"Does it ever feel like you can't leave work?" Darcy asked her over his menu.

"Every once in a while. Most of the time, I'm grateful I'm not refilling drinks."

"Jane told me you are an excellent manager."

"Jane talks too much."

Darcy chuckled. "She was kind enough to tell me about you and help me set everything up. I don't exactly spend much time dating—"

Elizabeth raised her glass and interrupted. "Couldn't tell. You're doing very well."

"Sarcasm, Oklahoma? No, honestly, I haven't been on a real date in over a year. I feel like I'm doing everything wrong."

"Not *all*." Elizabeth touched his hand. "You improve on further acquaintance."

"You're generous." Despite her attempt at reassurance, Darcy looked awkward.

"Out of curiosity, if this was any other first date, what would you want to do?"

"With you?" Darcy raised an eyebrow. "Or with any other first date?"

"Would the person involved change the scenario?"

"Absolutely. Now that I've met you, you aren't just any first date. You're amazing."

Heat from his compliment spread from Elizabeth's stomach, down to her toes, and through her chest. She stopped short of fanning herself with the menu which had become blurry and unreadable.

"Are y'all ready to order?" the waitress asked, having approached the table without Elizabeth noticing.

"Yes, I would love the duck and you were interested in the steak bites, right, Elizabeth?"

The way he said *Elizabeth* sounded like a caress. After twenty years of hearing it, she had never *felt* her name before.

She pulled herself together enough to nod at the waitress as she took the menus.

They sat for a moment, his eyes never leaving her face. She took a drink, intending to sip; instead, she gulped half of her water, trying to cool the fire he had lit within her. "What were you saying?"

"I wasn't saying anything. I've just been thinking about your eyes and how I've never seen anything like them."

"Brown isn't the most interesting color."

"You have the most beautiful eyes. They aren't just brown, they're like honey."

This time, the heat lit up her cheeks, but she held his gaze. "Thank you."

The spell lingered in a haze between them until Elizabeth could not help herself: "I heard you—on the phone before you came to the door. When you were on the phone with Charlie. I was taking the garbage out. And I heard what you said about me and my Instagram…"

Darcy's face turned white and then he flushed. "I am so sorry, Elizabeth. I was being an ass and reacting badly to being fixed up again." Darcy took a drink, licked his lips, then said, "It's just that since my father has fast-tracked me to head the company, my social life has taken a header and I have no real time to meet anyone. Here in Oklahoma, my assistant has taken it upon herself to find a single female exec to accompany me for at least work social functions. She hates seeing me go to business dinners and events alone but, honestly, it just feels like more work. We do the work socializing bit and then a driver almost always ends up taking her home. There's usually some reason I have to stay later for work anyway."

"So, you just dump them?"

"If it's work, does it really count as d-dumping? I told you I haven't asked anyone on a real date in a year."

Elizabeth cocked her head, trying to decide whether to be offended or not. "You didn't ask me. This was set up through Jane and Charlie, so should I expect a ride home?"

They both laughed, though Elizabeth noticed he had not

responded when their waitress arrived with their meal. They savored gourmet beef and delectable seared duck while watching the pre-game festivities through the glass windows of the lounge area. To roars of applause, the Sooner Schooner mascot shot across the field.

"What on earth is that?" Darcy asked pointing at the white covered wagon being pulled by a pair of white horses and driven by a young man with a beauty queen waving to the crowd. Several other male students ran next to the wagon urging the horse team along.

"It's the Sooner Schooner," Elizabeth said matter-of-factly.

Darcy pointed. "There's some guy hanging by his legs from the back."

Elizabeth nodded and considered Darcy's confused expression. "Sorry, I didn't realize you really didn't know what it was. The Sooner Schooner is a wagon like the Sooners used in the nineteenth century when Oklahoma was settled. It's driven by the RUF/NEKs, the male spirit organization. The girl is the RUF/NEK Queen. And that guy hanging by his legs is one of the younger members holding the school flag." Elizabeth shrugged her shoulders. "It's one of the oldest traditions in football."

"Oh." Darcy cleared his throat and took a bite of duck.

Maybe I shouldn't be so pedantic. He's already told me he doesn't know much about football.

The cheerleaders led the *Boomer Sooner* chant, and the players ran on to the field with raucous introductions before kick-off. Elizabeth, Darcy, and the other diners cheered along with those in the stadium, watching the coin toss.

The festivities distracted Elizabeth, so she did not notice the silence between them until her plate was nearly empty. Darcy appeared to be eating contentedly, holding his fork and knife in opposite hands and at the same time, like a European. He ate his salad with precision, cut each piece of meat into perfect little cubes. He watched the action on the field intently, turning to her from time to time and smiling, but never speaking.

The silence, except for the silverware on the plates, grew oppressive. *Do I have something in my teeth? Maybe that's why he's not talking to me?* Elizabeth assiduously ran her tongue along her teeth, checking if something was stuck in them.

They watched the kick-off.

Elizabeth checked her dress for dribbles, stains, or other potentially embarrassing particles. *Okay, maybe I'm overreacting.*

Seventeen downs passed without Darcy saying a word. At seventeen, he cleared his throat.

Maybe I should be figuring out the Uber situation right now...

Five downs later and she began to look at Darcy strangely.

After nearly three more minutes, she freaked.

"Did I do something wrong?" she asked, hearing her voice much louder than she had expected it to be.

Darcy's eyes widened in shock. "Not at all. I just thought you'd want to watch the game while I finished."

"In silence? I'm not asking for expert commentary, but I have never sat for more than fifteen minutes with someone in complete quiet."

He shifted in his seat. His gray eyes squinted as he looked at every part of her face.

"Can I tell you something I haven't told anyone since sixth grade?"

Elizabeth nodded, suddenly anxious to know what he wanted to reveal.

"I stutter."

Elizabeth stared at him for a moment, waiting for him to continue.

He took a deep breath and words spilled out. "I stutter. That's why I'm quiet. I don't want to embarrass myself by stuttering in front of anyone. I can keep it under control when I'm very particular about what I say and when I say it, but if I get flustered or too excited, it all comes back."

Nodding slowly, she said, "I actually had already noticed."

"Really? I thought I had only had a couple slip-ups."

"You know I'm a speech pathology student? I noticed, but it isn't something to be ashamed about. I just assumed you were nervous. You do a good job masking it. No secondary characteristics and only a few slight repetitions. You may stutter, but it isn't very bad at all."

"I did therapy for years, but it was boarding school where I learned how to control it most. Kids are mean at the best of times, but kids without parental supervision can be downright cruel."

"It sounds like it really affected your life."

"It's probably why I don't try harder for much of a social life. Or why I haven't been out with someone I'm even vaguely interested in for a long time, and that's how I expected tonight to go."

Ouch. Elizabeth turned back to the field to watch the quarterback narrowly avoid a sack and throw the ball away to the sideline.

Darcy timidly placed his hand over hers. "Then, I met you. You are nice, *and pretty*, but you are also so…real. You say things, and you mean them. You aren't trying to get me to buy anything; you aren't trying to impress me. You are just—you. I was halfway through dinner before I realized how much I was enjoying myself. I'm enjoying my time for once instead of biding it, and that's all because of you. You're fun and beautiful and smart and know way more about football than I probably ever need to know. I like you, Elizabeth."

Darcy's thumb glided softly against her own fingers. A current ran through her hand and Elizabeth's whole body hummed as he touched her. She had never reacted so strongly to a man before and certainly had never heard a man make so eloquent a case for liking her…especially from someone who doesn't like to talk. She found herself moving her legs toward him and allowing her knees to press against his under the table. There was a return of pressure, and her heart raced.

"Can I get y'all any dessert or did you want to grab something later?"

Elizabeth registered that the waitress was talking to them. Darcy, however, clasped her hand tighter. Darcy looked at her with a mischievous gleam in his eye and Elizabeth swore he winked at her. "Thank you but we'll go check out the game from our seats. Any chance we could get some popcorn?"

"Of course. I can bring it out to you."

After paying the bill, he said, "Ready, Elizabeth?" Once more, Elizabeth noticed that when Darcy said her name, it was closer to a prayer than a name. All at once, it frightened and thrilled her.

Once they sat down in their seats, Darcy asked, "So, can you explain what's going on now? Why is the referee with the white hat talking to the other ones?"

"Well, the one in the white hat is the head referee, the others all have different jobs. There's a head linesman, a line judge, an umpire, a back judge, a side judge, and a field judge..." As Elizabeth explained, Darcy nodded and asked questions. She answered most of them, admitting that even she did not have the encyclopedic football knowledge of her father, despite his first impressions.

"I don't think I've ever seen someone speak about something so passionately."

Elizabeth laughed. "You really haven't watched much football, have you?"

Darcy laughed too. "This"—he gestured to the field and around the stadium—"is fun for you, but you talk like it is the most fascinating thing in the world. I love hearing you talk about something you really love. Something you care so much about. I'd love to have your passion."

Elizabeth thought for a moment and wondered what it must be like to live a life that you did not love. "You don't have anything you're passionate about?"

"Don't get me wrong. I love crew. And reading. And my family is important, but most of them are scattered across the US now."

"Do you wish you lived closer to your relations?"

"Well, there's holidays. But I guess I spend so much time working for my father, and with finding my way with the company, that other interests have become low on my priority."

"Sounds lonely."

"That's what happens I guess when you move to a new city, new job. Don't get me wrong, I'm proud of the work we do. As one of the largest family-owned corporations in the United States, we can provide benefits, financial and otherwise, to our workers that other companies simply can't afford. If my lack of a social life means we can feed another family, it's worth it, I think." Darcy shook his head and went on. "I-I didn't mean to talk about work. I'm sure you wouldn't want to give up your family. You want to stay nearby?"

"I don't want to settle too near my parents. Too much drama."

"Where would you want to move?"

"Once I graduate, I want to travel around for a while. Growing up here was great, but I feel like I've missed a bigger part of the world."

Darcy nodded and there was the slightest pressure as she clasped his hand.

"I want to try new things. You'll probably think this boring, but I've always wanted to get Chinese food in those little boxes, like in the movies. I want to drink tea in some fancy English tearoom. I want a croissant in France or a schnitzel in Germany." Her voice faded off as she imagined the wonders she could see and the places she could go.

"So, what you're saying is, you're hungry and enjoy ethnic cuisine in far-off places?"

Elizabeth burst out laughing, and Darcy shook with the same. After she calmed, she said, "I guess that's true. I guess I shouldn't mention wanting to eat naan in India or Fideo in Mexico."

"Your food adventures sound amazing. I'd go with you on that journey. I'd probably drag you to a few art museums to walk off every meal."

Elizabeth smiled at the thought of Darcy accompanying her anywhere. "I think I would like that."

From the corner of her eye, she caught the Sooner Schooner moving rapidly through the in-zone. But she could not look away from Darcy; her blind date had turned out to be amazing. Maybe she had been the blind one, unwilling to even give him a chance initially; she had decided to come to this game to prove to Jane that her life was not missing anything. Instead, all she had proven was how much she was missing. She wanted this adventure—him.

Suddenly, the stadium thundered in cheers.

"I think we scored," Darcy said.

"We certainly—"

His lips stopped whatever she was about to say, but she didn't mind. Elizabeth closed her eyes as Darcy kissed her, the roar of the crowd fading away. They kissed on, without knowing or caring what direction the players on the field ran. There was too much to be thought, and felt, and said, for attention to any other. In Elizabeth's opinion, happiness in any relationship was merely a matter of chance, but she reminded herself she must thank Jane again and again for insisting she take a chance on this blind date. As she was enveloped in Darcy's embrace, one last thought crossed her mind: *This—he—is one chance I am willing to take.*

LEIGH DREYER is a huge fan of Jane Austen variations and the JAFF community. She is blessed to have multi-generational military connections through herself and her husband, who she met in pilot training. She often describes her formative years in this way: "You know the 'Great Balls of Fire' scene in *Top Gun* ('Goose, you big stud!') where Goose and Meg Ryan have their kid on the piano? I was that kid." Leigh lives with her pilot husband, a plane obsessed son, a "pink pilot" daughter, and a newborn boy, who at two months had already been on six flights.

Elizabeth: Obstinate Headstrong Girl

The
Age
of
Nescience

J. Marie Croft

"But in such cases as these, a good memory is unpardonable. This is the last time I shall ever remember it myself."—Chapter LIX

THE AGE OF NESCIENCE
J. Marie Croft

When I was ten, my father told me I was precocious. Glowing with pride, I beamed at him.

Ten years later, another gentleman told me, "Where there is a real superiority of mind, pride will be always under good regulation."

Turning away, I hid a knowing smirk.

What becomes of pride, though, when real superiority exists purely in one's own narrow mind?

Only now, after throwing a retrospective glance over my adolescence, do I comprehend how prideful and energetically wilful was my youthful conduct, how flawed was my biased discernment…and such it had been from the innocent age of ten to the equally nescient age of twenty.

COMING OUT
1806

IN HONOUR OF A FORMER MERCHANT'S ELEVATED STATUS, A *SOIRÉE* WAS hosted in Meryton by my aunt and uncle Philips. On that moonlit evening, I was permitted to attend in company with my parents and older sister.

Those of higher circles might have argued I, at fifteen, was not of an age to be introduced into society; but it was the country, and children often accompanied their elders to social events. Upon any objection to the scheme, my mother defended the propriety of her decision by claiming a certain right, as sister of the hostess, to bring whomever she pleased to the gathering.

Neither Mama nor I was satisfied with the results when I donned my first half-dress gown and had my ringleted hair dressed rather than left loose. She lamented my looks were nothing to Jane's, and I experienced a mixture of excitement and mortification at being on display in such an adult fashion…especially since boys I had romped with in childhood might be in attendance as eligible men.

In the habit of running, I was saddened to relinquish spirited antics and submit to more ladylike behaviour. *How suddenly we are expected to emerge from girlhood to womanhood, from maiden to wife.* The thought of being viewed as marriageable was as uncomfortable as the hairpins poking into my scalp and the lightly boned stays thrusting my bosom unnaturally upwards.

"Elizabeth Margaret Bennet! You are *not* leaving the house looking like *that*!"

"But… Mama!"

Tut-tutting, she removed the fichu I had tucked into my bodice and flailed the triangle of muslin in my face. "What were you thinking, child?"

"Of modesty. You went against my wishes and had the bodice lowered. I cannot face our neighbours with so much of my…with so much of *me* exposed. New meaning might be given to my *coming out*."

"Oh, pish! 'Tis the latest evening fashion. Every elegant lady wears that cut, and no daughter of *mine* will be seen as a dowd. Compared to Jane, you must flaunt whatever meagre, redeeming features you own."

Despite my mother's hopes upon launching a second daughter into the society of adults, my coming out was not an overwhelming success. Although I had been well liked as a precocious youngster, *my* new status was paid scant attention by the local populace. The guest of honour, Sir William Lucas—my friend Charlotte's father—did pay me a number of "Capital, capital!" compliments; and, after imbibing too much port wine, Uncle Philips proclaimed my altered looks charming.

Home from university, a friend bowed over my hand and, in doing so, his eyes came to rest on my bodice. Eyebrows hitched, he smirked, saying little before turning to speak with my drunken uncle. It took willpower to still my hand from cuffing the back of his stupid head. *Being genteel will require tremendous effort, I fear.* Discomfited over my erstwhile playmate noticing the changes in my figure, I was—as if of a contrary nature—annoyed he found me unworthy of further attention. *Well, I would not marry you anyway, William Goulding, even were you the last man on earth.*

Other than admiring glances, even Jane failed to attract overtures from the few single gentlemen in attendance. Neither our looks nor characters could be at fault, at least not *hers*. Jane's dance card, I heard, was never empty. 'Twas our paltry dowries—a disincentive commonly known amongst the two dozen families with whom we associated.

If one listened to Mama, Jane was destined to espouse a peer of the realm—preferably an heir about to assume his father's mantle—or a military hero sporting a tunic replete with medals. Either man would have deep, deep pockets and brothers enough for Kitty, Mary, Lydia, and me. Alas, suitors of noble birth, noble qualities, ample wealth, and ample male relations lived not in nearby manors but in castles in the air—specifically, the air between Jenny Bennet's ears.

Mama, vexed at having to henceforth address her friend Esther as Lady Lucas, waxed lyrical, yet again, about a London gentleman so enamoured of Jane two years previously that he had penned an ode to her. To my sister's mortification, the doggerel—treated as a work of poetic merit and a rightful tribute to her daughter's beauty—was fetched from Mama's reticule and read aloud to a coterie of enraptured women hiding yawns behind fans and gloved hands.

Back at Longbourn, freed from torturous hairpins and stays and having donned comfortable nightclothes, I turned from the wardrobe and found Jane kneeling by the fire, feeding oily verses to greedy flames.

"I pray," said she, "that when I receive a marriage proposal, it will be from a gentleman who can, at least, write reasonably well."

"Above any other defects in his character, if a gentleman has poor penmanship and can neither aptly apply the rules of grammar nor spell correctly, it must significantly weaken his chances of ever having his hand accepted." With a grin, I added, "The writing is on the wall for such a maladroit suitor."

"As you well know, I speak of a man's ability to express sentiment." Gaining her feet, Jane pointed me towards the dressing table. "I find little pleasure in comparison to an herbaceous plant. 'Eyes alike two linseed flowers, hair akin to flaxen bower.' Was that supposed to be romantic?"

Taking the proffered seat, I set aside my candle and handed Jane my brush. "A man might find as much solace in the sleek strands of your hair as in a pleasant, shady place. Sadly, there is no comfort whatsoever to be found in this mousey rat's nest of mine." Jane insisted my curls were a brindled nut-brown, but I saw naught but dun tangles compared to her silky, flaxen locks. Breathing in her jasmine scent, I contemplated my reflection. "I *am* quite pretty. But if you, with beauty, grace, and sweetness, have not yet captured a man's heart—one Town versifier notwithstanding—there can be no hope for the likes of me. Alas, I shall marry tomorrow-come-never."

"Good gracious." Jane gave my hair a yank. "You are full young yet, as am I. Give us time."

"Better yet, give us decent dowries. There are far too many pretty fishes in the sea and far too few eligible gudgeons waiting to be caught." Passing over my shoulder a length of ribbon to secure my thick plait, I caught Jane's eye in the mirror. "Perhaps, given enough time, a *sightly* knight of the shire, and of large fortune, shall trot in on a white charger and fall violently in love with you."

"What nonsense have you been reading lately, Lizzy?"

"I am struggling through *Le Morte d'Arthur*. Alas, the only knight hereabouts is married and neither handsome nor wealthy. Can you imagine Charlotte's father on a courser? Sir William cannot even keep his backside, broad though it may be, atop that long-in-the-tooth mare of his. As Papa would say, he sits like a toad on an upping block —bounce, bob, jounce."

A fit of giggles overtook us until Papa, walking past our door, admonished us to quieten.

Unlike me, rarely did my paragon of a sister reveal a less forgiving side. I loved Jane dearly but secretly rejoiced whenever she erred or behaved poorly. Such offences made her more human, less angelic, my own faults more tolerable.

She was all sweetness and honeyed mildness, attracting admirers like bees to nectar. No one would ever call *me* "honey." It was not in my nature to be sweet. I was, instead, sharp, keen, with a razor-edged wit—honed at Papa's knee. I had yet to fully understand that sharp-tongued remarks could cut and wound like a knife; but, propitiously, most of my barbs were aimed over others' heads, and no one was hurt.

Apologising for such unrestrained laughter, Jane claimed fatigue as an excuse. "Sir Galahad might be better advised to fall in love with *you*, dear Lizzy."

"One can dream, I suppose." Rising from the dressing table, I kissed my sister's cheek. "Good night and may all your dreams be sweet but not so outlandish. A wealthy man of consequence and integrity in love with *me*. Pshaw!"

Well, why not? Why should he not fancy me? I have certain qualities a gentleman might appreciate. Such as...

Tossing and turning in bed, I wondered with what qualities—other than sharpness and a couple meagre, redeeming features—I might entice a suitor. I could run but not sit still, dance a reel but not a minuet, sing in French or Italian but not speak it. I could play the pianoforte, but my hands were all fingers and thumbs. I could be outspoken but also entertaining...provided the other party was an equally skilled conversationalist.

AYERS AND GRACES
1807

CONVERSATION AROUND OUR BREAKFAST TABLE WAS OFTEN DIVERTING... or disturbing...or both.

"I hope, Mr. Bennet, you have remembered Mr. Ayer is expected today. I shall require the carriage."

"Is there some correlation"—Papa scratched his temple—"between Mr. Ayer's arrival and your departure? A secret assignation, perhaps? If so, you will have to use some other means to arrive at your tryst. I shall not be party to my own cuckoldry."

"My dear sir,"—Mama preened herself—"you flatter me."

"I do?"

"Why, yes. Mr. Ayer is a handsome man of thirty or so, and here I am almost a decade older."

Papa gestured for Jane to refill his teacup, though the pot was sitting right in front of him. "I hope the fellow does not cause me a great deal of trouble or lead me a merry dance. I have already shelled out a substantial amount so he may caper about with my womenfolk."

Mama huffed. "You enjoy provoking me."

"That I do, and I set great store in your facilitation." Papa unfolded his newspaper, disappearing behind it. "Unoccupied as I expect to be today, you and the girls are welcome to the carriage."

Papa's being at leisure was hardly an exception. The sweetening of his tea each morning likely was his day's most stirring event.

For our part, my sisters and I—depending on our age, inclination, and diligence—were in various stages of learning, under Mama's tutelage, the basic accomplishments a prospective spouse might expect should one of us manage to snag an unwary bachelor.

I, alone, learnt from my father in his book room—our sanctuary from Mama's highly-strung nerves, the silliness of my two youngest sisters, and poor Mary's unique cries for attention.

As to the rest of our education, using meagre funds allotted by their husbands, the mistresses of Lucas Lodge, Haye-Park, and the great house at Stoke occasionally pooled resources with those of Longbourn and hired masters to instruct their assorted offspring.

One such skilled practitioner, a caper merchant named Cornelius Ayer, had returned to teach formal movements of the dated minuet to beginners and to refresh various steps in those, like me, who had not given ample practice to the art. I loved to dance but, at sixteen, did not like being criticised or told what to do.

"The last time our dandy dance master was here," I complained to

Jane as we exited the carriage, "I was proclaimed too exuberant for stately dances and more suited to reels." Jane agreed the livelier, merrier tunes better suited my nature, but she insisted my steps had become more fluid, more graceful, since Mr. Ayer's previous visit.

And so, we entered Lucas Lodge and received instruction while, along one wall, Mama and other matrons sat discussing matters of life-and-death import—war and its impact on their daughters. The aftermath was, of course, Hertfordshire's dearth of eligible aristocrats, war heroes, nabobs, and their four brothers.

"Miss Mary and Mr. Lucas!" Mr. Ayer stopped playing his fiddle. "You are to engage in polite conversation while awaiting your turn. It would appear peculiar to be mute for your half hour. Say something to your partner."

Charlotte's younger brother opened his mouth, but nothing came out.

"I have read," said Mary, "silence is a woman's best ornament."

Another point on which she and I disagreed.

Mr. Ayer pinched the bridge of his nose then, tucking his fiddle under one arm, clapped his hands. "Come, now. I shall persevere. Before this tutelage is over, every one of you shall dance and engage with your partner effortlessly. I pride myself on engendering refinement and poise in even the most difficult cases. Who says a silk purse cannot be made of a sow's ear?"

Our foppish dance master apparently enjoyed some degree of patronage from members of the *ton*. Whilst mincing about amongst country folk, he used *beau monde* names to impress upon us his importance. "Even the mushroom sisters, the Misses Hoggard—speaking of glossy bags and sows—are, thanks to me, accomplished dancers."

At that point, in company with Charlotte's father and Miss Mary King, in swaggered a tall, handsome gentleman, drawing the eye of every female. *Has that mousey creature, with neither wealth nor connections, somehow captured a dashing buck? Is such a thing possible? How imprudent of me would it be to ask her? Terribly, I suppose.*

Oblivious to their arrival, Mr. Ayer took that particular instant to settle a gimlet eye on me. "Miss Elizabeth! One does not skip like a milk maid at a harvest festival. One glides, like your graceful sister." Whilst scolding me, Mr. Ayer gazed with affection on Jane.

She has always had that effect on men...and women and children and dogs and woodland creatures...*and* the approaching Adonis, who wore neither mantle of aristocracy nor decorated uniform but was far beyond any other mortal male I had ever seen in picture or in person.

As everyone congregated around, Sir William introduced the young man as Mr. Archibald Crosbie, a well-regarded attorney from Liverpool, who had come to Hertfordshire to visit his niece. Having learnt of his arrival in the neighbourhood, Charlotte's father invited Mary King and her uncle to join us.

"I thank you, Sir William, for acquainting me with such charming company. So many lovely ladies," Adonis said, gazing at Jane, "and, of course, the fortunate fellows partnering them."

Delighted by Mr. Crosbie's outward appearance and by his innocent relation to Miss King, I was equally impressed by his finesse at the minuet, reels, and Boulanger. Good humour sparkled in his eyes; scintillating conversation flowed from his lips. The man was, in short, perfection...except he hardly noticed me. I suspected bad eyesight.

Afterward, while Mama and my younger sisters rode home in the carriage, Jane and I walked to Longbourn, extolling Mr. Crosbie's magnificence. It was, though, a shame he had arrived when I was to leave the next day to spend a se'nnight at my uncle's London home.

"Dearest Jane, I know how fond you are of all the Gardiners. It would be no sacrifice to give up my turn for the sake of your happiness. Would you care to trade places and go in my stead?"

"No, Lizzy, I would never deprive you of such an opportunity. Besides, Hertfordshire is so handsome in late spring, I shall happily remain here."

"Handsome, indeed. Devilish smile. Cleft chin. Eyes a deep, forest green. I hope, for Mama's sake, he has four equally handsome brothers"—grinning, I glanced at Jane, gauging her reaction—"enough for *all* my sisters."

Jane commented on the attorney's good breeding, but the same

could not be said of Mr. Ayer. A discussion ensued about the uncharitable way he had denigrated others. Actually, as my tender-hearted
sister held forth on the subject, I listened half-heartedly while imagining the adorable children Mr. Crosbie and I might produce
together.

"And it was in poor form for him to belittle those Hoggard ladies.
Were we to meet, his derogatory remarks might influence our
opinion before we even had a chance to know them." Jane hooked the
crook of my arm through hers, and our walk continued in that sisterly
fashion. "One should only speak charitably of others. Hearsay should
never be taken as fact. We have all been guilty of hasty judgements
and voicing unkind comments, especially Papa and y–"

"Oh, look," I cried, sidestepping her and further chastisement. "The
comfrey I planted alongside the bourn has flowered."

"Comfrey is not alone in prickliness. You are quick to take offence,
Lizzy." Jane walked away in serene exemplariness.

*What an unfeeling sister she is...refusing to take my place in Town and
then calling me prickly.*

The last time someone—Mama, no doubt—had called me miffy, I
had stomped towards Lucas Lodge, hoping for a sympathetic ear.
Instead, Charlotte had supported my mother's bilious opinion, adding
such adjectives as "pettish" and "peevish."

After Jane's insult, I—clad in gardening clothes, old gloves, and
sturdy boots—tended my prized herb patch. In the yanking of
weeds and pinching off of flowered stems, my humour improved to
such a degree that I laughed at myself and admitted they—Jane,
Mama, and Charlotte—had the right of it. A resolution was formed
to be less quarrelsome and more mature. *Failing that, sarcasm and
criticism shall be masked with such a playful, teasing tone that no one will
notice.*

With a little less enthusiasm than in the past, I left for London, still
suspecting Jane might go behind my back and become betrothed to
Mr. Crosbie in my absence.

At Gracechurch Street, having listened to my aunt's plans for that
sunny June morning, I longed, instead, to be amongst verdure, not an

odious city street. "I have a better idea…Hatchard's. Afterward, we can stroll through the park, sit upon a bench, and peruse our purchases."

"No, Lizzy. We are for the linen-draper and dressmaker. You are here so I may array you in other than Jane's second-hand, altered gowns and your mother's unique, shall we say, notion of fashion. Your letters have been rife with grievances, and no niece of mine shall be forced to expose more flesh—or wear more flowery flounces—than is decent. My dressmaker will create gowns to appropriately flatter your figure." Patting my hand, Aunt Gardiner tut-tutted at my pout. "Harding Howell & Company is also a haberdashery. Most of our shopping can be done there. Heaven forbid I should drag you to separate establishments for gloves or millinery."

Walking about, I admired the room's knick-knackery. "But I do not care to go fabric shopping. I wish gowns and such were to be bought ready-made." It came out as more of a whinge than intended; and, having left behind childish behaviour, I checked my foot before it stomped itself into disgrace. Had my companion been any other than my beloved aunt, I might have protested longer and louder.

"Sacrilege! Browsing through London shops—with wares in all the latest style—is an irresistible pastime for *most* young ladies up from the country." Sighing, Aunt Gardiner gestured for me to sit beside her. "It is time, dear heart, to recognise and adhere to society's expectations for refined young ladies. I will help you cultivate poise and good deportment, but I have no wish to quell your exuberance, your ebullience. 'Tis what makes you the singular, beautiful person you are."

"Beautiful? Pish! I am nothing to Jane and shall always walk in her shadow. *I* might have been considered a beauty, if not for *her*. No gentleman, let alone an amiable, handsome attorney, will ever look twice at me when *she* is near."

"Yes, yes. Wherever she goes, whatever she wears, Jane is admired. If it is any consolation, you have less feminine bounty to conceal than your more roundly proportioned sister. Oh, do not be missish. Leave the squeamishness to Mary. Now, stand, and let me look at you." Obeying, I endured her scrutiny. "Your figure is—as the French say —*svelte*. Your brunette tresses have a richness Jane's blonde hair cannot rival, and your complexion has a pleasing, peachy undertone. Your eyes... Oh, your eyes, Lizzy! They are your best feature. Such compassion. Such warmth and intelligence. A sparkle when you tease, a fire when angered. Such heat, such passion!"

"Such flattery!"

"None of it false. With your high spirits, provocative nature, and cleverness, certain men will find *you* more alluring than Jane."

Ah. So those are qualities a gentleman of wealth and consequence might fancy. When pigs fly. "Men do not want clever wives." Flinging my *svelte* figure beside her, I crossed my arms. "If a woman has the misfortune of knowing anything, she should conceal it as best she can." Head resting against the sofa back, I glared at the ceiling. "Had I been born the male of the species, I might have been happier. Free to express insightful opinions without censure, free to engage in more physical activities, free to choose my own mate, free to cover myself with shirts, cravats, waistcoa—"

Aunt Gardiner scoffed. "Why would you want to wear all those layers when you can dress in cool muslin, brandish a fan, twirl a parasol? If you are so concerned about covering yourself, purchase several lengths of dainty lace to embellish your necklines. Jenny Bennet could hardly object to a wisp of lace."

It was true. Mama went into raptures over lace and frills, but I preferred a simpler style. "Please, Aunt, do not make me resemble one of those tawdry dolls sold at the Bartholomew Fair."

"Of course, not. Come now, Lizzy. Our carriage awaits."

En route to St. James's district, my aunt pointed out gas lighting along the street and spoke of being in attendance in January during Mr. Winsor's demonstration. "I mistrust such unnatural sources of light," she said. "They must surely pose some danger."

"Mama scolds me for exposing my face to another dangerous source of light—the sun. I have been instructed to hide my freckles under a beauty aid, lest some urbane suitor disparage my country ways. Will you help me find such a cosmetic?"

"Balderdash! Your freckles are hardly noticeable. No such preparation is necessary. A lip balm, made from mashed beets or red berries, might be nice, though. Apply the juice to your lips for five minutes and top it with beeswax." Winking, she suggested Mr. Crosbie might prefer raspberry or strawberry to a vegetable flavour.

"Aunt!"

"He seems a good sort of man. Your uncle knows of him through a mutual Liverpool acquaintance and has heard nothing disparaging." As we pulled up alongside the kerb, she huffed at a curricle racing by. "*Some* young bucks, on the other hand, are nothing but scoundrels with penchants for drink, gaming, and causing mischief. There are many of that ilk who care for nothing but carousing and corruption. While they may look respectable and may act charming and honourable, some men's intentions are anything but."

"I am an excellent judge of character. You need not fret about me. I shall never be hoodwinked by a man."

At the linen-draper, fabric after fabric was held against my complexion and up to the light for flaws. While I fidgeted, Aunt haggled with the shop assistant over a variety of muslins and a bolt of exquisite sarsenet. When he pressed upon us a measure of brassy satin, she shuddered, informing him no young lady in her right mind would wear that ghastly hue.

Beside us, two young ladies exchanged looks of derision, tittering into kid gloves. The taller, more angular, made a point of catching my eye before turning to the other. "They are much to be pitied who have not been given a taste for fashion early in life. Imagine, Louisa, having to shop with one's mama and heeding dated notions of style."

"Too true, Sister. I make it a point to never listen to outmoded advice."

"And there you have it," I whispered to my impeccably dressed companion as we strolled towards millinery. "Fashion, for some ladies, goes in one *era* and out the other."

"Be serious for a moment, Lizzy. Why not buy something pretty for your sisters while we are here?"

Clutched to my breast, my reticule held all my worldly wealth. "Excellent idea." Dissuaded from so rash a step by the thought of Jane and Mr. Crosbie together, I had, by day's end, as much wealth as ever.

Nevertheless, by week's end, I returned to Longbourn with kid gloves for Jane and a variety of ribbons for my younger sisters. For myself, I had an empty reticule, a bottle of violet fragrance, and a gown created from a soft, silky fabric with ivory warp and golden weft that subtly changed colour as it moved. I liked it exceedingly... and not just because Mama thought it modest and plain.

More proficient in dance and proud of my new apparel, I prepared for my first public ball and, with any luck, another encounter with Adonis, who, I learnt, had been—happily—nowhere near Jane the entire time I was gone. The event was anticipated with great impatience, and I hoped Mr. Crosbie might be the sort to appreciate intelligent eyes, violets, and a *svelte* figure in iridescent silk.

Feeling grand, indeed, I entered the assembly room—wherein my sarsenet was openly admired by Charlotte and my aunt Philips, and secretly, I imagined, by everybody else in attendance...except Mr. Crosbie. *How can Adonis admire my finery? He cannot even see me for all those stupid flirts surrounding him.*

That, I found, was the attorney's one and only flaw...that and poor eyesight. He was *too* handsome. Every young lady—including a few married ones—had set their caps at him. Adonis spent the entire night besieged by female worshippers and had not the freedom to gaze across the room and appreciate brunette tresses, peachy complexion, and raspberry-flavoured lips. With a bad case of sour grapes, I abandoned any scheme of gaining the peacock's admiration.

Who wants to live as far north as Liverpool? Besides, men like Mr. Crosbie are dangerous...attracting women like moths to a flame. Such a man could hardly be constant. Nothing shall ever induce me to marry a too-handsome gentleman. And I shall never pursue any man. I would rather be the flame than some stupid, fluttering insect.

IGNOBILITY
1808

"SUCH WEALTH! SUCH CONSEQUENCE! SIR JACK ASHE! OH, HOW WELL

and grand that sounds! 'Tis almost as good as a lord! Rumour has it he leased Ashworth, sight unseen, on the merit of its name alone. Imagine!" Practically bouncing, Mama piqued Papa's curiosity.

"Who, pray tell," he asked with asperity, "is this nincompoop you keep prattling about? Judging by their eager faces, at least *some* at my breakfast table have no objection to hearing it."

"Well! According to Hill, who heard it from Ashworth's housekeeper, Sir Jack is a handsome bachelor of the *ton*—a baronet who, at the age of one and twenty, inherited his father's wealth and title. He has almost *six thousand* a year! Enough to keep dear Jane in comfort."

"Why would this Jack Ashe hand over his wealth to her?"

"He must *marry* her, of course."

"Must? In the name of heaven, woman! Did this rake, this gentleman rogue—whom none of us ever met—spend a half hour alone with our daughter? And, during such reckless behaviour, was Jane's virtue called into dispute by some scandalised witness? Alas, my dear, it is a hopeless business. We are ruined, and it shall be the hedgerows for you when I die of shame." So overwrought was he that Papa calmly bit into a slice of buttered, grainy toast, washed it down with a sip of tea, and reached for his newspaper.

"What nonsense you talk." Mama flapped her handkerchief at him while Kitty and Lydia giggled.

Smirk hidden behind my serviette, I composed myself before speaking. "Her design is for Sir Jack to fall violently in love with Jane. *Everyone* falls in love with her."

"Yes, they *do*! And my dear Lydia will be just as well-favoured in a few years. Only think! Lady Jane Ashe! Oh, Mr. Bennet, you must call on him the instant he arrives."

Ashworth remained an inconvenient ten miles distant, Papa would not be moved, and the introduction was deferred.

On the day before Mary's coming out, she was even more resistant to the scheme than I had been about mine. Flatly refusing to wear the gown Mama had selected, my younger sister protested it was wrong to be judged by outward appearances. "*I* shall choose a right-eous gentleman," she insisted. "One who will appreciate my innate character and talents."

I wished her much success and, rather than practicing scales on our pianoforte, I ventured out for a walk, thereby improving my well-being through extensive exercise and not having to listen to my younger sister plunking at the keys.

The next evening, my parents, Jane, Mary, and I finally made the baronet's acquaintance at a *soirée* hosted by Sir William, who was fond of announcing, *ad nauseam*, he had met Sir Jack at St. James's.

Pleasing me exceedingly, the baronet had not the disadvantage of being *too* handsome. In a genteel, agreeable manner, he fell easily into conversation with everyone present that night, including me and—*Drat it all!*—Jane. But *she* could claim none of the to-and-fro banter comprising *our* exchanges.

He and I met often, thereafter, in large, mixed parties, but our time together never sufficed. Sir Jack proved as changeable as the seasons—flirting, going away, returning, and repeating the cycle. *Teasing man! What does he mean by making me set my cap at him then doffing his and leaving?*

After dining thrice in company, I knew he stupidly preferred cards to reading and cold souse to sweetmeats. Such information proved inadequate to understand each other's character; but, by the time I had known him a few months, I believed myself in love.

The improvement of *his* regard for me was suspended until a much-anticipated annual November event—the private ball at Mr. Standish's Netherfield Park.

By then, Jane and I had become as close as two sisters could possibly be and were no longer in any sort of competition. She, of course, remained blissfully unaware there had ever *been* rivalry. Donning gowns purchased during a joint visit with the Gardiners, we prepared for the ball with more than usual care. Why Jane did so, I knew not; but *I* was determined—like some romantic novel's heroine—to conquer a baronet's heart.

The crush of revellers and perspiring, drunken dancers was more than Netherfield's ballroom could comfortably hold. We were, thereby, ensured a rout of highest quality. Sir Jack certainly did *his* part to ensure its success by inviting, so it seemed, *all* the single ladies to stand up with him; but *I* was the gloating, lucky one he asked for *two* sets.

"You dance divinely, Miss Bennet." I thanked him before remarking on his prolonged absences. He apologised without explanation. "I understand *you* often spend time in London." Giving my gown a glance, he posited it had been purchased in Town, and I congratulated his discernment. "Did you obtain anything else of note there?" He clasped my hand as we went down the dance. "A suitor, perhaps? Are you promised to anyone?"

"To my inexpressible astonishment, I am not. You, Sir Jack? Are you now betrothed?"

"I escaped, entirely unscathed, having fought hard for my freedom. Lionesses have nothing on the huntresses encountered in *my* society."

The dance separated us, and I savoured his lingering citrusy scent until he returned and asked of what we had been speaking. "Of lions… and of *your* society. I could make some comment about lionesses taking great pride in *their* society but shall not. Pray, have you come to your estate to evade leonine claws, or are *you* on the hunt, here for some sport?"

"A bit of sport is agreeable from time to time. In fact, I went out early yesterday, in my shooting jacket. Despite being a crack shot, I came home empty-handed. But, after the bustle of Town, I appreciate Ashworth's peacefulness. Why shatter tranquility with ugly firearm blasts? Some *other* pursuit shall have to be taken up. Tell me, how *does* one occupy oneself here in the wilds of Hertfordshire?"

"My tastes may seem rustic to a sophisticated baronet from Town. But—as elsewhere—calls are paid and received, news and ideas exchanged, reels danced, songs sung, books read, *trees climbed*." At his shocked expression, I retracted my last comment. "Your attention was tested and, happily, found not wanting. Now, prepare yourself for a *truly* shocking confession. Above all else, I love solitary walks and nature."

"I suppose it might be pleasant to stroll along a bourn—apple in one hand, book of poetry in the other, a faithful hound at my heels. The only element missing from such a tableau is a human companion, preferably of the fairer sex, with whom to share life's simple pleasures. I expect you and I might be similar in that regard."

"How presumptuous to suppose such a thing, especially after I just mentioned my love of walking. I suspect we have nothing else, at all, in common."

"Must you always be so contrary?"

"Quite. I daresay, however, I would be most obliging if ever you praised my good sense."

"I shall happily oblige, madam, if ever I have occasion to witness such."

A mixture of good nature and archness in his manner made it impossible to be affronted, plus he provided all the honour an illustrious dance partner could bestow.

It had been a glorious night; and, to my happy surprise, two days after the ball, Sir Jack called on me at Longbourn.

Mama's matchmaking scheme had us out of doors within minutes, scandalously unchaperoned and watching a litter of kittens frolicking in the grass outside the barn. While stroking and cuddling one, I became unsettled by the baronet's intense stare, wondering if it was indicative of disdain. Dismissing that notion, kissing the cat's head and placing it on the ground, I laughed at the antics of its roly-poly brothers and sisters.

"Aha! You, madam, *do* take delight in the simplest things. Yet you are an intelligent and remarkably vivacious woman." Facing me, he smiled, leaning one shoulder against the side of the barn. "Have you ever been kissed?"

Before remembering I was supposed to be a lady, I swatted his arm. "Of course not." Lowering his voice, inching closer, he asked if I would *like* to be kissed. I asked if he was mad.

"Come now." He tapped my nose. "As an inquisitive, natural sort of country maiden, are you not the least bit curious, hmm?" He grasped bare fingers, my gloves having been tossed aside while petting the kitten.

"Well, yes. I mean... No." My gaze lifted from our entwined hands to his eyes. "Can you imagine if someone caught us?"

"No one is near. Your father's coachman hurried off in the direction of the house minutes ago."

Uneasily, I looked around the barnyard. "'Tis unconscionable." Raised to his lips for a perfunctory kiss, my hand trembled.

"Did you not like that? Or..." He began softly kissing each fingertip. "Is this better?"

Heart racing, I surrendered to a raging, inordinate curiosity. *Where is the harm? No one will see, no one will know.* A lingering kiss upon my cheek sent tingles down my spine. As he moved back a bit, my eyes strayed, unbidden, to his lips. He told me *that* was a blatant provocation, kissed the corner of my mouth, and drew back.

"Gauging by the passion in your eyes, Elizabeth, you want this as much as I."

Bowing my head, I fought shame against desire.

Sir Jack tilted my chin up to his face and—

Bang!

The loft door swung outward, slamming the barn's exterior, followed by a deluge of loose hay pelting our heads. I squealed, and Sir Jack jumped away just as Papa poked his head out of the open hayloft door, expression nothing short of thunderous.

Standing next to his employer and holding the pitchfork, Longbourn's coachman scowled down at the baronet until Papa thanked James for his assistance and waved him away.

One hand braced against the jamb, Papa brushed from his coat a stalk of hay which wafted past our upraised faces. "And *that*, young man, was the proverbial last straw. Apologise to my daughter. Then leave Longbourn, and never set foot here again."

Sir Jack obeyed Papa's first order but dallied long enough to gain my whispered promise to meet him at Oakham Mount at eleven the next day.

Then he left me alone to face my father's disappointment, his disgust. The former was spoken of at length, the latter only evident from Papa's sour expression. Cheeks burning, overcome with anger and humiliation, I raced to my room, flinging myself on the bed, soaking my pillow with tears.

Sir Jack had earned my good opinion, and I was loath to relinquish it just because we had been caught behaving impulsively. As an honourable man, he would offer marriage on the morrow. I would accept, and Papa would eventually and reluctantly give his blessing.

With high expectations, I set out for Oakham Mount, hoping to encounter my noble suitor along the pathway.

It was at the top that I spotted him against the impressive view; and it was there he tried again to kiss me before making another—far less welcome—advance. Rife with references to carnal desires, his words spoke of amorous pursuits and offers of his "protection"—all of which were heatedly declined.

"You cannot be in earnest, Elizabeth. With your inferior connections and a family so beneath mine, this is the best proposition you shall ever receive from me. You cannot have expected any *other* sort." My stricken look prompted ugly laughter. "Dear god, girl, you *did!*" For the second day in a row, I received a gentleman's disgusted look. "Compose yourself. I cannot abide crumpled faces, snivelling, and bleating. Here." He passed me a handkerchief. "Dry your eyes. You look a fright."

I shoved aside his hand and, sight blurred, ran as I had not done in years. Reckless, I neither bothered to look behind to see if he followed nor paid mind to my footing or the branches snagging my clothing.

And I told no one, not even Jane—ever!—of my disgrace. When anyone questioned my dolour or why the baronet had gone away, I explained there had been no hope of—no interest in—an attachment on either side.

Papa assumed my despondency was due to the impropriety he witnessed outside the barn. I let him believe that. Mama was inconsolable over the loss of a baronet as her son. Jane, concerned, was brushed off with as much solicitude as I could manage. Mary pontificated until I applied to her vanity for some soothing music. She obliged by performing a dirge. Kitty and Lydia whispered and giggled over a folly of which they knew nothing.

Just as I know nothing. He is not the man I thought him to be, and I am naught but a foolish, green girl.

The brave face presented to others became less of a facade. Not formed for ill-humour, I wiped away tears no one else beheld and forced up my chin. I had not been in love. What I shared with Sir Jack lacked the pure, elevating passion I expected, craved. There *had* been ardour—a longing, an intensity—but it was passion of a baser nature. *No wonder he made assumptions about me. Stupid girl! I shall never again make such a mistake. But what a fine fellow he was to deceive me into admiring him. I cannot but compliment the man's ingenuity and discernment.*

I buttoned my pelisse and grabbed a wrap for additional warmth against the biting wind. After being confined in the house for two days due to inclement weather and heartsickness, I was gladdened by the morning sun streaming through my window. About to open the front door, intent on a brisk, solitary walk, I was stopped in my tracks by a voice from behind.

"The horses are not needed on the farm this morning. Now is as good a time as any for your next lesson." Clad in riding boots and the worn, woollen coat he wore for shooting, Papa unlatched the door, gesturing towards the barn.

Drat. "After my last disastrous attempt, I thought we settled on the hopelessness of further instruction."

The farther the walkway led, the stronger became the smell of hay and animal. Slowing his pace to match the dragging of my feet, Papa tucked my hand in the crook of his arm and insisted he had agreed on no such thing.

Gravel crunched underfoot as I gazed at my intended destination, the chalk ridge in the distance. "May I wear breeches and ride astride?" Admonished that a genteel lady such as myself should never conceive such a travesty, I disengaged my arm from his. Fidgeting with my glove's cuff, I pouted. "Riding sidesaddle is too hard."

"No." He chucked me beneath the chin. "The hardest thing about learning to ride, my dear, is the ground."

"My point exactly. I shall surely fall off again."

Eyes trained on a Royston crow taking flight in our direction, Papa beckoned me forward. "Our greatest glory is not in never falling but in rising every time we fall." He spoke, I suspected, not only of riding but of being crossed in love.

"Confucius," I huffed, "never had to ride in skirts with both feet on the same side." My step faltered as we neared the barn. "We cannot afford the luxury of pleasure horses. There is no real need for me to learn. Honestly, I would rather walk like the commoner I am than ride on a high horse like the nobility of yore. Right now, I have not much use for either nobles or ignoble baronets."

Slinging an arm across my shoulders, Papa hugged me close to his side. "If it puts your mind at ease, Ashworth is up for lease again. You will likely never cross paths with the baronet again...unless you marry some other man of the *beau monde*."

"Ugh. Other than bobbing the slightest of curtsies, I shall not pay any undue respect to *that* lot."

Papa patted my arm. "Good. Now, as for noble *steeds*, I would never put you at risk and am not expecting you to gallop or hunt. But I encourage you to learn to ride at a walk and, eventually, a trot."

Watching as the hooded crow alighted on the barn's weathervane, I pointed it out to my father. "Do you know of the Northern legend in which a maiden throws a stone, a bone, and a clump of turf at one of those birds on Candlemas morn?"

"Much more efficient to shoot at it, I should think."

"If one wanted to slay the creature, yes. But a maiden curious about her marital prospects needs to observe the crow. If it flies away, her husband will be a foreigner. If it perches on a farm or house, he will be a man from her own country."

Papa's eyes narrowed, focusing on the bird. "And what is the girl's fate if the crow stays put?"

"Spinsterhood."

"I see. Well now, Lizzy, are you ready to give it a try?"

"'Tis far from Candlemas."

"I have no desire to learn about the man to whom I must one day relinquish you. And, despite your attempt to change subjects, I was asking if you are willing to try riding again."

Rolling my eyes heavenward, I again espied the crow on the weathervane. Hefting a piece of gravel, I flung it at the bird with admirable accuracy. The startled crow ruffled its feathers and settled a moment before taking wing. We turned, watching, as it flew towards the house and landed on the roof above our front door after—to our amusement—leaving a nasty deposit on Mama's lacy cap. Whatever purpose my mother had for ducking her head out of the house at that particular moment was forever lost to subsequent wailing and fluttering. Despite the frantic flapping going on below, the crow remained unmoved.

"Well, well." Papa chuckled. "I am unsure whose aim impressed me more, yours or the bird's."

"Poor Mama. I should go. She will need much placating."

Grasping a sleeve, he stopped me in my tracks. "Ruffled feathers can be smoothed later. News of your English husband will go a long way in mollifying your flighty mother. But that countryman will expect his wife to have *some* knowledge of horsemanship." Holding up a hand, he stifled any protestation. "Face your fears, Lizzy. Conquer or quell them. One's courage should arise apace with intimidation."

At Papa's insistence, I became an overly cautious rider and learnt to drive a gig. As a means of getting around my environs, though, I would always prefer Shank's mare. Such would be well suited to my lot in life—wife of a humble clergyman or brave soldier. I was not formed to endure a handsome, debauched man of higher station.

EMBROIDERY & BEAUS
1809

SUNLIGHT, SLANTING THROUGH THE WESTERLY WINDOW, GAVE MEAGRE warmth to the draughty room on a chilly January day. Moving in and out of the sunbeams, Mama paced, continuing her rant. "Foolish girl! Rather than acting like a hoyden, you should take Jane as a model. Why can you not be more like your demure sister?"

"Need I remind you, Mrs. Bennet, that Lizzy and Jane are two completely different people with dissimilar personalities?" Setting aside his book, Papa removed his reading spectacles. "Very well. What have you done, Lizzy, to earn your mother's disfavour...other than having seen the backside of a potential suitor a month or so ago? What a distinction you have earned. Not many of your sex can afford such an indulgence."

"I invited the Lucas brood to play leapfrog and quoits out there." I pointed through the window to the uncultivated section of our brown lawn.

"You"—Mama aimed her handkerchief at me—"are too blithe, too energetic, too playful, and too noticeably happy for your own good."

"Liveliness and good cheer are, I suppose, to be avoided at all costs." Wrapping fingers around his cup, Papa sipped spicy, coddled ale. "'Tis comforting to know *I* am rarely tempted by such wickedness."

Lace-trimmed square raised to her eye, Mama dabbed nonexistent tears. "Lizzy's unbridled behaviour and ungovernable tongue are influencing her younger sisters. If—in having discouraged a baronet's favour—she has not already done so, one day, mark my words, she will bring disgrace on our good name."

"I image she had her reasons for eschewing him, but let the girl have her secrets. And wherever Lizzy is known, she is respected and valued. Except here"—Papa spoke so only I heard—"in her own home, by her own mother." Setting his drink beside the abandoned book, he roused himself from the comfort of a fireside chair. Hands clasped behind his back, he watched from the window as a merry band of boys and girls capered around his two youngest, most boisterous daughters. "Is there some duty you are neglecting, child?"

"Not that I am aware of." I resented being called away from the games, but Mama insisted I was too old.

Papa turned towards her. "Is it not admirable she offered to amuse the children while Jane teaches Charlotte the intricacies of"—pausing, he furrowed his brow—"what vital technique?"

"Whitework embroidery."

"Ah, yes, those loops of colourless thread indispensable to the tapestry of a maiden's life." Turning back to the window, he grinned as squeals of glee sounded from without. "I daresay Charlotte is glad for the respite from her brothers and sisters and grateful for Lizzy's thoughtfulness."

Mama resented the way Papa always took my side. At eighteen, I was accustomed to her disappointment in me—and in Mary and, to a lesser extent, Kitty—but such acceptance did not lessen the hurt. In public and within her hearing, however, woe betide any person with the effrontery to disparage *any* of Jenny Bennet's daughters. In that fierce loyalty, I was not unlike her.

"We must take measures now to preserve our girls' reputations." Presented as if I was not in the same room, a lengthy lamentation of my dismal marriage prospects ensued. "Oh, Mr. Bennet, if only the baronet had made *Jane* an offer instead of paying attention to Lizzy." Mama's tone matched the bitter look cast in my direction. "I suppose *you* will one day run off with a lowly naval or army lieutenant and think it nothing but a lark."

Papa signalled my silence. "Does one run off with a seafaring man? I imagine they might sail away. And, Daughter, I presume you are able to differentiate between a soldier and a songbird." Moving from the window, he nudged his wife's side. "Need I remind you of a lively, young woman who almost ran off with a redcoat many years ago? We can always hope, my dear Jenny, that Lizzy might share that girl's fate and be saved by a foolhardy, infatuated country gentleman."

Mama narrowed her eyes. "Are you insinuating Lizzy is, in any way, similar to me?"

"No, no." Shoulders slumping, Papa shuffled back to his chair. "She is nothing like you, and I am grateful for small mercies."

Later, tracing a forefinger over the embroidery on the muslin my sister and Charlotte had worked, I complimented Jane on its perfection. After carefully passing her the delicate gown, I shivered in the chill, hugging my shawl closer. "That shall do nicely for the morning you plight your troth to some fortunate man." I slipped off my shoes, climbed atop the four-poster and flopped on my stomach. "Describe him for me."

"Who?" Jane's perfect brow furrowed as she placed the garment in our wardrobe. "You know I have no suitor."

"Pretend you do. What is it about this man that tempted you to accept his offer of marriage?"

Jane obliged with a slight shake of her head and a gentle smile. "Kind and protective, he has happy manners and sufficient means to keep me in relative comfort."

Sitting, I adjusted the shawl snugly around my shoulders. "Good grief. What an unsentimental, practical answer. You obviously spend far too much time with dear, unromantic Charlotte. Come now, you can do better. Start anew."

Settling beside me, Jane hugged knees to chest, tucking cold, stockinged toes beneath a blanket. "My intended is a sensible, good humoured man, warm-hearted, lively, gently bred. And he writes well." Upon my coaxing of a physical description, she added, "He is not ill-favoured."

"Details, Jane, details! Is the man tall or squat? Broad shouldered or hunchbacked? Dark or fair? Does he have more hair than wit, or is he balding? Lean or fubsy? When he looks upon you, do his eyes shine like sapphires, emeralds, or ebony? Are his calves shapely, or is he spindle-shanked?"

"He is amiable and can keep me in comfort. That is what truly matters." Jane laughed at my huff of annoyance. "Although his looks are unimportant, the man of my dreams is tall, fair, and lean. Now, your turn, Lizzy. Describe your suitor."

"He is neither baronet nor of the *ton* and is not devastatingly handsome. If ever I marry, it shall be to a gentleman of modest means, someone from my own sphere—most likely a second son, just as I am a second daughter. Likely he will be a clergyman or brave soldier. In fact, I rather fancy the thought of a uniformed admirer."

"Go on." Jane nudged my shoulder. "Tell me about him."

"He has a splendid smile and a dry sense of humour…but…um…" My face crumpled as I feigned a sob. "Oh! 'Tis a sad, sad story." With a corner of my shawl, I dabbed imaginary tears. "My suitor is a soldier in the, um, Royal Artillery." Warming to the subject, I grasped Jane's hand. "My beloved—the valiant, um, Lieutenant Mann—was badly injured while fighting far, far away for King and country."

"No! How terrible." Jane squeezed my hand. "What happened?"

"He was blinded."

Jane gasped. "How tragic. Good gracious, the poor, dear man."

"As far as I am concerned, it is a blessing…as is his loss of hearing due to, um, cannon fire." Watery-eyed, Jane asked how such dreadful afflictions could possibly be a godsend. I hugged her, apologising for causing distress. "'Tis all fanciful, you realise."

Jane sniffled. "One must never, ever make light of a person's hardships." Fidgeting with the fringe on my shawl, she gave it a tug. "Why, of all things, would you imagine a blind and deaf suitor?"

"We would be well matched. He could neither see my defects nor hear my impertinence. Now, despise me if you dare."

Pinching my arm, Jane grumbled that she *should* despise me but could not. "You are too utterly endearing. And, one day, Lizzy, some intelligent, fortunate man will discover just how loveable you are."

"Pray tell," I said, rubbing my arm, "is this fortunate man also a man of fortune?"

"You tell me. He is *your* imaginary beau."

"Well, since you find the unfortunate Lieutenant Mann too tragic a figure, what think you of a *Mister* Mann? I shall now go against my inclination and proclaim him a fine, tall, wealthy gentleman with patrician features, noble mien, aristocratic connections, and a palatial country house the size of Blenheim or Chatsworth, no less. Despite perfect eyesight and unimpaired hearing, he will admire me, warts and all, for the liveliness of my mind. There. Have I not painted a striking portrait of a most improbable suitor?"

"He sounds somewhat similar to Sir Jack, and the baronet *did* single you out. So, other than the fact you have no warts, the rest is unconditionally believable...especially the part about your future home."

Bursting into uncontrollable giggles, we—like the refined ladies we were—collapsed onto the mattress, rolling about and laughing ourselves silly.

LAW? WHAT A JOKE!
1810

"MR. BENNET! MR. BENNET!" CRIED MY MOTHER, BURSTING, UNBIDDEN, into Papa's sanctuary. "Have you heard? Mr. Standish is retrenching and has moved to smaller lodgings in Town. My sister just told me so." After being informed that Uncle Philips, the attorney handling the affair, had provided Papa and me with all pertinent details, Mama sat, fluttering her handkerchief. "Well! Heavens! Netherfield is to be either let or sold. What are we to do?"

"We?" Papa leaned back in his chair, lacing fingers together over his waistcoat. "It seems a cut and dried business to me. We wait and see who leases or purchases the place. Then, I suppose, I shall sit idly by until you badger me into paying our new neighbours a call, which I will have already done by that time, being the exemplary, gregarious gentleman I am."

Mama, brow furrowed, glanced around the room. "Where did Mr. Philips go? He did not leave with Margaret."

"He went to meet with Morris." Papa winked at me. "Our brother has a good *deed* to take care of with Netherfield's land agent."

"Oh?" Mama gripped the arms of her chair. "And what good deed would that be?"

"Never mind, my dear."

"Well! I still do not know what to think of this business with Netherfield. Who will be our neighbours now that Mr. Standish has gone? If only the manor were purchased by a bachelor swimming in lard and in search of a wife. What a fine establishment it would be for Jane." Lacy cap bobbing, face beaming, she moved about the room, speculating—with astonishing accuracy—on the monetary worth of someone in a position to purchase Netherfield Park. Garnering only our disinterest, she swept from the room.

"Good *deed*, Papa? You distracted me from my novel to witness *that*?" He apologised then asked what I had been reading. Holding the book forward, I watched as he, squinting, read the title. *"The History of Sir Charles Grandison*. What, again?"

"I grew tired of Sir William's back issues, specifically the society pages announcing absurdities of the *ton*. There is, apparently, a fashionable swell of the first stare from Derbyshire, some earl's grandson, who has every Quality female—youthful or not, pretty or not, single or not—panting after him."

"Elizabeth!"

"'Twas a quote from the newspaper, Papa. It is to be assumed those ladies were breathless from running after the fellow. It seems he, no doubt a rake of the first-order, cannot be caught."

"Hence your rereading of a novel about a morally *good* man."

"Well, is that not the kind of husband I should find?"

"I do not recommend seeking a husband at all...too dangerous a pursuit." At my puzzled expression, he grinned. "My advice, Lizzy, is to seek a *single* man."

"Fine advice. Thank you. But do you suppose a morally decent gentleman can be found only in fiction?" Pacing between cluttered desk and window, I riffled the book's pages. "I *hope* there are men with good principles out there...somewhere."

"*Most* young men have a bit of the devil inside, my dear, but it is no mean feat to sketch a fellow's character upon first acquaintance. Do not criticise yourself excessively for once being foolish over an unworthy swain."

"I am much wiser now. The folly of my youth shall be forgot." I was warned, instead, to *remember* my mistakes and learn from them. "I shall. But I *am* still curious about that rakish Derbyshire fellow. Do you suppose his sphere devoid of all decency?"

"What a thought, Lizzy. Following the prime example set by our

Prince of Wales, how can members of the aristocracy be aught but paragons of proper behaviour?"

"Tut-tut, Papa. Such sarcasm."

"Do you understand, now, why I prefer to keep at Longbourn? Heaven forbid I should spend time in London Town, Brighton, or Bath...finding my foot in my mouth and my neck in a noose. Worry not about a corrupt society in which we have no part. Conduct yourself properly and allow a man no liberties until he has the privilege of being your wedded husband. Also, try to instil a similar modicum of decorum in your two youngest, bacon-brained sisters. Mary we need not worry about. She is too pious by half. There. You see? Not only the royal family has embarrassments."

I feigned horror. "Surely you do not mean *our* family."

"Recently, I told your mother I knew of a family with two outrageous sisters. 'Their brother, though,' I said, 'is an amiable, prosperous fellow who earned his fortune through trade.' My dear wife claimed she knew of no such family and asked if the man was married."

"Uncle Gardiner's character *is* entirely different from his sisters'. But, Papa, my sisters and I are all dissimilar. Jane, for instance, would never have been caught in such a predicament with the baronet."

I could never forget my folly, could not entirely cast Sir Jack's proposition from my mind. Mortified over that degradation and resentful at being asked to parent Kitty and Lydia, I sought comfort from my older, wiser sister, our paragon of proper behaviour. She was found alone in the sitting room, engrossed in her embroidery, and I asked the whereabouts of the rest of the family.

"Mary has taken my poor mother to her chambers. Done in by speculation about Netherfield, Mama is overwrought, convinced the manor will be purchased by a wealthy bachelor in search of a bride and expects *me* to become its next mistress. 'Tis too much."

"You are perfect for the position, but only if the fellow himself is worthy."

"Mama speculated about that, too. His worth, I mean." Furrowing her brow, Jane pulled out a misplaced stitch. "Imagine how she would badger an unwary bachelor settled at Netherfield. It would be better for some crotchety old crone to take the place."

"I beg to differ." Taking the chair across from her, I rummaged through my work basket. "Any number of single gentlemen between the ages of eighteen and forty would be welcome. How are we to find husbands when there are no candidates within twenty-five miles? No one stays. Eligible men leave—for university, to join the militia, enlist in the Regulars, or to make a fortune in the navy—and rarely return. We females remain, awaiting our fate instead of going forth to make it happen. As much as I love Longbourn, I yearn to broaden my horizon."

"If you *could* go, what would interest you at university, Lizzy? What occupation might you choose?"

"The legal profession, I suppose."

"Law? What a joke!"

"Brava. What an impressive imitation of dear Lydia."

"Thank you. But can you envision a woman ever being called to the Bar?"

"I have faculty enough to imagine it, yes. Why not? We are intelligent, rational creatures."

"Can you honestly picture Lydia in that role?" Jane apologised for the unkindness and, setting aside her work, contemplated me. "Would you truly wish to be a barrister?"

"Perhaps. I *am* capable of formulating good arguments to plead my case."

Jane's lips twitched. "At nineteen, you *have* come a long way from the pouting poppet stomping her foot, exclaiming, 'Because I *want* to!'"

Raising my nose in the air, I claimed no recollection of such childish behaviour. "Speaking of which... Where are Kitty and Lydia?"

"Aunt Philips took them to Meryton. Uncle has gone to meet with Mr. Morris at Netherfield...something about a good deed. I wonder what that might be." Laughing, I told her it was not worth mentioning and set about stitching the ripped seam in a shift. "But, Lizzy, noble acts should not be dismissed as unimportant. Good deeds are not be laughed at."

"Yes, yes, you have provided sufficient evidence and may rest your case." Tossing aside the shift, I strode to the window. "Instead of a barrister, I should like to become a solicitor and manage a grand estate." Hand splayed against the pane, I gazed at the horizon. "As land agent, I could be involved in outdoor pursuits rather than confined to some musty office or pompous courtroom all day. I drive a gig well enough to traverse my employer's home farm, parkland, and tenant farms. I enjoy chatting with others. Mama taught me about household accounts and ledgers. And, in one easy lesson, Papa imparted his own invaluable advice about bookkeeping." Jane asked if I would share his advice. Turning, I leaned against the sill. "Of course. He told me the best way to *keep* books is to never *lend* them."

"Seriously, dear Lizzy, I know you. You *do* wish to broaden your horizon. It saddens me you cannot do so from here and that one day we will part."

Settling beside her on the sofa, I admired Jane's handiwork. "We must not cling to this local attachment, strong as it may be. A woman goes where her fate—her husband—takes her. We cannot always be at Longbourn." Nudging her shoulder, I grinned. "Do not forget *you* will be advantageously married and settled at a neighbouring manor, not three miles distant."

That night, elusive sleep had me pondering the future. Parting from Jane *would* be painful, and I prayed that—if my destiny had *me* remaining at Longbourn—*she* might also stay in the vicinity as Netherfield's mistress.

Having settled her fate, I woke to a glorious autumn morn.

Besides the great outdoors and Papa's small but well-stocked book room, the sweet-smelling stillroom was one of my favourite places at Longbourn. I loved its entire wall of windows and its hanging bunches of dried flowers and herbs. Adding to its appeal, it was also where cakes and other sweetmeats were stored. Standing at its threshold, I breathed in the mingled aromas and observed the activity within as Mrs. Hill and her underlings bustled about an enormous trestle table—pickling, preserving, drying, and distilling.

Directly outside, song thrushes descended upon the hedges of currant and gooseberry enclosing the kitchen garden. Wafting in through the open windows, their musical phrases went unnoticed by the workers intent on individual tasks.

Farther afield, another crop of grass had been cut and dried, and bundles of fodder were being loaded onto wagons. Catching a whiff of the sweet, sunny smell of new-mown hay, I inhaled deeply. Everywhere I looked, workers were busy harvesting nature's bounty. The Bennets, and those families and livestock under our care, would not go hungry that winter.

As much as I loved Longbourn, my eventual leaving would not much signify. I could be content elsewhere. A greater state of peaceful happiness might even be achieved—provided my new home was near fields and woods to roam, had a small book room in which to curl up with a novel, a sunlit stillroom to putter about in, and picturesque views from every window. But only a wealthy gentleman could afford the tax on such light and air. The scheme diverted me beyond moderation until reality intruded. *Unless it is within my power to find a husband with four or five thousand a year, I must entirely surrender these absurd notions. I will more likely end up in service—dusting those bookshelves and washing myriad casements. Ugh.*

Standing at the same window the next morning, I glowered. The day before, abounding in activity and sunshine, had given way to a starless night. The morn had dawned halfheartedly, with grey skies and a relentless rain. Inclement weather put an end to outdoor occupation for all, it seemed, except worms and garden slugs. Going for a walk would provoke Mama's disgust, and I had already made languid attempts at needlework, reading, and practising scales. With a start, I noticed a reflection in the window and whirled round. "Papa!"

"I became concerned when you abandoned your book and did not return. Are you well, Lizzy?"

"A little melancholy, perhaps." Reaching overhead to a bundle of herbs drying upside-down, I plucked and crushed a leaf, releasing its piquant fragrance. "I cannot bear the thought of always hanging on your sleeve, becoming a burden, ending an old maid, or going into service."

He led me to the trestle table. Once we were both seated on the bench, he patted my hand. "I apologise for failing you and your sisters. My indolence is to blame for the insignificance of your dowries. But you and Jane are lovely young ladies, and I am proud of all you have achieved despite being raised by deficient parents. As long as your sights are not set too high, you will be discovered by a man worthy of your regard."

"But would he be a sensible man? I have not much to offer."

"An intelligent fellow would see your true worth." He stood, gazing at me with concern. "Find some activity, child, and shake this pensiveness; so unlike you." He kissed the top of my head and invited me back to his book room for a round of backgammon.

As I silently contemplated the board, the sounds of the house drifted in and out of my awareness—the hiss and pop of the fire, the bang of something being dropped above us, Lydia's raucous laughter, a slamming door. Mary clanging at the pianoforte. A clock chiming. Kitty's cough, a chair scraping, Mama calling for her salts.

"Are we not fortunate, Lizzy? We can proudly boast of a pair of the silliest girls in the country, one pedantic young woman, one paragon of perfection, and one middle-aged matron with nervous flutterings of both heart and handkerchief. How dull life would be without them to make sport of, eh?"

Having lost the game, I took a turn about the room, floorboards creaking in their customary pattern, dust motes rising as I ran fingertips along bookshelves. "What of the Golden Rule? Do as you would be done by."

"Ah. Do you see, now, why I prefer to spend time alone in here? Less chance for others to make sport of me. Or, if they do, I do not hear of it."

My father rarely acknowledged his own family's improprieties, preferring to look the other way and feign ignorance. My eyes, however, strayed to the shelf upon which sat a book containing a woodblock print depicting three monkeys. "One does not care to be reminded of one's foibles. Like the proverb says, 'see no evil, hear no evil, speak no evil,' I want to cover my ears whenever Mama scolds me to curb my tongue."

"Your mother is always the soul of discretion, is she? Speaking of which, for my part, discretion is often the better part of valour. 'Tis better to avoid a dangerous situation than to confront it."

Aye, there's the rub. Correcting your family's behaviour would mean confrontation...a situation to be avoided at all costs. Such is not the course for me. I would not back down from an argumentative situation. "Kitty and Lydia certainly make sport of others—calling them plain or ugly. 'Tis unfair to ridicule someone for the way they look. One's character should be more important."

Papa reminded me I had, several months previously, assigned one-word characteristics to friends and family. "Your dear mother was pronounced *overstrung*, Jane *naive*, Mary *pedantic*, Kitty *susceptible*, and Lydia *brash*." Tapping his chin, he frowned. "How was it you described me? Ah, yes, *sarcastic*."

"Surely not. I believe the word was *witty*."

"*Witty* was how you defined yourself. No, no, my mistake. You referred to yourself as *clever*. Others earning positive pronounce-ments were your *industrious* uncle Gardiner, his *paragon* of a wife, the *gregarious* Sir William Lucas, and our *dedicated* Mrs. Hill. On the other hand, poor Lady Lucas and Mrs. Long were declared *busybodies*. Your dearest friend Charlotte was deemed *desperate* and her sister Maria *vacuous*. Mr. and Mrs. Philips were described respectively but not respectfully as a *sot* and *gauche*."

"Surely not! My temper must have been ungovernable that day, my judgements immoderate. Jane should have been proclaimed *beautiful*, for she is certainly that, inside and out."

"And *you* are blessed with not only comeliness but a good head on your shoulders. I hope you are not feeling in any way inferior because of Jane's exceptional beauty."

"No, but all our family's hopes seem to rest on her shoulders because of Jane's looks. A man should choose a wife based on character and intelligence rather than beauty and fortune. I resent the fact women are often judged by appearance alone." I stopped to study my reflection in the mirror. "Unlike a person's mind or conduct, not much can be done to improve one's outward form."

"Tell that to your uncle Philips. He stuffs paper layers into his shoes in an attempt to appear taller and tries to conceal his balding head by combing the last remaining strands to either the left or right. And those, for now, shall be my *parting* words."

BURIED TREASURE
1811

FOR WEEKS ON END, ALL MAMA COULD TALK OF WAS A NEWLY-ordained, bachelor cousin of her brother, and I was declared particularly suited to a parsonical suitor and life in some idyllic country parish...until my aunt arrived with a letter detrimental to my prospects and to Mama's frangible nerves.

Aunt Phillips, with spirits greatly shaken, rushed to embrace me and explain that the eligible vicar had met another gentleman's daughter, fallen violently in requited love, married after the third reading of the banns, and gone off on a five-day wedding tour without me.

"Oh, Sister, Sister!" Mama's handkerchief fluttered with each syllable. "How could he be so heartless?" She—in convoluted logic, for I had never even met the cleric—blamed me for the ruination of all her dreams.

"Now, now, Mrs. Bennet." Papa patted his wife's shoulder. "'Tis just as well Lizzy missed her chance to wed him." Upon being asked how he could say such a thing, he reminded her the man had the living in Wakefield. "Do you not see the problem?" At Mama's puzzled expression, he sighed. "Having never finished an entire book in the decades of our marriage, you, I suspect, are unfamiliar with the protagonist in *The Vicar of Wakefield*, a novel of family endurance and—"

"But a novel is just a fanciful story." Mama sputtered, waving her arms about. "This, Mr. Bennet, is real life!"

"And I thank God the account is fictitious." Papa swiped theatrically at his brow. "One man's idyllic country life...beset by so many woes. Imagine having a vain, social-climbing wife eager to splendidly marry off her daughters. Imagine six children—including a luxuriantly beautiful paragon of forgiveness with an overwhelming desire to please. Imagine another alluring—although not so striking at first— female offspring. Imagine another daughter, abducted, then married to an evil man. Imagine *that*, if you will, Mrs. Bennet."

Mama called for her salts before retiring to her bedchamber, aggrieved with an entire world bent on her personal suffering.

Spared more of Mama's sentiments on being the wife of such an unfortunate man, Jane and I strolled along the sweet-scented cutting garden, baskets slung over arms, and soon welcomed our dear friend Charlotte who had come to call.

Our voices, birdsong, and the clipping of shears were the only sounds disturbing the clear morning as we selected the fullest, most vivid, late blooms.

Setting aside our implements, we perched on a bench while I continued, for Charlotte's benefit, an account of Mama's disappointed hopes. "Then she declared that if I did not jump at the next opportunity to capture some man's heart, she would never again see me."

Adjusting her brim so no rays beset her face, Charlotte laughed. "Your mother has made similar threats before and will again."

"You know well all our idiosyncrasies, Charlotte. We, therefore, must promise to always be friends, no matter what our futures hold... even should one of us end up the wife of a vicar in another county." Raising my face to the sun's warmth, I closed my eyes. "Such an establishment might actually be a cosy existence if a woman held affection for, and respected, her mate. I, however, shall never marry. What man in his right mind would tolerate this malapert mouth? Instead, Auntie Elizabeth shall end an old maid and teach her forty nieces and nephews"—grinning, I nudged Charlotte's side—"and her dear friend's ten children, to be boldly disrespectful."

But I longed for more than spinsterhood. *The importance of marriage is universally acknowledged, but happiness in such a state must be paramount.* I yearned to experience, again, the intense feelings roused as Sir Jack embraced me. *How divine such affinity, such intimacy, must be with a man one actually loves. I want to be in love. I want to fall so deeply in love that I never find my way out again. Though I may proclaim otherwise, I pray marriage is in my future. If such does not come to pass, however, I may smugly say I knew it all along.*

"You could always wed Lieutenant Mann." Jane rescued a ladybird from one of her snipped dahlias, setting it free on the gentle breeze.

"Who," asked Charlotte, "is Lieutenant Mann?"

"Lizzy's deaf and blind imaginary suitor."

"Good grief. Do not conjure up that unfortunate soldier after all these years. Although, compared to the aggravation of having me for a wife, his affliction would be as nothing." Fists gripping the fabric of my apron, I grimaced. "As much as I admire Papa's sarcasm, his amusement in others' faults is, in itself, a fault. I am, I think, an odd mixture of my parents—offspring of Papa's aloof cynicism and Mama's injudicious volubility. Ergo, I *should* never marry."

Jane tut-tutted. "There must be a tolerant, intelligent gentleman of moderate fortune out there, somewhere, for you."

"Oh, fie! Must he be intelligent? A clever man would quickly perceive my follies, foibles, and flaws."

"If a man comprehends your meaning and engages you in a battle of wits, you will have met your intellectual match." Jane nodded while Charlotte spoke. "If, on the other hand, he is unable to understand your repartee, you might be perceived as feeling yourself superior."

"So, I have an impressive aptitude for inventive thought and quick understanding. What am I to do? Hide my lamp under a bushel basket?"

"Not at all." Jane reached for my hand. "Light is to be revealed, not concealed. I envy the gleam in your eye, the fire within you. Promise me you will let no one extinguish that light."

In turn, I made the gentlest, most delicate creature on earth promise she would never let anyone hurt her. "If anyone dares, they should prepare to be harangued by your loyal, sharp-tongued spitfire of a younger sister." Jane, paragon of forgiveness that she is, said she would pity such a person.

At times, I could be flippant, but Jane and Charlotte deserved good men. All three of us were worthy of being cherished. *We are treasures waiting to be found. Treasures buried deep in Hertfordshire. And some of us need to be extracted sooner rather than later. Perhaps treasure maps could be drawn up and circulated throughout England...but not as far north as the Midlands. If one's husband had sufficient fortune to make the expense of travelling unimportant, distance could be no evil, but that will be an unlikely prospect for the three of us.*

A week later, on a night bathed in pale moonlight, Meryton's monthly assembly was expected to be a dull event with neither treasure hunters nor bantering dance partners in attendance.

JANE WAS INDISPOSED, AND MARY REFUSED TO ATTEND. KITTY AND Lydia argued they should be allowed to go in their sisters' stead. Mama agreed and... *Voila.* Both youngest Bennets were out at once.

Clad in well-fitted muslin, I had two wishes upon setting off. First, Lydia would stop acting the giddy ox. Second, by night's end, I could not say I sat as well as my gown.

Five years earlier, on the night I came out, I had sat quietly chatting with Charlotte, not snorting in laughter or drinking too much negus. Never had I been like Lydia and Kitty—head full of the opposite sex, imaging a man's admiration, putting myself forward, trying to catch the eye of two handsome militia members scouting our shire for encampment possibilities.

Entirely at Lydia's importunity, Sir William, our Master of Ceremonies, introduced us to the newcomers. Minutes later, snuggled up to the lieutenant's arm and smiling smugly, Lydia was led to the lines of dancers while the captain—lip curled in disdain, hard-heeled boots clap-tapping—glared at them with brooding eyes.

After the set, while sipping punch and dying of embarrassment, I overheard the captain haranguing his subordinate with words such as "hoyden" and "money-grubbing chit." Laughing, the lieutenant added, "Not to mention fishwife of a mother!"

"Did you see me, Mama?" Flushed with excitement and negus, Lydia gushed about the young officer. "Is he not handsome? And he singled *me* out. Oh, I pray the Derbyshire Militia decides to encamp here in Meryton!"

Taking my youngest sister in hand, I chastised her for being stupidly swayed by a man's good looks. "First impressions can be misleading, Lydia. You entirely misunderstood the situation and him. What were you thinking? What did you hope to accomplish by such shameless behaviour?"

Shrugging, Lydia said she wanted the lieutenant to notice her, like her. "And he *did*, Lizzy! I was the only girl he asked."

"Above being liked, Lydia, a person needs to be, first and foremost, respected. And, believe me, you were *not* respected by those men."

"How would *you* know?"

"I *heard* them, Lydia. Besides, knowing a person's true character takes time. Deep admiration and respect are earned through one's qualities, abilities, or achievements. Handsome looks matter not a groat if one cannot follow through with regard for the feelings and wishes of others. I shall only be satisfied if a gentleman demonstrates his love for me through his deeds and deep trust. In return for his faithfulness and support, he will have all that, and more, from me."

But will I ever find such a man myself...someone to love and laugh with?

An ominous billow obliterated the full moon as I departed the assembly hall in a dark mood, under my own cloud. While waiting for the carriage to be brought around and shivering as a sprinkle of rain chilled my bones, anger heated my face. That the officers ridiculed my sister and mother was distressing enough, but I could not decide the night's most intolerable offence—their harsh contempt for Lydia and Mama or my own shameful embarrassment over my own family.

Lydia acted the giddy ox on the drive home, while I was the opposite. After all, I *had* sat as well as my gown. Not once had I been asked to dance. Perhaps envy, as well as sisterly concern, had impelled my rebuke of her.

I slept poorly that night, praying for clear skies at dawn. A long, solitary walk amongst verdure often soothed frustrations and solved problems. Vast, open skies compelled me to count my blessings and to gain a true understanding of the relative importance of things.

It was not to be.

Under usual circumstances, an unremitting drizzle would not keep me indoors, but our dear little maid-of-all-work had been abed with fever two days in a row. Mrs. Hill was hard-pressed to keep up with her regular duties while tending a patient, so Mama put her foot down. No more muddy muslin was to be added to the mound of soiled clothing and linens amassing below stairs. My sisters and I were ordered to drop whatever held our interest and attend to over-flowing work baskets. If Papa's shirts and our shifts could not be laundered, new ones must be sewn.

Needlework had been learnt at an early age, as evidenced by five rudimentary samplers gracing our walls; but I held the distinction of being even worse at it than my youngest sister and also of having the most clothing in need of repair. Such work was as unrelenting as the drizzle and ten times as monotonous.

The entire routine of life in my little corner of the world had become increasingly dull. Every landmark, every tree, every rock in the vicinity was familiar, and I longed for new vistas. *Hang that narrow horizon! If one could travel, one might learn to better appreciate the comforts of home.*

New blood might have relieved such mundaneness, but Ashworth and Netherfield remained uninhabited. Like hungry but tentative fish, several prospects had nibbled at the bait, but those nibbles had not been to their taste.

"Well!" Mama sniffed with disdain. "If Netherfield was deemed unworthy, there could be no pleasing such pernickety people. We are better off without them."

In the event pernickety visitors might call, utilitarian work and mending was abandoned in favour of more genteel embroidery projects. *Heaven forbid Lady Lucas might drop by and discover Mama darning Papa's stockings.*

Bending to the tedious chore of intricate stitchery, I nudged Jane's foot. "Old Mother Twitchet had one eye and a long tail that she let fly. And every time she went through a gap, she left some tail in the trap."

"What nonsense is that, Lizzy?" Upon my reply it was a charade, Mama scoffed. "Mother Twitchet must be a one-eyed nag passing through a hedgerow." Squinting, she threaded her needle, pushing floss silk through the tiny hole.

"Speaking of hedges," said Mary, "I wonder if the gentleman who eventually purchases Netherfield manor will be for or against Enclosure."

Lydia stabbed at the cushion she was embroidering. "La! Netherfield Park is already enclosed by hawthorn shrubbery."

"If he is for Enclosure," said Mary, "he and I shall never see eye to eye. The working class should not be deprived of common land. The village of Longbourn may be enclosed, but I am thankful Papa is a lax enough landowner that the poor may poach from us all the food and firewood they can use."

"Heavens, Mary!" I gaped at her. "How liberal of you. Tell me, what happens once they have felled all our trees and killed all our game?"

"One might as well poach on our neighbour's territory." Kitty chimed in. "The place will be overrun with hares should Netherfield not be let or sold soon."

"Any poacher climbing through those spiny hedgerows will get a thorn in his side." Lydia's laugh erupted as a snort.

"Hunger is no laughing matter." Mary, who prided herself upon the solidity of her reflections, paged through her book of extracts. "And the generous will themselves be blessed," she quoted, "for they share their food with the poor."

Talking over her, Mama lamented Netherfield's prolonged vacancy. "If only a single gentleman would come and—"

"I am come, Mrs. Bennet." Papa stood in the doorway. "Alas, a single gentleman amongst a houseful of women." Sauntering over, he admired Jane's handiwork but—evincing his discernment—not mine. "By the bye, you may all be happy to learn a young gentleman—and no ladies—came from London yesterday in a chaise and four to inspect Netherfield Park."

Mama opened her mouth but was forestalled. "I am further pleased to report hawthorn is an emblem of hope and a mender of broken hearts. So, should Netherfield be taken, its new owner may give us false hope and, at the same time, have the means of remedying heartsickness...thereby killing two birds with one stone." His piercing glare settled on Mary. "The young man, however, will *not* be permitted to poach upon *my* estate."

WHERE I AM TODAY

HAVING THROWN A RETROSPECTIVE GLANCE OVER THE LAST FIVE YEARS, I understand my own behaviour has dictated the course of my life. One's persuasion, however, cannot help but be nurtured by one's family.

Under Papa's subtle influence, I became somewhat prejudiced, thinking meanly of the upper levels of society and tarring them all with the same dark brush. In truth, many denizens of the loftier sphere *do* deserve to be taken down a peg or two.

To my chagrin, so did I.

Months ago, a handsome but arrogant, taciturn gentleman of the *ton* made me a marriage proposal. Soundly spurned, he politely handed me a letter the next morning. Now, memorised verbatim, his written words speak to me like a monologue in Mr. Darcy's deep, resonant voice. The particulars contained on two sheets of letter paper and an envelope made me realise how utterly flawed was my discernment, how narrow was my mind. And I regretted every —*nearly* every—nescient word hurled at him.

He—of noble birth and deep, deep pockets—owns an estate situated nearby. The question is... Does he own noble *qualities*? Does a gentleman of honour and integrity exist only in fiction or in castles in the air...specifically, the air between my stupid ears? I could not have been as mistaken in his character as I was about his treatment of Wickham, *could* I? He seems to care deeply for his sister, but I wonder what kind of master he is.

Two evenings ago, when my aunt suggested this visit, I affected a great disinclination for further intimacy with great houses and displays designed merely to impress. My true objection was—still is— that I have absolutely no business going thither. When my aunt added "delightful grounds" as an incentive, my curiosity piqued; but I could neither acquiesce the scheme nor conceive the mortification, the dreadfulness, of meeting *him* while viewing the place. Good heavens, I still blush at the very thought.

Last night a chambermaid claimed the family was not currently in residence. So, to Pemberley we are headed.

The first appearance of Pemberley Woods is anticipated with no little perturbation on my part. Heart pounding and spirits in such high flutter as would make Mama seem serene, I consider asking that we turn back. Instead, we turn in at the lodge. Mind too full for conversation, I silently admire every remarkable point of view. At length, Pemberley House itself is espied, and we are all warm in our admiration. *Well, well. To be mistress of Pemberley might be something, indeed...something as unattainable for one such as me as...as stupid castles in the air.*

I am all apprehension as our carriage crosses a bridge, arrives at the sweep, and stops at the front door of a large, stone building. *His* building. His *home*. Anxiety at the possibility of meeting him over-comes me, but I keep reminding myself he is *not* down for the summer. Still, my hands and knees tremble as Uncle Gardiner applies to see this magnificent place...which would have been my home had I accepted the gentleman in April.

Always have I been the architect of my own fortune, my own future. Alas, the spring of my life—my adolescence, my time for learning—unfolded with more nescience than prescience. I learnt more of myself this April than in the past twenty years together, but such knowledge shall be put to good use now that summer has come. As I enter adulthood, I shall seek my own identity apart from my parents and, somehow, find fulfilment...and, perhaps, a husband. This past year's wrongs haunt me, though, as we are admitted into the hall.

And, while we await the housekeeper, I wonder at my being where
I am.

J. MARIE CROFT is a self-proclaimed word nerd and adherent of
Jane Austen's quote "Let other pens dwell on guilt and misery."
Bearing witness to Joanne's fondness for *Pride and Prejudice*, wordplay,
and laughter, are her light-hearted novel, *Love at First Slight* (a
Babblings of a Bookworm Favourite Read of 2014), her playful
novella, *A Little Whimsical in His Civilities* (Just Jane 1813's Favourite
2016 JAFF Novella), and her short stories in the anthologies *Sun-
kissed*, *The Darcy Monologues*, *Dangerous to Know*, *Rational Creatures*, and
Yuletide. Joanne lives in Nova Scotia.

Elizabeth: Obstinate Headstrong Girl
A Mate for Life
Christina Boyd

Her heart did whisper that he had done it for her. –Chapter LII

A MATE FOR LIFE
Christina Boyd

*I*f I can offer you any advice, my dear, do anything but marry without affection. Do not give yourself away so cheaply."

"You know he is rich as Croesus?"

"I do not mean his money, Adelaide. You, your heart, is worth everything, and if you cannot love and respect him, then I would wait for another. Let me not have the grief of seeing you unhappy with your partner in life."

My granddaughter takes off her broad brimmed hat and turns her face up to the sun. A spray of freckles on her nose reminds me of how my mother used to plague me for going out without my bonnet. I hold my tongue about the dangers of the sun. No grandmother wants to be thought of as a shrew.

"I think of him all the time. I believe I do love him. But how can I be sure? I have never been in love before. And we have not known each other very long to be certain, have we?"

"Two years would be insufficient to make some people acquainted with each other and two months, nay, two weeks are more than enough for others. My old friend Charlotte once said in our youth, 'Happiness is a matter of chance.' She believed it was better to know as little as possible of the defects of the person with whom you were to pass your life before you married him."

"Gram, how did you know you were in love?"

"Oh my dear, it was so long ago. I was in the middle before I knew I had begun."

"Now that is what I said to you!"

"I daresay I fell in love with your grandfather—"

"Tell her how it really happened. You fell in love with me when you first saw Pemberley—"

"After seeing these beautiful grounds at Pemberley." His laughter sounds in my ears and fills my heart. Even after all these years, he enjoys having his way.

"That cannot be true. It sounds absolutely mercenary. Not you, Gram," my sweet Adelaide says, kissing my cheek.

"But it really is a long story about an obstinate, headstrong girl and a fine, noble man. He was rich as Croesus too, my dear. He had too much pride and she had too much prejudice, or was it the other way around? But surely, you have other things to do. You do not want to sit here and listen to the ramblings of an old lady."

"Oh no. Ramble on." Taking my hand and tucking it into her arm, she pulls me from the stone bench, and we start down to the lake. "Tell me. How did you fall in love?"

"I hate to disappoint your romantic sensibilities, but I did not fall in love with him upon first sight. In fact, I believe I despised him from almost the very beginning."

"Whyever would you not like Grandfather?" Motioning to all about us, she asked, "Were you not enchanted by all of this?"

"Yes, dearest, whyever did you turn me down?"

His teasing makes me chortle, and I say to my granddaughter, "Well, he insulted me when I first met him."

"No!"

"Yes. I overheard him tell your uncle Charles' papa that I was tolerable but not handsome enough to tempt him."

"How could he?"

"I know"—patting her hand—"shocking! Worse, every time we were in company thereafter his conceit and prejudice, his standoffish behavior towards the good people of my village, confirmed he was the last man in the world who could ever interest me."

"Elizabeth, darling, now you know that comes later. And I believe you said I was the last man in the world you could ever be prevailed upon to marry."

I smile at the memory of that impudent girl, that audacious young thing…. Well, that's youth.

"Adelaide, you know that my family estate was much smaller and nothing grand like Pemberley, and as the second daughter to an unremarkable country squire I should have been using my arts and allurements to draw in eligible men." My granddaughter snickers, and I am pleased she appreciates my humor. "Such amenable behavior might have eased my own mother's nerves. She was always going on about being thrown into the hedgerows the moment my father died and Longbourn passed to my cousin Mr. Collins. I suppose, had your grandfather not wounded my pride, I might not have been so predisposed against him from the beginning. As it was, we sparred much and had many misunderstandings, too many misunderstandings, before I fell in love. It's a wonder he even asked me to marry him after I refused him the first time."

"The first time? He asked you twice?"

"Yes, I loved her that much. But she was right to refuse me then."

"Well, my darling, he did not know I did not like him. He had no reason to believe I would refuse him."

I stop at the edge of the lake, observing the pair of swans glide toward the reeds and remembering how my beloved told me once that swans mate for life. "After all, he was rich and handsome. But you must understand me, my child, your grandfather really had the most ungentlemanlike manner…then."

"My behavior was unpardonable. I cannot think on it without abhorrence."

My granddaughter's eyes are wide with wonder. "I do not see how you could fall in love with someone you had such prejudice against if all you did was argue."

Looking at the hat still at her side, Adelaide seems reluctant to wear it and makes a little face. With a sigh, she lifts the straw thing to her head as if it weighs a stone and ties the ribbons at her chin. So like me, this grandchild of mine, and yet she seems to carry the world on her shoulders like Atlas.

"Just because you are asked to marry does not mean you are obliged to say yes."

"But that's the thing, Grandmother. I must love Talbot. He is the most handsome man I have ever beheld. His eyes are blue as a robin's egg, and his voice is so deep and clear. And he speaks to me about things. As if he wants to know my mind. And his keen wit makes me laugh. And he's so very sweet...at least to me." I swear the child blushes to her roots! It warms my old heart to think of such happy tidings, of my granddaughter in love. "I hate to imagine he would marry some other girl. That his house would not be my house. That some other woman would bear his children...."

"And has he asked you? Because if he has not, you may well be putting the cart before the goat."

"Not yet. But last night after dinner, he asked to speak with me today. He said he has something very particular to discuss." I raise my eyebrows at this and start to wonder if maybe this is coming about too quickly after all. "I think that when he left us two weeks ago for his family seat, he left to speak with his father about me. And I ought to know what I should like to say before he asks, don't you think?"

"I'll not sport with your sensibilities then and ask what if he comes only for your opinion on the removal of newspaper stamp duty." She shoots me a look that tells me she needs my guidance, not my cleverness, and so I pat her arm, encouraging her to go on.

"But what will happen to me after I leave my family and am no longer Miss Adelaide Darcy? Will I cease to be...me? The church says I will go unto my husband's house and become his property."

"Oh, my sweet. You will always be you. Do you respect him? Does he respect you? Do you trust him? With your heart? Your whole being?"

She does not reply but worries her bottom lip with her teeth.

I continue. "Do you not think he is rather prideful?"

"At first, I did. A little. But on further acquaintance, you know, I believe that is how he likes to appear to strangers. Or even those he considers...inconsequential." After a breath, she says, "Well maybe he can be rather prideful."

"Inconsequential indeed"—that rich timbre of laughter echoes in the warm breeze, and I press my lips firmly together to keep from laughing out loud, too.

"Well, since your grandfather was very much like him when we first met, I suppose I should not hold pride against your young lord."

"When there is a real superiority of mind, pride will always be under good regulation." I cannot help but roll my eyes at that.

Dreamily, she twirls my large chintz parasol to the side, no longer shading us, and I accept that my daughter-in-law will not be pleased when she sees how Adelaide and I will have caught the sun. And yet, as there are no Caroline Bingleys present, we are safe—and I wave the thought away.

"Before your grandfather proposed, someone else asked me to marry him. And I refused him too."

"Did Grandfather know? Did you love him?"

I hear the echoed chuckle of my beloved, and I cannot help but smirk at the thought of how much I *did not* love Mr. Collins.

"In the autumn of 1811, before my twenty-first birthday, my cousin Collins came to Longbourn, and as he was the heir apparent, he felt incumbent to marry one of us Bennet daughters. I suppose it was a generous act—he surely thought he was magnanimous, and entitled, all at once—but when it fell to me to marry him, when it was obvious I would be his choice, I could not do it."

"Was he handsome?"

"Goodness, no. He was pompous, boorish. Absolutely ridiculous. Well, I suppose he might have been appealing to my sister Mary, but I could never respect nor be satisfied with such a man. My mother expected me to marry him, as I suppose to her, he was a good match. And when she learned I had refused him, she demanded I relent. But no matter how much it would benefit my mother and even my sisters if I were to become Mrs. Collins and the future mistress of Long-bourn, I could not sell myself into a marriage of convenience, for any amount of security."

"Your parents must have been terribly angry." Adelaide hands me the parasol as she steps away to brush her hand through a clump of daisies that grow wild along the lake. She plucks a daisy and carelessly begins to pull the petals off.

"Your great grandmother Bennet was livid and took to her bed but not before swearing *she would never see me again*. But my father, bless his soul, said *he* would never see me again if I married my cousin."

She tosses the now bare daisy head and loose petals into the air, laughing. "Thank heavens for your father. But I suppose that was a very brave thing for you to do then—not marry when you could have secured the happiness of your family."

"I did not look at it like bravery then. All I knew was that I could not possibly be happy with a man I did not respect. Besides, I was certain that my sister Jane would marry for love, and Charles Bingley was quite rich enough. So why sacrifice myself on the altar to Mr. Collins? I suppose Charlotte was the brave one. Marrying Mr. Collins and taking him to her bed." Adelaide looks at me, slightly scandalized, then peals of laughter ring out around me.

Wrinkling her brow, she asks, "But I thought you and your sister married on the same day...?"

"You are getting ahead of my story. You see my cousin Mr. Collins asked my dear friend Charlotte to marry him soon after I declined his suit, and despite how sensible I had always thought my friend, it was a while before I could reconcile the sense in such a match."

"But if you didn't want him, and she did, I don't see why you might mind."

"I suppose, in my heart, I knew that I only wanted to marry for love and could not see what she saw. Looking back, I understand that Charlotte made a very shrewd choice. *For her.* She was no longer a burden to her family and could be mistress of her own home. And become a mother to her own family." We begin again along the lake toward the footbridge. "But oh, how it rankled my mother that Charlotte would one day be the mistress of Longbourn."

"But it hardly mattered about Longbourn if...but how...if you and Great Aunt Jane married so well...when did you fall in love with my grandfather then? It seems an unlikely match if you were prejudiced against him from the start."

"Indeed, it was an unlikely match. We had several obstacles to overcome before I understood him. Before he loved me as he should."

"Oh, I always loved you, my darling. I only needed to be a better man, a man worthy of your love."

After all this time, his words still pervade my heart. To have experienced the love of such a man, who filled my life with...so much. My throat constricts and I reach for my handkerchief in my pocket.

As I dab at my eyes, my granddaughter puts her arm around my waist and relieves me of my parasol of chintz. It all seems so cumbersome with both our full skirts, crinolines, and numerous flounces. But that is the fashion these days. How I long for the simpler sprigged muslin gowns of yesteryear.

"With your hem six inches deep in mud?"

I smile at that, and put my handkerchief away, because I know how he had adored my youthful tramps across the muddy countryside.

"You will be surprised that your grandfather did not approve of my sister Jane as a wife for his friend... He could not recommend a match where there would be an unequal marriage. He wrongly thought her heart untouched. And when I had discovered that he had been an architect in driving his friend away...well, let's just say it was rather poor timing because that very day, he asked me to marry him. Of course, I said no—"

"Oh, I believe you said more than that, dearest—"

"I refused him, although I did recognize the compliment he had bestowed upon me. Our entire acquaintance had always been a joust —parry and riposte. So, when he pressed me for justification, fueled by old resentments, I could not resist. I unleashed the manifold reasons against him: for separating my beloved sister from his friend and breaking her heart; for his unrelenting pride and disdain for others; for his actions toward another of our acquaintance, who I later learned, I was entirely wrong about. All of my vitriol only wrought his temper. Obviously, he retreated, feeling scorned and much the injured party. And I was flustered and not a little cross by his lack of remorse. The next day, while walking in the park, he approached me with a letter. Later I learned he had stayed up half the night writing, confessing his actions and clarifying my ignorant assumptions. You can imagine how hesitant I was to accept his letter, but there it was, in my hand. And as quickly as we met, he left me alone in the lane."

"How romantic!"

"Ha! It was anything but. Not a love letter by any means." Pitching my voice, I said, "'Be not alarmed, madam, on receiving this letter.' Are those the words of a lover? The words were designed to mitigate my ignorance. I read them over and over again. And the more I read them, the more his words shamed me for my mistaken beliefs, for accepting lies and half-truths about his character...all because I had believed someone who had flattered me and had used me to slander your grandfather. Fitzwilliam explained why he had separated his friend from Jane—and I could not help but recognize his wish to be of service to his friend."

"*And then* did you tell him you understood him better after reading his letter?"

"Goodness, no. He left Rosings shortly thereafter and we thought never to see one another ever again."

"Well, now I am all anticipation to know how you came together because *that* seems like an impossible situation."

"Indeed. I returned to Longbourn, regretting my behavior. Mind, I did not regret that I had rejected him, but I did regret having been blinded by my own prejudice and behaving so badly. To my chagrin, I was dealt some truths that were humiliating to my pride; and admitting I was wrong...well, that is never easy to accept.

"Anyway, my aunt and uncle Gardiner had invited me on a trip to the North, and later that summer, I found myself touring great houses in Derbyshire."

"And you visited him here, and you reconciled?"

"Well not entirely, but yes, I did encounter him here. Quite by chance in fact. When my aunt and uncle had suggested we tour the house, I knew I had no business here and made every excuse to avoid Pemberley. I was wholly worried that if he was in residence, and we should meet, I would look like...a grasping upstart. That evening I had learned from a chambermaid at the inn in Lambton that the family was not down for the summer yet, and so we made our way here the next day. Little did I know that he was on his way to Pemberley with the Bingleys and your great aunt Georgiana. He had ridden ahead of the party, only to discover me wandering about his garden."

"*And then* you apologized to one another and became engaged?"

"I abhor spoiling your love of drama and fairytale endings but not for a couple more months. And not until after we had taken more fences...but yes, we finally confessed our misunderstanding, and understanding, and love for the other." I continued, re-counting George Wickham's many betrayals of Darcy, his attempt to run away with Georgiana, his elopement with my own sister Lydia, and how Darcy found them and contrived the marriage, saving my family from shame. How his aunt Lady Catherine de Bourgh had traveled from Kent to Longbourn to demand from me a promise to never marry her nephew. And all the rest...

"But the point I want to make, Addy darling, is that you must know your heart. Know your own worth. Do not marry out of obligation to your parents. Or because you think you should like to have a wedding celebration. Or because someone flatters you. You must know that this man, who you will betroth all you are and all you own, is someone you can honor and respect. Because when the wedding gifts have all been acknowledged, when your parents have moved on to think of a match for your sister, and when the fresh passion has waned, you will be bound to him."

Across the park, a rider approaches. His tall, athletic frame seems hauntingly familiar. The way he sits atop the great black beast... My heart...my heart surges. I put my hand to shade my eyes from the sun but, almost at once, I realize my mistake, recognizing young Matthew Stanton, Lord Talbot, as the light glints on his auburn hair when he waves his hat in salute. These days my mind plays strange tricks, and I sober, contenting myself with only the memory of a younger Fitzwilliam when he would ride out across his lands nearly every day.

At the sight of her handsome beau, Adelaide blooms like a rose. "He has come," she whispers. As he swings his lean limbs to the ground, leaving his horse to stand in the grasses, I am reminded of last June when we first encountered the eldest son of the Earl of Airlie.

MY GRANDSON WILL HAD BROUGHT A FRIEND HOME AFTER THE SEASON. I remember being seated under a broadleaf elm, watching Adelaide and the younger girls busy at their archery. My eldest granddaughter was poised to release her arrow and win the match when her brother called out from across the lawn, startling us all. Adelaide's arrow went far left of the target and she rounded on Will, chastisement on her lips. Upon glimpsing his comely friend, quite fine in his long jacket, checked waistcoat, and the trousers that are so popular these days, she promptly closed her mouth.

Will presented Lord Talbot to his mother and me, and I could not help but notice his carelessly tousled gold and auburn locks when he took off his hat and swept a courtly bow. He had offered some pretty remark about his parents sending their regards and then thanked my daughter-in-law for her hospitality. I was fascinated as Adelaide quietly put her bow aside and made her way to her brother, eyeing his friend with curiosity.

After kissing my cheek and his mother's, Will picked up his sister and swung her around, making her laugh and beg him to set her down. Her bonnet had long been discarded to the lawn, and her chestnut coils had started to come loose. "Now look what you have done?"—tucking a whorl behind her ear—"I must look positively medieval."

"To Talbot? Nonsense. I've already told my friend here all about you. I daresay he would be disappointed if you were to appear anything but perfectly imperfect. We can find *perfect* in London."

Lord Talbot then offered his hand to Adelaide and drawled, "Ah, yes, Miss Darcy. Just as I imagined. Perfectly imperfect."

The poor girl only looked at his hand, not knowing what to do. Looking at her mother, then me, then back to Lord Talbot's clear blue eyes, she shyly took his hand and said, "My lord."

My grandson snickered (the scamp) at his sister's hesitancy, her inexperience, and resulting awkwardness in shaking hands with a gentleman of rank, and she stiffened. Recovering, she smiled sweetly, but I saw it. Her eyes had cast daggers at her brother, and I am sure she was thinking how she might repay the humor he enjoyed at her expense. I suspected young Lord Talbot often found diversion putting young ladies off balance with this new custom that has become so popular.

"And common." I bit my lip in amusement thinking of Darcy's old-fashioned opinions and my poor girl's pique.

Straightening herself to her full height, my darling girl said, "Oh yes. And we have been expecting you. Will has written us tales of your perfectly imperfect gentlemen exploits."

"I wouldn't believe a word your brother says. You know him. He enjoys spinning a colorful—"

"You wound me, Talbot!"

"Your brother—"

"La! My brother! That last letter justly disquieted me as I ponder my own presentation and first Season in the coming year—"

"Adelaide…" her mother warned.

"Fair to say, my lord, between the two of you, many hearts have been broken across the capital."

Fanning herself quickly, my daughter-in-law exclaimed, "And that is why young ladies are not presented until they have matured enough to temper their words. Forgive my daughter, Lord Talbot. She forgets herself as she does like to run on in a wild manner here at home."

Adelaide colored in humiliation, or anger, I know not which, but then His Lordship, like a balm to these filial reproofs, said:

"Nonsense, madam. I daresay, Miss Darcy shall be the one breaking hearts."

And so, for the next se'nnight, I was almost enchanted by such pretty speeches and electric exchanges between my granddaughter and the young lord, but I admit, I was a little disappointed. I was confounded why she offered him so little encouragement, because it was not like she had been slighted upon *their* first introduction. And who would not love to see their beautiful granddaughter married well! Lady Talbot—how well that sounds!

"I recall Mother Bennet expressing similar—"

My granddaughter drops my arm, leaving me with the unwieldy parasol and hurries out to meet her young man, and I smile at his long, purposeful strides, thinking what a lovely picture they make. He extends his hand and they laugh as she takes it. He then carries her hand to his lips and says something I cannot hear but makes her laugh again.

Tucking her hand in his arm, they walk toward me. "Good afternoon, ma'am"—as he makes a correct bow to me, and I welcome him to Pemberley. He asks if he might join us on our walk, and so we continue about the lake. With wry delight, I notice His Lordship has abandoned his characteristic imperious hauteur and seems *unsettled*, tugging at his neck cloth.

"Grandmother was telling me how she fell in love with my grandfather who, it would seem, shared many of your own characteristics." She looks up at him, offering a sly grin. The imp!

"Oh, ho! Well, in that case, do tell. I can only be encouraged by the compliment of comparison to your excellent husband, madam."

"I was only telling my granddaughter that often first impressions may not always be correct, and sometimes our pride, our prejudices, get in the way."

I catch an exchange of secret looks before Lord Talbot says, "I believe my first impressions of you, Miss Darcy, were very true."

"Oh, how so? I recall the word 'imperfect' or something to that effect. You made me think you thought me still in the schoolroom."

"I thought you the loveliest creature I had ever beheld. How you crossed the lawn to greet us…your youth, beauty, and elegance. How delighted you were upon seeing your brother." Lord Talbot's cheeks pink when he remembers he has me, too, as an audience—"Meeting you as well, ma'am. Very memorable."

"To be sure." I can only smirk at the young man's gallantry and wonder if he would only get on with it. Just ask her! What a fine match—to unite both houses. I shudder at my thoughts, remembering how I loathed both my own mother's matchmaking and Lady Catherine's interference, and I feel discomposed by the heat again.

As we come upon the little chapel, I stop at the gate. "Why don't you two lead me to the bench there? I have a mind to rest under that leafy oak. You might gather some flowers for me, my love."

Sitting on the cool bench, out of the sun, my pulse steadies and I am once more at peace. I hear murmurs amongst the birdsong, words like "Would you wear an engagement ring?" and then "It would depend who gave it to me." I smile at this exchange and rest my hand on the stone bench, studying the gold band Fitzwilliam gave me so long ago. My eyes are drawn across the chapel lawn to the family vault, and I feel my throat tighten; my eyes blur as tears spill down my cheeks.

These days I feel especially lonely having lost Jane, my dearest sister, a year ago, and with Fitzwilliam gone these three years, my grown children and now grandchildren are my whole world.

I was blessed to have forty years with Fitzwilliam before he left this earth, but my heart still aches at the hole that remains. I hear him in my thoughts, and as I wander the grounds of his ancestral home, his voice is on the wind, a whisper at my nape, the thudding in my heart. Until we meet again, I will feel gratitude; gratitude, not only for how he loved me, or for all he had done, but for loving him still. Like the swans on our lake, we are mates forevermore.

I look at Adelaide and her beau as they collect flowers, and I am reminded again of the life before her, hopeful she has chosen well.

"Has she chosen well?"

Time alone will tell, my darling, but I like that she knows our story now. That once her grandmother was an audacious woman who spoke her mind, took charge of her own destiny, and did not conform to what was expected of gently bred ladies. And then, like some wonderful, glorious fairytale, I lived happily-ever-after with the love of my life.

CHRISTINA BOYD wears many hats as she is an editor under her own banner, The Quill Ink, a great reader and reviewer, and a ceramicist. A life member of Jane Austen Society of North America, Christina lives in the wilds of the Pacific Northwest with her dear Mr. B, two busy young adults, and a retriever named BiBi. Visiting Jane Austen's England was made possible by actor Henry Cavill when she won the Omaze experience to meet him in the spring of 2017 on the London Eye. True story. You can Google it.

ACKNOWLEDGMENTS

"Follies and nonsense, whims and inconsistencies do divert me, I own, and I laugh at them whenever I can." –Chapter XI

Elizabeth: Obstinate Headstrong Girl has been a journey a long time coming. After *The Darcy Monologues* was published in 2017, and as early as the day after publication, readers suggested an Elizabeth anthology—and I kept putting it off, wanting to pursue *Jane Austen's Rakes & Gentlemen Rogues, Rational Creatures*, and even *Yuletide: A Jane Austen Collection of Stories*—because I thought all the Elizabeth Bennet point-of-view stories surely must have been told. Last year, on a whim, I floated this project idea out to a few authors and was heartened by how keen they were to write *Elizabeth*. This Dream Team of authors—Elizabeth Adams, Karen M Cox, J. Marie Croft, Amy D'Orazio, Leigh Dreyer, Jenetta James, Christina Morland, Beau North, and Joana Starnes—joined me on another adventure with no promise of success but countless hopes. Like many journeys, we encountered unexpected turns, and even a few disappointments, but *"it was our business to be satisfied"* and prefer to *"think only of the past as its remembrance gives you pleasure."* I am forever indebted for their creativity, inspiration, great suggestions, and adherence to schedule.

And for bolstering my own offering of an Elizabeth story. All of you, I can easily count as friends.

I had heard that New York Times and USA Today bestselling Regency romance author Tessa Dare had once upon a time written some Jane Austen fan fiction. When author Beau North suggested we ask her to write the foreword, there was a resounding "Yes!" You might say we were audacious to even ask but, in the temperament of Lizzy Bennet, our *"courage always rises..."* When she ardently accepted, you might imagine us: *"What delight! What felicity!"*—well, more like fangirl squeals! Dare's love of Elizabeth Bennet and her deft understanding for the scope of this anthology left me wholly gratified, knowing we asked the right person to introduce this fifth anthology of the Quill Collective series. *She* is just like us, but awesome!

Thank you again to Shari Ryan of Mad Hat Books for helping to create another eye-catching cover that we think is a good companion to *The Darcy Monologues*. And a huge thank you to Karen M Cox for formatting the interiors so beautifully! Blessedly, you have great patience and a calming nature more like Elinor Dashwood than Lizzy Bennet though. Much gratitude to Elizabeth Adams and Joana Starnes for lending fresh eyes to the final eyes stages.

Special thanks to blogmistress Meredith Esparza of Austenesque Reviews for her enthusiasm in the project from when it was but a whisper. Reviews and encouragement from readers and many bloggers have kept us motivated. *"You give me fresh life and vigor. Adieu to disappointment and spleen."* We are grateful for the continued support of this anthology book series, the Quill Collective.

As always, my dear Mr. B is my rock as he sustains me while I chase my dreams in this wild west that is modern day publishing and continues to care for me *"as a woman worthy of being pleased."* And for Finnegan and Ellary, never forget *"you are the sun of my life, gilder of every pleasure, the soother of every sorrow..."*

We hope this homage to one of Jane Austen's best beloved heroines was all you expected, especially for those that suggested an "Elizabeth" anthology back in 2017. Like Darcy, we *"had never been so bewitched by any woman"* and writing this collection has been diverting/gratifying/delightful. Please accept these stories in the same affectionate spirit they were written.

–Christina Boyd, editor

Thank you for reading *Elizabeth: Obstinate, Headstrong Girl*. If you enjoyed this anthology, please consider leaving an honest review at Amazon. Your words matter.

For more anthologies in the Quill Collective series, check out Amazon and Audible:

The Darcy Monologues
Dangerous to Know: Jane Austen's Rakes & Gentlemen Rogues
Rational Creatures
Yuletide: A Jane Austen Collection of Stories